Cassie Miles, a *USA TODAY* bestselling author, lived in Colorado for many years and has now moved to Oregon. Her home is an hour from the rugged Pacific Ocean and an hour from the Cascade Mountains—the best of both worlds—not to mention the incredible restaurants in Portland and award-winning wineries in the Willamette Valley. She's looking forward to exploring the Pacific Northwest and finding mysterious new settings for Mills & Boon Heroes romances.

Karen Whiddon started weaving fanciful tales for her younger brothers at the age of eleven. Amid the gorgeous Catskill Mountains, then the majestic Rocky Mountains, she fuelled her imagination with the natural beauty surrounding her. Karen now lives in north Texas, writes full-time and volunteers for a boxer dog rescue. She shares her life with her hero of a husband and four to five dogs, depending on if she is fostering. You can email Karen at kwhiddon1@aol.com. Fans can also check out her website, karenwhiddon.com

Also by Cassie Miles

Mountain Retreat
Colorado Wildfire
Mountain Bodyguard
Mountain Shelter
Mountain Blizzard
Frozen Memories
The Girl Who Wouldn't Stay Dead
The Girl Who Couldn't Forget
The Final Secret
Witness on the Run
Cold Case Colorado
Find Me

Also by Karen Whiddon

Colton 911: Soldier's Return
The Texan's Return
Wyoming Undercover
The Texas Soldier's Son
Texas Ranch Justice
Snowbound Targets
The Widow's Bodyguard
Texas Sheriff's Deadly Mission
Texas Rancher's Hidden Danger

GASLIGHTED IN COLORADO

CASSIE MILES

FINDING THE RANCHER'S SON

KAREN WHIDDON

MILLS & BOON

First Published in Great Britain 2022
by Mills & Boon, an imprint of HarperCollins*Publishers* Ltd
1 London Bridge Street, London, SE1 9GF

www.harpercollins.co.uk

HarperCollins*Publishers*
1st Floor, Watermarque Building,
Ringsend Road, Dublin 4, Ireland

ISBN: 978-0-263-30336-0

0322

MIX
Paper from responsible sources
FSC™ C007454

This book is produced from independently certified FSC™ paper to ensure responsible forest management.

For more information visit: www.harpercollins.co.uk/green

Printed and Bound in Spain using 100% Renewable electricity at CPI Black Print, Barcelona

GASLIGHTED IN COLORADO

CASSIE MILES

To Jackie and Christian, the ballerina and the surfer.
And, as always, for Rick.

Chapter One

A waning moon dimly lit the forest. The trees, shrubs and rocks looked like something she'd already run past, but she couldn't tell. No idea where she'd been. No hint of where she was headed, but she had to stop. Seconds away from a full-fledged anxiety attack, her energy was spent.

Staggering, she came to a halt. The palms of her hands were scraped—couldn't say how or where. *Fight the pain. Don't give up.* She braced her hands on her thighs and bent nearly double, gasping for breath. Her lungs burned. Her throat was raw. Gradually, she uncurled her spine and stood erect.

Acting on instinct, she glanced over her shoulder, peering into a tangle of branches that rustled in the dry spring breeze and smelled like pine resin. *Not paranoid.* Or was she? She couldn't tell if she was being chased, couldn't see him or her or whatever was in hot pursuit.

The canyon filled with echoing sounds, none of them reassuring. She heard the lonesome howl from a coyote, the screeches of owls and an indefinite growl. Though the wind held a distinct chill, she was sweating. Reaching up, she touched her forehead to wipe the moisture. Her fingertips came away sticky with blood. Under her dark brown hair, she felt a lump and more bleeding. What the hell had happened?

Instead of recalling the events of a few minutes or hours

ago, her memories went backward in time, all the way to childhood when she was a kid at a summer camp led by a burly woman named Braddock, who called the campers "Scout." Mrs. Braddock told her that if she ever got lost in the woods, she should go downhill until she found a creek and then follow the water to civilization.

"Do you hear me, Scout?" she'd asked.

"Yes, ma'am."

Wishing she could once again be an innocent child, she zipped her red sweatshirt and carefully lifted the hood to cover her head wound. She raised her arm to check the time on her silver Cartier watch. Her wrist was bare. The watch—a gift when she graduated from high school—was gone. Her cell phone was also missing, along with her purse, wallet, driver's license and ATM card. Had she been robbed? Later, she'd worry about that. Now, she needed to find a creek. The toes of her sneakers aimed downhill.

Mrs. Braddock wasn't an expert, but having a plan felt better than dashing aimlessly. At the edge of a cliff, she scanned the landscape and realized... *I'm in Colorado, in the Rocky Mountains.* The memory gave her hope. Everything would be all right.

Though she didn't see the reflection of starlight off a creek, she spotted something even better: light from the windows of a cabin that cast an orange glow into the forest. Where there was light, she'd find her rescue. The closer she got to the small log cabin, the more familiar it seemed.

Smoke plumed from the stone chimney. The porchlight was lit. A red-painted door stood between two windows. A one-step porch with three rocking chairs stretched across the front, and she imagined herself as a child sitting there, inhaling the fragrance of the flowering honeysuckle vines that wove through the banister. She'd been here before. Remembering so clearly should have relaxed her.

But not all memories were soothing. Some varieties of honeysuckle were toxic.

The bump on her head hammered in time with her pulse, warning her. More trouble lay ahead. She tiptoed across the porch and peeked through the window. Inside, she saw a man with stringy gray hair sitting in a rocking chair facing toward a stone hearth and away from the window. The lamp on the end table had not been turned on. The fire sputtered its dying flames.

She went to the door and knocked. At least she wouldn't be waking the man. She knocked again. When he didn't answer, she returned to the window. It didn't look like he'd moved. Maybe he'd fallen asleep.

This time when she knocked, she called out, "Hello, is anyone home?"

Back at the window, she saw him sitting immobile in his rocker. The room with the fireplace connected to a dining area and a kitchen, where the lights were on.

She knocked one last time to no avail, then grasped the knob and tried to open the red door. It was locked. But she had to get inside. She needed a phone, needed to find her way back to civilization. The sounds of the forest closed around her, and she felt the predators watching her from behind the rocks. She imagined their powerful muscles coiling as they prepared to attack.

Circling the cabin, she went to the Dutch door in the kitchen and peered through the window. Again, she knocked. Beyond the kitchen lights, she could see the outline of the man in the chair. Silently, she prayed for him to wake up and open the door for her. *Help me.*

Gathering her courage, she twisted the knob. It turned easily in her hand, and she pushed the door open. She hurried inside and closed the door as she called out, "Sorry to disturb you."

She entered the room where he was sitting with his elbows resting on the arms of the chair and his boots planted a solid eighteen inches apart. His head lolled forward on his chest. "Sorry," she repeated, "but I've gotten lost in the forest and need to use your phone."

In the flickering light from the fireplace, she saw the bloodstain on his long-sleeve plaid shirt. Around his neck, he wore a bolo tie with a bucking-bronco design. When she was a kid, she'd seen one just like it. Again, she'd recalled something from the distant past, which was the only time in her life when she'd been in the Rockies. Or was it? Had she been here before?

She pivoted away from the man in the chair and ran to the kitchen to find a phone to call an ambulance. An old-fashioned landline hung from the wall beside the light switch. She grabbed the receiver and listened to dead silence. Glancing over her shoulder, she saw the man in the chair. He still hadn't moved.

She ought to try CPR or feel for a pulse. Standing beside his rocking chair, she reached down and lifted his wrist. The movement upset his balance. With his arm no longer holding him in place, his upper body slipped sideways in the rocker. Trying to keep him from falling, she caught him under his arms and braced his body against hers. The bloodstain smeared across her sweatshirt. He toppled from his chair onto the rag rug in front of the fireplace and dragged her down with him, spreading his slippery blood over her hands.

She heard a heavy thud, looked and saw a black automatic pistol that had fallen from the chair. Had he been shot? She had no idea what a bullet wound looked like, knew nothing about firearms, couldn't remember ever holding a pistol.

Until she felt for his pulse and found nothing, she wouldn't accept that he was dead. She scrambled to her feet and stared down at him, not wanting to get closer but knowing that she couldn't hide or run away. The firelight picked up a sparkle from the end table. She turned on the lamp and saw her silver Cartier wristwatch, which had an engraving on the back: "With love, Popsy." Who was Popsy?

She eased her hood back. Her wound was tender, still bleeding. She unzipped her sweatshirt. When she knelt beside the gray-haired man, his blood smeared her yellow T-shirt. Wet blood meant his wounds were fairly recent. The person who attacked him could be nearby. She picked up the automatic, leaving her bloody fingerprints on the grip—probably not a smart move, but she needed a way to defend herself.

With trembling fingers, she reached for the man's gnarled wrist and pressed against his blue veins. No pulse. And his flesh was beginning to feel cold in spite of the recent fire in the hearth. Leaning closer, she swept aside the strands of hair that clung to his forehead. The pupils of his eyes were opaque, lifeless. His skin sagged from prominent cheekbones and a hatchet jaw. His face had turned into a death mask, and yet she knew him. She had seen that face before. He haunted her nightmares.

She stood over the monster who had made her childhood a living hell. He couldn't hurt her anymore, but she still wanted vengeance, wanted to hold the gun in both hands and empty all the bullets into the lifeless husk that was lying before her.

She heard the thud of boot heels on the wooden porch. A heavy fist hammered at the red door. "Open up, Virgil, I don't have time to mess around."

Without thinking, she responded. "Just a minute."

"Who's in there with you? Why did you call me, Virgil? Dammit, are you okay?"

She looked down at the blood on her clothes and the gun in her hand. Though she'd done nothing wrong, she looked like a murderer. It crossed her mind to run, but that would make her appear even guiltier. And what if this late-night visitor had a gun of his own?

"I mean it, Virgil," the man on the porch growled. "Open the door or I'll kick it down."

She flipped the lock on the red door, pulled it open and raised the gun. "Don't move or I'll shoot."

Her voice caught in her throat, and she nearly strangled when she saw the bronze five-pointed star pinned to his black L.L.Bean vest. He was a deputy sheriff. She was holding a gun on a lawman. *Great!*

He stepped into the room. In the sort of low, soothing voice used to talk to small children or dogs, he said, "I want you to put the gun on the floor and take a step back."

"Of course." She did as he asked. "I didn't mean to threaten you."

"Step back."

"Another step? Well, okay. Listen, I know this doesn't look good, but—"

He picked up the gun. "Is Virgil okay?"

How could she explain? Nothing made sense, and she was digging a hole that got deeper every time she opened her mouth. "I tried to find a pulse, and that's when he fell out of the chair. I couldn't feel one. A pulse."

"What's your name, Miss?"

She drew a blank, didn't know, couldn't even remember her own name. *Oh, my God...* "It's Scout," she said. "Scout Braddock."

He touched the brim of his black cowboy hat. "I'm John Graystone, a deputy for Peregrine County. I've got to be honest with you, Scout. Finding you like this… Well, it doesn't look good."

"I know." Her legs were stiff, and she moved disjointedly as she went toward the kitchen. "Why are you here?"

"Virgil called the dispatcher at the station and said something about danger. He's not the sort of man who complains needlessly," John said. "When I called back, he didn't answer."

She came back toward him, passing the dining-room table, and returned to the fireplace. She wanted to be honest and straightforward, especially while she was talking to this tall, handsome deputy with the translucent gray eyes. Never mind that she couldn't recall her true identity or where she was from—she had a feeling that Scout Braddock was a decent person who tried to do the right thing. If Deputy John got to know her, he'd like her. Most people did…at least, she hoped they did.

"Stop pacing," he said.

"I feel like there's something I ought to do."

"Stand still." She watched him kneel beside Virgil and feel at the base of his jaw for the carotid artery. John stood and shook his head. "He's dead."

"I'm sorry," she said automatically.

"Me, too. He was a good man."

"There's nothing I could have done for him."

"I don't suppose there was."

With one-hundred-percent honesty, she said, "I came to the cabin looking for help. You see, I have a head wound, and I don't exactly remember how I got it. I'm kind of disoriented."

"You might have a concussion."

When he approached her, she darted away from him. "What are you doing?"

He pointed to the wall opposite the fireplace. "Over there, Scout. Take a seat on the sofa."

"I'm all bloody. I don't want to wreck it with stains." The furniture was old but clean. Virgil had taken care of his place. "I'll find a towel to sit on."

"Stay," he said.

Why was he gruff and treating her like a dog? Why so

suspicious? "What's the deal? Do you think I'm going to run off and escape into the forest?"

In response, he reached into a pouch attached to his belt and took out a pair of handcuffs. Without asking, he seized her right hand and snapped on the cuff. *This isn't happening.* Then, the left. "Don't move. I'll be right back."

She stared at her hands, cuffed in front, and took what she hoped would be a calming breath. It made total sense that he considered her a suspect, and she wouldn't seem innocent when she told him that she couldn't remember her name and didn't have her wallet.

He had left her alone with the dead man. Though not a superstitious person, she had a sense that Virgil's ghost hovered nearby, smiling while he sang a song about unicorns and bluebirds. That memory couldn't be correct. When she first saw him, she thought of nightmares.

When John returned, he was talking on his cell phone and carrying a couple of blue towels. He ended his call and spread the towels on the sofa. "Sit down and let me take a look at that head wound."

She cooperated. What choice did she have? He took off his hat, placed his hands on her shoulders and looked down at her skull. He leaned close to inspect her wound, and she caught a warm, masculine scent from him. He smelled woodsy, like the forest after a rainfall.

"That's a nasty cut," he said. "You don't remember how you got it?"

"I must have fallen."

"I already called the ambulance. You'll need to go to the hospital."

"Not necessary," she said. "I can take care of myself."

"You need a doctor to stitch up that wound, and I'm guessing they'll want to keep you under observation if it's a concussion."

"I hate hospitals." Did she? Why? "They'll say I need a CT scan, maybe an MRI."

"Sounds like you know something about brain injuries."

"It's how my mother died." The statement surprised her as much as it did him. In a flash, she glimpsed a vivacious red-haired woman. Her mother. Always surrounded by laughter and light, she'd passed away unexpectedly. For a moment, the loss of that remarkable lady caused a hard knot of unassuageable grief to twist around her heart. "Car accident. She'd sustained a head wound resulting in a subdural hematoma. An aneurysm eventually killed her."

Her mother had regained consciousness for a few days after the crash, and she was supposed to be okay, but that wasn't how it worked out. Mom's death inspired her to pursue a career in medicine. She'd taken classes, but…

"Scout, are you all right?"

She jolted back to the present, unsure of whether she'd completed her studies or dropped out. The memory that she'd been in nursing school was significant—the entry point for more complex, deeper recollections. She pushed off the sofa and stood on wobbly legs. "I'm feeling better already. Please take off the cuffs."

"Not until I have your statement," he said. "Where are you staying?"

A question she couldn't answer. She groped inside her brain but couldn't recall the name of the nearest town, much less a hotel or motel. Moving cautiously, she crossed the room and stood at the fireplace. "I didn't hurt him. Don't even know who he is."

"Then you've got nothing to worry about." He joined her and moved the screen so he could look directly into the dying flames. "It's not a cold night. Wonder why he started a fire."

She glanced down at the hearth. "Looks like cardboard

and papers. Maybe he was burning something to get rid of it."

"Could be."

"Or somebody else could have started the fire to get rid of evidence," she said. "The murderer."

"I can't be talking to you about this."

She leaned against the wall beside the brick fireplace, anchoring herself against a feeling of light-headedness. "I'm a suspect."

He didn't deny that obvious fact. Using the fireplace tongs, he reached through the embers and pulled out a scrap of paper, then another and another. "Looks like correspondence and legal papers."

"I've never been a suspect before." At least, she didn't recall a criminal history. "What happens next?"

He fished another half sheet of paper from the ashes. "We'll test your sweatshirt and your hands for GSR—that's gunshot residue. At the hospital, they'll take a DNA swab. And the forensic technicians will look for your fingerprints in the cabin."

She heard the distant wail of the ambulance siren. "If I agree to go to the hospital, do I have to ride with Virgil?"

He stepped back from the fire. "Mr. Hotchner needs to stay right where he is until the coroner legally declares him deceased. That could take an hour or longer. You need to see a doctor sooner."

Hearing a knock on the red door, John called out, "It's unlocked. Come in."

The black-haired man who rushed inside radiated a sense of urgency and was almost as tall as John. His complexion was flushed, and he stared at her with a worried, intense gaze. "Thank God, you're all right."

He dashed across the room and wrapped her in a tight, possessive embrace. Clearly, he knew her, which was good news because he'd have her name and some kind of explanation about what was going on.

"Was it hard to find me?" she asked.

"You wandered off. I didn't know what had happened to you."

She placed her cuffed hands against his chest and pushed him away, creating a distance between them. "We came here together, right?"

"Of course, we did." He hooked a long, skinny finger through the cuffs. "What's this all about? What's wrong with you, Caroline? You're acting like you don't know me."

Caroline, her name was Caroline. She liked it. Unfortunately, she couldn't say the same about this guy. She recognized his angular face and the neatly trimmed goatee. A long time ago, they'd dated, and she remembered the sensation of his mouth pressed against hers. He was not a great kisser, and she was fairly sure they'd never slept together.

John stepped forward, shook hands with the guy and introduced himself. The man with the goatee straightened his shoulders and said, "I'm Max Sherman. And I'm her fiancé."

Her eyelids slammed shut, and she crumpled to the floor.

Chapter Two

Outside Virgil's cabin, John Graystone watched the ambulance drive down the narrow, gravel driveway that merged onto a two-lane graded road. Lying on a gurney in the rear was the woman whose real name was Caroline McAllister. She didn't appeal to him as much as Scout Braddock, who was gutsy and strong, saddened by the death of a man she didn't know and confused enough to face him with a Glock 13 in her trembling hand. Judging Caroline was unfair because she didn't have a chance to prove herself and hadn't been fully awake after she fainted.

The paramedics had taken a quick look at her injury and backed up his advice to get a doctor's opinion. Treating a head wound was tricky, especially in this case, when Caroline couldn't remember her name or what had happened to her. Amnesia wasn't uncommon with a concussion, but the effect was usually losing a few minutes or an hour. It seemed that Caroline had forgotten much of her life, including the fact that she had gotten engaged and planned to get married in Reno.

John was glad she hadn't gone through with the wedding. He didn't like Max Sherman who was driving his Chevy Tahoe behind the ambulance. Max treated his fiancée like an idiot, as if losing her memory was an inconvenience. He barely acknowledged her injuries. The third vehicle in this convoy had a Peregrine County Sheriff's

Department logo on the side and was driven by Deputy Miguel Ochoa, whom John had assigned to guard Caroline—the number-one suspect in a murder case.

John knew he'd been too friendly and open with a woman he found standing over the dead man with gun in hand and blood on her sweatshirt. He should have placed her under arrest instead of fussing over her head wound. But his instincts told him that she wasn't a murderer. He had the opposite reaction, believing she was innocent and in need of his protection.

When the taillights of the ambulance and the other vehicles disappeared behind a curve in the road, he called Sheriff Roger Bishop, who'd been the law in this county for over twenty years. First, John apologized for disturbing the old man after nine o'clock, and then he outlined the situation and proposed a course of action. "I already called the coroner and arranged for Deputy Ochoa to keep an eye on Caroline McAllister at the hospital. Should I talk to the Colorado Bureau of Investigation and get their forensic team to process the cabin?"

"You betcha," the sheriff said. "And the CBI will likely want the M.E. in Pueblo to do the autopsy."

That was a given. Peregrine county was small and didn't need a full-time coroner. Bob Henry had been appointed to that position. He was a full-time pharmacist who was capable of filing a death certificate, but autopsies weren't part of his skill set.

John said, "Ochoa can handle the processing for the suspects. DNA swabs, prints, tests for GSR, but I'd like to do the interviews on both Caroline and her fiancé."

"Too bad about Virgil. Every year I gave him a ticket for not buying a fishing license, but I always liked the old goofball."

"I know you did." Virgil and the sheriff were probably

the same age—a couple of old goofballs. "Can you think of anybody who'd want to kill him?"

"Virgil had his share of enemies, but nobody hated him enough to shoot him in cold blood. Nobody I know, anyhow." When he hesitated, John could almost see the man stroking his thick, luxurious mustache. John was accustomed to the sheriff's way of communicating. Bishop was a deliberative man who made a habit of thinking before he spoke.

The old man continued, "There was a guy—a petty criminal named Derek Everett—who was always running scams. He got caught robbing a jewelry store in Durango where the clerk was shot. Virgil witnessed the getaway and testified in court. When Everett was convicted to twenty-two years, the scumbag swore revenge against Virgil."

A viable suspect. John wished he had a notebook to jot down the name. Instead, he repeated it inside his head. Derek Everett, Derek Everett. "When is his sentence up?"

"Doesn't matter," the sheriff said. "He died in jail."

Before they'd started down that path, he hit a detour. "Maybe he had friends or family who came after Virgil for revenge."

"It's worth looking into." He cleared his throat. "You ought to contact Dolly Devereaux tonight. She's been Virgil's best friend for a long time."

"Girlfriend?"

The sheriff scoffed. "A pretty blond gal like her and a knucklehead like him? No way."

John considered other motives for murder. "Did Virgil have any money? I heard that he hired Teresa Rosewood to clean his cabin and do his laundry."

"Is that so?"

"It's what I heard."

"I'll tell you what, John, I'm tired. This is going to be

your case. I'll just be a…what do you call it? A consultant. You're the quarterback. You carry the ball."

If he was the QB, he wouldn't be the ball carrier. But he didn't correct his boss. Having a homicide handed to him represented a step forward in his career. "I'm going to need to call all hands on deck."

In their small county, the entire sheriff's department, including a file clerk and dispatcher, consisted of ten full-time employees and twelve part-timers. Bishop usually kept a tight rein on overtime expenses, but he said, "Do what you need. We haven't had a homicide that wasn't an open-and-shut case in over ten years. Just don't mess it up, Johnny."

John ended the call as the coroner's Range Rover turned into the driveway. He greeted the owner of the Sagebrush Drug Store. "Sorry to drag you out so late, Henry."

The small, wiry pharmacist bounded from his vehicle as through his skinny legs were on springs. His bald head was covered by a dark blue baseball cap with a logo for the Peregrine County Fair. He carried a black leather case with his documents and information for the coroner's report. Though Henry had seen John earlier in the day, he grasped his hand and shook vigorously. "Tragic circumstances, me, oh, my. Virgil wasn't much older than I am."

"The sheriff said much the same."

"Oh, Sheriff Bishop is way older than me." He tugged on John's sleeve. "Listen, I hope you don't mind but I told my wife I was coming to Virgil's place. She was shocked that he was dead. I'll bet she's on Facebook right now, telling all her friends."

John wasn't thrilled but he expected the Sagebrush gossip mill would be churning at top speed, echoing the news of Virgil's murder throughout the San Luis Valley, from Wolf Creek Pass to the Apache Reservation. The old man had been a fixture in this area.

Bob Henry stomped onto the porch. He was wearing galoshes, as though he expected to be wading through blood and gore. "Old Virgil was a loner. Didn't have any regular prescriptions, so he didn't stop by the store often. Just occasionally to pick up a six-pack of soda or a bag of pork rinds."

While Henry kneeled beside the body of Virgil Hotchner and started inspecting him, John leaned against the mantel, where he'd stood beside Caroline less than an hour ago. Her story about coming to the cabin looking for help made sense, but why was she in this area? Her fiancé said they were from Portland. Why had they come to these remote mountains? He had a lot of questions for them and wanted to get to the hospital as soon as possible. But he couldn't abandon the crime scene.

Since the sheriff said this was his case, he took out his cell phone and called in two other deputies who were off duty until tomorrow. They could process the crime scene. Then he contacted the Pueblo CBI office, told them he had a murder victim and verified that the ambulance should deliver the body to the M.E.'s department in Pueblo.

As soon as John lowered his cell phone, Henry said, "Medical examiner, eh? Time to call in the big guns."

"I don't think your pharmacy is equipped for autopsies."

"And you'd be right." He gave a knowing nod. "The CBI has to be involved."

"They can use all their fancy forensic equipment and the computer programs that identify suspects faster than you can say 'mass spectrometer.'"

"I hope you catch the person who did this." Henry packed up his leather bag. "I'll email you the paperwork and the death certificate when it's done, but I've got to wait until I hear from the autopsy doctor to fill in the COD—that's cause of death."

"Isn't it obvious?" John asked.

"I can't declare this a homicide until the M.E. says so."

He ushered Henry from the cabin and watched him drive

away. As soon as the other deputies showed up, he'd leave them to dust for fingerprints, look for footprints and take photos of the scene, including Virgil's body. Right now, there wasn't much else he could do. Might as well take a look around.

The hallway off the living room led to a bathroom and two bedrooms. One was set up as an office. A gunmetal gray file cabinet had a drawer pulled open and appeared to be mostly empty. John thought of the paper scraps he'd rescued from the fire. One had a piece of a letterhead for an attorney whose name was Edie Valdez. Her office was in Durango.

On the desk in the office, there was only one photograph: a five-by-seven print of a snapshot that had been taken in the mountains. In the background was a barn that looked familiar. A much younger Virgil held the reins for a tall chestnut horse. Beside him was a woman with thick red hair and a brown-haired girl with a bowl cut who held a stuffed bunny. The serious expression on her face made him grin. He recognized her dark brown eyes and her button nose. This little girl was Scout. Or Caroline. Or whatever her real name was. Apparently, she'd known Virgil for much of her life.

AT THE MERCY Regional Medical Center in Durango, John strode down the hallway on the second floor, passed the nurses' station and found Deputy Ochoa sitting in a square waiting-room chair outside a room, drinking coffee from a cardboard cup. He stood as soon as he saw John. Though they were both deputies with the same rank, John had started with the sheriff's department as a part-timer during the summers when he was eighteen. That was thirteen years ago, which meant he had seniority. Ochoa and most of the other deputies were happy to step back and let John take the lead.

Ochoa's round, cheerful face could barely contain his grin. "This woman has real-life amnesia. She's not faking it."

"Why would anybody fake a memory loss?"

"Amnesia makes a good alibi." He glanced to the left and right, then lowered his voice. "You found her covered in blood with a Glock in her hand. She needs an excuse."

He wasn't wrong. "You've had a chance to observe her. Do you think she shot Virgil?"

"I'd have to ask my wife, she's the expert."

Lucinda Ochoa recently had started taking psychology classes in night school at Adams State in Alamosa. "Do you think Lucinda wants to be a criminal profiler?"

"Si," he said. "She watches all the crime shows and always guesses who's the perp. I'm thinking she'd pick Max Sherman, Caroline's fiancé. That guy has a bad attitude. He made a big fuss about Caroline needing a private room, like he was the king of the world."

John didn't like Max, either. "I want to interview both of them, then I'll head back to the cabin. Can you stay here until morning?"

"No problem."

"Do you need to take a break?"

"Good idea. I'll go downstairs and grab a sandwich. And I can call Lucy and tell her that you think she should be on *CSI*."

He didn't blame Ochoa for being excited. This sort of murder case was a long way out of the norm for Peregrine County. The two other deputies who were at Virgil's cabin right now were stoked about collecting forensic evidence, hanging crime-scene tape and using computer programs to research. Tomorrow, they'd compare notes with the team from CBI.

He entered Caroline's room—the private room that Max had insisted upon. She sat up in the hospital bed. A solution fed into her wrist through an IV. Other tubes and wires monitored her breathing and heart rate. Her head was wrapped in a white gauze bandage above her eyebrows. Her straight bob hung neatly to just below her chin. When she saw him, she broke into a smile and waved her wrists.

"No handcuffs," she said. "Deputy Ochoa said he checked with you, and you told him that as long as he was here watching, it was okay."

She looked like the absolute opposite of a dangerous criminal who needed constant restraint. "Where's your fiancé?"

"Consulting with doctors. I really hope he's not bothering them."

"What do the doctors say about your condition?"

"I've got a concussion and had eight stitches. My head wound is considered superficial."

"Do you remember how you were injured?"

"I don't. Probably I stumbled, fell forward and tried to catch myself with my hands, which was when I got the scrapes. Probably banged my head on a rock."

Her explanation sounded plausible, but he sensed an undercurrent. There was something she wasn't telling him. "What else?"

She lowered her gaze to her hands, which were wrapped in gauze. "I remember after I hit my head and was running in the forest, I thought someone was after me. Max says that sounds paranoid. Do you agree?"

"I try not to judge how other people feel. What else?" The more that witnesses talked, the more likelihood they'd say something to give him a clue. When she looked up with wide brown eyes, he noticed the left one—on the side where she'd been injured—was bloodshot.

"I was scared," she said. "Really scared."

"Did you see an attacker?"

"I didn't see anything, but I heard coyotes howling and

owls screeching. It felt like predators were everywhere." She shook her head. "Max might be right. I imagined the danger. I'm taking meds for depression. Sometimes, I get dizzy. And sometimes, confused."

"Good to know." And unexpected. He wanted more information. "How long have you been on this medication?"

"Don't remember." Her brow crinkled as she concentrated. "I didn't think of them until Max gave me my purse, and I found the bottle. My therapist suggested I try this brand, but she can't prescribe. She's not a medical doctor."

Talking to her therapist might help him understand Caroline. "What's her name?"

"I don't know. Maybe it starts with an *L*. Wait! It's Lola. Lola Powell."

Even if he could reach her therapist, John expected to be thwarted by doctor-patient privilege. "What do the doctors here at the hospital say about your medical condition?"

"They seem to think I'll be okay after I get caught up on sleep."

Pretty and petite, she was the picture of innocence with her button nose and smiling lips. But he recalled the other picture that he'd taken from Virgil's desk—visual proof that she'd known the man who had been murdered. Why hadn't she told him? Ochoa had been right when he said that amnesia was a handy excuse for forgetting inconvenient details, especially ones from a long time ago.

Accompanied by a young, clean-cut doc wearing a white lab coat, Max stalked into her room. The doctor was talking. "We'd like to monitor her condition for a few days."

"Is she all right to travel?" Max asked.

"She appears to be healthy and in good shape, but concussions are difficult to treat."

"Have you seen other patients who completely forgot their past?"

"No, sir."

Max sneered. "But you're not a neurologist."

"Specialists will be in tomorrow, and they can give you a more complete picture. With her permission, they'll want to take more scans and X-rays."

"I don't think so," Max Sherman said. "I don't want anyone using my fiancée as an experimental subject. As soon as she's well enough to travel, we'll be on our way."

John stepped up. "I have a few questions."

Max folded his arms across his chest and glared. "So do I, starting with this one. Why is there a deputy sitting outside her room as if she's a suspect?"

"Because I am," Caroline said from her bed. "I was right there with the dead man and I was holding the gun that killed him. At least, I think that was the murder weapon."

John watched the doctor's expression turn to stone as he took a step away from Max and Caroline. It might be best to interview Max without having Caroline or anybody else listening. "Mr. Sherman, I'd like to get your statement. There's a cubicle at the end of the hall where we can talk."

"In a minute," Max said. He went to Caroline's bedside and kissed her forehead. "Try to rest, my darling."

Instead of an adoring gaze, she averted her eyes and turned her head away from her fiancé. John had the distinct feeling that this engagement wasn't going to last.

When Max snapped another question at the doctor, John left the room. He waited outside until Ochoa returned and took his position. Then John escorted Max to the private cubicle, which he'd used before when interviewing witnesses and suspects at the hospital. The upper half of the walls were glass on three sides. Not the best circumstances for an interrogation. But he could close the door for privacy.

John pulled out one of the uncomfortable hospital chairs and sat at a rectangular table, as did Max. He took a small recorder and placed it between them. "Do you mind? This helps me remember details."

"I understand why you'd suspect Caroline, but why me? I wasn't there."

"You might be in danger." Not likely, but it gave John a reason for maintaining surveillance on them other than the obvious fact that they were suspects. "Until we have more information, I'll have to ask you and Caroline not to leave town."

"Or else?" He smoothed his goatee.

"I could arrest you."

"Then I don't have a choice." He pushed back his chair, stood and paced in the small cubicle. "I don't like this room. It's a hamster cage."

Not an unusual reaction. "Do hospitals make you nervous?"

"Not at all. I'm a vet."

"Thank you for your service."

"A veterinarian," he said with a condescending smirk.

John really didn't like this guy. He regretted letting him off the hook by not labeling him a suspect and slapping on the handcuffs. "Tell me what happened when Caroline was injured."

"We were lost on these twisty dirt roads that all seem to be dead ends. Made me glad that I didn't bring my Lexus. Late in the day, it was getting dark. I parked her Tahoe. I'd given up on the GPS and started looking at maps. You really ought to do something about that, Deputy. Better street signs or something."

"I'll pass that suggestion along." A slam dunk into the trash can.

"Caroline was antsy. She took off, saying something about getting a better visual perspective from the top of the hill. That must have been when she fell." Inside his goatee, his mouth twisted in a weird, inexplicable grin. As if falling was what she deserved. "After twenty minutes, I went looking for her. She was gone, vanished into the ether. I looked all over the place and finally found her at the cabin."

His story was fairly straightforward, and there was no way to disprove Max's assertions. "When you were studying the maps, were you looking for a specific location? What was the reason for your trip to this area?"

"It's ironic." Again, his mouth twitched. "We were looking for Virgil Hotchner."

Chapter Three

Forcing himself to stay calm, John kept his face from betraying his surprise. With very little prompting, Max had revealed a mountain of circumstantial evidence by admitting that he and Caroline were connected with the dead man and had been in the area looking for him. Next, he'd be claiming ownership of the Glock 13—the murder weapon.

Oblivious, Max said, "The old man was Caroline's great-uncle on her mother's side."

A relative? "Were they close?"

"I don't think I should say anything more about this. It's personal and doesn't portray Caroline in a good light."

Murder investigations had a way of bringing out the worst in people. "I hope to discuss this relationship with her therapist."

"Oh, she told you about Lola, did she? Well, I'm sure you've heard of doctor-patient confidentiality. Lola doesn't have to talk to you."

Really don't like Max Sherman. "This is your opportunity to give me a more positive focus on Caroline and her great-uncle. Is he the reason she's on antidepressant meds?"

"Oh, well, yes. I absolutely blame him." He leaned back in his chair, behaving as though he'd won this skirmish even though he was giving a response instead of keeping his mouth shut. "Have you ever heard of post-traumatic stress disorder, commonly referred to as PTSD?"

"Yes." He hadn't been living under a rock for the past fifteen years.

"The symptoms don't apply only to soldiers in battle." Max steepled his fingertips and looked over them. "PTSD is common with people who have suffered trauma, such as rape victims or those who have been in an accident or have been abused."

Those parameters covered a wide sector of society, and John wasn't about to play a tragic sort of guessing game about which label applied to Caroline. Though he wanted to grab the other man by the lapels of his hipster jacket and shake the truth out of him, he bit his tongue and bided his time.

"Caroline's therapist worked with her for almost four months before they had a breakthrough—"

"Excuse me," John interrupted. "How long has she been seeing this woman?"

"Eight months or so," he said. "Anyway, after four months, Caroline remembered the trauma that sparked her depression. As a child, she was abused by her great-uncle."

His story didn't fit with what John had heard about Virgil, who was weird and a loner but not cruel, certainly not to a child. Still, he didn't discount the accusation. Abusers came in all shapes and sizes. "Why was she coming to see him?"

"Lola suggested that Caroline confront Virgil and clear the air. I came along for support. It's a long drive from Portland, and I didn't want her to be alone. As it so happened, we stopped in Reno. That's when we decided to get engaged and married."

"Spur of the moment."

"Romantic," Max said. "I didn't mind the plastic flowers or the obviously drunk justice of the peace wearing a mint-green tux. But Caroline was too exhausted and wanted to go back to her room. Doesn't matter. I will marry her. I'll be with her, no matter what."

"I suppose congratulations are in order." But John didn't offer them. Marriage to this jerk was a big mistake. "Let's back up. When you say the therapist wanted Caroline to 'confront Virgil,' what does that mean?"

"Talking." Apparently, Max wasn't interested in the therapy part of this conversation.

"Why did it have to be in person?"

"Who knows?" He stared through the glass wall as if he saw something fascinating behind John's shoulder. "I suppose she couldn't call him because telephonic interactions are too easy. Virgil could simply disconnect if she said something he didn't want to hear. And she wouldn't have been able to read his body language. What if she wanted to slap the old bastard?"

"Did her therapist tell her to use physical contact?"

"What are you suggesting?" His tone went higher. "That Caroline came to Sagebrush to get even?" His voice was full-fledged soprano. "That she planned to murder her great-uncle?"

Max's attitude was garbage, and John wouldn't dignify it with a response. "That was not my intention."

"It certainly sounds like it's what you're saying."

It was a good thing that Max specialized in the treatment of animals because he didn't do well with humans. John tried to drag him back on topic. "I was asking about possible procedures suggested by Caroline's therapist. Had Caroline communicated with Virgil before? She must have let him know she was coming and planned to meet with him. In a letter? By telephone? When she faced off with him, were you supposed to be in the room?"

"Me? What a terrible idea!" He rolled his eyes like a bratty teenager. "I didn't want to get near that old man.

When I thought about him hurting my sweet girl, I wanted to kill him."

Was that a confession? "You might want to rephrase that statement."

"Why?"

"It sounds like something a murderer might say."

"Don't be absurd. I would never risk going to jail because I rid the world of an old cheapskate like Virgil."

His tone was dismissive but lacked the ring of truth. Max wasn't telling him everything. "Why do you think he was cheap?"

"Well, look where he lived. He didn't have a fancy car or a glamorous lifestyle."

Max wouldn't waste his efforts on a penniless cabin-dweller. If Virgil had been a wealthy man, Max would be singing a different tune…perhaps a two-part harmony with a lawyer.

MORNING LIGHT FILTERED around the edges of the window shade while the hums and chirps of medical monitoring equipment encouraged Caroline to wake up. *Where am I?* A hospital in Durango, Colorado. *What's wrong with me?* A concussion plus scrapes and bruises. She squeezed her eyes shut and groaned, not from pain but from the realization that she'd somehow gotten engaged to Max Sherman. At least, that was what he said. She couldn't remember. *Wait! That's the important part.* She didn't remember much of anything that had happened before she stumbled into a log cabin, discovered a bloody murder victim and met Deputy John Graystone.

She opened her eyelids again. John had called her Scout, and she liked the way it sounded. As Scout, she felt independent and strong, while Caroline was kind of a wimp. Caroline McAllister, CPA, was the kind of woman who could be talked into becoming engaged to a phony like

Max, with his manicured fingernails and his splotchy goatee that he thought made him look like Robert Downey Jr. Scout knew how to stand up for herself, and that energy was needed. A man had been murdered, and Caroline ranked as the most obvious suspect.

What time is it? She looked for her wristwatch, remembering that she'd found it at the cabin. The watch was taken from her when she checked in at the hospital. Did Max have it?

And where was Max? He'd made a big deal of taking care of her, but then he left. Last night, they'd argued, and he took her car. Where did he go? Did she care?

Her thoughts scattered. Nothing made sense. *Settle down.* If she was going to get herself out of trouble, she needed clearheaded focus. She was surprised that John hadn't already arrested her. To be frank, she couldn't swear that she hadn't fired the shots that killed that man. *What was his name?* Virgil—Virgil Hotchner. She needed to solve this murder, but first she needed to get unhooked from these devices and go to the bathroom. Rather than disturbing the nurses, she figured that she could stretch the monitoring equipment. It wasn't far to the louvered bathroom door, not far at all.

She lowered her legs from the bed and stood. Her IV for hydration was hooked to a portable stand. No problem with that. She plucked out the nasal cannula that was pumping oxygen into her lungs. The heart, temp and blood-pressure machines were attached by sticky patches tied into long cords, which weren't easy to navigate. Halfway to the bathroom, she gave up and unfastened the nodes on her chest. The machines burst into a cacophony of beeps as she stepped into the hallway and looked toward the nurses' station.

In a waiting-room chair with minimal padding and wooden arms, John stretched out with his long legs straight in front of him, his arms folded below his chest and his black cowboy hat tilted down to cover his eyes. Looking at him, she automatically smiled. She had no logical reason for the grin she felt spreading across her face, but it made her happy to see him outside her hospital room—a hundred times happier than she would have been to see Max.

A nurse in daffodil-yellow scrubs marched toward her. Her Crocs made a squeaky noise on the patterned vinyl floor. "What do you think you're doing, young lady?"

She placed her finger across her lips to signal quiet and pointed to the sleeping deputy.

The nurse scowled and raised both palms silently asking "Why?"

Caroline mimed the need to go to the bathroom, pointing to her crotch and twisting her legs in knots.

Annoyed, the nurse repeated the "why" gesture.

"I'm awake." John lifted his hat and gazed up at her. "I wouldn't be much of a bodyguard if I could sleep through all this racket."

"Were you supposed to be guarding my body?" she asked.

"Something like that."

"I thought you were here to make sure I didn't try to escape."

"That, too."

To the nurse, she said, "I have to pee."

The nurse hustled her back into the room, sat her on the bed and finished removing the sticky patches that attached to the monitors. "The next time you need to use the bathroom," she said, "press the call button and I'll get you unhooked."

Dragging the IV stand behind her, Caroline went into the bathroom, relieved herself and stood at the sink to wash her hands, which meant she had to remove the gauze wrapping. *Ouch, ouch, ouch.* The abrasions on her palms were sore but healing. She'd need fresh bandages.

Her reflection in the mirror with the bandage wrapped around her head made her look like a disaster victim. Inside her skull, she felt a residual ache. Her knee hurt, and she left that bandage in place. Injuries weren't going to sidetrack her. There were more important things to worry about.

When she returned to the room, the daffodil nurse had smoothed the sheets and light blanket on her bed and was waiting to hook her up to the monitors again. "Let's go."

"I'm ready to be awake," Caroline said. "What time is it?"

"Still early, it's just after six o'clock. You need to get back to sleep."

Instead, Caroline went to the window and raised the shade. The view was amazing. A hopeful pink sunrise lit the sky. Cottonwoods and aspens were turning green. Buffalo grass spread across the hills outside town.

She looked over her shoulder at the nurse and at John. "Beautiful day."

"Here's the deal," the nurse said. "If you lie down and put the cannula back in your nose, I won't hook you up to the rest of the equipment. However, I can't let you leave the grounds until a doc signs a release."

"That works for me. Are my clothes in the dresser?"

"Do not, I repeat, *do not* get dressed until you see the doctor."

"Okay." She perched on the edge of the bed. "This might be a long shot, but do you happen to know where I can find my wristwatch?"

"I do," she said. "It's at the nurse's station. I'll bring the watch to you if you promise to be more cooperative."

"Yes, ma'am."

When the nurse left, she transferred her gaze to John, who dropped his hat on a chair and raked his fingers through his dark brown hair. His light stubble outlined a firm jaw, and she decided her first impression of him was accurate: John was a very handsome man. She needed his help to solve this crime, which meant she had to find a way to make him trust her. Starting with something small might be a good plan. "What happened to the clothes I was wearing last night?"

"The sweatshirt is pretty much ruined," he said. "The good news is that we tested all of your clothes for GSR and found only trace amounts consistent with handling a weapon, not shooting it."

She nodded slowly, not wanting to set off a renewed burst of pain inside her head. "Last night, Deputy Ochoa took swabs from both my hands and Max's to test for gunshot residue."

"And he found nothing," John said. "Neither you nor Mr. Sherman fired that gun."

"Does that mean I'm in the clear?"

"Slow down." He held up his hand, indicating a halt. "It's too early for me to issue a free pass. However, there's other info that looks positive for you."

"Give me the news."

"Your criminal record is clean. You were arrested once, but charges dismissed."

She didn't recall the circumstances. "What did I do?"

"Protested outside a chemical lab that used bunnies for cosmetics testing."

"Good for me." She grinned. "I'm not sure what I can do, John, but I want to help with your investigation."

"How's your memory this morning?"

"I know my name. I can list the last three Presidents of the United States. And I can recite most of the Gettysburg Address."

"Max says you came to Sagebrush to visit Virgil."

"He told me that, too. Virgil is, supposedly, my great-uncle on my mom's side. I wish I could tell you more."

"You mentioned a woman named Lola Powell."

"She's my therapist back in Oregon. I told you I was seeing someone for depression."

"And for PTSD."

Her once-a-week sessions, every Tuesday at eleven in the morning, had seemed to be wrapping up after she'd established a regimen of morning exercise and her daily dose of antidepressant meds. Lola wasn't an M.D. and couldn't prescribe, but she'd discussed Caroline's case with a psychiatrist.

"Lola suggested we go deeper into my childhood memories. I've had trauma in my life that I haven't dealt with, starting with my father who left when I was a toddler."

The deputy's gray-eyed gaze held a warmth that comforted her. "I'm sorry," he said.

Though she needed for John to be on her side, she hated that he might feel sorry for her. "It seems to me that everybody has some kind of trauma. I mean, that's life."

"Do you remember anything about your great-uncle?"

Slowly, she shook her head. "Sorry."

"There's a woman in town who was close to Virgil. I talked to her last night, and she says she met you when you were a kid. Her name is Dolly Devereaux."

She didn't recognize the name. "What does she look like?"

"Why don't you tell me? Just take a stab at it."

"The name Dolly makes me think of Dolly Parton." She shrugged. "That's all I've got."

"You wouldn't be far from wrong. Ms. Devereaux is blond, and she has—" he gestured with both hands as though he was holding a cantaloupe in each "—big ones."

"She sounds like an interesting character. I wish I remembered her."

The nurse breezed back into the room holding the silver wristwatch in her outstretched hand. "Here you go, Caroline."

"Thanks so much." She took the watch and flipped it over to read the inscription aloud. "'With love, Popsy.'"

"Who's Popsy?" he asked.

"Can't remember, but Popsy must be important. This watch is one of my few mementos, and I always keep it with me."

"Are you still in a hurry to leave us?" The nurse automatically smoothed the blankets.

"Nothing personal, but yes."

"I'm not insulted." The nurse went to the door. "The doc should be stopping by within the hour."

John lowered himself into a chair at her bedside and unzipped his leather satchel. "I'll be having breakfast with a couple of CBI agents while I'm in Durango. Deputy Ochoa will be back here to keep an eye on you."

"I'm not going to run away. Where would I go? Obviously, Max has a room, but he might not be happy to see me."

"Trouble in paradise?"

"We argued last night," she admitted. "And he's the kind of guy who holds a grudge. I don't know where he's staying, and he hasn't made any attempt to get in touch with me."

"Here's a thought," John said. "Dolly runs a bed-and-breakfast in Sagebrush. She'd be happy to have you as a guest."

"I'd like that." She could learn more about Virgil from his friend.

"In the meantime, she sent along some clothes for you." He dug deep into his satchel and pulled out a soft, buff-colored sweatshirt, blue-striped T-shirt and khaki cargo pants. "These might be too big, but they're clean."

"Thank you."

"One more thing." He took a five-by-seven photograph from his satchel and smoothed the blank side. "I found this in a frame on your great-uncle's desk."

He placed the picture on her lap, and she was drawn into the scene. She could feel the warmth of the sunshine as it filtered through the pine trees and could smell the hay, the leather and horse manure. Her beautiful, redheaded mother was laughing, sharing a joke with the skinny, bearded man who wore a cowboy hat and a shiny silver belt buckle. Standing in front of them was a girl with straight, bowl-cut hair. Her small, pointed chin stuck out at a stubborn angle. Her lips tried to smile, but terror filled her deep brown eyes.

"It's me."

Even now, the picture frightened her. She saw tension in her fingers as she clutched a stuffed bunny that she'd won at a local carnival. Her mother rested her hand on Caroline's shoulder, reassuring her. Nothing to be afraid of.

This appeared to be an innocent family photo. Now, two of them were dead.

Chapter Four

"I'll tell you what, John. You'd better keep a watchful eye on that lady."

"I intend to." Deputy Graystone tasted the hot, strong, no-nonsense black coffee that made Wilbur's Café famous in the San Luis Valley. "She's still in the hospital, and Ochoa is with her."

"Do you believe her cockamamie amnesia story?"

"Yes, sir, I do." The deputy looked across the table at Sheriff Bishop, who had arranged this breakfast meeting with the CBI agents from the Pueblo office and had already ordered his huevos rancheros scrambled with green chili on the side, extra tortillas and extra bacon. "I also believe that Caroline McAllister will be the key to finding out who murdered Virgil."

"I hope you're right."

With his forefinger, the sheriff smoothed his thick silver mustache. In other aspects, Bishop was an average-looking older guy with a little potbelly and thinning gray hair. But he had impressive facial hair. Respectfully, John addressed the 'stache. "I hope to learn more about her relationship to Virgil after I speak to his attorney, Edie Valdez. Her office is here in Durango, and I have an appointment at half past nine."

"I know Valdez. She's a tough customer, and she's been around for a long time." Bishop craned his neck and looked toward the kitchen, apparently eager for his breakfast. John knew that the old man's wife would never approve of the extra bacon, but Wilbur's Café was named for the pig in *Charlotte's Web*, and pork products were part of every meal. "Seems to me like there are a lot of females involved in this investigation."

Mentally, John ticked off a short list: the lawyer, the therapist, Caroline's mother and Dolly Devereaux. They all had their part to play. "Not a problem."

"Tread carefully," the sheriff advised. "You've always been a soft touch for the ladies."

The waitress arrived with a tray full of side dishes, plus the giant platter of over-easy huevos, refried beans and salsa for the sheriff. At the same time, the two CBI agents—Mike Phillips and Larry Wright—entered the café. Both wore jeans with blazers and button-down shirts. The sheriff focused intently on his breakfast while greeting the agents, then handed them off to John. "Deputy Graystone is in charge of this investigation. Communicate directly with him, and he'll keep me posted. Have you eaten here before?"

Phillips nodded, and Wright said, "No, sir."

"You're in for a treat. I recommend the pork-belly sausages." He looked toward the other man. "Am I right, Agent Phillips?"

"You are correct, sir."

John had already spoken on the phone to Phillips, who was the senior agent and had made the arrangements for Virgil's autopsy in Pueblo. "We appreciate help from the CBI. There are a couple of deputies at the cabin right now, collecting evidence. They're excited to work with your forensic people."

"Our crime-scene unit is the best in the business. If there's evidence in that cabin, our guys will find it."

John liked these two agents. They were direct, efficient

and proud of their work. "Are you planning to drive back and forth from Pueblo?"

"We'll set up an office with the Durango police and stay in a local motel. It's too far to drive every day."

"Let me know if I can help," John said. He was ready to get down to business. "Our victim didn't have many enemies. I'm hoping you can fill in the blanks about Derek Everett, the guy who died in jail. Did he have friends or family who wanted revenge against Virgil?"

"He wasn't officially married, but there was a woman who claimed he was the father of her kids. She's deceased. As for friends, nobody liked this guy. He got knifed in jail. We'll keep digging into his associates to see if we can find a lead." Phillips leaned back in his chair. "Tell us what you've got, Deputy."

While John launched into a summary, they ordered eggs, sausage, hash browns and coffee. Interest from the CBI agents picked up when he started talking about Caroline and her memories, or lack thereof. "According to her supposed fiancé," John said, "she's related to Virgil Hotchner. She claims that she doesn't remember him, but there was a photograph of Virgil, Caroline's mother and Caroline as a child on his desk."

"We'll find out more when we access his bank records," Phillips said, "and his phone records and talk to his lawyer."

"Ms. Valdez," John said. "I have an appointment with her in less than an hour."

The junior agent—Larry Wright—was built like a thick-necked brahma bull and had already devoured the sausages on his plate. He dabbed at his mouth with surprising delicacy. "The autopsy hasn't started yet, but the body is in the morgue. Here's a photo of a tattoo on his forearm."

Wright held up his cell phone and showed them a tat of a bunny rabbit. The fancy script surrounding it said, "Sweet Caroline," like the classic Neil Diamond song.

"She meant something to him," Phillips said. "You've found out a lot. That's good, so good, so good."

AT TWENTY MINUTES past nine, John entered a two-story redbrick office building on Main Street in the historic section of Durango. Across the hardwood floors in the front lobby was a door with Law Offices etched in gold on the frosted glass window. He opened the door and stepped inside a tastefully decorated waiting room with a long counter and a nameplate that read, Becky Cruz, Paralegal and Receptionist.

The young woman in a pinstriped pantsuit stood behind the counter while arranging a bouquet of red roses in a vase. She smiled. "Deputy Graystone, what did you bring me?"

He glanced over his shoulder and saw Max seated in the center of the leather sofa. His skinny arms stretched across the back of the sofa and his legs were crossed in a figure four, taking up as much space as possible. With a simpering grin, he repeated Becky's question. "What did you bring? I felt certain that roses would ensure an appointment with Ms. Valdez."

John's hand went to his belt. "Handcuffs."

"For me? Very kinky." Becky fluttered her long eyelashes. "When Edie is done with her spin class, you can go first."

John was signed up for the nine-thirty slot, and he wasn't about to let Max snake his appointment away from him. The nearest fitness studio—called the Burn—was around the corner. "Spin class?"

Becky nodded. "Every morning at eight-fifteen. Feel the Burn."

If he hurried, John figured he could catch her after she left her exercise bike, showered, dressed and walked to her office. Promising to be right back, he slipped out the door.

He hadn't even rounded the corner when Max trotted up and joined him.

"Slow down, Deputy. I'm not letting you get a head start."

"What are you doing here?"

"After your aggressive handling of Caroline with the handcuffs and the armed guard, I thought we might need legal counsel."

"Why this particular attorney?"

"Why not?" He stuck out his jaw, emphasizing his patchy goatee. "I have the right to select and hire whomever I choose."

"I'd have thought an important vet like you would have an attorney on call."

"Of course, I do. But he's in Portland. I want somebody local."

A fiftysomething woman wearing a chic black suit and carrying a leather briefcase stalked toward them at an energetic pace. Max tried to block her route, but she held up a slender hand to direct him out of her way without breaking stride.

"Let me guess," she said. "You gentlemen are Deputy Graystone and Max Sherman. My nine-thirty and nine-forty-five appointments. Deputy, you'll go first."

Max scampered along beside her. "Ms. Valdez, I believe I should go first. My concerns are far more complex and important. Not to mention, I would be a paying client."

"Good point." She glanced at John. "Why do you need to see me?"

"Murder investigation," he said.

She gave a short, sardonic laugh. "You win. Nothing tops murder."

Stifling an urge to gloat, he followed Ms. Valdez into her building. She paused at the counter and glared at Becky, and then at the vase of long-stemmed roses. "Get rid of the flowers. This is a law office. Not a boudoir."

"Yes, ma'am." She smiled at Max and shrugged.

"Deputy," Edie snapped, "come with me."

Natural light from an arched, south-facing window and a glass-paned French door spilled into her stylish, modern office. Potted plants, most of which were cacti, lined the windowsill. The fenced-in patio outside the door featured similar high-desert landscaping as well as a circular, glass-topped table and chairs. John suspected that the patio allowed her to make a quick escape from meetings she'd rather not attend. Smart lady.

The only artwork was a Georgia O'Keefe-style cow skull with mountains in the background that hung above a long sofa. Her framed diplomas took up a significant portion of the wall space. Other photographs showed Edie shaking hands with local politicians from both parties. John wondered if she changed them after each election.

She lowered herself into a swivel chair behind her sleek L-shaped desk with a gleaming agate top. He sat opposite her desk in a gray upholstered chair and waited while she combed her fingers through her short salt-and-pepper hair, then placed black-frame glasses on her nose and fixed him with a steady gaze. "Deputy Graystone, I looked you up on the computer when you contacted my answering service after hours last night."

Apparently, she was a night owl. "I was surprised when your service called me back and offered an early morning appointment."

"You aren't the only person who works long hours," she said. "Your credentials and background are impressive. When I read about your mother's years of service in the Colorado Springs Police Department and your father's career as a decorated US Air Force lieutenant colonel, I wanted to get in touch with you. Sheriff Bishop is on the brink of retirement, and you're qualified to replace him."

"Thank you." John knew the sheriff's job was within his grasp but wasn't sure if he wanted to stay rooted in Sagebrush.

"How are your parents?"

"Happily retired. Currently, they're living in Australia."

"Good for them." The smile disappeared from her face. She appeared to be disappointed that she wouldn't be able to arrange a meet with his mom and dad. "Let's get down to business. You're here about the murder of Virgil Hotchner. How did you get my name?"

This was not a woman who suffered fools gladly. If he answered wrong, she'd toss him out on his bottom. He responded honestly without embellishment. "Last night at the crime scene, there was a fire in the hearth. I couldn't tell exactly what had been burned but managed to save several scraps. Letterhead with your name was among them."

"Was there enough of the document to see what it was about?"

"I'm afraid not."

"You are correct in assuming that I did legal work for Virgil. There isn't much more I can tell you, Deputy. I'm restrained by confidentiality from talking to you about my work with Virgil. Not without a court order."

"I understand." John had expected this roadblock. "I have a few general questions starting with Ms. McAllister's relationship to Virgil. Was he her great-uncle on her mother's side?"

"Yes." She rested her elbows on her desk and leaned forward.

Her dark eyes challenged him, daring him to proceed, while at the same time she seemed to be anticipating the moment when he would fail to meet expectations. He asked, "Did Virgil have a will?"

Her upper lip curled in a sneer. "I don't know what you've heard about me, but I'm proficient at my job. There's no way I'd allow a client who was worth as much as Virgil Hotchner skate by without a will."

He sensed a crack in her stone wall and pushed for more information. "Exactly how much was he worth?"

"I'm sure your CBI friends will clarify his finances when they subpoena his bank and savings records. I'll just say that he was quite well off."

If John had an idea of the old man's net worth, he could gauge whether monetary gain provided a motive for murder. Would sweet Caroline kill her uncle for his wallet? He didn't want to suspect her, but the facts pointed in her direction. He tried a different track. "Who is the executor of his will?"

"You're looking at her, Deputy Graystone."

"In addition to Caroline, did Virgil have other family?"

"Not that I'm aware of," she said. "Like me, he was smart enough to never get married. And he didn't have children."

He asked, "Is Caroline the primary beneficiary of his estate?"

"I'll file the documents with probate today and make the will available shortly after that. Be patient, John."

This was the first time she'd used his given name, and he wondered if this small step toward familiarity meant she approved of him, or if it indicated a lack of respect. He didn't push his luck by calling her Edie. His next question was open-ended and important. "If I hope to find Virgil's murderer, I need more information as soon as possible. As his attorney, you'd know his investment advisor, his real-estate agent and partners he might be working with. Are there any names you can give me?"

Instead of answering, she deflected. "I heard that Caroline is suffering from long-term amnesia and can't recall her own name. Is this true?"

"She's beginning to remember." He thought of the expression in her eyes when she looked at the family photograph. She had been surprised and excited, as if she'd found a valuable piece of jewelry—a treasure—that was supposed to be lost forever. "The neurologists expect her to make a significant recovery."

"And this fellow in my waiting room, Max Sherman. What's his angle?"

"He claims that he and Caroline are engaged and intend to get married right away. She doesn't remember and doesn't seem all that fond of Max."

Ms. Valdez leaned back in her chair and tapped on her desktop with a sharpened, polished fingernail. "You don't like Max, do you?"

"A sudden, unexpected engagement is suspicious." This idea had been rolling around in his head ever since he met Max, but he hadn't articulated it until now. "If Virgil was wealthy and Caroline was his only heir, Max's desire to get married makes sense. As Caroline's husband, he'd inherit."

She shook her head. "Is that what they call the long arm of the law? Because your logic is quite a reach."

"Is it?"

"Not my problem. I don't investigate. I prosecute or defend, and Max is about to become my client." She paused. "That means I don't have the luxury of personal opinions."

John rose from his chair. "I appreciate any help you can give me."

"I like you, John." She stood, came around her desk and shook his hand. "Rafael Valdez, my nephew, played in a weekly poker game with Virgil. He's a broker and might have given him financial advice."

"Thank you, ma'am."

As he exited her office, he donned his black cowboy hat. If this was how she treated the people she liked, he was glad not to be her enemy.

Chapter Five

Though the nurses at Mercy Regional Medical Center in Durango swore things were moving as quickly as possible, it seemed to take forever for Caroline to get one of the doctors to sign a release form. The scrapes on her hands had been treated with small, almost unnoticeable, bandages. Her head wound had a fresh gauze patch and was covered by a denim baseball cap. The medical opinion was mostly positive, with an expectation that much of her memory would return over the next few days. There shouldn't be significant permanent brain damage, but the hours immediately before and after her injury might be erased forever.

She promised one of the neurologists that she'd stay in touch. Later, he could paste electrodes to her head and study the effects of amnesia. For right now, it was imperative to find out who killed Virgil. Otherwise, she might end up in jail.

Dressed in the clothes Dolly had loaned her, which were too big and too long, Caroline was ready to take on the world, but not entirely on her own terms. For one thing, she needed her car. Though she had her purse, license and car keys, she had no idea where Max had taken her Tahoe. Rather than tracking him down, she asked Deputy Miguel Ochoa if he'd give her a ride to Sagebrush. "Without handcuffs," she added.

"Only if you promise not to run away like a jackrabbit."

"Promise."

Riding in the passenger seat of Ochoa's official SUV, she was finally on her way to Dolly Devereaux's bed-and-breakfast, where she'd meet John. In her purse, she found a pair of sunglasses and slipped them on. She loved these Ray-Bans that she'd bought in San Diego. *Another memory.* Bit by bit, her identity was becoming clear. "Thanks, Deputy Ochoa, for helping me."

"It's my job. If you'd taken your own car, I was supposed to follow. I'm glad you're with me. This is easier."

"So I'm still a suspect?"

"Si." He glanced toward her. "Before you leave town, would you do me a favor?"

"Name it."

"My wife, Lucinda, is taking psychology classes at Adams State, and she'd like to talk to you about amnesia for her final paper."

"Cool. I've never been anybody's final paper before."

"Or maybe you have," he suggested. "But you don't remember."

Yesterday, she must have driven through the San Luis Valley with Max to get to Sagebrush, but she didn't remember the grass being so green or the wildflowers so bright. In this season, the rivers were high with runoff from the winter snow. The headwaters of the Rio Grande cut a winding swath through the valley at the start of a journey that went all the way to Mexico. In the distance beyond the foothills, she saw snow draped over the highest peaks of the Sangre de Cristo Range. "How could I forget this landscape?"

"You're lucky," Ochoa said. "Not many people see natural beauty for the first time. You get to see it twice."

She exhaled a contented sigh and tried to recall the first time she'd been here when she was a kid, traveling with her mom. Had they come here more than once? Did they go hiking or camping? Did they build a fire?

Deputy Ochoa announced, "Here's our turn for Sagebrush."

A small Western town unfolded before them. Center Street was two-and-a-half blocks with storefronts on both sides and slanted parking at the sidewalk. The businesses were typical: a couple of taverns, a bakery, a diner, a coffee shop and a hardware store. A gas station and auto repair shop were on the first corner. In the middle of Center was a two-story bank and office building. At the far end, Ochoa turned right and drove two blocks to a hanging sign for Devereaux's Bed and Breakfast. In the front yard were yellow potentilla shrubs, wild daisies, three slender aspen and a tall blue spruce. A long, asphalt driveway led around to the front entrance of a three-story, redbrick house with crisp white trim and a forest-green door.

With his arms folded across his chest and his hat tilted back, John Graystone leaned against the center pillar of the covered porch that stretched across the front of the house. With his five-pointed bronze star pinned to his khaki uniform shirt and the sleeves rolled up to the elbow, his posture was iconic. He was the archetype of a Western lawman.

When Ochoa parked in a small lot to the left of the house, she leaped from the passenger seat and rushed toward John. She called to the other deputy. "Thanks for the ride."

"De nada."

Her sneakers were filthy from last night in the forest, but she was glad she'd kept them with her in the hospital. Unlike the rest of her clothing, the shoes fit. When she was close enough to throw herself into John's arms and encourage him to pursue the investigation, she held back. Max had shuffled out the door and onto the porch. His presence reminded her of a dark, nasty storm cloud.

"About time," he said. "What took you so long?"

"In case you forgot, I was in the hospital."

"I'm not the one with memory problems." His laugh was cold and fake. "Come on, sweetie, I'll take you back to our motel, and you can catch up on your beauty sleep."

She glanced over her shoulder, noticing her green Tahoe parked at the end of the small lot. Though she wanted her SUV, spending the day with Max wasn't on her agenda. If he took the car, he'd be out of her way. "You go ahead. Maybe I'll join you later."

He stroked his goatee and pursed his lips in a childish pout. "Is that any way to talk to your fiancé?"

What had she ever seen in this man? She'd met him about year ago at a Save the Spotted Owl rally, and she'd liked that he was a veterinarian. They'd dated for about a month, but their relationship had never gotten serious, and she'd *never ever* had sex with him. He was clingy, selfish and snobby. Not good traits for a lover. The only things they had in common were a deep fondness for animals and an appreciation of good sushi. She paused for a moment, realizing that she'd just remembered quite a lot about him. "The doctors were right. I'm recalling things."

"Good for you. Now, let's get moving."

In a firm but quiet voice, she said, "I'm sorry, Max, but—"

"Say no more." He waved his hands. "I get it. You want to hang around with Deputy John and play detective, even though he thinks you're a suspect. By the way, I've engaged an attorney."

"Why?"

"Because you have a talent for getting into trouble." He handed her a business card. "Her name is Edie Valdez. Call her if you need to be bailed out."

He stomped down the porch stairs and went to her Tahoe as if he owned the SUV. Another of his obnoxious traits was treating her property, like her car and her condo, as his own. He liked to take advantage of people and make himself feel superior. As if she was a peasant who should be thrilled to serve King Maxwell.

Deputy John—who was, by contrast, a real man—held open the green door. "Dolly had to run some errands, and she left me in charge. Would you like water, coffee, tea? Or tequila?"

Several shots of tequila might take away the bad taste of Max's attitude, but the alcohol would also destroy the shards of memory that had resurfaced. "I'd better stick to coffee."

"This way to the kitchen."

He directed her through the charming house, which was decorated with overstuffed furniture, oak tables and floral pattern drapes. Beyond the living room was an extra-large dining room that had a table with twelve place settings. There was also a woven runner and small planters for violets and primroses, along with eucalyptus candles that cleansed the air.

In the huge kitchen, she sat at a casual table and accepted a gold-striped, ceramic mug from John. The first sip was coffee-scented heaven. Though she'd had breakfast at the hospital, the tiny muffins in Dolly's kitchen beckoned. John put together a plate for her.

When he took a seat at the small table, she couldn't hide her smile. A tasty breakfast with a good-looking man came close to her idea of a perfect morning. The only way it could be improved was if she and the handsome man had just tumbled out of bed together—it was an idea so inappropriate that her cheeks burned.

She cleared her throat. "Okay, where should we start?"

"Tell me about the photograph I gave you," he said.

Though she'd brought the photo with her in her purse, she didn't take it out. The fear she'd felt when she'd first seen it was still too strong, new and confusing. "I had a stuffed bunny, and I remember winning it at a local carnival by tossing coins in a bowl. A stupid game. The only way to win is sheer luck, but I did it and I got Miss Bunny Foo Foo. For years, she was one of my favorite toys."

"That's a solid bit of memory."

"I'm improving," she said. "The docs expect an almost full recovery."

He gazed at her across the rim of his own coffee mug. "Where was this carnival?"

"Somewhere up here in the mountains. I can't really remember but that's not the amnesia. I was only seven years old, and not great on locations. Plus, that was twenty years ago."

"Do you remember where the photo was taken?"

"I don't know." She peeled off the paper cupcake liner and bit into a muffin with a crunchy cinnamon-and-brown-sugar topping. *Delicious.* "Hanging around a barn isn't my idea of fun. It smells like manure and hay."

"You're a city gal."

She wanted to deny the girlish label, but Caroline honestly did prefer the city to the untamed wilderness. "You're the native. Do you recognize the barn?"

"It looks familiar, but I couldn't place it until I showed Dolly a copy of the photo. She said the barn was now painted yellow and belongs to a Russian guy named Yuri Popov. He plays in a regular weekly poker game with your great uncle."

She noticed his use of the present tense when he said "plays" in a poker game. How long would it take for John to shift Virgil to past tense? "Have you spoken to Mr. Popov?"

"Tonight is the poker game. I'll see him then." He rose from his chair, went to the counter and poured another cup of coffee, finishing the pot. "I want to ask you a couple of personal questions, starting with your occupation."

"I'm a CPA," she said with wonderment, as though that

simple fact was a revelation. "I have a feeling you already knew. That kind of info is easily available in a computer search."

"I did a search."

Looking into his luminous gray eyes made her tingle inside, and the pleasant sensation spread throughout her body. "What did you find?"

"You work part-time from a small office in Portland with other CPAs, secretaries, typists and attorneys. With each of your specialties, you're like an office staff for rent. In addition to helping clients file their taxes, you do accounting work and billing for several charities, including Save the Spotted Owl and Feral Cat Rescue."

She was a little bit uncomfortable having him know so much. "Is my background relevant to your investigation?"

"Leads to another question," he said. "With your part-time work and pro bono accounting, you don't earn enough to pay for your four-bedroom condo in the Pearl District. I'm guessing that you have another source of income."

"Pearl District." When she thought of her condo, memories bombarded her. Views of snow-capped Mount Hood from a high-rise window. Sounds of boats and lapping waves from the Willamette River. Tinkling bells on the doors of vintage shops. Parks filled with trees and fragrant rhododendrons. She adored the Pearl District—it was hip and historic with great restaurants. She licked her lips. "Sushi. Empanadas. Barbecued oysters. Fresh croissants."

"Memories," he said.

"All the good stuff. In answer to your question, I have a trust fund."

"You don't have to tell me how much. The CBI agents will be digging into your finances. But I want to know two things. First, did you inherit from your family? Second, did Virgil also have family wealth?"

"My family has always been small. Mom and I didn't

start wealthy, but nest eggs and investments have funneled down to me, including a half-million-dollar insurance policy payoff when Mom was killed. I really can't say much about Virgil." She crinkled her brow, trying to figure out why John was asking about her finances. The answer came in a flash. "If Virgil was wealthy, that's a motive."

"Certainly among the top four." He ticked them off on his fingers. "Lust, love, loathing and loot."

"That sounds like something Hercule Poirot would say."

He stood before her, sipping his coffee. "For the next part of my questioning, we need more privacy. Shall we go to the bedroom Dolly has arranged for you?"

"Deputy Graystone, are you asking me to go to bed with you?"

He hesitated a few seconds too long, and an image of rumpled sheets and entwined limbs flashed in her mind. He said, "I spoke to your therapist in Portland. She tried to explain how her treatment for PTSD works, but I didn't follow. She offered to do a phone session with you."

Her therapy with Lola Powell touched on the most personal, intimate parts of her life. Her reactions were unpredictable. She wept or laughed or screamed like a banshee. John was correct—she wanted as much privacy as she could get.

After trooping through the front foyer, she followed him up the wide staircase to a landing on the second floor, where a long hallway bisected the house. Each direction had several closed doors with gold numbers fastened to them. He took her to number seven at the right corner and opened the door. "Dolly calls this the master suite, with its own bathroom attached."

A color scheme of lavender and soft green was reflected on the duvet of a king-size bed and the tufted backings on the Victorian-style chairs that sat beside a marble-topped table. The four-drawer dresser with attached mirror was also covered with a variegated marble slab. The window seat had a stunning view of the mountains. In spite of all the antiques, the room didn't look prissy. The soft duvet and furniture felt welcoming. "This will be perfect for therapy."

"Do you have any special needs?" he asked.

"Just to be comfortable."

He sat in one of the Victorian chairs and took out his cell phone. "I'd like to stay in the room during your session."

She didn't think of herself as a shy person, but she barely knew John Graystone. And she liked him. *There. I admitted it to myself.* Despite the fact that he slapped a pair of handcuffs on her the first time they met, she was attracted to him. And she didn't want to ruin any chance of a relationship by bursting into a Niagara Falls of tears or blurting out some ridiculous phobia. But she didn't want to create barriers. The investigation came first. If John thought he might learn something that would help the investigation by being in the room, she couldn't say no.

"Try not to judge me," she said. "And don't interrupt."

"You're brave to do this," he said.

"Brave?" If true, why did her hand tremble? Why was her stomach clenched in a knot? "Before I change my mind, put through the call to Lola."

She went around the room, pulling down the shades to block the midday sun. She took off her cap and smoothed her straight brown hair around the gauze bandage. Then she stretched out on the soft duvet and arranged the pillows. Eyes closed, she tried to remember as much as she could about the PTSD therapy. The process was similar to guided meditation or hypnosis, and the goal was to uncover memories of bad things that had happened in her past. *Ironic!* The stress that disrupted her life and dragged her into depression came from repressed memories of traumatic events. And now she had amnesia. Shouldn't that be a cure?

She heard John speaking to Lola as he walked across the

room toward the bed. "Thank you, Ms. Powell, for agreeing to do this session with Caroline. She's given me permission to stay in the room. I'm going to put you on speaker and leave the phone on the bedside table."

Lola's gentle alto voice flowed through the speaker. "Deputy Graystone, is there anything specific that you're hoping to hear?"

"General impressions," he said. "Virgil Hotchner is as much a mystery to me as he is to Caroline. I'll step back now."

Caroline spoke up. "Hi, Lola. Guess you heard about my amnesia."

"Are you in any pain?"

"A little headache. Nothing much."

"Are you taking pain medication?"

"No."

"You don't need to remember the phases we developed to get into your subconscious," Lola said. "We're returning to a mental state where you've been before. The process should be as natural as falling asleep or breathing in and breathing out."

"I'm tense," Caroline admitted.

"That's to be expected. You've experienced a fresh trauma, something we'll have to work on when you get back to Portland." Her voice took on a rhythmic cadence. "I want you to hum along with me. Do you remember the song?"

For relaxation, Caroline had chosen a tune from childhood, "Little Bunny Foo Foo," because it always made her smile. She hummed along without the words, the first verse through the third, and then started over. Gradually, her stress flowed away from her body like the ebb tide left the shore. She kept humming, emptying her mind, thinking of nothing.

Lola counted backward from her current age to seven

years old. "You're in Colorado. In the mountains. What do you see?"

"So many trees and branches and bushes with berries. I see blue skies." Caroline spoke in her adult voice. Though she was aware that she wasn't a little girl, her identity was the same whether a grownup or a child. "I hear chickens cackling. And other sounds. Hush, do you hear the rustling in the forest?"

"What is it?"

"Something scary like a bear. But not so big. A snake in the grass." A heavy shudder ripped down her spine. "I need to find Virgil."

"Why?"

"He'll help me. He can keep me safe. I have to go to the barn."

"Slowly, slowly," Lola urged. "You've never talked about the barn before. What does it look like?"

"Huge." Caroline spread her arms wide to illustrate. "Big animals live in there. Horses, I don't like horses. I want to love them like my mom. She's teaching me to ride, and I'm trying really hard. But the horses scare me."

"What else is inside the barn?"

"Hay bales and tools and stuff you use to go riding, like saddles and bridles. Virgil calls it tack. I see the horse, the one in the picture. He's mean."

"Why do you think so?"

"I know he is. The chestnut stallion is Baron, and he's not in his stall." Her legs curled up in a fetal position. Her forehead twisted with worry. "He's so big."

"Let's leave the barn."

"He's pushing me. I can't get away. What if I fall down? He'll crush me."

"Caroline, listen to me. We have to leave the barn."

"Too late. He's going to kill me."

Panic overwhelmed her.

Chapter Six

John had agreed not to interfere with her therapy, no matter what. But how could he sit idly by and watch while she was in so much pain? Her breathing came in tortured gasps. Her complexion flushed a mottled red, and she trembled. Though nothing had touched her physically, Caroline's fear was real.

Her therapist on the cell phone urged her to breathe and to hum but didn't offer words of comfort or reassurance. Instead, Lola advised her client to confront her memory and to fight the terror. Caroline's small bandaged hands drew into fists as though she could punch her way out of this nightmare.

Not what he'd expected. John never thought therapy would be so visceral. He'd imagined there was some kind of safe word to end the session. He'd seen a magic act in Reno where the magician clapped his hands to wake up the people who were in a trance. But this wasn't a stage act. Caroline claimed this therapy had helped her deal with depression. Had it? To him, Lola's directions seemed cruel.

In a barely audible voice, Caroline babbled about the demon steed with eyes like glowing embers and hooves of sharpened steel that would slice into her arms and legs. When she moaned, John shifted his weight in the chair. Uncomfortable, he was helpless and hated the feeling.

"Listen to me," Lola snapped. "Forget about the damned horse, Caroline. Tell me about Virgil."

"But I mustn't turn my back on Baron."

"Where's Virgil? Find Virgil."

"He's not here. Nobody is in the barn but me and Baron. Nobody is in the saddle." Her head whipped back and forth on the pillows as though she was searching for help, though her eyes were closed. "Here's Baron. He's coming at me. He lowers his big head. Drooling. Stinky. I'm trying to sneak away but he won't let me. He shoves me with his nose. I'm up against the stall. The rough wood scrapes my hand and gives me splinters. Baron slobbers on my arm. He pushes me again. Ow!"

Her lips compressed into a tight horizontal line. With her right hand, she grasped her left wrist and cradled it against her chest. "It hurts, hurts so much."

She went silent. Her eyes were still closed, and he wished he knew what was going on inside her head. He rose from the chair and walked toward the bed, ready to scoop her into his arms and rescue her…from what? He couldn't save her from a memory.

Less than an hour ago, he'd wanted her to remember everything about her great-uncle. Now, it was the opposite. As he waited for Lola to continue, he heard traffic noises in the background on her phone. Was she attempting to manage this delicate situation while driving? He didn't like her methods or her attitude. As far as he was concerned, she had the bedside manner of Lizzie Borden.

"Come on, Caroline." Lola's voice was demanding. "You need to leave the barn and go to the cabin, the place where Virgil lives."

"Okay." Though Caroline continued to gently clasp her wrist, her attitude changed. She was more confident, reminding him of when they'd first met. "Virgil's cabin is made from logs. There's a red door. I never told you that before."

"Maybe it wasn't always red."

"Last night, it was locked, and I couldn't get inside."

"This isn't about last night," Lola said. "You're seven years old, visiting your great-uncle. Go into the cabin and find him."

"Okay." Though she didn't open her eyes, she said, "I see him. He's in the kitchen, making chocolate-chip cookies."

A smile played on her lips, and John was relieved. Though Max had told him Virgil was an abuser, this old cowboy baking treats for his little niece didn't make him seem like a monster. Caroline sat up on the bed and held up her arm. "Look, Virgil. The bad horse hurt me. We better go to the doctor."

If there was a regular doctor she saw as a child, he might be able to find records of her injuries A doctor would tell whether she'd been attacked by an abuser or had an accident with a "bad horse." John needed facts to back up her memories.

Her smile widened. "Uncle Virgil hugs me really tight."

He braced himself. Some abuse started with inappropriate touching from an adult. He needed to be alert to that possibility. The therapist reflected his concern.

Lola said, "How do you feel, Caroline? Where is he touching you?"

"His whiskers tickle."

"Is he threatening you?"

"He wants to give me a special present from the treasure chest that's hidden in the wall in my bedroom. He has a necklace with a gold coin."

John made a mental note to look for a wall safe in that room when they returned to the cabin. Hiding precious metal in the wall counted as weird and possibly suspicious behavior. The coins might be contraband or stolen.

Caroline raised her arms over her head and yawned. "I'm ready to wake up, Lola."

"In a minute, Caroline. First, you need to relax and hum your song, meditate."

"And then…what?"

"Then we'll be done."

John stepped forward and picked up the cell phone. Speaking softly, he asked, "Ms. Powell, is this session finished? Can I wake her?"

"Please take the phone into the hallway," Lola said. "We should talk."

"Is it safe to leave Caroline alone?"

"Perfectly safe, Deputy Graystone, but if you're concerned, leave the door open so you can keep an eye on her."

In the hallway outside the master suite, he watched Caroline as she slept on her side. Her hair was mussed, and the gauze patch had slipped away from her head wound, but her breathing was steady and calm. The outer sweatshirt tangled around her body and the too-large cargo pants hung low on her slender hips, making her look like a kid playing dress-up. She'd kicked off her sneakers, and her bare feet curled under her.

He spoke into the phone. "Was this a typical session?"

"Actually, no. And the variations worry me. Caroline and I have been working on her PTSD for months with sessions once or twice a week. A change in her central narrative could unravel her recovery."

"What is that change?"

"She has identified Virgil as her abuser, the source of her traumatic memories. Now, she's talking about him as a cookie baker and blaming a horse for her panic."

"How can you tell which version is correct?"

"Maybe it's both," she said. "It's no secret that she used to hate horses."

"Used to?" Her fear had sounded clear and present to him.

"When she was a kid. As she grew older, I believe the animals were symbolic of speed and related to her mother's death in a car crash."

"You got all that from what Caroline just said?"

"Of course not." Her tone was brusque. "My conclusions are drawn after months of sessions similar to this one and from talk therapy. In some of our early sessions, I encouraged her to face her equinophobia, the psychological term for fear of horses. She signed up for riding lessons and is no longer crippled by that panic."

An impressive victory for the therapist. Again, he heard traffic noises on her end. "Are you in your car?"

"As a matter of fact, I'm just pulling out into traffic. I was parked while I was directing Caroline. I have a full schedule, Deputy. This was the only way I could work in an appointment at short notice." Briskly, she demanded, "Switch your phone to FaceTime so I can see you."

After adjusting a setting, he and Lola were staring at each other on their tiny screens. Though he could only see her face and a colorful gold-and-green scarf around her neck, he had the impression that she was thin. Her long nose drew a straight line down the middle of her face, and her mouth was a narrow slash highlighted by scarlet lipstick. She was probably in her early thirties, and her brown hair was scraped into a high ponytail. With the tip of her little finger, she touched the corners of her mouth. "Nice to meet you, John."

"Same here, Ms. Powell." He didn't presume to be on a first name basis. John didn't know much about psychology, other than criminal behavior that applied to addicts and drunks. But he didn't like the haphazard way Lola Powell had only dedicated partial attention to Caroline while parked at the side of the road. "Where did you learn your methods?"

"Are you questioning my training?"

"Should I?"

"I went to Berkeley, and I've taken dozens of specialized courses on depression and PTSD. Caroline has been seeing therapists off and on for most of her life. After her mother died, eight years ago, her depression worsened, and she went more regularly. I'm the first to make progress with her. Not that I owe you an explanation."

"Ms. Powell, this is a murder investigation," he explained. "If you're called to testify on Caroline's behalf, you will damn sure need to outline your credentials for the court. A recommendation from Maxwell Sherman isn't enough."

"Max told me you had a problem with him."

John put a lid on his temper. It wouldn't do any good to erupt. "Since we're on the subject of Max, what do you think of their sudden engagement?"

"I can't say. You understand, patient-therapist confidentiality."

"I'm not asking for a diagnosis, just an opinion."

"Sorry, John." He could hear the smirk in her voice.

He was done with this conversation. "Is there anything I need to do after Caroline wakes up?"

"Frankly, I'm concerned about her. She's sliding back into denial about Virgil and his abuse. I ought to fly out to Colorado and spend some time with my client."

Much as he wanted to keep her and Max at bay, he couldn't stop either of them. "I'm sure we all want what's best for Caroline. In the meantime, please send an email with your credentials to my office for my files."

"Why? Are you planning to take her to trial? Put her in handcuffs again? Charge her with murder?"

"I can't talk about my plans." He took pleasure in turning her confidentiality comment back at her. "Not during an ongoing investigation."

Before she could snarl a hostile response, he disconnected the call. He wasn't establishing good rapport with the women involved in this case. Edie Valdez brushed him off like an annoying gnat, and Lola Powell was openly hostile. Sheriff Bishop wouldn't be surprised; he thought John didn't handle women well. Possibly true. Not that it mattered. The only woman he cared about and wanted a connection with was Caroline.

At the far end of the hallway, two of the other guests at the Devereaux B and B headed toward their room. A white-haired couple, they were giggling and trying to hide the bottle of red wine from Fox Fire Farms in the Valley, as if Dolly would mind. After a friendly wave, he closed the bedroom door, crossed the room and sat beside Caroline on the bed.

On her back, she was lying—still and relaxed—with her right hand still holding the left wrist. Below her straight bangs, her complexion was pale. A light sprinkle of freckles was scattered across her button nose. Her thick, black lashes formed crescents on her cheeks. She blinked. Slowly, her eyes opened. For a moment, his questions and concerns faded while he focused on this lovely, delicate woman. How had sweet Caroline gotten entangled in a bloody murder?

He gazed into the depths of her deep brown eyes, noticing flecks of gold at the outer rim of the irises. Thinking of their connection, he was tempted to kiss her forehead, her cheek or her full, pink lips. For most of his life, he'd done what was expected, what was honorable and right. With a cop for a mom and a lieutenant colonel for a father, he hadn't been encouraged to take risks. Kissing a murder suspect fell into the category of super-inappropriate.

Lightly, he stroked her smooth brown hair and removed the gauze pad. The area surrounding her head wound had been carefully shaved to avoid creating a large bald spot. She'd mentioned eight stitches, and he could see where she had been treated. "Not much blood," he said. "You might want to wash it off."

"Would you do it for me?" she asked. "I can't really see the top of my head."

He stood and held out his hand to help her to her feet. "We'll clean your wound in the bathroom."

As she trotted along behind him, she said, "I'd really like to get my suitcase so I could change clothes, but I don't want to see Max. I can't believe I agreed to be engaged to him. He's not even a good friend."

John couldn't help grinning. He wanted to do a fist pump and victory yell but held back. "Does that mean you'd rather stay here at Dolly's place?"

"Absolutely. It's charming."

And, he'd noticed, Dolly didn't have many guests. She'd be happy to rent out another room. "After we get you cleaned up, we'll go down to the kitchen and see if we can talk Dolly out of lunch."

She closed the toilet seat and sat so he could see her head wound clearly. "What did you think of the therapy session?"

"I could use more explanation." Lola was too hostile and defensive to be much help. "How does it work?"

"My sessions with Lola are like dreams or nightmares. Some bits I can recall in detail. Others are vague. Mostly, the session floats out of my mind." She paused, frowning. "It's not like amnesia, where the memory is nonexistent until I get it back, and then it fills out."

"Give me an example."

"You mentioned my condo in Portland's Pearl District. In my mind, I can see those streets and I know the menus of my favorite restaurants."

"And this recent session. What do you remember?" He reached into a drawer beside the sink and found a comb with wide-spaced tines. Carefully, he stroked through her straight, chin-length hair, trying not to pull at the stitches. "Tell me if I hurt you."

"It's fine." Without moving her head, she peeked up at him. "Let me think. What do I recall? Oh, the horse in that photo. His name was Baron, and he was mean. I got stuck in the barn with him, and he scared me. I was certain that he was going to stomp on me with his giant hooves or knock me to the ground."

"Did he hurt you?"

She held up her left hand. "He pushed me up against a stall, and I sprained my wrist."

"Did you go to the doctor?"

"I must have." She stared at her wrist. "I think I remember. The doc wrapped it in a pink wrist brace. Virgil always took good care of me."

He made a mental note to check on medical records for her. "Do you remember the doctor's name?"

"No."

"What did your mother say when she heard about the injury?"

"I guess she was okay with it. Mom was back in Portland doing her art while I was staying with Virgil for a few months in the summer. Mom wanted me to learn how to ride, but I couldn't get over my fear of horses. Not until recently, when I took riding lessons."

"Lola told me that was her idea." He took a clean white washcloth from the shelf and dampened the end to gently dab at her stitches. "Is that true? Were the lessons her idea?"

"Maybe. I don't know," she said. "Lola can be really insistent. The first time I talked about Virgil hurting me, she labeled him an abuser."

"And you don't think that's true," John said.

"Sure, he was gruff, and he didn't hesitate to scold me

or give me a swat on my bottom. But abuse?" She shook her head. "I don't know."

"Max said you intended to confront him."

"I was angry," she admitted, "but I just wanted to talk. Lola advised me to meet him, and she's given me good advice. I've been to psychiatrists, psychologists, psychics and faith healers. She's the only one who has made a difference."

But was the difference positive? Was she coming closer to the truth? "Do you know where Lola got her training? She said she went to Berkeley."

"But I don't think she graduated, not that it matters to me. Do you know what's really unfair?"

"What?"

"My insurance won't pay for my sessions with Lola. Just because she doesn't have some kind of whoop-de-do degree."

Not often did John agree with insurance companies, but in this case…he could understand. Lola wasn't necessarily a phony, but she didn't have the credentials to practice psychotherapy and meddle in people's lives. "You mentioned a necklace with a gold coin and a treasure chest hidden in your bedroom wall."

She quickly nodded. "Virgil had secret hiding places all over that cabin."

He needed to contact his deputies and the CBI forensic investigators immediately. While they were at the cabin, they could search for the old man's caches. Virgil had more to hide than anyone had expected, and one of those secrets had gotten him killed.

Chapter Seven

Usually after a session with her therapist, Caroline felt invigorated, energetic and in desperate need of a hamburger or other protein. The long-distance phone-call session she'd just finished wasn't much different, except she had renewed concerns about whether or not Virgil had abused her when she was a kid. From the beginning of her relationship with Lola, the therapist pointed to indications of PTSD, due to a trauma unrelated to her mother's death and her father's abandonment. It hadn't taken long for Virgil to emerge as a potential abuser.

She shuffled down the staircase, following John and trying not to trip on her overlong cargo pants. As far as she could tell from a glance in the bathroom mirror, he'd done a good job cleaning her head wound. With her hair combed, she could hardly tell it was there. Still, she decided to wear a gauze pad and the denim baseball cap to protect the stitches.

"How are you feeling?" John asked.

"Not bad but disconnected. I don't feel like me."

If she ever hoped to figure out who she was, she needed to understand her memories about Virgil. Most definitely, her great-uncle had a temper. She remembered how his face blazed a fiery red when he scolded. His growly voice grated on her eardrums like sandpaper. But he also baked chocolate-chip cookies. They sang songs together, told jokes and he listened to her stories about Bunny Foo Foo. He never really spanked her, just gave her a little smack on her bottom. And he always forgave her after she apologized.

Hopping down the last two stairs into the foyer, she was pleased to find her legs weren't stiff or sore in spite of last night's wild run through the forest. *Thank you, Lola, for insisting that I exercise on a daily basis.* After her stay in the hospital, she'd pretty much recovered, physically. Her memories would take longer to come back.

John greeted another couple who were staying at the B and B as he held the door to the front porch for her. "Let's wait for Dolly out here."

"Or we could go into town and grab lunch," she suggested.

"I get it. You're hungry."

"Starving, and it's going to take more than a couple of muffins to fill me up." She settled into a rattan chair with a floral seat cushion while he leaned against the clean white banister at the edge of the long porch. She asked, "What are we going to do this afternoon?"

"Let me make something clear," he said. "You aren't part of an investigative team. The other deputies in Peregrine County and the agents from the CBI are professionally trained to handle the information we're gathering. And they will be looking for Virgil's secret hiding places. However…"

"You need me," she said. "I'm the closest thing to a witness you have."

He tossed his cowboy hat onto a vacant rattan chair and looked at her with a steady gaze. The shine from his silver eyes had faded to a troubled gunmetal gray. "Until we know Virgil's financial status, we won't know if money is a legitimate motive for murder."

"What about the lawyer? Can't she tell you?"

"She has to do what's right legally, which means she

needs to file with the probate court and contact heirs and perform all the duties of an executor. You'll have the right to know what you're going to inherit in the next couple of days, maybe even tomorrow, but Edie Valdez didn't offer to tell me when I saw her this morning. And I don't want to push her."

"Does she scare you?"

"Naw." He shrugged and grinned. "Maybe a little."

The screen door on the front of the B and B swung open, and a mature woman with expertly applied makeup and long, curly blond hair stepped onto the porch carrying a tray with several glasses and a pitcher of iced tea. As soon as she spotted Caroline, she froze in midstride.

John took the tray from her hands before she dropped it. "Dolly Devereaux, this is Caroline McAllister."

"I know." Her hands flew to cover her mouth. "I haven't seen you since you were a little girl, but I'd recognize you anywhere."

Dolly came forward and pulled Caroline into an aggressive hug. As her arms encircled Caroline's shoulders, she made a sound that was half sob and half laughter. Then she deflated like a balloon and sank onto a rattan chair. "Your great-uncle was a decent guy. Good sense of humor. Always made me laugh. Doggone it, I'll miss the old coot."

Until this moment, when confronted by an honest display of grief, Caroline hadn't recognized the depth of sadness caused by Virgil's murder. She was recalling more and more about him but didn't have a clear picture. They'd lost contact. For some reason, he'd written her and Natalie McAllister, her brilliant mother, out of his life.

A memory tickled the back of her mind. She'd gotten Christmas cards from Uncle Virgil and birthday cards, always with a hundred-dollar bill inside. Mom's family was small, and Caroline didn't know anyone from her father's side. Virgil might have been her last living blood relative.

Dolly dabbed at her eyes with an embroidered handkerchief that had appeared from nowhere. Her outfit—shirt, vest and slacks—was entirely black, saved from being too severe by the addition of silver and turquoise jewelry. She poured the iced tea and gave Caroline a smile. "I'm sorry for falling apart like that. Virgil hated when I made a scene."

"I understand. You were close."

"A long time ago, I thought we'd get married, but it wasn't in the cards." A heavy sigh puffed through her pink-painted lips. "Over the years, he helped me so much. I never would have purchased this big old house if he hadn't loaned me the down payment."

John drank half his iced tea in one gulp. "Remember how I told you that Caroline had lost her memory?"

"Oh, my dear, are you feeling okay?"

"I just have a little headache." She touched the denim cap. "But it would help me a lot if you could fill in some of the blanks about my relationship with Virgil."

"He loved you to bits, even got a tattoo. 'Sweet Caroline' it said, with a picture of Bunny Foo Foo. Do you still have that thing?"

Oddly, she hadn't thrown away the stuffed toy, even though it was raggedy and smelled like licorice. Caroline couldn't say why she kept Bunny Foo Foo, but she'd dragged the thing along with her for years. "Foo Foo sits on my dresser behind a jewelry box."

"I'm glad."

"I remember that Virgil sent me cards for Christmas and my birthday. I'm wondering if you're the person who actually bought the cards."

"Guilty," she said. "You know how men are. They forget the nice things."

"And he always put money in the cards."

"A hundred-dollar bill from his stash." Dolly rolled her

saucer blue eyes. "I told him to put his cash in the bank. But did he listen to me? No, he did not."

John stepped forward. "I never thought of Virgil as the kind of guy who kept a stash of hundred-dollar bills. Was he wealthy?"

"Well, I don't think that's really any of your business."

He tapped the five-pointed star pinned to his chest. "It's my job to ask questions."

"So sorry, Johnny boy." Her pretty face crinkled in a frown. "When I look at you, I see a naughty little kid stealing sips of beer from his father. Or a skinny teenager kissing Belinda Meyer behind the garage."

"That was a long time ago, Dolly."

"Okay, I'll be cooperative. Ask me anything."

"Was Virgil rich?"

Dolly tilted her head to one side as she considered. "He wasn't Bill Gates, but Virgil had a goodly chunk of do-re-mi. At one time, his family owned half the land in this county. He didn't have much of a head for business and might have blown through every penny, but he was lucky to have a sister in Portland who made smart investments."

"My grandmother." Caroline still missed her grandma who passed away ten years ago. A smart lady, Grandma got in on the ground floor with some important businesses in Silicon Valley. She budgeted and planned and had more in common with Caroline than the artistic Natalie. "Grandma was a CPA, like me."

John asked, "Dolly, do you know where Virgil's stash was located?"

"A lockbox he kept in a floor safe under the Navajo rug. Do you think he was robbed?"

The possibility of robbery made sense to Caroline. An old man living alone in a remote cabin with lockboxes of cash and other secret hiding places made a tempting target. "What did he say when he called nine-one-one?"

John whipped out his phone. "The dispatcher sent me a recording of his call. I'll play it for you."

She listened to the standard what-is-your-emergency message, which was followed by a raspy voice that had to be Virgil. "Some dang fool stole my Glock, and I think they're creeping around outside the house. I'd like for John Graystone to come check it out. Tell him I've got ice-cold Guinness."

The lively sound of her great-uncle's voice touched her. "He doesn't sound like the sort of man who'd give up without a fight. Didn't he keep his weapons locked up?"

"He has a gun safe in his office," John said. "It was unlocked. The Glock, which ballistic tests determined was the murder weapon, was registered to him."

"I didn't see any sign of a robber," Caroline said. "When I got there, his cabin didn't look like it had been searched."

"You might have interrupted the intruder," John said.

Running through the forest, she'd felt the presence of danger. Back in the old days, before she'd gotten her depression mostly under control, she was prone to anxiety attacks. Tension in her lungs, fog in her brain and the metallic taste in her mouth that came before she vomited. Paranoia would overwhelm her. "I didn't actually see anyone."

Dolly stood and grasped both their arms. "You kids keep talking and come into the kitchen. I have leftover roast beef and potato salad for lunch. And I'm going to get some leggings for you, Caroline. They won't be a perfect fit, but anything is better than those baggy khaki pants."

Caroline had expected Dolly to serve finger sandwiches and hors d'oeuvres to go along with her feminine decor but was happily surprised with hearty slices of beef on rustic artisanal bread with horseradish, sprouts, onion and tomato. She was equally pleased with the conversation, which mainly consisted of Dolly telling stories about Virgil and the men he hung out with in Sagebrush. Among them was Sheriff Roger Bishop, John's boss. His friendship with the sheriff might be why Virgil wanted John to respond to his 911 call. According to Dolly, the older generation wanted John to take over as sheriff.

After devouring a wedge of chocolate cake, Caroline tossed down her napkin in surrender, unable to eat another bite. She wished she'd stayed in touch. Regular trips to Colorado would have been pleasant, especially after her mom was killed and she'd been left without family ties. Instead, she'd stayed in Portland and buried herself in work. Why? The answer was horribly simple: depression.

There had been days when she barely got out of bed, and at the same time, her insomnia got worse, and she only slept only a few hours a night. Her sadness sank deep into the marrow of her bones. Of course, it was natural to grieve the death of her Mom, but she couldn't seem to climb out of that dark pit of despair and sorrow. In the deep blue throes of her depression, she was doing well to get dressed and force herself to eat one meal a day.

The work she'd done with Lola had given her a new perspective. Maybe it was the meds prescribed by the psychiatrist Lola recommended or the regular exercise regimen. Whatever the cause, the results gave her relief and a burst of energy. She wasn't so sure about Lola's PTSD diagnosis but couldn't discard the suggestion of abuse when her therapist had been correct about so many other things.

Before she climbed into the passenger side of John's SUV with the Peregrine County logo on the side, Caroline changed into a pair of multicolored leggings that looked like a riot in a paint factory but fit better than the cargo pants. She wanted her own clothing from her suitcase to be returned, which meant she had to talk to Max. With great reluctance, she took her cell phone from her purse and punched in his number.

He answered on the second ring. “It’s about time you called.”

“I want my suitcase and my car,” she said. “I’ve decided to stay at Dolly’s B and B.”

“Fine, that’s just fine.” He was huffy. “I suppose you’re rooming with Deputy John.”

“I’m not, but if I was, it wouldn’t be any of your business.”

“Listen up, Caroline. I’ve got rights. We’re engaged. You and I need to make wedding plans.”

She’d made embarrassing mistakes in her life and getting engaged to Max was one of the worst. “I don’t believe I accepted your proposal.”

“I have proof,” he said triumphantly. “I’ve got photos. Where are you going to be? I’ll show you.”

Whether or not they were engaged, she owed him the chance to explain. “We can meet at Virgil’s cabin. Please bring my suitcase.”

She disconnected the call and glanced at John. She probably should have consulted him before inviting Max to the crime scene. When it came to the investigation, she seemed to do everything backward. “That was a mistake, right? Should I call him back and tell him not to come?”

“We don’t have a problem as long as Max waits outside and stays out of everybody’s way. Don’t even think about inviting him inside.”

“I won’t,” she promised. Not that she wanted to see Max but their relationship needed to be clarified. “Were you ever married?”

“A long time ago,” he said. “It was a familiar story. We dated in college, graduated and got married before we moved to Denver for law school. We never had much in common but hung in there, even after I dropped out.

She wanted a big house, a family and a golden retriever. I couldn't do it for her."

"Divorce?" she asked.

"You bet, and she kept the dog."

She listened, nodding. In the course of the last day, they'd shared some difficult and intimate experiences, but they barely knew each other. Her excuse was amnesia. And his? His conversations were typically terse and direct. She was glad that he'd opened up, just a little bit, to her. "What made you want to be a deputy?"

"My mom was a cop in Colorado Springs, so I knew I didn't want to deal with big city problems. But I like the motto of Serve and Protect. Law enforcement appealed."

"From the way Dolly was talking, I thought for sure that you were a local kid, growing up in Sagebrush."

"My dad came up here in the summer to hunt. That's where I got to know Sheriff Bishop. After Dad retired from the air force, he worked part-time as a deputy." He exhaled a weary sigh as if all this talking had worn him out. "That's pretty much my life story."

She suspected there was a great deal more to John Graystone than a bare-bones outline of marital and employment history. Digging for the pieces that made up his life might be a journey she'd enjoy. "What was your major in college?"

"Philosophy." He cast a curious glance in her direction. "Yours?"

"Art history."

For the rest of the drive, they bounced an array of topics back and forth, ranging from sports to cinema, and discovered that they shared a love of baseball and cheesy horror movies. When Virgil's cabin came into view, she was sorry their talk was about to end.

Several other vehicles were parked along the driveway and at the side of the road, which meant he had to drive higher up, make a U-turn and come back down to find a space to park. When they walked back to the cabin, Max was waiting for her.

Unlike the laconic John Graystone, brassy Maxwell Sherman was delighted to brag about every detail of his life, from how long his mother had been in labor to his favorite necktie. He signaled for her to follow as he hiked up a winding trail into the trees.

At a clearing that was still in sight of the cabin, he pivoted to face her. "We don't have to argue, Caroline. I'm willing to forgive and forget."

She planted her fists on her hips. "Let's see this proof of yours. It had better be good. You didn't even give me a ring."

"Because this was spur-of-the-moment and romantic. If I buy you a diamond, will you accept the fact that we're going to be married?"

"That's doubtful."

"Stubborn woman." He reached into his backpack, pulled out a folder and slapped it into her hand. "Here's the paperwork and photos of the wedding that never happened because I was being considerate."

Nevada was an easy state in which to get married. The basic requirements were to be eighteen years old and show valid photo ID. Any of the chapels along the Las Vegas or Reno strip would perform a ceremony. She looked over the application for a Marriage License. "It's not signed."

"Because you were too tired."

He showed her an eight-by-ten photo of them together. Her shoulders were drooping, and she wore a veil. "This was taken by the official who was supposed to read the vows."

She squinted at the photo. Her arms were loose and her posture sloppy, as though her legs weren't capable of supporting her. She looked like she was going to pass out. *Why can't I remember?* The flimsy veil blurred her features, but it was clearly her face. Had she been drunk?

Behind her in the forest, she heard the snapping of twigs as though someone was approaching, moving fast. Her head swiveled, and she looked in the direction of the noise. There was no one in sight. She whispered, "Did you hear that?"

Max flipped through photos on his cell phone. "What am I supposed to be listening for?"

A gust of wind rattled the tree branches. A chill washed over her. Someone or something was out there in the thick, impenetrable forest. She held up a hand as though she could stop the invisible presence.

A single gunshot popped and echoed through the trees. The sound was muffled. A silencer?

She dropped to the ground and ducked her head.

Max stared down at her. He hadn't moved an inch. "What the hell is wrong with you?"

"Somebody took a shot at us."

"Stop it, Caroline. You sound like a raving paranoid."

Being attacked by an unknown person was terrible, but there was something worse. If there was no gunman, if she'd made up the attacker, she was delusional. She was losing her grip on reality.

Chapter Eight

Caroline was no stranger to panic attacks. The bone-chilling fear she felt right now might have sprung from her subconscious. But what if it didn't? What if the gunshot was real? Her arms and legs drew in close to her body as she curled herself on the pine-cone-strewn forest floor in the clearing behind the cabin. She gritted her teeth and pried open her eyelids as she desperately tried to summon the willpower to search for the shooter,

Fearful of what she might see in the shadows of late afternoon, she scanned the wall of pine trees and craggy boulders. Was that sunlight gleaming on the barrel of a pistol? Or was it only a gray branch?

"Come on, Caroline, stand up." Max was angry. "You're going to get filthy."

"Someone is trying to kill us."

"Us?" Inside his scraggly goatee, he sneered. "Don't include me in your fantasies. I'm an innocent bystander. Nobody wants to kill me."

"Why me?"

"Because you murdered Virgil."

"No," she shouted. "How can you say such a thing?"

Peering into the heavy forest, she saw the flash from the gun's muzzle. She heard a pop. And another, which was definitely not loud enough to be gunfire. He had to be using a silencer. Her pulse skittered. Her breathing fluttered. If she did nothing, the bullets would find her. She pulled her knees under her body. The fresh dressings on her scraped hands were already dirty, and the flashy leggings were smudged. Her plan was to spring to her feet, make a wild dash to the cabin and wrap herself in John's embrace. Even if he didn't see a monster in the trees, he wouldn't make fun of her the way Max did.

She needed to go now, to run from the danger. What about Max? She had to take him with her, couldn't abandon him. Even if he was a first-class jerk, he didn't deserve to die. She leaped to her feet, grabbed his arm and tugged him toward the cabin. "Come with me. Now."

"I don't think we're welcome at the crime scene."

John had specifically told her not to allow Max into the cabin, but that instruction didn't apply in this situation. No way would John advise her to be a sitting duck for a mystery shooter. They had to run. No time to talk. "Now, Max."

"All right, if it'll make you feel better."

She dragged him to the Dutch door that led to the kitchen and pulled the yellow crime scene tape aside. She opened the door and dragged Max inside with her.

John stared at her. "This is an active crime scene. You have to leave."

"Up the hill in the clearing," she said, "there's a shooter. I think he has a silencer."

"Or maybe he's not there at all." Max patted her shoulder. "Nobody blames you for seeing things. You've been through a lot, sweetie. You need a little nap."

"Don't patronize me." She shoved him away from her. "I heard three gunshots. Didn't actually see the shooter, but I saw the flash from the muzzle of his gun."

"You're frightened," Max said. "It feels like you're being attacked."

He made that statement sound like an accusation, and

she protested. "Damn right, I'm scared. But I'm not making this up."

"To you, the shooter is real."

She turned to John. "Are you going to investigate or not?"

"You can't be here."

"But the shooter…"

"I'm on it." He signaled for two other deputies to accompany them to the nearest police vehicle. With their weapons drawn, they hurried along the gravel driveway packed with cars. When she and Max were in the back seat, John leaned in and said, "Stay here. The deputies will check the hillside. You said the shooter was in the clearing, right?"

"On the hill above the clearing." She nodded, grateful to be taken seriously. "Three shots."

She sat stiffly, staring through the car window. Her pulse continued to race, and a cold sweat trickled between her shoulder blades and down her forehead from under her cap.

When Max reached over and rested his hand atop hers, she tried to pull away from him. But he held firm. "I'm worried about you."

She refused to meet his gaze. "Is that why you accused me of killing my uncle?"

"You can't blame me." He ticked off reasons on his fingers. "Number one, you came here to confront the guy. Number two, you were angry. Three, you were alone with him. Four, and this is the biggie, you had a gun."

"It wasn't my weapon."

"I heard," he said. "The police checked registration, and the Glock belonged to Virgil. You found it here in the cabin. Convenient?"

"I'm not a murderer," she said with quiet intensity. "I'm a good person, and it's not in my nature to kill anyone."

"You're confused and upset, but don't worry. I'll take good care of you after we're married."

"Here's the deal, Max. Your so-called proof that we're engaged doesn't work for me. And it doesn't matter. If there was ever anything between us, it's over."

"You don't mean that."

Caroline stuck out her chin and glared at him. "I'll be staying at Dolly's. I want my suitcase and my car."

"Fine." He spat the word. "Your suitcase is still in the Tahoe so I can give it to you right now. Then you can change into one of your boring little T-shirt-and-jeans outfits to go with your boring denim cap."

When he flicked the brim, she snapped. "I'm wearing this to cover the dressing on my head wound. By the way, I'm feeling okay after my stay in the hospital. Thanks for asking."

"I'm going to need your car until I can arrange for a rental."

"No longer than a day."

"Why are you being so bitchy? I talked to Lola earlier. She's as worried about you as I am. She said that she might come to Colorado to help you."

"She doesn't need to." But Caroline would be glad to have her therapist here. "Why is she talking to you? She should contact me."

"Or you could make the call."

Which was exactly what Lola would say. Caroline needed to take charge of her own life. "Maybe I will."

He grasped her hand again and squeezed her fingers. "You don't remember what you were like before Lola helped you manage your depression and PTSD. You used to be constantly struggling, like you were just now in the clearing. You thought people were after you. Paranoid. Depressed. Whenever you misplaced something, you were certain that it had been stolen. And those were on your good days."

"I remember..." She shook loose from his touch. "I remember enough."

Some of his accusations struck a chord within her, but she didn't trust his opinion. Yes, she'd been depressed, but she had dealt with her problems. She earned a living as a CPA, worked in a setting with other professionals and lived in a pleasant condo, where she paid bills, shopped for groceries and made her bed just like everybody else.

And then she remembered the most difficult issue in her personal life: the lack of a true, committed relationship. Approaching the Big Three-O, her biological clock was bearing down on her. She wanted to find love, wanted a real home and children. She and Lola had talked about her situation many times. Why was Caroline so guarded? Why did she find so many reasons to break up and so few to stay together? Was she afraid of men? Afraid of love? When was the last time she'd gone on a third date?

As if on cue, John strode into view as he approached the police car. Easily, she could imagine a relationship with someone like him, even though he lived three states away from her home in Portland. Long-distance relationships almost never worked. Getting involved with him was exactly the wrong thing to do.

"The deputies didn't find signs of a shooter on the hill," he said as he opened the car door. "There were no shell casings. No bullets."

Her heart sank. "I didn't invent those gunshots from thin air."

Max gave a disbelieving snort.

"I didn't say I was done investigating," John said. "I'd like for you to come with me and pinpoint the place where you saw a muzzle flash."

"Waste of time," Max muttered.

"And you," John said. "I have to ask you to leave. This is an active crime scene."

She stepped out of the car. "First, I should get my suitcase from the Tahoe and stow it with the deputy. He'll give me a ride back to Dolly's B and B."

Aware that she was suspected of paranoia and panic, Caroline made sure that her gait was measured and her posture erect. Though her emotions were in turmoil, she wanted to create the appearance of calm control.

Somehow, Max had snagged a good parking place on the crowded road outside the cabin. The three of them approached her Chevy Tahoe as a man in a tailored charcoal suit strode toward them. He was the classic image of tall, dark and handsome. If she'd been searching for a mate based solely on physical appearance, this guy would have won. John introduced him. Rafael Valdez was the nephew of the Durango-based lawyer, Edie Valdez, and he was an investment counselor.

He took her hand and made sizzling eye contact. "My condolences, Caroline. Your great-uncle was a wise man and a good friend."

Max acknowledged him with a nod. "We already met. At your aunt's office."

Her first impression of the man with the shining black hair and smooth caramel complexion was tainted by his association with Max, though it wasn't Rafael's fault that he'd been in contact with her soon-to-be ex-fiancé.

John asked, "What can I do for you, Rafael?"

"I'll be seeing you at the poker game tonight," Rafael said, "but since I'm in Sagebrush this afternoon, I thought I'd find you and offer my assistance in your investigation. As you know, I was Virgil's financial advisor."

John glanced at Max, then at her, before he gave Rafael his full attention. "My questions can wait."

"Don't be discreet on my account," Max said. "We all want to know if Virgil was rich."

"Well, that depends on your definition of rich." Rafael

arched his sculpted eyebrows and looked toward John. "Would you prefer to talk privately?"

Though she didn't approve of squeezing Rafael for information, she had to admit the parameters of Virgil's wealth made her curious. His log cabin seemed like the home of a man who had very little expendable cash. But he'd always sent a hundred-dollar bill for her birthday and Christmas. He'd loaned Dolly enough to buy her B and B, and he had enough capital to require the services of a financial advisor.

"You and I can go into detail later," John said. "But I see no harm in giving ballpark figures."

"Well, in Virgil's case, the home team hit a grand-slam home run. He had *beaucoup* bucks. I've made investments for him in the high six figures."

Caroline felt her jaw drop. She saw a similar reaction from John. Oddly, Max was calm, perhaps too calm, as he said, "That's a handy motivation for killing the old man."

He turned away from the icy disgust radiating from John and Rafael, who had more gracious sensibilities about the recently deceased. Max pulled her suitcase from the back of the Tahoe, placed it at her feet and climbed into the driver's seat. Before he drove off, he waved. Though Caroline didn't care if she ever saw him again, she was concerned about her Tahoe.

After John bid farewell to Rafael and promised to talk to him tonight at the poker game, she was finally alone with the deputy. "Now what?" she asked.

"I want to check the hill behind the clearing, maybe find a clue about the shooter."

"Thank you for believing me."

"Why wouldn't I?"

"Max didn't," she said. "He thinks I was having a panic attack. And he says Lola feels the same."

"I base my opinions on facts. If you heard a gunshot and saw a muzzle flash, there was a shooter."

"I could have made it up." *No shell casings, no bullets.* "I didn't, I swear I didn't. But I could have."

"Follow me." He turned and hiked into the forest on a dirt path. "If you're in danger, it's my job to protect you."

She inhaled through her nostrils and counted to five, then held her breath for four and then exhaled to a count of six—a mindful technique she'd learned from Lola. Concentrating on her breath, her muscles released the tension she'd been holding. Walking behind John on the path, she felt safe. Nobody would dare attack her when she was with him. She asked, "How well do you know the drop-dead-gorgeous Mr. Valdez?"

"He's smart, successful and well-connected. Durango is growing, becoming more of a city, and Rafael fits in with the new crowd. Oh, yeah, and he's gay."

He led her into the clearing. Though the ground was dry and not good for taking footprints, he was able to show her where the ground had been disturbed. "Max stood here."

She pointed to the scrapes and shuffles in the pine needles, twigs and dirt where she'd curled up in a ball. "Here's where I ducked down to get away from bullets."

"Is this where you were when you saw the muzzle flash?"

She nodded.

"I need to get your perspective to understand what you were seeing." He placed her in the center of the vague imprint. "Show me your position when you saw it."

She lowered herself to the ground and got down on her knees. This memory was recent and strong. She peeked up from the ground and pointed into a thicket of pines and rocks. "Up there."

He joined her. With his head even with hers, he took off his hat and stared up the hill. "Like this?"

"Lower." Lying flat on her belly, she dropped to her elbows, arched her back and lifted her chin. Looking straight up from this position, the trees were closely packed and thick against the surrounding granite boulders.

John stretched out beside her and mimicked her position. "Like this?"

There was a strange intimacy about their side-by-side pose, as if they had awakened in bed together. Her gaze slid down his body. His legs were so much longer than hers. She imagined what it would be like if she and John were entwined. When his arm rubbed against her shoulder, her careful breathing accelerated, and heat prickled across the surface of her skin.

She raised her arm and pointed. "There. In the middle of those branches. That's where I saw the flash."

His silver-gray gaze linked with hers. In his eyes, her attraction was mirrored. If she moved more than six inches, their bodies would connect. If she tilted her chin and eased toward him, their lips would meet. If she opened her mouth…

He rolled away from her and stood. After slapping the dust off his jeans, he reached down to help her stand. Her hand was small in his grasp. She felt his strength as he pulled her upright.

Together, they hiked up the hill to the thicket of pines and shrubs. John focused on the ground and the bushes. He was a tracker, noticing broken twigs and scrapes through the dirt. "No clear footprints," he said, "but plenty of partials. Over there is a heel mark. This is a place where a toe dug out a small divot. I see plenty of signs that someone or something has been up here."

"Something?"

"Could be deer. Squirrels, chipmunks or rabbits."

"Squirrels wearing boots?"

"The forest is a habitat for all kinds of animals. And men." He stalked past her to a waist-high rock nestled in the trees. "Your shooter could have ducked behind here, hiding. He might have rested the barrel of his gun on this surface to steady his aim. But I doubt that happened."

"Why not?"

He gestured for her to come closer to him. When she stood in front of him, he turned her to face downhill. "Can you see where you and Max were?"

"Yes." She leaned against him. Her back molded against his broad, solid chest.

"If the shooter bothered to take aim, he could have easily scored a hit. But he fired three times and missed."

She appreciated his logic and was grateful for his willingness to believe that she'd been attacked, but her focus was on listening to the way his voice rumbled inside his rib cage when he spoke. They were close enough that she could smell his woodsy scent, which mingled with the faint whisper of soap from a morning shower. He hadn't taken a break since then. His day had been filled with investigating, trying to clear her name. More than anything, she wanted to turn around in his arms, reach up to hold his face and kiss him hard on the mouth. The urge to do so was nearly a compulsion. Unable to stop herself, she turned.

She didn't remember ever being so attracted to a man. Amnesia? Or maybe this unexpected chemistry had never happened to her before.

Chapter Nine

For fifteen long seconds, John stared into her coffee-brown eyes, noticing the lighter hues of green that textured the iris and the thin gold rim. He sank deep into the ebony pupil. Anybody who thought brown eyes were dull hadn't taken the time to look. He imagined her memories recorded in those mesmerizing eyes and hiding from her. She was as much a mystery to herself as she was to him.

If he didn't put distance between them, he'd be drawn too close. He wanted to caress her smooth, pale cheek, to kiss her lips and to enclose her slender body in his embrace. Moments ago, when she leaned her back against his chest, he almost lost control—a potential lapse in judgment that would have been a mistake.

Though she wasn't a suspect anymore, not from his perspective, anyway, Caroline was central to the murder. She was a witness and a blood relative of the deceased, which meant she would, very likely, inherit a substantial sum of money. For these reasons and many more, she was off-limits and supremely unkissable for him—the deputy in charge of the investigation.

He looked away from her lovely face and dug his hands into his pockets to prevent himself from reaching for her. "We should check out the cabin, look for some of these hiding places you remember from childhood."

"But it's a crime scene. I'm not supposed to go inside."

"You'll be an expert consultant, helping us find Virgil's caches and hiding places."

"Did you find the lockbox under the Navajo rug that Dolly talked about?" Her voice was breathy, unintentionally sexy. "Virgil's stash of cash."

"We got it." His crew of deputies and the CSI team from the CBI had been embarrassed by overlooking such a blatant clue. "Right where she said it would be."

"What was inside?"

"Treasure." He sidestepped away from the area between the waist-high boulder and the trees, pivoted and headed downhill toward the cabin, talking while he picked his way through the forest. "The cash wasn't all that much—less than five thousand in different denominations. And there were a dozen books of stamps. The cool part was the coins—twenty-seven Gold Eagles from the Carson City mint."

"He gave me a gold-coin necklace. Is it valuable?"

"Those coins are worth a couple thousand dollars apiece."

"Why would he have them?"

"People who don't trust banks—like your great-uncle—prefer keeping their wealth in precious metal or other physical treasures." Which made him wonder what kind of investments Virgil had made with Rafael Valdez. "You're a CPA. I'm sure you've run across other people who handled their money like this."

She nodded. "People can be very weird when it comes to investing or collecting."

"Anyway, finding the coins gives us a good reason to go through his cabin again with a fine-tooth comb. There was the floor safe and the gun safe in his office. Who knows what other secret hidey-holes he has? You thought he might have a cache inside the room you used as your bedroom when you stayed here as a kid. That room is now the office."

When he took another step toward the cabin, she touched his arm, sending a jolt of awareness into his bloodstream. "Wait."

He froze in place and scanned the area around them. "What is it, Caroline?"

"Don't go to a lot of trouble based on my memories. Maybe I didn't get it right. I can't promise that we'll find anything. Lola and I spent a lot of hours deciphering my memories of Virgil, and the specifics are still hazy."

As he directed her downhill, he kept an eye on her. "Would it help you remember if we contact Lola and she does more sessions with you?"

"I'm not sure if seeing her will help, but I'm planning to invite her to Colorado. It's hard to separate reality from memory. When I suffered childhood traumas, my mind protected me by burying the fear and hurt. I pretended it never happened, erased the incident, which resulted in PTSD."

He was familiar with the concept. Suppressed memories were similar to an infected wound that would eventually erupt in festering disaster, like her depression or anxiety. But there was a lot he didn't understand. "Give me an example."

She looked up and to the left, which supposedly indicated she was telling the truth. "My father left me and Mom when I was a toddler, too young to form coherent memories, but Lola showed me how having my father take off created abandonment issues. The resulting post-traumatic stress makes it hard for me to trust men."

He landed on another question—an important one. "Is Lola ever wrong?"

"This isn't about my therapist," she said.

She was a little too defensive, and he wondered if those doubts had also occurred to her. Shrinks make mistakes just like everybody else. He walked the last few steps toward the cabin. “Why would you have a memory that takes you in the wrong direction?”

“It happens,” she said. “And it even has a name—false memory syndrome, or FMS.”

He’d heard of false memories as they pertained to eyewitness testimony, especially when it came to identification of a perpetrator. A witness could steadfastly point to the wrong person and might be so certain that they could pass a lie-detector test. “Which is one of the reasons why eyewitness testimony is considered unreliable.”

“False memories,” she said with a nod.

“How do you know what’s true?”

“You don’t. That was part of my rationale for coming to Colorado. Though I expected my meeting with Virgil to be angry and hostile, I wanted to face him and find the truth.”

Before entering the cabin, he glanced up the hill toward the place where a shooter might have taken a position. He almost hoped that she was suffering from an illusion. If she was right and someone had fired three gunshots at her, Caroline was in danger. He needed to find a way to keep her safe.

AN HOUR LATER, Caroline trudged behind John as he carried her suitcase up the staircase to the feminine, green-and-lavender bedroom at Dolly’s B and B. Tired, her feet were cement blocks. Her head ached with the drumbeat of a steady *throb, throb, throb.* It had been a disappointing day.

At the cabin, the CBI crime-scene unit and the Peregrine County deputies had followed her memories of a long-ago time with her great-uncle. They looked for a secret hiding place, tapped on walls and even pried off strips of paneling. The search was fruitless. One of the deputies pointed out that Virgil had done some remodeling over the years, turning the larger guest bedroom into an office. He might have torn out one of the walls. Still, she felt responsible for wasting their time.

John stepped aside so she could use her key on the locked bedroom door at the B and B. She entered first, crossed the cheerful room and stumbled to an overstuffed chair beside the window. Exhaling an audible sigh, she deflated as she sank into the flowered cushions.

John placed her zippered suitcase on the bed and turned toward her. "Earlier, you mentioned false memories."

"Like imagining I saw a hidden cache in the bedroom wall?"

He was kind enough not to point fingers. Unlike Max, John hadn't once accused her of being illogical or untruthful. "You told me *how* FMS works. But not *why*? What causes a memory that's bogus? It might come from association with something else. Or you might make it up."

"Not consciously." Dealing with Max and his obnoxious accusations was easier than facing John's well-meaning interrogation. "Can we please drop this?"

"I need to know."

"And I want to help in the investigation." She rubbed her forehead. "Listen, John, I'm not a neurologist or a therapist, so my explanation isn't guaranteed to be accurate. This is how I understand false memories. They're like dreams. They don't make sense until I work through the details with a therapist."

"So, Lola points you in the right—or wrong—direction."

"Why would she point me in the wrong direction?"

"You're a client," he said. "It's to her benefit to keep you hooked and coming back for more. You'll keep paying her bills."

If she hadn't been so tired, she would have fought back. "I'm sorry we didn't find another collection of Gold Eagle coins, but you can't blame Lola."

"I'm not accusing her."

He sat in the other chair beside the table at the window and sprawled out. In the delicate, ladylike room, his rugged male presence, with his long legs, broad shoulders, large hands and…his aggression, was a definite contrast. Men were hard to understand. She and John were on the same team, but they seemed to be at odds with each other. "Do you have other suspects? Besides me?"

"I'm grasping," he admitted. "I need a direction to follow in the investigation. Tonight, when Virgil's pals gather for their regular weekly poker game, I might make some progress."

"Do you suspect Virgil's old buddies?"

"I won't know until I talk to them." He leaned forward. His forearms rested on his thighs. "Also, I'm worried about your safety."

"Me, too." Though she tried not to think of the shooter on the hillside, her brain had recorded the popping sound of the gunshot and the resulting fear. "I can't think of a reason why anybody would want to hurt me."

He shot her a sidelong glance. "You haven't been in town long enough to have enemies who want to kill you."

"But I have an enemy." This idea had been rolling around in her head while she'd been in the hospital. She held out her left hand and allowed the light to catch on the silvery wristband of her watch. "I must have been unconscious with my concussion. That's when my enemy stole it."

"Your watch? You never told me about this."

"I didn't have it when I was running in the forest. At Virgil's cabin, I saw it on the table beside the chair where he was sitting," she said. "Almost like it had been planted."

"The murderer took your watch, probably intending to frame you." He was obviously excited by this possibility, couldn't keep himself from pacing. "The killer couldn't know that you'd stumble into the cabin before anybody else. The watch was supposed to be a clue to implicate you."

When he drew these conclusions, the question seemed inescapable. "Why didn't I figure this out sooner?"

"An understandable lapse," he said. "There's been a lot of distraction. But now, we know, and we can use this clue to our advantage."

She was delighted to hear him saying "we." Maybe she had sneaked her way on to the investigation team without either of them realizing it. "We can start tonight at the poker party."

"Show off the watch and see if we get a reaction." To her surprise, he took her hand, studied the watch and dropped a light kiss above her knuckles. "We'll solve this."

Her gaze met his, and for a moment they were linked. She wished they could be closer, but she was so tired she could barely keep her eyes open. "At the hospital, the docs told me I might need to take a nap. I think they were right. I'm exhausted."

"Do you need anything for pain?"

"I'm okay with Tylenol. And I have enough of my regular antidepressant meds to get me through a week. If I need more, the prescribing doctor can contact the local pharmacy."

"You're planning to stay for a week?"

"At least a week." She hadn't given her agenda a great deal of thought, but she knew from the events following her mother's death that the next-of-kin had certain responsibilities. "I need to make arrangements for a funeral and burial. And I'll have to talk to the lawyer about what happens to Virgil's cabin…if he left it to me, that is. Tomorrow, I have an appointment with Edie Valdez in Durango to hear about the will."

"First, a nap." He took her other hand and pulled her to her feet. "For now, I want you to stay here in your room with the door locked. If you have any problems, call me. Don't let anybody in."

"Not even Dolly?"

"Make sure it's her." He went to the dresser and gestured to a wicker basket packed with goodies. "Looks like she left you a hospitality gift with fruit, cookies and bottled water. I'm guessing the cookies are fresh baked."

She was beginning to develop a girl crush on the bouncy, blond, home-cooking Dolly. "Is there anything else I should think about?"

"Lola," he said. "I'm not a fan, but it might help sort things out if she came to Colorado for in-person sessions."

Much as Caroline wanted to handle the amnesia by herself, Lola could help her cope. "I'll call her this afternoon."

After John left, she locked the door, hauled the suitcase off the bed and unzipped it. Though she had considered taking a shower before getting dressed in a nightshirt, she didn't have enough energy to do more than peel off her borrowed clothes and slide into the comfort of freshly laundered sheets beneath the green-and-lavender duvet.

John had promised to be back in time for dinner at seven. The poker game—which was always held in Dolly's game room—started at nine, and he thought he might find a suspect among Virgil's old buddies. Was it possible? The small mountain town seemed peaceful and even quaint, but Sagebrush was teeming with intrigue.

Chapter Ten

Unlike the first and second floors of Dolly's B and B, which were decorated in pastels and florals mixed with old-fashioned froufrou, the garden-level game room reminded John of a casino. Two heavy, round-topped tables covered with green felt lurked beneath hanging lamps. The chairs matched the polished oak of the tables and were upholstered in leopard print. If poker wasn't your game, a pool table bisected the room. Five slot machines, blinking with silent encouragement, lined the far wall. Nearer to the staircase was a wet bar with sofa and chairs facing a giant TV screen.

Caroline descended the stairs ahead of him, entered the room and turned to him with raised eyebrows and a wide grin. "I'm guessing Dolly enjoys gambling."

"And she's a damn fine poker player."

"I thought slot machines were illegal in Colorado."

"Not in a private residence." It didn't hurt that the sheriff was known to occasionally join the poker game. "What about you? Are you a gambler?"

"As a CPA, I know casinos are not a good place for investors, but I'm good—very good—with numbers." She flashed another smile. "At poker or blackjack, I usually win."

He was glad to see her cheerful. Dinner with Dolly had been subdued. In spite of the seemingly unstoppable energy of their bubbly blond hostess, she'd been quiet. Not surprising, only a day had passed since Virgil's murder, and she was mourning the loss of a good friend and former candidate for husband. She'd served T-bone steaks and baked potatoes with sour cream.

Though Caroline had picked at her food and turned down the offer of beer because she was taking a bunch of nonprescription pain meds, she looked wide-awake and alert after her nap and shower. Her straight, dark brown hair fell neatly to her chin, and she wasn't wearing the gauze patch over her head wound. Her clothes were simple: jeans that actually fit her slim hips and a red plaid cotton shirt. He liked this normal version of Caroline.

"If you want," he said, "you can sit in on the game."

"I'd like to meet all the players, but I'm still tired. I'd rather go back to bed. After all, tomorrow is going to be a big day. I see the lawyer in the morning and Lola will arrive in the afternoon."

"She can stay here at the B and B."

"I suggested that," she said, "but she thought it might be wise to have some distance between us."

Lola was going to be a pain in the bottom. "Let me get this straight," he said. "She's willing to drop everything, hop on a plane and come to Colorado. I'm guessing that you're on the hook for her expenses."

"Of course."

"But she doesn't want to be too close."

"That's what she says, and I agree. Sometimes, our sessions don't go smoothly, and I have trouble letting go of whatever we talked about. If she was down the hall, I might be knocking on her door."

"It's up to you. Lola can stay wherever, but I'd rather have you stay here." The gunman on the hill behind the cabin convinced him that she was in danger. "This place is safer than most. Last year, Dolly had a burglary, and I oversaw the installation of a new security system, including updated cameras. The alarm activates if locks are rattled or windows busted."

"How can you maintain security when guests are coming and going all the time?"

"There's a midnight curfew. After that, guests have to buzz Dolly to get the door opened for them. All the rooms have top-of-the-line door locks, and you might have noticed the backup manual latch that fastens from inside. Be sure to use it."

Before she went to bed tonight, he'd warn her again and advise her not to open the door for anybody. The best security measure would be for him to sleep beside her in her bed, but that plan carried its own threat. If he slept with her and didn't make love, John was fairly sure that he'd come undone. And if they had sex…well, that was a whole other ball game.

He placed his hand at the small of her back and guided her to a stool at the bar. Decorated like a miniature version of an old-time saloon, the polished oak bar had brass spittoons in front. Behind the serving area, there was an artsy, nearly nude painting of Dolly in an elaborate gold frame.

In the minifridge, he found an orange soda, the same brand Caroline had been drinking at dinner. He scooped cubes from the ice maker, poured her a drink and served her. When she reached for the glass, their fingers brushed. The warmth in her hand startled him. Either she was running a fever or something else was making her hot.

If he hadn't been looking forward to this opportunity to question several potential suspects in one place at one time, he would have blown off the card game and focused entirely on this woman. He wanted to test their attraction but had to force himself to hold off until he had Virgil's killer under arrest.

The first poker player to arrive was Rafael, who came down the stairs into the Sagebrush version of a gambling den carrying a bowl of corn chips and a container of guacamole that Dolly had made. He set both on a serving table, which already held a supply of paper plates and napkins. Rafael shot them a gleaming white smile. Beneath his sculpted black eyebrows, his dark eyes actually seemed to twinkle. He'd changed from his suit to a sleek leather jacket and jeans. As handsome and stylish as a cover model, he could have swept Caroline off her feet, but John knew this guy wasn't looking for a conquest. Not a female conquest, anyway.

After Rafael gave Caroline a hug, he reached across the bar to shake John's hand. He slipped his polished, manicured fingers into the inner pocket of his jacket and pulled out an envelope. "This is a compilation of investments I've made for Virgil over the years. I'm not usually this well-organized, but my aunt asked for documentation, and I thought this might be helpful for your investigation."

"I appreciate it." John accepted the envelope. "How did Virgil come to be your client?"

"I have Aunt Edie to thank," he said.

In his meeting with Edie Valdez, John didn't think she was family-oriented. The opposite, in fact. The only way she'd recommend her nephew was if she had something to gain from his association with Virgil. "Why you?"

"Ask her yourself. We all have appointments with her tomorrow to talk about Virgil's will." He eyed the bottles behind the bar. "Can I get a chardonnay?"

John hadn't intended to play bartender, but he wanted to pump Rafael for possible evidence and figured alcohol might loosen his tongue. He looked into the under-the-counter wine cooler beside the regular fridge and selected a bottle. "It's from Fossil Rock, a local winery."

"Perfect. Their CEO is one of my clients." Rafael raised an eyebrow as he looked toward Caroline. "You're not drinking?"

"Not tonight."

"Wise move. You're probably taking meds for the…oh, my God—the amnesia. Who gets that in real life?"

"Me." Beneath her wispy bangs, her forehead crinkled with what John suspected was embarrassment. "Does everybody know about me?"

"You're a local celebrity. Tell me all about it."

While Caroline chatted about her accident, John uncorked the chardonnay and filled a stemmed wineglass. He wasn't surprised that Rafael kept abreast of local gossip. Much of his business revolved around personal relationships with his clients, which meant he had inside information on practically everybody.

Before the others arrived, John came out from behind the bar. Unlike Rafael, he wasn't smooth and glib. He didn't carefully transition into a change of topic. "You know all about money as a motivation. Who do you think murdered Virgil?"

"He had enemies. Some of them are going to be here at the poker game, but I don't want to slander any of these people, some of whom are clients."

"What can you tell me about Doc Peabody?"

"A sweet old guy, he's about a thousand years old. I'm not sure he could lift a gun, much less shoot one." He sipped his wine and glanced at Caroline. "He claims to remember meeting you when you were a kid."

From upstairs, John could hear the rest of the poker players arriving. He didn't have time to get sidetracked. "How about Bob Henry, the pharmacist?"

"I stopped by his store to pick up some vitamin supplements, and he was delighted to talk about Virgil. I'm guessing that Henry resented his old friend's success, but the local coroner is too law-abiding to be a killer."

John tried to remember who else was attending. "The

Rosewoods, Teresa and Luke. I heard that Teresa had recently taken a job as a housekeeper for Virgil."

"Which means," Caroline said, "she had an opportunity to search for his treasure."

"You're talking about the Gold Eagle coins," Rafael said, making a good guess. "Weren't those stashed in a floor safe?"

How the hell did he know about that? Rafael sucked up juicy rumors like a sponge absorbed water. John dragged them back on topic. "We were talking about Teresa and Luke."

"It's no secret that Luke argued with Virgil about renovation jobs in Durango on a couple of his properties. One reason why Teresa was working for the old man was to increase the family income. Luke hasn't been doing well lately."

What about Rafael as a suspect? John had been thinking about how Rafael had appeared at the cabin at the same time the shooter fired at Caroline and Max. Coincidence? Though he didn't appear to have a motive for the attack, he was in the right place at the right time to pull the trigger.

"You haven't asked about Yuri Popov," Rafael said.

"Should I?"

"An interesting guy. He's a former jockey and now owns a horse ranch. He might have been Virgil's oldest friend. Popov is nowhere near as wealthy, but he does quite well with his horses, and I've been trying to land him as a client for years. Ask him about the time when he and Virgil went in together on a thoroughbred horse that ran at the Kentucky Derby. Losing the race was a sore point."

John switched gears, trying out their new clue. "Have you noticed Caroline's watch?"

"Cartier," Rafael said. "It's a quality piece. Of course, I noticed. Why do you ask?"

"No reason."

The sound of footsteps on the staircase mingled with conversation as the Rosewoods, Doc Peabody and Bob Henry trooped into the casino. Each of them carried a homemade treat from Dolly. More chips and dips, crackers, hummus, nuts, olives and a platter of buffalo wings. Much to John's relief, Rafael took a position behind the bar and began preparing cocktails, opening beer bottles and uncorking a bottle of red wine for Teresa Rosewood.

Doc Peabody, a stocky man with white hair, a ruddy complexion and a Santa Claus beard, marched across the room and went directly to Caroline. He held both her hands and gave her a genial smile. "I'm sorry about Virgil," he said.

"I appreciate your condolence. You and Virgil were friends for many years."

"Good lord, yes." Behind his wire-frame glasses, his eyes widened. "I doubt you remember me, but I saw you a couple of times when you came to visit."

John eased himself into the conversation. When asking about her childhood injuries, he was careful not to make accusations. If the doctor suspected child abuse, he surely would have informed the authorities. "When Caroline was a little girl, was she accident-prone?"

"Not more than any other kid." His bushy white eyebrows lowered. "I remember one time when Virgil brought you into my office, he was pacing and fuming, worried that your mother was going to be mad. And you were scared to death. A skinny little thing, you quaked like an aspen leaf."

"What happened?" John asked.

"I had to order Virgil out of the examination room. He was near hysterical. Never saw him so upset." Reliving the past, Doc Peabody held her left wrist and pushed up her watch to examine it. "One of Yuri's horses bumped into you, and you tumbled backward into the stall. Ended up with a badly sprained wrist."

"I remember." Her voice was soft and wistful. "You gave me a pink wrist brace."

"And you wanted a matching brace for that stuffed rabbit you were always dragging around with you."

"Bunny Foo Foo."

"A week later, your mother ambushed you and Virgil in my office." He exhaled a sigh. "A handsome woman, Natalie McAllister had the prettiest red hair I ever saw. A perfect match for her fiery temper. She gave Virgil an earful."

"But it wasn't his fault," Caroline said.

"According to your mom, it was. He was supposed to be keeping an eye on you, and he let you wander off to the barn by yourself."

They were joined by a very short, wiry man with curly gray hair. Yuri Popov. "The injury was my fault," he said in a heavily accented voice. "I warned Virgil about Baron, a spirited horse, but I should have done more. I apologize."

Without a word, Caroline threw her arms around Yuri and hugged him close. Her returning memories seemed to be surfacing in unexpected flashes. Apparently, she'd been close to the former jockey, even though she hadn't mentioned him to John.

With a melancholy smile, she held up her left wrist and pointed to her silver Cartier watch. "This is my favorite keepsake."

It was John's turn to have a sudden recollection. The inscription on the back read "With love, Popsy." The name had been a mystery, but now he knew that Popsy was Popov.

She glanced at him. "He gave me the watch when I graduated from high school. Not only was it beautiful but it suited me perfectly. Popsy and I often talked about the importance of setting goals and using time wisely. He never treated me like a dumb kid."

"Never dumb," Yuri said. "You were bright as a star."

Rafael joined them and placed a highball glass filled

with ice and vodka in the Russian's hand. He toasted with a glass of his own. *"Nostrovia."*

"*Spasibo.* Thank you." Yuri took a big swallow.

Dolly came down the staircase, carrying a plate of macadamia-nut-and-white-chocolate cookies. Still dressed in black, she gave them a smile that didn't quite reach her eyes. In a casual tone, she spoke to the group. "Out of respect for Virgil, I considered canceling our poker game tonight, but I decided not to. Maybe because I think he would have wanted us to keep our game going. And I wanted to be around other people who knew Virgil and loved him."

"We love you, too." Teresa Rosewood enveloped Dolly in a hug. Tonight, she'd worn her waist-length hair unfastened, and the auburn waves fell around her like a curtain.

"Thanks, sweetie." Dolly gave her a peck on the cheek before addressing the others. "I'm thinking this poker game takes the place of a wake. As for the funeral and such, Caroline will probably have something to say about that."

"Hear! Hear!" Doc Peabody stood. "Now let's get started with the games before my beard grows another six inches."

Settling at the tables was a slow process since they all wanted to freshen their drinks and put together a plate of snacks. John turned to Caroline and asked, "Have you changed your mind about playing a few hands?"

"I'm too tired. After I say good night to Yuri, I'm going upstairs to my bedroom."

"I'll walk you up."

Before he left the room, he gave Dolly a light hug and reassured her that she was doing the right thing by having the game and bringing people together. Then he followed Caroline through the house to the foyer, where he noticed a red light blinking on the camera aimed at the front door. The light indicated a malfunction. Though the security had been upgraded, breakdowns occurred with annoying regularity. After he got Caroline tucked in, he'd figure out what was wrong with the system.

"What did you think of the poker gang?" he asked.

"Teresa Rosewood kept looking at me sideways, like the way you watch someone standing on the ledge of a tall building." Caroline shook her head. "She made me feel like I was on the verge and ready to jump."

"But you're not."

Outside her bedroom, he took the key from her and unlocked the door. Recalling the red light on the downstairs camera, he prepared himself to find an intruder and placed his hand on the butt of his gun before stepping across the threshold. His gaze scanned quickly. There weren't many hiding places, and it only took a minute to check the closet and look into the adjoining bathroom. "All clear."

"No monsters hiding in my bedroom, eh? What about under the bed?"

He ducked and flipped up the spread. "No monsters."

She went to the dresser, where Dolly's welcome basket took up most of the surface. Though she'd had a nibble downstairs, she took a granola bar and peeled off the wrapper. "Tomorrow is going to be a busy day."

"You've got the lawyer at eleven. I'll pick you up, and we'll drive to Durango together."

He warned her again about latching her door on the inside and not opening up for anyone. If she needed help, she should call him. He turned and opened the door.

Standing just outside was Yuri Popov. His wizened face twisted in a scowl. He inhaled a deep breath, stretching his height to five feet, four inches so he could look her directly in the eye.

"Caroline, you must not remember everything," he said. "The truth will break your heart."

Chapter Eleven

When Popov took a backward step, John caught his arm and held him in the open doorway to Caroline's bedroom. *What shouldn't she remember? Why not?* Her amnesia had hidden much of her past, and she seemed to have little control over what emerged from her subconscious mind. Popov's warning was cryptic, but his words were a clue…or a threat. He knew something, and John wasn't going to let the Russian drop a bombshell and walk away.

"What's the truth?" he asked. "What shouldn't Caroline remember?"

"I must not say."

"Is she in danger?"

"Perhaps."

Caroline joined them. She enfolded Popov in an embrace and spoke softly into his ear. "I need your help, Popsy. I need to know why Virgil was murdered. And I've got to know why, after years when I didn't see him or hear from him, except for Christmas and my birthday, why he shut me out. What happened between us? Did I do something to upset him?"

"You were a child, an innocent lamb." He looked up at John. "I cannot tell her. But I can share with you. Come. We will talk."

John didn't want to cut her out of the loop. If he talked privately to Popov, she'd be angry, and rightly so. But he needed to hear what Popov had to say. He lobbed the ball back into her court. "What do you think? Should I go with him?"

She glared at him, then at Popov. Her expression conveyed outrage at being treated like a child who couldn't handle the truth. "Do what you have to do."

Slowly and deliberately, she closed the door, and he heard the latch fall into place.

John suspected he'd pay for this slight later. He led Popov across the landing and down the staircase to the security camera with the flashing red light that was mounted high on the wall. Before dealing with the malfunction, he looked to the Russian. "Talk."

"First, you must promise me that you won't tell Caroline."

"No games. No promises." They needed to act like adults not children keeping secrets. "Either you tell me or I arrest you for obstruction of a criminal investigation."

"You would do that?"

"Damn right." John squared his shoulders. "I want to hear what you have to say."

"The danger started with Natalie, her mother."

"When?"

"Caroline was a child. The incident happened the year after she was injured by Baron. In those days, Natalie brought her daughter every summer. In Colorado, she had time to paint." His mouth twitched into a melancholy grin. "Natalie was an artist. Very good but not genius. When she was not working at her easel, she found other projects. One was named Derek Everett."

John had wondered when Everett's name would surface again, but he hadn't considered Caroline's mother as the key player. He asked a pointed question. "Were they lovers?"

The Russian's shoulders rose and fell in an eloquent shrug. "Yes."

"Did she help him commit the crimes?"

"*Nyet*, of course not. But she was blinded by passion, unable to imagine her boyfriend would rob a jewelry store and wound the guard."

John had read the criminal record provided by the CBI. "Prior to the robbery, he'd been charged with fraud for several scams, convicted and ordered to pay reparations plus hefty fines. No jail time, though."

"I was the victim of one of his schemes," Popov said. "I purchased a share in a racehorse that did not exist. Virgil confronted Everett and got my money back. He also told Natalie she must not see him again."

If Natalie was an independent woman, like her daughter, she wouldn't be pleased about her uncle making rules for her. "What did she do?"

"Cut her visit short and went home to Portland. The real trouble came at the start of the next summer." His tone dropped. As he continued, his expression became more intense. The furrows across his forehead deepened. "She and Caroline arrived at the cabin for their visit. Instead of being greeted by her lover, Natalie learned that Everett had been arrested, and her Uncle Virgil was partially responsible for his arrest and intended to testify against him in court."

"I'm guessing that Natalie exploded," John said.

"I was there."

His conversation with Popov was interrupted by Dolly, who stalked across the dining room and foyer toward them. "There you are. Will you boys be joining us for poker?"

"In a moment," Popov said. "You were kind to invite me. I will not be a bad guest."

Instead of answering, John pointed to the blinking red light on the camera. "How long has this been broken?"

"Since this morning. I haven't had time to fix it."

He didn't like the coincidence of having the camera

go out when Caroline moved in. "We'll be downstairs in five minutes."

"Better hurry or the others are going to be too drunk to hold their cards." She pivoted and hurried toward the basement staircase.

John looked back at Popov. "What happened when Virgil told Natalie that her criminal boyfriend was going to jail?"

"I took Caroline and her stuffed bunny into another room. I had hoped to spare her the rage from her mother and Virgil. But they were shouting too loud. We heard glassware being broken. I held the child close to shield her, but Caroline broke away from me. Sobbing, she ran into the other room."

His voice choked into silence, and he took a moment to compose himself. His story had given John a new perspective on Caroline's PTSD. If what Popov told him was true—and the old man didn't seem to have a reason to lie—the little girl hadn't been abused or frightened by Virgil. The violent fight between her mom and her great-uncle was the real trauma.

Popov spoke quietly. "Natalie was threatening Virgil with a poker from the fireplace. She said she would kill him. When little Caroline tried to stop her mother, Natalie pushed her aside and she fell to the floor."

John was no stranger to incidents of domestic violence. Whenever he responded to a 911 call on those situations, he knew he'd be facing a nightmare. "What did you do?"

"I dragged Virgil from the room before he could fight back. During those few minutes I spent with him, Caroline was taken to the car by her mother. Natalie yelled at me before she drove away, told me that she and her daughter would never return."

"Did she stick to her word?"

He nodded. "She cut off all communication with Virgil and never came back to Sagebrush."

"But you gave Caroline that wristwatch," John asked. "Did you attend her graduation?"

"My gift was delivered through Edie Valdez, the attorney. Virgil and I were banned from her life, but we thought of the child often. And Virgil made sure to cover Caroline's expenses and college tuition."

"I have a few more questions," John said. "Just now, when you stood at her door, why did you warn Caroline? Why do you think the truth will hurt her?"

"Her life has been filled with disappointment and abandonment, starting when her father left. But Caroline always loved and admired her mother. I would not give her reason to think otherwise."

"After Natalie's death, did Virgil try to patch things up with Caroline?"

"Her mother had poisoned her mind against him. She kept him at a distance."

As far as John was concerned, family fights were the worst. Natalie had dug in her heels and refused to relent. Virgil and Popov had been equally stubborn and didn't try to heal the rift. And Caroline had paid the price by losing contact with her beloved great-uncle and her other friends in Sagebrush.

"Last question," John said. "Do you know any friends or family of Derek Everett who might have killed Virgil for revenge?"

Instead of a categorical denial, the Russian hesitated. "There was a woman who visited him in jail. I do not know her name."

"Who told you about her?"

"Edie Valdez."

"I'll look into it." He clapped the small man on the shoulder. "You'd better go downstairs and join the poker players before Dolly scolds us again. I'll stay here and repair the security camera."

Stretching to his full height, John reached up and detached the camera from the mounting. When he cracked open the case, he found nothing in the basic system that would cause the flashing light. But he was no expert.

He took out his cell phone and contacted the 24/7 service number for the security company that installed the camera. The repair guy promised to be there within two hours, and there was no need to open the door for him. He had the codes to override the system. Problem solved.

John climbed the staircase to Caroline's room. He wasn't expecting a welcome. When he'd left with Popov, she'd unleashed a laser-edged glare that could have peeled the flesh from his bones. And he didn't blame her for being mad. They were supposed to be working together as a team.

Actually, the story about Natalie wasn't as important to his investigation as the details about Derek Everett. Did Caroline recognize the name? Ever had contact with him?

He tapped on her door. "It's John."

"I'm fine. Go back to your poker game."

Oh, yeah, she was angry. Exhaling a deep breath, he said, "I'm sorry."

"You should be." Her hostility told him that she wasn't in a forgiving mood. "We'll talk in the morning on the way to Durango."

He didn't want to leave their conversation like this, but it might be best to let her cool down. "Don't open the door for anyone but me. And call my cell if anything bothers you."

"I can manage by myself."

He heard echoes of her strong-willed mother in her clipped tone, but he didn't believe Caroline would discard a friendship. Her ongoing relationship with that idiot Max was proof enough. She obviously disliked the guy, but she was still kind to him. John placed the flat of his hand on the wooden door and whispered, "Sleep well."

Downstairs in Dolly's casino, he took the open seat between Doc Peabody and Bob Henry. The game was five-card stud poker with no wild cards. Doc folded and took a drink of craft beer straight from the bottle. Henry asked for two cards from Luke Rosewood, who was dealing. Though the coroner was trying to play it cool, he kept fidgeting with his cap, tapping his bald head and rubbing the fringe of hair around his ears.

"You must have a good hand," John said.

"You don't know that. Could be I'm bluffing."

"Could be." John tilted back in his chair and looked over at Doc, who was staring off into space and absent-mindedly stroking his Santa beard. "Do you think he's bluffing?"

"I'm remembering," he said. "Caroline's mother was a fine-looking lady."

"If you like redheads," said Henry.

Across the table, Popov drained his vodka on ice. He tapped the felt-covered table three times and discarded his rejected cards. "Natalie McAllister was magnificent. A natural wonder of the world."

"I'm with Popov," Doc said.

Rafael asked, "Did she look like Caroline?"

"Pay attention," Henry snapped. "Didn't I just say that she was a redhead? Caroline is a brunette."

Rafael indicated that he wanted one card. "Hair color doesn't define a woman, you know. They wear wigs and switch hair dye. Am I right, Teresa?"

She twirled a lock of her waist-length hair. "Change can be fun."

"But not for you." Her husband patted her hand. "You'll never cut your hair."

"I might." She usually kept it braided and wrapped around her head. "Nobody gets to tell me how to wear my hair."

They went around the table twice more with some holding and others folding. Finally, the betting was down to Henry and Rafael.

The handsome investment counselor arched a sculpted eyebrow. "Shall we make this more interesting?"

"No side bets," Dolly said. "This is a friendly game, and you're not going to trick us into playing for high stakes."

"Not even for this?"

Rafael flipped a gleaming gold coin onto the table. The size and weight of the Gold Eagle was a sharp contrast to the plastic chips gathered in the pot. John knew the worth of the coin was upward of two thousand dollars. He noticed Teresa gasping and covering her mouth with both hands.

Her husband stood. "What kind of game are you playing, Rafael?"

"Poker." He gestured to the table. "Obviously."

John asked, "Where did you find the coin?"

"It was a gift from my dear friend Virgil."

"A keepsake." Dolly stood and snatched the coin. "And yet, you throw it into a game as if a precious coin from a precious friend is worth nothing at all."

"To the contrary." Rafael stood to face his accusers. "This game is our remembrance for Virgil, and the Gold Eagle is how I want to remember him. He kept his wealth hidden, but he never hesitated to share with others."

In John's mind, Rafael's statement was a challenge to the others and a touching eulogy from his own perspective. "What should Henry put up to match your bet?"

"He decides," Rafael said. "What did Virgil's friendship mean to you, Henry?"

With one hand, he held his cards against his skinny chest, hiding them from view. With the other, he dug into his pocket and took out his car keys. He showed them an oblong silver medal. "This is St. Peregrine."

"Like our county," said Teresa.

"One of the reasons I love living here," Henry said. "St.

Peregrine is also the patron for cancer patients. When my daughter was diagnosed, I didn't know how we'd pay for her treatment. An anonymous donor took care of our bills. Later, I found out it was Virgil."

"A precious keepsake," Dolly said.

"Much too important to waste on a bet."

"And your daughter." Teresa looked at him with sympathetic eyes. "How is she?"

"In remission for seven years." Henry kissed the medallion and put his keys in his pocket. "You win, Rafael."

"Wait." Dolly spread her arms, encompassing the whole table. "This isn't fair. Rafael, show your cards."

He had a straight flush in diamonds from the eight to the queen. Henry had a pair of kings. Dolly smiled at them both. "Rafael would have won, anyway. Without all the show-off tactics."

After getting himself a beer, John played a couple of hands, losing both times. When the third hand was dealt, he had a pair of tens, not a bad start. He asked for three more cards and didn't get another match.

His phone buzzed, and he read the text message from Caroline. Help me. Hurry.

He folded his hand and left the room. Upstairs, he rushed through the house and drew his gun before climbing the staircase to the second floor. The B and B seemed quiet, but there had to be a serious threat. Caroline was too angry at him to call without a good reason.

He tapped on her bedroom door. "It's me, John."

Her door whipped open and she hustled him inside. She was breathing hard. Her eyes darted wildly, looking for danger in every corner. She thrust a piece of lined yellow paper into his hand. Written in red marker, it said, "Caroline: Get out of town, bitch."

No wonder she was upset. "Where did you find this?"

"In my bed." Her lower lip trembled. "When I slipped

between the sheets and stuck my hand under the pillow, I felt the piece of paper and heard it crinkle."

"I'll check for fingerprints, but I doubt there will be any. Every criminal knows they should wear gloves."

"The worst part..." She inhaled a ragged sob. "That's my handwriting."

Chapter Twelve

The red letters spilled across the lined yellow paper and swirled before Caroline's eyes like a whirlpool, sucking her deeper into panic. *Caroline: Get out of town, bitch.* The threat frightened her, but she couldn't allow herself to give in. She had to fight.

How had the person who wrote the note gotten into her room and mimicked her handwriting? Somehow, he or she had bypassed the security measures. And why did they want to get rid of her, make her leave town? She hadn't forgotten the other warning from Popov that she shouldn't try to remember.

Concentrating hard, she fought the shivers that shook her to the bone. *Think!* She couldn't let her panic overtake reason. *I'm a sensible person.* At least, she used to be.

John grasped her arm and turned her toward him. "It's okay, we'll figure this out."

She clung to him, buried her face against his broad chest and hung on tight, needing the sense of safety he effortlessly provided. He was a lawman—he knew right from wrong and would protect her. His warmth wrapped around her like a wool blanket, and her panic subsided. He was her anchor, her sanctuary from one more trauma. As disasters went, the note wasn't so awful. No one had died. She wasn't hurt.

She inhaled and exhaled slowly, counting her breaths.

Their physical contact became something more than an expression of his kindness. In a flash, her senses awakened. His scent, like a forest after a spring rain, sank into her consciousness. She felt the hard strength of his muscles. Her hands on his back caressed the fabric of his shirt. When she tilted her head and looked up at him, the sharp angles of his features created a mesmerizing vision, but she knew full well that she must not allow herself to melt into his arms.

Loosening her grasp, she stepped back. "If I crossed a line, I'm sorry."

"I'm not." He held the note so she could see. "Tell me what you see."

She focused on the shapes and slant of the writing. All of the *o*'s were perfect, detached circles. The *f* and *t* letters were written in a smooth, cursive style, tilted toward the right. And the capitals were heavy blocks. There was nothing particularly remarkable about the writing, except that every part matched her penmanship habits. "My name at the top could easily pass for my signature."

The conclusion was inescapable and horrible: she'd written a scary letter to herself, referred to herself as a bitch and hid the note under her pillow. But she had no conscious awareness of having picked up a marker and written on the yellow paper. Did she have an alter ego? A split personality?

Adrenaline surged through her veins and punched her energy level to the top of the charts. Before John had entered her room, she'd debated with herself: Should she tell him about the match with her handwriting or not? She didn't want him to think she was losing control. Thus far, he hadn't doubted her sanity in spite of her amnesia, her offbeat therapy and her ridiculous engagement to Max. He had believed her when she told him about the gunfire and the shooter on the hill, even though they didn't find shell casings, spent bullets or footprints.

When he looked up from the note and met her gaze,

she searched his eyes for doubt or anger. Instead, she saw something even worse—pity. She snapped at him. "Don't you dare feel sorry for me."

"Okay, we'll break it down into two parts." He crossed the room and sat in the straight-backed chair at a small writing desk. "Step one, analyze the note itself. Step two, determine how someone got past security to hide it in your room."

His logical approach made her feel more rational. Drawing on her wavering grasp of reality, she asked, "Starting with the note, where did the paper and marker come from?"

John pulled open drawers on the desk. "There's stationery in here with letterhead for the B and B. Also, brochures for local businesses and a handful of cheesy postcards. I know Dolly uses yellow legal pads, but I don't see one in here."

"Of course not. That would have been too simple."

He took a pair of blue latex gloves from a flat pouch on his utility belt and handed another pair to her. "Put these on. If we find the paper, I don't want to get your prints all over it."

After putting on the gloves, she shuffled through the dresser drawers, the bedside table and the cabinets under the countertop in the bathroom. She discovered that Dolly was an extremely proficient housekeeper who left no dust bunnies under the bed. There were no hidden legal pads. "If the paper isn't here, the note must have been written somewhere else."

"Keep looking."

She shouldn't abandon hope so easily, but the situation seemed futile. Maybe she'd been hypnotized into writing and hiding the note. According to Lola, she was a highly suggestible subject, which made her a good candidate for the meditative sessions. She looked behind the dresser, lifted the cushions on the chairs by the window and peeked behind the curtains before she went to the closet and watched as John brushed his hands along the top shelf.

She returned to her bed and perched on the edge. Her pink-and-yellow striped nightshirt wasn't deliberately sexy, but the soft jersey fabric hugged her curves and the hem was above her knees. She grabbed Dolly's oversize sweatshirt and put it on before resettling at the foot of the bed. She sat on something harder than a mattress. Could it be?

She stood and threw back the duvet. There was a yellow legal pad with a red marker clipped to the top. "Hello, evidence."

"Don't touch." John stepped up beside her. "I'll give this to the forensic team. There might be prints or fibers. Maybe the person gaslighting you made a mistake."

"Gaslighting?"

"The term comes from an old movie starring Ingrid Bergman. I'm surprised you haven't heard of it. The theme of mental manipulation seems right up your alley."

"Tell me."

"An evil husband tries to make his young wife think she's having a breakdown by hiding her things or causing her to hear mysterious noises or dimming the gaslights when it appears nobody is touching the switch."

The idea sounded horrible and familiar. "Like hearing gunfire when nobody is there to shoot the weapon," she said, "or finding this note."

"Who could have copied your signature?" he asked. "Max has spent time with you. He probably knows your writing style."

"He does." It would be typical of Max to leave a creepy note. "And he'd like to have me out of town and back in Portland, where he'd have more control. Max is the most obvious person to take my wristwatch. Everything points to him."

"Maybe too obvious," John said, "which makes me think

someone else could be framing him. Your writing wouldn't be too difficult to copy, especially using a marker. I've heard analysts say that the nib of a marker is too thick and covers much of the character of the person writing."

She sat on the bed and tucked her legs under her bottom. "What do you know about handwriting analysis?"

"Not much," he readily admitted. "Graphology was covered in a class I took on fraud and forgery. If this note was a sample of your actual writing, I'd point to the perfect, little *o*'s that are separate from the other letters—an indication that you like to have your space. The rounded letters show creativity. The dominant capital letters indicate strength and confidence."

"Do you believe that?"

"I believe you're independent, strong and smart." His gentle grin reassured her. "But not because of the way you put letters on paper."

Digging for the implied compliment, she asked, "What makes you think I have such admirable traits?"

"Instinct. I liked you from the moment you lied and told me your name was Scout."

"Did you know I was lying?"

"Not a bit. I thought the name suited you. But Caroline is just as good. Maybe better, sweet Caroline."

He stayed across the room, keeping his distance from her. Would it be so bad if she launched herself from the bed and bridged the abyss, once again joining her body with his? "If you liked me so much, why did you handcuff me?"

"Dead body. Glock in hand. Blood on your sweatshirt. My instincts were telling me that you were a witness, but the facts pointed to suspect."

"I don't blame you." She probably would have done the same thing. "I'm sorry for all the trouble I'm causing."

"None of this is your fault."

"Not unless I wrote this note, faked the gunfire and killed Virgil."

"And gave yourself amnesia? Not likely."

She was tired of the confusion and the threats. The smart decision would be to leave town as soon as possible. But she was stuck here. Tomorrow she had a meeting with Edie Valdez, then there were funeral arrangements and handling whatever Virgil dictated in his will. With a sigh, she resigned herself. "What's the proper outfit to wear for a reading of the will?"

"It's not a formal occasion," he said. "Contrary to what you've seen in movies, the family doesn't have to gather in the attorney's office for a dramatic reading. Ms. Valdez has already filed with probate. That process might take months before assets are disbursed, but the will is a public document. She can send out copies or call people in to her office, which is what she's doing with the primary heirs like you. When we get to her office, she'll explain what you'll be inheriting and tell you what to expect."

She thought back to when her mother passed away. An attorney arranged for the sale of the house and many of Mom's paintings. He also set up a trust fund for Caroline's inheritance. "I didn't pay much attention after Mom died. There were a couple of significant gifts to deserving friends, but I was the only heir."

"Virgil's estate won't be that simple. I suspect there will be those who contest the terms and think they deserve more. It's a job for the lawyers." He grinned. "Let's get back to the note. The next question is, how did someone get the note past Dolly's security system? I have a partial answer. The camera aimed at the front door is broken. I've already called for a repair."

She noticed that he didn't say how the camera had been broken or how it could be fixed, which was fine with her. Electronics were not an area of her expertise. "A broken camera doesn't explain how somebody got past the lock on my bedroom door."

"It would take an expert to disarm that lock, but we can't rule out the possibility. Dolly has copies of all the keys. I think they're in her desk downstairs, which she keeps locked up."

"Does she?" Dolly was a great housekeeper and fantastic cook, but she was also open and friendly. Security would not be one of her top concerns, even if the B and B had been burglarized. "Is it always locked?"

She saw her doubts reflected in John's gaze. He said, "Let's go downstairs, rifle through her desk and find out."

"Wait." She was afraid of drawing attention to the possibility that she'd threatened herself. "If you don't mind, I'd rather not tell anybody about the writing looking like mine."

He crossed the room and sat on the bed beside her. "Are you asking me to lie?"

"Not exactly. You can tell people about the note but leave the part about my signature out of the equation. It's embarrassing."

"If they don't understand that somebody's trying to scare you, it's their problem. Not yours."

"Yeah, yeah, I get it." She tucked her hair behind her ears. "The opinions of other people shouldn't be important to me. I shouldn't give a damn about what they think. After all, I'm going to be leaving Sagebrush."

"I couldn't have said it better."

"But I can't help caring. Popov is an undeniable link to my childhood. And I would have liked Dolly, even if she hadn't been involved with my great-uncle." She wanted their acceptance. These folks—whom she'd known for only a few hours—were more like family than most of her friends and acquaintances in Portland. When she thought of the people of Sagebrush, a pleasant sense of normalcy blossomed in her heart.

He rested his large hand atop hers on the bed. "I won't give away your secrets."

She leaned toward him, intending to give him a kiss on the cheek. As she came closer, her gaze locked with his, and she was drawn in a different direction. Her lips bypassed his jaw, rough with stubble, and homed in on his firm yet pliant lips. His kiss sent an electric current charging through her body, setting off a chain reaction of sensation. Her free hand clutched his collar and held him so he couldn't escape.

His arm swooped around her, and he pulled her across the bed and onto his lap. He continued to kiss her. His mouth pressed harder against hers.

Though the possibility of a relationship was nearly impossible to contemplate, she was happy to grab these moments of pleasure. Her body melted against his, fitting into a nearly perfect embrace. His tongue parted her lips. A small, sensual moan climbed her throat.

Truly, she felt like she'd come home. She was meant to be with John.

Chapter Thirteen

At three o'clock in the morning, John staggered out of bed in the room next to Caroline's, took his Glock from the bedside table and went to the window. The temperature in Dolly's B and B was nippy, but he welcomed the bracing chill that made him feel awake. Every ninety minutes, he'd done a quick patrol of the house he formerly thought was safe.

The repairman from the 24/7 security company had replaced the camera that focused on the front entrance rather than fixing it. He explained that the digitized recorder had been disarmed, probably hacked, and nothing from the last day was recorded. The lock on Caroline's room—requiring a key to open because Dolly didn't like key cards or an electronic system—wasn't immune to a competent lockpick, and Dolly's desk had been left unlocked. Anybody could have swiped her master key. Caroline still had the interior dead bolt and chain, but she wasn't well-protected at the B and B.

He slipped into his jeans and stuck his cell phone in his pocket. His all-night patrolling wasn't the best system, but he couldn't sleep in Caroline's room, especially not after that awesome kiss. No way could he lie in bed beside her without taking their attraction to the next level. Unfortunately, he didn't think either of them were ready. And so, he'd stayed at the B and B and patrolled the hallways, sending her an all-clear text after each circuit of the house.

The window in his bedroom faced Via Vista Street, and the only movement he saw was a handsome buck, his doe and two fawns who were munching in Dolly's strawberry patch, even though she'd planted deer-resistant marigolds to keep them away from the berries and roses.

He left his room and went onto the landing. Since there were only three couples occupying the guest bedrooms, John had his pick of windows facing in different directions. He padded barefoot across the carpet to the room with a view of the front lawn. The corner streetlight shone on a vacant sidewalk. There was zero traffic. Apart from a few night owls at the tavern, nightlife in Sagebrush was nonexistent. The residents were mostly the early-to-bed-and-early-to-rise types. Rafael, an exception, had probably left Dolly's and driven back to Durango—a place with a more exciting vibe.

From the corner of his eye, John caught a glimpse of movement to the right side of the yard near the area where most of the cars were parked. A shadowy figure crept toward the house. John didn't take the time to return to his room for his shirt and shoes. If he hoped to catch the intruder, he had to move fast. He descended the staircase.

The downstairs was faintly illuminated by night-lights so guests who went in search of a midnight snack wouldn't crash into the furniture. John took advantage of the semi-darkness, dashing through the kitchen to the attached mudroom. Using the keypad, he punched in the code to deactivate the alarm. When he opened the door, he saw the motion-sensor lights had already activated. The parking area was nearly as bright as day. The white-tailed deer bounded away from him. Had they set off the lights?

Wishing that he'd worn shoes, he ran down the four stairs to the backyard and took a few steps across the grass toward the parking area. Gun in hand, he paused. If he went too far, he'd leave the back door unprotected.

He squinted into the night, unable to spot the shadow, and he had to wonder if he'd actually seen anything. *Hell, yes, I did.* John was a hunter, accustomed to tracking and watching in the dark. Someone had been out here, lurking.

After he returned to the house, he reset the alarm on the back door and texted an all-clear to Caroline's phone. Immediately, she answered with a text of her own: I heard something.

No doubt, she'd heard him and the deer, but he didn't want her to worry. He answered: I'll be there ASAP.

As he made his way through the house and up the front staircase, his bare feet left a trail of twigs, grit from the backyard and prickly pine needles. He tapped on her door and whispered, "I'm here."

She whipped open the door and took a step toward him as though she'd dive into his arms. Before she made her move, she halted. In the glow from her night-light, he realized that her gaze was riveted on his bare chest. He sucked in his gut.

"You're breathing hard," she said.

"I was chasing something that I spotted from an upstairs window." He shrugged. "When I got to the back door, it was gone."

She stepped aside. "Do you want to come in?"

More than anything. He absolutely wanted to spend the rest of the night in her bed, but his prior reservations about their relationship were still valid. "I'll go back to my room and you stay here. We both need more sleep."

"Right," she said, "before we see the lawyer at eleven."

"At ten, we're meeting a CBI agent for a cup of coffee. I want to give him your note so a handwriting analyst can study it. And I need CBI to check a guy who had history with your uncle a long time ago."

"Who?"

He wouldn't be betraying Popov's confidence by mentioning the name. He'd heard about Virgil's enemy the first time he talked to the CBI. "Derek Everett. Ever heard that name?"

"I don't think so." Her chocolate-brown eyes were guileless, and he believed her. "Or maybe I do know him. You can't trust anything I say. I have amnesia, you know."

"A joke?"

"Yep."

She was so damn cute. If he stood here much longer, his resistance would crash and burn. Firmly, he said, "Good night, Caroline. Be ready to go at half past nine."

"Sleep well, John."

As if he could relax? Chasing shadows had gotten his adrenaline pumping and seeing her trim little body in a clingy nightshirt was a major wake-up call. He needed to find a way to keep her safe. Maybe tomorrow night, he would take her to his cabin, and they'd get a good sleep. *Yeah, right. That'd happen when frogs grow beards.* Having Caroline spend the night in his cabin would inevitably lead to something far more intense. Imagining the happy possibilities, he went to his room and flopped across the bed.

HER MOM HAD taught her that first impressions were important. In spite of what John told her about the reading of the will being casual, Caroline took care in choosing an outfit. A meeting with the Colorado Bureau of Investigation and another with Virgil's lawyer seemed to require the type of clothes she wore on a first interview with clients in Portland—a peach silk blouse with cream-colored slacks and strappy beige sandals. The long, striped, silk scarf tied around her head both protected and camouflaged her stitches. Her mascara and lipstick were applied with care. The end result was classy but not stuck-up. She projected the image of a woman who was professional, organized and in full control of her mental abilities.

Settled in the passenger seat of John's SUV with the Peregrine County Sheriff logo on the side, she glanced at him and asked, "Do I look okay?"

"Like one of those Popsicles that's orange sherbet mixed with vanilla," he said. "A Dreamsicle. Only hot."

"And you look nice, too." He'd shaved and was wearing a khaki uniform shirt with his jeans. His black cowboy hat was in the back seat, and his thick brown hair was neatly combed. Though he tried to sweep it back, a longish piece fell across his tanned forehead. Her fingers itched to stroke the unruly hair into place. "I thought about the name you mentioned, Derek Everett. Maybe if you give me a clue about who he is, I'll remember something."

"I'd rather not force your memories, but there are details you're going to pick up when I talk to Agent Phillips." He gave a frown and a shrug. "Everett knew your mom, your great-uncle and Popov. He was convicted of armed robbery and died in prison."

"Is he the person Popsy was talking about when he pulled you into the hall?"

"Partly."

"Even if Everett was dangerous, why should we think about him? He's dead and can't hurt me."

"Change of topic," John said. "When is Lola getting into town?"

"This afternoon." And she'd be glad to see her therapist. The confusion and chaos of the last few days had turned her life inside out. She was suffering from amnesia, had witnessed a murder and was being gaslighted. Clearly, she needed counseling. Not that her time in Sagebrush was all terror and trauma. Caroline smiled to herself. She'd also kissed a deputy.

On Main Street in Durango, John took a left and found a

space to parallel-park on a side street. They walked around the corner to a coffee shop with a long display case for donuts and other baked goods. It smelled like sugary, buttery heaven, but Caroline wasn't hungry. Dolly had insisted on feeding her and John a full breakfast.

Agent Mike Phillips sat waiting for them. When introduced, he politely shook her hand. His outfit was business-casual done cowboy style, which meant jeans, a plaid cotton shirt, a blazer, cowboy boots and a big, fancy belt buckle. His hair was longer than she'd expect from a CBI agent, and his grin barely touched his lips.

After he offered his condolences, he said, "You're the lady with amnesia."

"Am I?" She smacked her forehead. "I can't remember."

He didn't acknowledge her attempt at a joke, and she decided to make it her mission to get a real chortle—or, at least, a grin—from this guy.

After they ordered, John got down to business. He explained, "We have an eleven-o'clock appointment with Edie Valdez, and I don't want to be late."

"From what I've heard, Ms. Valdez doesn't like to be kept waiting."

John dug into his pack and took out the original threatening note on yellow-lined paper, which he had encased in plastic. "I checked for fingerprints. Didn't find any, but your forensic people might have more sophisticated methods."

"No doubt."

Beside the original, John placed the notepad they'd found under her duvet, the red marker and a different piece of paper where Caroline had copied the threat. John pointed to her writing. "You can see the similarity."

Phillips squinted at her name and asked, "Is that how you sign your name?"

"Unless I'm using an alias." She watched him for a grin and got nothing.

"I know a little something about forensic graphoanalysis." He nodded slowly. "You have some interesting characteristics in your penmanship."

"Do I?" Here was another chance for a joke. "Am I a psycho serial killer? Or a nymphomaniac? Or both?"

"Neither." He rewarded her with a slightly amused smile. "I don't ascribe to the fortune-teller aspects of graphology, but the study of writing is a useful scientific tool for comparing signatures and uncovering forgeries. The way you write your *o*'s can be easily copied but not duplicated. An expert graphologist will verify if you wrote the first note or not."

"I'll be relieved to know the answer." And that was no joke.

"Here are the autopsy results." He passed a nine-by-twelve envelope to John. "Nothing unexpected. Three shots to the upper body. The first bullet nicked his heart, and he died within seconds. We're calling it a homicide."

A smart aleck comment about stating the obvious occurred to her, but humor wasn't appropriate. Not when talking about her great-uncle's death. She figured the job of a CBI agent didn't allow for a lot of chuckles, and she shouldn't give Phillips a hard time. When the waitress brought her Americano coffee, Caroline quietly sipped.

"About Derek Everett," John said. "Were you able to check on his visitors in prison?"

"Not yet." He scowled. "Come on, John, what do you expect? You called only a couple of hours ago, and not everybody is as worked up about the investigation as you are."

"You're right about that. I've got to dig up some leads."

"It'd help if you give me names of suspects," Phillips said.

Before answering, John gave her a steady gaze. "Would you excuse us, Caroline?"

"I didn't appreciate being dismissed last night when you

and Popov were talking, and I feel the same way now. I'd rather stay and drink my coffee."

"I get it." He turned to Phillips. "Was Everett visited in prison by Natalie McAllister?"

Her mother? He was dead wrong. Mom wasn't the type of woman who hung out with criminals, even though her lifestyle was passionate and unusual. As an artist, she had a lot of offbeat friends, and she never understood how Caroline—a child of hers—could be interested in something as mundane as accounting. But visiting a man in prison? Never!

Phillips frowned and shook his head. "I don't recall anybody named Natalie, but I'll keep looking. A friend or relative of Everett would have motive to kill Virgil."

"Why?" she asked.

"Revenge. Your great-uncle's testimony contributed to getting Everett convicted."

Why didn't she know about this? How was this man connected to her mother? She needed to find out and had the sense that the answer was something she already knew, something buried in her unreliable memory vault.

When they left the coffee shop, they walked side by side past the Main Street storefronts in historic Durango, a charming little town where other pedestrians strolled. Her hand nearly touched his. It would have been natural to lace their fingers together, but his investigation stood in the way of their intimacy. Though he claimed to no longer consider her a suspect, he couldn't deny her involvement in the murder. And now, her mother was also connected?

John cleared his throat. "The law office is at the end of this block."

"Will Ms. Valdez ask for any documents?"

"Doubtful," he said. "I think she just wants to explain how the will works. You know Max has visited her, right?"

"He made sure to tell me about retaining a lawyer." As if he was so very important. "I don't know why he needs one."

"Think about it, Caroline. According to Max, you're engaged. If you got married, he'd share in your inheritance."

She dug in her heels and screeched to a halt in the middle of the sidewalk, causing the woman walking behind them to bump into her. Automatically, Caroline excused herself for being clumsy. Her brain was elsewhere. Fireworks exploded inside her head when she faced the obvious: Max was trying to marry her to get his hands on the inheritance. "That means he has a motive to kill Virgil. A big one."

"How much did he know about your great-uncle?"

"I don't know." She stepped out of the way of the other pedestrians on Main Street. "Can't remember. I can't think. I hate being so confused."

"It's only been a couple of days. Give yourself time."

"You're right." She straightened her spine. "Let's get this meeting over with."

Inside the two-story redbrick building, John escorted her across the lobby to a door with a frosted glass window and Law Offices written across it in gold letters. A long reception desk stretched across the waiting room, and a cheerful honey blond with dimples greeted John.

"My favorite lawman," she said with a flutter of her ridiculously long eyelashes.

He brought Caroline forward like a shield and introduced her to Becky, who beamed an even wider smile. Apparently, the receptionist was enthusiastic about everybody she met.

"This is for you," she said to John as she handed him an envelope. "As for you, Caroline, I was told to send you in as soon as you got here. Ms. Valdez's office is at the end of the hallway on the left."

"Thank you."

She went quickly toward the office with a closed door.

The nameplate read Edie Valdez, Attorney-at-Law. Caroline gave three brisk taps and got no response.

From the reception area, Becky called out, "She might be out on her patio. Just go right on in."

Caroline pushed open the door. The first thing she saw when she stepped inside was a large painting of a dead cow's skull, which struck her as ominous. "Ms. Valdez?"

Though sunlight poured into the office, the atmosphere was chilly. No one sat behind the modern, L-shaped desk. No one occupied the long, maroon sofa. A row of spiked, desert plants sat along the windowsill. The French door was open.

Outside, Caroline glimpsed a garden with yucca, saguaro and barrel cacti. She went to the door and stepped through.

Edie Valdez was lying facedown on the brickwork beside a glass-topped table and overturned chair. Her arms were thrown up as though she'd belatedly tried to protect her head from the bloody wound that matted her salt-and-pepper hair.

Chapter Fourteen

In shock, Caroline froze and stared for a long minute before she dashed back through the office and yelled toward the receptionist's counter. "Becky, call nine-one-one. We need an ambulance. John, come here."

He rushed toward her. "What is it?"

Instead of answering, she grabbed his hand and dragged him to the French door. The second time she saw Ms. Valdez was more horrible than the first because it was so awful and real. Beside the overturned chair, there was a coffee cup that had fallen to the bricks and broken. The attorney must have been sitting there when she was attacked. What was used to hit her? A ceramic planter? A loose brick?

John squatted beside Valdez and felt in her throat for a pulse. He shook his head. "She's gone."

Before Caroline had a chance to understand or react, she saw Becky stalking through the door from the office. Caroline should have jumped into her way, but the young receptionist was moving fast. In an instant, she'd joined them at the French door, and she stared at the murder scene. Her ankles wobbled on her stiletto heels. Her eyes squeezed shut, she threw back her head and screamed in a high-pitched wail that was both horrified and horrific.

When Caroline tried to comfort her, the scream rapidly became hiccupping sobs. Caroline guided her through the office to the maroon sofa and made her sit before she collapsed. "Did you call nine-one-one?"

"Is she dead?"

"Nine-one-one," Caroline said insistently. "An ambulance."

"Yes, I called."

"Good." She patted the young woman's hand and lied. "We won't know her condition until the paramedics get here. We need to stay calm."

"How can I?"

"I don't know." Caroline was on the verge of a panic attack herself, but she refused to give in to the emotions raging inside her like wildfire. Under long, peach scarf, her forehead was damp. Sweat gathered in her armpits and under the line of her bra. "We need to think and be rational. Do you know who was on the patio with Ms. Valdez? Did she have an appointment?"

Becky shook her head and looked down. Her coppery hair cascaded around her face. "Nobody came through the front, but there's a gate from the alley. It might have been unlocked."

If the gate was open, she must have been expecting someone. Caroline heard voices from the front. "How many other people work here?"

"Three other lawyers have offices, only one of them is in right now. And there are four paralegals. Ms. Valdez had a full schedule today with several people coming in. I think they're all heirs, like you."

"Can you cancel her schedule?"

"I can try." She gasped. "Who will give me the okay? Tell me what to do?"

"If anybody complains, I'll take responsibility." She held both of Becky's hands and offered words of encouragement. "You're going to have to be strong. It's up to you to take care of the people in your office. I know you can do it. You have tons of enthusiasm and the best smile ever."

The receptionist recovered some of her poise as she stood. "What should I tell them?"

"The truth," she said simply. "Tell them that Ms. Valdez has been injured."

Becky practiced her smile. The result was more ghastly than brilliant. When she spoke, her voice sounded like a creaky hinge. "You're wrong. I can't do this."

"You can." Caroline guided her to the office door and gave a little shove. "You're tough. You're cool. The others need you."

Stiffly, Becky marched down the hallway toward her desk, where the staff had gathered. She stumbled when she heard the wail of an ambulance signaling the arrival of the EMTs, but she recovered her balance and flashed a thumbs-up signal.

On the patio, Caroline watched while John snapped photos with his cell phone. When he turned his head and saw her, his eyes changed from stormy anger to a cool, hazy gray. Purposely, he positioned himself to screen her from the sight of Edie Valdez, except for her calves and feet.

"Another body," he said. "This has got to be hard for you. We should find a place for you to lie down and catch your breath."

Not what she wanted. "I can handle this."

"It's up to you."

She stared at the lawyer's sensible black pumps and muscular legs. Hadn't John said something about how she took spin classes every morning before work? Even the best, most healthy habits couldn't protect her from a murderer. "Is she dead because of Virgil?"

"I can't say. She was a lawyer, and I'm guessing she made plenty of enemies." He took a step closer and focused on her face and throat. "You're flushed."

I'm burning up. Her fear and panic had ignited an inferno in her belly, which was better than manifesting in screaming, trembling or fainting. What was the worst that could happen from a rising temperature? She'd worn antiperspirant. "It's under control."

"Can I get you some water?"

He was coddling her, similar to the way she'd handled Becky, and that wasn't what she needed. If she hoped to be taken seriously and not have others believe the gaslighting, Caroline had to project strength and resilience. "Treat me like a partner, John. Tell me what I can do to help."

"I wish I could. Jurisdiction is going to be a problem. Technically, the Durango police are in charge, even if Edie's death is connected to your great-uncle. I put in a call to Agent Phillips to find out if he can oversee both investigations. I want access to whatever evidence comes from this murder."

"What are you saying?"

"I'm not giving the orders." He didn't look happy about that turn of events. "I can't tell you or anybody else what to do."

When the paramedics from the ambulance entered through the office and saw John—who looked every inch a lawman in his uniform shirt and badge—he waved them out onto the patio, then pointed to the gate. "That will probably be the easiest way to move her."

After they determined that Valdez was dead, they stepped back to wait for the coroner and the police. The small patio became even more crowded when Agent Phillips joined the others. Caroline felt herself shrinking, fading into the background, while the investigators jockeyed for position. When Becky poked her head into the office and signaled to her, it was a relief to excuse herself.

"What is it?" she asked Becky.

The formerly perky receptionist pointed toward the front desk and said one word. "Rafael."

Caroline cringed inside. Rafael was slick, sophisticated...and demanding. He'd want answers and action. Since he was Edie Valdez's nephew, he had a right to know what was happening. "I'll talk to him."

In the front lobby, she noticed that the handsome investment counselor seemed uncharacteristically shaky. His striped, silk necktie was loosened, and he repeatedly combed his long fingers through his black hair. When he saw Caroline, he pounced on her.

"What's happening?" he demanded. "Where's Edie?"

She put off his question with one of her own. "Why are you here?"

"The same reason you are. My aunt wanted to talk with me about Virgil's will."

"I might be able to help," Becky said. She tapped a letter-size envelope on the top of her long, receptionist counter. "She wanted me to give this to you."

He snatched the envelope, which was marked with his name, and ripped it open. When he perused the top sheet of paper, he grinned like a sleek cat with a bowl of cream. When he read the second page, he sank into a beige leather chair and groaned. *"Dios mio."*

Caroline sat on the sofa beside his chair. "Bad news?"

"Your uncle left me his collection of Gold Eagle coins."

That should be cause for celebration. If she recalled correctly, the coins were worth over two thousand dollars apiece, and there were more than twenty of them. Rafael had inherited close to fifty thousand dollars. "Why does this upset you?"

"My aunt had an addendum about a problem with the inheritance." His grip tightened on the second page, and he crinkled the edge of the paper. "She says I should know what she's talking about."

"Do you?"

"Hell, no." More vehemently, he added, "Absolutely not."

His reaction was too much. Though he denied knowledge of his aunt's "problem with the inheritance," Rafael was showing the classic signs of a guilty conscience. He avoided her gaze. His fingers massaged his temples, where she suspected a tension headache had taken root.

Though Caroline wasn't an investigator, she was a practicing CPA, and she sometimes encountered clients who hedged on the numbers for their taxes, loans, valuations of property and other forms. These deceptions ranged from slightly fudging the amounts of charitable contributions to outright fraud, like discounting the value of an apartment building by hundreds of thousands of dollars. Rafael's attitude made her think he was lying.

"You know I'm a CPA, right?" She leaned toward him and placed her hand on his knee, hoping that physical contact would encourage him to come clean with her. "Is there anything you want to tell me?"

He shoved her hand away and narrowed his gaze. "Is this where I'm supposed to confess to you about the millions of dollars I swindled from your great-uncle's estate?"

She thought of the documents from Edie Valdez's office that were burning in the fireplace when she found Virgil's body. Had the lawyer been reviewing Rafael's transactions with her great-uncle and finding discrepancies? She also recalled that Rafael had appeared at the cabin when someone was shooting at her. Was it him? He'd been at Dolly's B and B last night and could have placed the threatening note in her room. And now, Edie had been murdered.

"You can talk to me about anything," she said. "I understand how finances and investments work. Sometimes, it's necessary to take a risk to earn a decent profit."

"You look so innocent in your peachy blouse and scarf,

but I know you're trying to trip me up. I'm done with you." He jolted to his feet. "Good day, Ms. McAllister."

After a sharp pivot, he left the outer office. The Rosewoods—Luke and Teresa—came through the opened door. In his obviously outgrown suit with buttons that would never fasten over his belly, Luke looked uncomfortable. Teresa had also dressed up in a blue flowered dress and a short jacket. Her hands clutched a dark blue purse so tightly that her knuckles were white. Her long hair was fastened in a messy bun on top of her head.

From the corner of her eye, Caroline saw Becky pick up an envelope similar to the one she'd given to Rafael. Not wanting to open another can of worms, she went to the counter and whispered to Becky, "Would you mind waiting a few minutes before giving the Rosewoods their part of the will?"

"My instructions were clear. Ms. Valdez told me to hand over these envelopes if there was any reason why these people couldn't see her."

Being deceased counted as a reason for skipping a person-to-person meeting. But taking orders from a dead woman was irrational. "Before you do anything, let me check with John."

"Well, I guess I can wait that long. But make it snappy."

Was this the same woman who had been screaming and weeping? Talk about a brilliant recovery. "Thanks, Becky."

The receptionist waved to the Rosewoods. "Please have a seat."

"What's going on?" Teresa's voice trembled. Her hazel eyes swamped with unshed tears. "Why is there an ambulance outside?"

"Ms. Valdez has been injured," Caroline said. "Please wait here. I'll be right back."

In the patio behind Valdez's office, more investigators had gathered, including Agent Phillips, two police officers with Durango patches on their sleeves and a man who must be the coroner, who was kneeling beside the body. She tapped John's arm and whispered, "Other heirs are arriving. You should be at the front desk to meet them."

"Why?"

"Ms. Valdez left envelopes for everybody. Like the one Becky gave to you. Rafael has already come and gone. When he read the note his aunt left him, he was shaken."

She noticed Agent Phillips watching them. He looked directly at John and gave a nod, which, apparently, indicated that he should go with her. John took her elbow and guided her away from the crime scene.

Before they went down the hallway to the front lobby, he asked, "Why do you think Rafael was upset?"

"I've worked with a lot of people who try to cheat on their financial documents. I'm good at spotting a liar."

"Are you? What about Max?"

"Point taken. I can't believe he talked me into being engaged. I must have been drunk."

"Or something."

"Usually, I'm good at knowing when somebody is telling a lie. It's part of my job." She was proud of this well-learned, practical ability. Finally, she might be useful in his investigation. "Rafael showed the kind of behavior that indicates guilt. As Virgil's investment advisor, he has his hands all over the money. In her note to him, Edie Valdez indicated that he'd done something wrong and he ought to know what it was."

"We can investigate the way he handled the cash." He gave her an approving nod. "Good work. Rafael is a viable suspect."

A happy dance would have been inappropriate, but she was proud of herself, and celebrated in her mind. "The Rosewoods have arrived, and I told Becky not to pass out any more envelopes from Edie Valdez."

"How many envelopes did she have?"

"I'm not sure. What was in the one she gave you?"

"A copy of the entire will." He gave her a smile. "By the way, congratulations. You've inherited a small fortune."

The money didn't matter to her. Her family had never been poor, and she had never wanted for anything. After her mom died, she'd received a substantial inheritance—more than she could spend in her lifetime. "I don't care."

"Not many people would say that."

"Money is my business. I understand how it works." She knew what wealth could do to people, turning them into greed monsters or miserable misers. Marriages broke up over finances. Children resented their parents and vice versa. Not that wealth was always a negative. "It's great to have a decent amount in the bank, enough to meet your needs and follow your dreams. But money isn't a solution to every problem."

His warm gaze caressed her. "Lead the way, partner. Let's keep this investigation rolling."

In the front lobby, Teresa Rosewood was perched on the edge of one of the leather chairs. Her tense fingers kneaded her purse. Her husband paced back and forth like a caged grizzly.

Luke Rosewood confronted John. "What's the problem? We had an appointment with Edie Valdez."

"Since the will has been filed with probate, it's basically a public document. You can read the section that applies to you. That doesn't mean you get your money right away. It has to go through the executor."

"But Edie can still tell us how much we're getting," Luke said. "Am I right?"

When his wife stepped up beside him, Caroline couldn't tell if Teresa was embarrassed by her husband's blatant greed or being supportive. "We can wait," Teresa said.

"You'll have to excuse us. We're not used to lawyers and documents and such."

Caroline nodded. "Official meetings always make me nervous."

"Teresa, you've been working for Virgil," John said, "as a housekeeper."

"Twice a week." Her tense expression lightened when she smiled. "Each time I come, I do one big job, like washing windows. Then I take care of the regular cleaning. Recently, I started making healthy casseroles that I'd store in the freezer."

"While you were working in his house," John said, "did you run across any of his hidden places for storing valuables?"

"Like the Gold Eagle coins in the floor space? And the cash?"

The door to the office pushed open, and Max Sherman stepped inside. An immediate burst of hostility flared in Caroline's mind and heart. What was he doing here? Max wasn't an heir to Virgil's fortune. He didn't even know the man.

He held the door for a slender brunette with her hair in a high ponytail. Red lipstick outlined her thin lips. Her sharp blue eyes flashed with innate intelligence. Lola Powell had arrived.

Chapter Fifteen

John recognized the therapist from their brief FaceTime meeting on the phone after Caroline's session. Lola wore a red-and-black scarf loosely knotted around her neck. Her appearance gave the impression of efficiency and organization—maybe too much organization. He wouldn't be surprised to find her closet sorted by matching things that were supposed to be worn together. Her elbow-length blazer was red and the rest of her outfit—silky shirt and slacks—was black. Her slim wrists were encircled by heavy gold cuffs that matched her chain belt. She greeted Caroline with a hug and then turned toward him.

In a few strides, she crossed the lobby and grasped his hand for a firm, no-nonsense shake. "Deputy John Graystone, pleased to meet you."

"We didn't expect you until this afternoon."

"I don't like to be predictable," she said. "Max has been filling me in, but I want to hear from Caroline. Will you join us for lunch?"

"I'm working."

"Very well." Her tone was crisp. "I'm sure we'll meet again. Caroline, shall we go?"

He wanted to tell this organized, pushy woman that Caroline was busy. She'd only been his partner for a few moments, but he'd miss having her at his side, pointing him in unexpected directions. While dealing with this fresh murder, she seemed to have regained her equilibrium. He wanted her to stay with him. "What do you say, partner?"

"Maybe I should go with Lola."

"You can't go far. The investigating officers will want to question you."

Her dark eyes stared at him beneath a furrowed brow. He could tell she was thinking, weighing her options, considering whether she ought to follow her therapist or join him. Time and again, she'd told him how much she wanted to help in the investigation. Finally, she had the chance. And he couldn't think of a single reason to suspect her.

"I need to stay here," she said to her therapist. "When I'm done, I'll call and arrange to join you."

"Do I need to remind you that I dropped everything and came here at great personal inconvenience?" Lola's expression remained impassive but her deep blue eyes exploded with rage, frustration, hostility and more. "My time is valuable."

"And I'm paying for it." Caroline maintained her self-control. "Not to mention that I'm covering the cost of your travel and housing."

Lola huffed. "I'm rather surprised that you've recovered enough from your injuries to work with the police."

"You're not the only one who likes to be unpredictable. Maybe I'm not behaving in an entirely rational manner, but I need to be involved in the investigation. Virgil was my last living relative."

"Except for your father."

"He doesn't count."

"Fine." With a sly smile, she said, "By the way, congratulations on your engagement."

"We're not engaged. If he'd given me a ring, I'd throw it back in his face. Not engaged."

Caroline's lips pinched together. John could see the anger building inside her, and he was glad she had the guts to stand up to the therapist who had suggested this perilous PTSD journey to meet Virgil. When Agent Phillips strode into the lobby from Valdez's office, John took the opportunity to emphasize Caroline's importance.

"Agent Phillips of the Colorado Bureau of Investigation, meet Lola Powell and Max Sherman." Pointedly, he added, "Caroline and I have been in contact with the CBI."

After cursory handshakes, Phillips pulled John aside. "I have some information for you about Derek Everett."

John waved Caroline over. "You should hear this."

She turned her back on Lola and Max. "Please continue, Agent Phillips."

"According to prison records, there was only one person who visited on a regular basis. A woman—her name was Sylvia Cross. She claimed to be married to Everett, and she had two kids that she said were his. He denied the relationship and the offspring."

"You mentioned her before."

"I didn't know she'd been a prison groupie. That can be a deep connection."

Barely noticing that Lola and Max had left, John focused on this new lead. Sylvia Cross might have gone after Virgil seeking revenge. Another suspect. Another woman. "What else can you tell us about Sylvia?"

"Not much. She moved to Denver after Everett was killed. Before that, while he was incarcerated, she visited him once a week. One of the older guards remembered her because she was tidy and attractive, worked as a librarian in Colorado Springs and was, by all accounts, a law-abiding citizen. Unfortunately, she died young."

"And her children?"

Phillips shook his head. "A boy and a girl. They disappeared into the foster system."

"Their names?" she asked.

"Twenty years ago, when Sylvia visited Everett, they

were called Maggie and David. They never accompanied their mom to the prison. Finding them won't be easy."

"But it might be worth it," Caroline said. "One or both of them might have come back to Sagebrush and killed Virgil, looking for revenge for their supposed father."

"This sounds like a project for Agent Wright." Phillips nudged John's arm. "The kid could use some experience in tracking down suspects and witnesses. And he enjoys working on the computer."

"I'd appreciate if Wright would handle the background search," John said.

Phillips pivoted and headed back toward the patio. "I'll keep you posted on the forensics and the autopsy for Ms. Valdez. The local police will notify next of kin. Nobody who works in this office is allowed to leave until they've given a statement. Tell the receptionist."

"I'll do it," Caroline volunteered.

"Thanks," John said. "You've established a bond with Becky."

When she escorted Becky into a vacant office and Phillips returned to the patio, John was free to concentrate on the Rosewoods. From his quick reading of the will, he knew that Virgil had left them the cabin, free and clear. Inheriting a home might count as motive for murder, especially since Luke Rosewood's construction business had been in trouble recently.

John sat on the chair beside the sofa and motioned for them to join him. "I've got a few questions."

"Ask us anything," Teresa said. "We want to help."

Unlike his wife, Luke didn't seem willing to cooperate. He reluctantly took a seat on the sofa. Slouched forward with his elbows on his knees, he stared down at his hands, avoiding eye contact. His attitude implied that he didn't have to answer John's interrogation if he didn't want to, which wasn't exactly true. John didn't want to arrest these two, but if he had to take them into custody to get answers, he'd damned well do it. "Earlier, we were talking about Teresa's job as a housekeeper."

"You know what," Luke said, "I've got a question of my own. What happened to Edie Valdez? I overheard that CBI agent talk about notifying next of kin. Is Edie dead?"

"Yes." There was no point in denial. They'd gone too far down the road for him to pretend. "She was murdered."

Teresa paled. "Like Virgil."

Without raising his head, Luke asked, "Without the lawyer, what happens to our inheritance?"

"There might be a delay while another executor is appointed, but the amount you receive will not be affected."

"It had better not be."

John returned to the questions that pertained to the first murder. "Teresa, we were talking about the work you did for Virgil. Did he pay you well?"

"More than minimum wage."

Under his breath, Luke grumbled, "What difference does that make?"

Losing patience, John turned on him. "I've heard that your construction business is going through a hard time."

He raised his chin and glared. "So what?"

"Maybe that's why Teresa needed to work for Virgil. She had to kick in her share to cover the bills."

"I've always taken good care of my wife. Who the hell are you to say otherwise?"

"I'm investigating a murder," John said. "Two murders. Your alibis for the time when Virgil was shot is each other. Where were you this morning before you came here?"

"We were together," Luke said.

"Once again, your alibi is Teresa. And vice versa."

"That's natural. We're married."

"Oh, Luke." Teresa exhaled a deep sigh. "He's just doing his job, trying to figure out who killed Virgil. And now,

Edie. Sounds to me like John thinks we have a motive because we want to grab Virgil's money."

John couldn't have said it better himself. "Do you know what you're going to inherit?"

"As a matter of fact," said Teresa, stiffening her spine, "I know that he intended to leave us his cabin. Virgil was a good man. He wanted to help our little family, especially when I told him that we're trying to get pregnant."

"Congratulations."

Luke reached over and grasped her delicate hand in his big, rough paw. They reminded John of *Beauty and the Beast*. "We've been waiting a long time to have kids. It's our dream."

"When Virgil found out, he said he'd help in any way that he could." Her voice trembled. "He was a very good man. Shame on you, John Graystone, for thinking we'd want to hurt him."

Less articulate, her husband growled under his breath.

John wasn't sure he could trust this statement of outraged innocence, but he leaned toward acceptance. It seemed clear that he wasn't going to learn anything new from them.

Caroline and Becky emerged from the inner office. Though the receptionist was young, flirty and a little scatterbrained, she seemed to rise to the occasion. Her voice was calm as she informed the Rosewoods that they needed to wait until they had given a statement to the Durango police. She left Caroline in charge of the front counter and went to speak to the other employees in the law offices. Not once, John noted, did Becky Cruz flash a smile.

Behind the counter, Caroline sorted through the envelopes that Becky had arranged. She held them up and went through them, one by one. "In addition to the one for the Rosewoods, there are also messages for Dolly, Popsy, Moira O'Hara and Lucas Jones."

"Moira is the owner of the Sagebrush Café," John said. "I don't know Lucas Jones."

"Virgil's barber," Teresa said. "Are these people getting bequests from the will?"

"I don't like to speculate," John said with a shrug, "but I'm guessing they are. Edie was starting to make final arrangements."

"Can we have the one with our name?" Teresa asked. "Virgil already told me we'd inherit the cabin, but I'd like to see it in print."

John figured that Caroline or Rafael knew more about the disbursement of a will than he did, but none of them were lawyers. "I'm going to leave this part of the investigation up to the Durango police. I'm sure somebody—maybe an attorney in this office—will be appointed executor in Edie's place. Handling the will is their responsibility."

Yuri Popov pushed open the door and stepped inside. His calloused hand trembled on the doorknob. His eyes were wide and wild, as though he'd seen a ghost. He strode to the counter, reached across and grasped Caroline's hand. "Thank God, you're all right."

"Why wouldn't I be? Who have you been talking to?"

He rattled off a stream of Russian that John guessed was either a curse or a prayer. Popov had, like Luke Rosewood, chosen to wear a suit for this meeting, but the similarity ended there. While Rosewood's suit was rumpled and dated, Popov had dressed in an elegant, dark green three-piece suit with a plaid vest of green, white and yellow. The small, wiry man reminded John of a curly-haired leprechaun. Popov regularly wore this outfit when he attended various sporting events—rodeos or horse races or livestock shows for breeders.

"So much danger," he said.

Caroline acknowledged his statement with a nod and quickly changed the subject. "You look nice."

"Spasibo."

Her smile seemed to chip away at his nervousness. Gently, she asked, "Did you talk to anyone before you got here?"

"*Da*, the lady who is your doctor and the other man. Tell me about this Lola person. Do you know her family?"

"No," Caroline said with a shake of her head. "Why do you ask?"

"She looks very familiar. What about the man who says he is your fiancé? His name is Max. Short for Maksim? A good Russian name."

"Maxwell," she said. "He's not my fiancé, and I don't know his family."

"A veterinarian?"

"Though I hate to compliment him, I've heard he's competent at his job."

"I'm glad, because I have invited him and Ms. Lola to my ranch this afternoon. Max will inspect Sasha who is pregnant."

John was struck by Popov's invitation for two reasons. In the first place, the Russian had procured excellent veterinary care for his racehorses and thoroughbreds, neither of which included Sasha, who was a plain old mixed breed he used at the county fair to give rides to kids. Secondly, Popov wasn't a person who enjoyed socializing. As far as John knew, the Russian didn't do much more than visit the Sagebrush Café a couple of times a week and attend the poker game. Why would he want to spend time with Lola and Max?

"I'll be there," Caroline said. She must have been wondering the same thing.

No way was John going to abandon her to the care of the twosome from Portland. "If you don't mind, I'd like to attend as well."

Caroline caught him with a glance. "You really don't have to come along. I'll get my car back from Max today."

He doubted that Max would willingly turn over the vehicle but didn't want to refute her. "You're my partner. We stick together."

Popov slapped his palm on the countertop. "I know Edie Valdez is dead. I heard the police talking outside."

Instead of giving an outright confirmation, John probed. He recalled that Popov had mentioned Valdez when he talked about the fight between Natalie and Virgil. "Were you close to Edie?"

"Our relationship was professional. She did legal work for me." When he lifted his chin, the veins and tendons on his neck stood out. "You might have heard that we were dating, but it was not serious."

John wasn't so sure about that. Both Popov and Valdez were unmarried. There might be more of a connection between them than others suspected. "I'm sorry to inform you that she was murdered."

"Two good friends in one week," he said. "This is not right."

John had to agree.

Chapter Sixteen

After she gave her statement, Caroline left Edie's office with John. While they walked to his car, questions swirled around in her mind. Edie's murder had to be connected to Virgil's. But how? Why was she killed? What did she know?

Somehow, the Rosewoods were involved. But how? Was Popsy having an affair with Edie Valdez?

Caroline's curiosity extended beyond the residents of Sagebrush to include Lola and Max. Though she believed in the treatment Lola provided, she had a nasty feeling that her therapist and Max were manipulating her. When she called Lola's cell phone, she got a pleasant voice message, promising to call back. Caroline sent a text message to Lola's phone. Nearly an hour later, when she and John left the law office in Durango, neither the call nor the text had been acknowledged. Was Lola playing games and avoiding her as punishment for Caroline's refusal to fall in line when she had swept unannounced into the law office?

With cell phone in hand, Caroline climbed into the passenger seat of John's SUV. They had planned to return to Sagebrush and get Lola settled at Dolly's B and B before they went to Popov's ranch at four in the afternoon. She glared at her phone as though the frustrating confusion was the fault of the cellular company. "I don't think we should leave Durango until I talk to Lola."

"Do you have other phone numbers where you could reach her?"

She'd disregarded the obvious alternative because she didn't want to use it. Now, she was stuck. With a groan, she said, "I suppose I could call Max."

"I hate to say this. But contacting him might be better than another trip back and forth between Durango and Sagebrush."

"I can't believe Lola went waltzing off with that neurotic narcissist."

"Wow, you're really into this psychology stuff, aren't you?"

"That's what he is. An egotistical jerk. And Lola isn't much better. Did you hear her congratulate me on my phony engagement? What kind of therapist does that?"

"Ya got me." His cheeks puffed out as he obviously suppressed a chuckle.

"Don't you dare laugh. Max is a creep and might be dangerous, but I can't wait any longer for Lola to respond." She punched the speed dial for Max's cell phone, hating that she had such a close connection with him. He answered quickly.

Her response was terse. "Let me talk to Lola."

"The battery on her phone is low and needs to be recharged."

Caroline wasn't interested in hearing his excuse. "Give her your phone."

"Did you see Popov?"

Why was he still talking? "Yes."

"The old Russian might hire me to do some vet work for him. That would be outstanding. This trip wouldn't be a total waste for me."

As usual, it was all about him. Her fingers tensed on the edge of her cell phone. "Lola. Now."

"I'll do it, but I don't appreciate your attitude. You never used to be so mean."

A bomb exploded inside her skull. Calling off this engagement wasn't enough to satisfy her rage. She wanted to kill him, hack him up into tiny pieces and—

"Caroline?" The therapist's voice was infuriatingly calm. "I hope you can meet us at Mr. Popov's ranch this afternoon. Afterward, we'll have our session. Will that be convenient?"

"Of course," Caroline said.

"I'm interested in seeing the location where you had your incident with the horse named Baron. A visit to the site might trigger other traumatic memories."

In spite of her misgivings about Lola, Caroline appreciated her opinion, and she was most anxious to talk to her about Derek Everett. His relationship with her mother seemed fraught. "Did you change your mind about staying at the B and B?"

"I think not. I've taken a room in the motel where Max is staying. That location is suitable for my needs since you're going to be occupied with the police part of the time I'm here. Also, Max can drive me around."

In my Tahoe? She hadn't given him permission to keep her car. "I think he needs to get back to Portland."

"Not true," Lola said. "Max, your fiancé, is dedicated to—"

"Not my fiancé," she interrupted.

"Dedicated to helping you through this difficult time. His worry is deep and sincere. When he picked me up at the airport, he couldn't stop talking about your amnesia."

"I'll see you at Popov's."

She disconnected the call. Frustrated anger crashed through her, and it took every bit of her self-control not to fling the cell phone out the window, bang on the dashboard and scream her head off. *Max had picked her up at the airport. Seriously?*

John started his engine. "Problem?"

"Nothing I couldn't fix with a machete or a butcher's cleaver." She flexed her fingers and twisted her hand in a gesture that provided relief for her occasional bouts of carpal tunnel syndrome. "Unless you have something else to do in Durango, we can head back to Dolly's until we go to Popov's ranch."

"Dolly's it is. Between the Durango police and the CBI, the ongoing investigation into Valdez's murder is handled."

A thread of guilt wove through her anger. She didn't want her problems to keep him from investigating. "Is there anything else you need to be doing?"

"I wish," he said. "A lot of police work involves the computer, hardware and software, and I don't have access to either. So I have to wait and leave the background research to Agent Wright. You've never met the guy, but he's big and muscular, doesn't look like somebody who'd be good at a computer."

"But Agent Phillips says he is."

"After he finishes digging into the background of Sylvia Cross and her two children, I asked him to check into Max and Lola."

"Why?"

"Gut feeling." He maneuvered out of the parking place and merged into the lazy afternoon traffic. As he navigated through Durango, he reached over the console, took her hand and squeezed. "Do you want to talk about what's going on with your therapist?"

No. Yes. No. Yes! "Why would Lola call Max to pick her up? I knew she probably wouldn't stay at the B and B, but I didn't think she'd take a room down the hall from Max. Why?"

"I can think of an obvious answer. You're not going to like it." His mouth pulled into a scowl. "Maybe there's something going on between Lola and Max."

"As in sex?" She'd never considered the possibility. Physically, they looked like a couple, what with their shared interests in trendy grooming and expensive clothes. Max's goatee and his manicures were a bit too urban chic for Caroline's taste, and she'd say the same about Lola's penchant for outrageously costly scarves.

John continued, "Max told me that he introduced you to Lola."

"He did." She dredged up a niggling little memory from her subconscious. In her first session with Lola, the therapist wore a red-white-and-blue scarf. "When we met, she made sure to tell me there was nothing between them, even encouraged me to date him. I really don't think they're having an affair."

"Why are you so certain?"

"I'm not," she admitted.

"I have another question for you, an important one. Ready?"

She turned her head and studied his profile. Without the cowboy hat, his brown hair was mussed and appealing. And natural. Unlike Max, John didn't waste time on things like stylists and designer jeans. *What you see is what you get.* And she liked what she saw. "Ask me anything."

"After everything that's happened in Sagebrush and everything you've found out about Virgil, do you intend to continue your program with Lola?"

"Of course, I will. She's my therapist." That answer was way too simple. Maybe she ought to consider alternatives. Or not. "Lola has made more of a difference than anybody else I've consulted."

"How so?"

"Since we're headed to Popsy's ranch later, I can give you graphic proof. Remember when we talked about my fear of horses? The trauma with Baron was one of many bad memories that I could recall if I tried." Not that she wanted to relive her episodes of horse terror. "Lola advised me to face my fear. She talked me through my panic and made me take riding lessons."

"How are you going to prove to me and everybody else that you're cured?"

"I'm going to march right up to the biggest, baddest horse in the barn, look him straight in the eye and stroke his flank." She wasn't thrilled with the prospect but knew she could pull it off. "That's not all Lola has done for me. She got me exercising every day, gave me a relaxation regime to help me sleep and worked with a psychiatrist to get me on the right medication."

"She's gotten results for you."

"Absolutely." She inhaled and exhaled, concentrating on her mindful breathing, which was another skill Lola had taught her. True, Lola's idea to confront Virgil had turned into a disaster, but she wasn't to blame for his death. How could she be? She didn't even know Virgil.

"Do you trust her?" John asked.

Caroline hesitated. She wanted to say that she believed in her therapist and was certain that Lola would never betray her or hurt her. But why was she siding with Max? "I've been disappointed a lot in my life, starting with my father leaving. It's hard to say whether I trust her…or anybody else, for that matter."

Outside the city limits of Durango, he drove onto the shoulder and parked before he turned to face her. "You trust me, don't you?"

As she gazed into his shining gray eyes, a pleasant warmth spread through her. John made her feel safe and protected. Though she'd only known him a few days, she believed he wasn't the sort of man who would lie to her or take advantage or betray her. "I do trust you, John Graystone. You would never hurt me."

The space between their seats seemed like a mile. He reached across and gently caressed her cheek, drawing her toward him. She unfastened her seat belt and bridged the gap. Her first kiss was gentle and swift, promising more to come. Her second kiss went deeper. She leaned across him, and her upper body pressed against his. His embrace was gentle but firm. She didn't want to escape from his grasp. She wanted to make love, but not now…not in the car.

"Tonight," he whispered. "I want you in my bed."

"Yes."

"At my cabin."

"Yes." A thrill went through her.

"You'll have to leave the B and B."

"Absolutely, yes."

Since Lola wasn't staying at Dolly's there was no reason for Caroline to keep her bedroom there. She could go to John's cabin. Maybe the therapist had done her a favor, after all.

WHEN SHE AND John arrived at Popov's horse ranch, Caroline sat for a moment in the SUV. She recognized the barn. Her memories of the house and other outbuildings were hazy, but the image of the tall, broad structure with the gambrel roof had left an indelible imprint in her seven-year-old mind. When she'd come here as a child, the barn had been a dull red with white trim around the huge door, big enough to drive a truck through. Now, it was painted a sunny yellow. The trim was still white, and she noticed a large opening above the door and smaller windows on either side of the loft.

Seeing the barn stirred up her old fears of the horses inside, but she was able to inhale a few breaths and dismiss them quickly. Popov's ranch was a well-kept, attractive place, as befitted a rancher who had a reputation as a breeder and was involved in the high-stakes world of horse racing. John had told her that Virgil's bequest to Popov was a fifty-one percent share in a Kentucky Derby winner.

"I still don't get it." John stared through the windshield at the house. "Why do you think Popov invited Lola and Max here?"

"Max seemed to think it was because of his brilliant rep as a vet, and I've got to admit that he talks a good game. He has positive reviews for his services on his phone app."

"Yuri Popov won't be easily conned. What does he have to gain from talking to those two?"

"No idea." She wiped her sweaty palms down her jeans, glad that she'd changed from her delicate silk blouse and switched the cream-colored slacks for a pair of blue jeans. Instead of the long peach scarf tied around her head, she'd gone back to the more comfortable denim baseball cap.

When she stepped out of his vehicle, she was hit by barnyard smells. Her memories became more intense, and she recalled Baron the stallion with the wind tugging at his manes and his nostrils flaring as he charged toward her. Impossible! That was twenty years ago. *Mindful breathing. Don't panic.* She dismissed her fears and mentally prepared to face her irritating therapist and the man who called himself her fiancé.

Max and Lola came out of the house with Popsy, who had changed his leprechaun suit for boots, jeans and a canvas vest. Max had the leather satchel he used to carry his veterinarian tools slung over his shoulder. He came toward her with his arms outstretched for an embrace, which she avoided by dodging around him to face her therapist.

"Nice scarf," Caroline said, referring to Lola's neck scarf of peacock-blue and green.

"I needed a pop of color with all this khaki."

From their visits to the riding school in Portland, Caroline knew that her therapist wasn't a fan of equestrian pursuits. "Have you seen the horses yet?"

"We're on our way to the barn," she said. "After that, you and I will have a private session."

"I'm looking forward to it." Caroline wasn't lying. In just a few sentences, Lola had put her at ease. Their sessions had been crucial to controlling her depression, and she was grateful for the guidance from her therapist.

"We have been talking," Popov said. "Ms. Powell has never visited Colorado. Not once. I am not sure I should believe her."

"Why would you think otherwise?" Caroline thought of John's questions about reasons Popov might have invited Lola and Max.

"She is very familiar to me."

Lola thanked him. "I try to fit in."

Max and John walked ahead of them on their way to the barn while Popov stepped between the two women. "I should take you both for a ride," he said. "Would you like that?"

Caroline shook her head. "You're thinking of my mother. Natalie loved horses and riding. I don't feel the same way."

"I have two of Natalie's paintings in my house," he said. "One shows three fillies in the corral. The other is my stallion, Baron, in his prime."

She wasn't surprised that her mother had immortalized Baron—the horse who terrified her as a child. That choice said a lot about how they related to each other. While Caroline had struggled to tamp down her panic, Mom believed her daughter could easily overcome her fears. She never stopped pushing. If she'd lived, what would their relationship have become? Caroline liked to believe that they would have found middle ground. She wished, desperately, that she could talk to her mother about John, the first man she'd been attracted to in a very long time.

In the corral bordering the barn, she saw four older horses grazing, pacing and enjoying the temperate spring weather. A big bay horse turned his head and looked directly at her. It had been over twenty years, but she recognized Baron.

Her memories returned in jagged shards. The stallion had aged. His long face was marked by veins and had turned gray around the eyes and muzzle. His coat was dull. His long black mane was matted. Warily, she watched him. *Mindful breathing, mindful breathing.* Her panic began to rise.

Baron swaggered toward her. His belly sagged. His dark, rheumy gaze locked with hers. Still big, he was so big… and dangerous.

Her right hand cradled her left as she remembered the pain from her badly sprained wrist. She'd been hurt before, many times, and didn't know how much more she could take. The horse was a harbinger of worse threats to come.

Chapter Seventeen

Inside the barn, John listened with half an ear while Max bragged about his veterinary skill and reputation, which was so stellar that—supposedly—even Popov should be impressed. Nothing was going to stop this big mouth from waving his cell phone and showing cute photos of him and his doggy and kitty patients. When Lola and Popov stepped through the wide doorway, John realized that he'd lost track of Caroline. Ignoring the others, he went outside to the long driveway that curved past the parking area, the house and the barn. He spotted her at the corral attached to the barn, where she was standing behind the sturdy, whitewashed boards of the fence. Her slender shoulders were tense, and she held her left wrist protectively.

On the opposite side of the fence, a chestnut horse stared at her with fierce attention. John remembered her therapy session, when she'd called Baron a demon steed, which was not what he looked like twenty years later. The bay stallion was still big, but he'd lost his regal bearing. His head drooped. His movements were stiff and arthritic, which was probably not the way Caroline saw him.

John stepped up beside her and gently draped his arm around her shoulders, just to let her know he was there if she needed his support. Wasn't this a job for Lola? Shouldn't the therapist comfort her client when she was distressed? Maybe Lola only offered that level of care and attention when Caroline came to her office, followed procedure and paid the tab.

Without turning her head, Caroline said, "In my rational mind, I know Baron isn't going to tear down the fence and attack me. He probably doesn't even remember who I am."

John wasn't so sure about that. He'd grown up around horses, liked and respected the animals. Sometimes, a horse—or a dog or a cat—bonded with a human. Seeing the adult Caroline might trigger a response from Baron. "I doubt he's held a grudge for all these years."

"Not like me." She inhaled and exhaled at a measured pace. "It's hard for me to stand here, looking into his cruel, dark eyes, and not think back to how badly he frightened me. He caused me to sprain my wrist, and it's never completely healed. I still have carpal tunnel syndrome."

"We can leave."

"I can face the damn horse." She shivered. "Do you think I should touch him?"

He understood that stroking Baron's long nose scared her but doing it might be a triumph. "It's up to you."

She shrugged off his arm and took a step closer to the fence. "At the riding school, they told us to approach the horse from the front, but not head-on. I should angle my body."

When she suited her actions to the narrative, John moved with her, staying close and preparing to catch her if she fell or ran. "What else did they teach?"

"To hold out my hand, so he can sniff it and understand that I'm not going to hurt him." Her right hand quivered as she reached across the fence. Baron cocked his head, watching her with unwavering focus. "What if he smells fear?"

John kept quiet, not wanting to put more pressure on her.

Caroline rested her hand on Baron's neck and stroked once, twice. She left her hand there until the stallion tossed his head and nickered. Abruptly, she stepped back. "I'm not sure if he's saying hello or if that's horse talk for 'I'm gonna kick you in the knee.'"

"Doesn't matter what he's saying, you're the boss. That's a good thing to keep in mind when you're facing other hostile beasts, like Lola or Max."

"Look at you, giving me life lessons." Before she left the corral, she waved farewell to Baron the demon steed. "Now that you've had a chance to observe Max in action, what do you think?"

"Can't stand the guy," he said with outright honesty. "But I have an idea about him that might pertain to our investigation, partner. Does he always carry his veterinarian kit with him?"

"Very often, he does. Just throws that leather satchel into the back of the car so he'll have his equipment if he gets called outside of regular work hours. Max prides himself on giving personal service. His practice handles some show dogs and superexpensive breeds. A lot of his clients are spoiled brats—not the animals, but the people who own them."

Inside the tidy, well-organized barn, horse stalls lined the walls on both sides. In the middle of the afternoon, most of the spaces were empty. John exchanged a greeting with the young cowboy, Clayton, who was mucking out the stalls—a task John had performed many times when he was growing up. These surroundings were comfortable for him. The smells of leather, hay and horses brought back pleasant memories.

At the rear of the barn, they joined Lola, who was standing outside a large stall with three walls and a waist-high fence that opened into the barn. Popov and Max were inside the fence with Sasha, a very pregnant dappled mare. She whinnied and wiggled and danced away from her owner, who kept talking to Max about symptoms, like viscous discharges and colic.

Max stood by with his stethoscope at the ready. "I recommend an ultrasound," he said. "Do you have the equipment?"

"Da." Popov called out to Clayton and told him where to find the portable ultrasound.

"If you don't mind my asking," Lola said, "why does a horse need an ultrasound?"

Max answered as though he'd been waiting for a question from his small audience. He stroked his goatee and lectured. "Ultrasounds are useful in pregnancy to make sure the fetus is in the correct position, and I've used that technology to study sprains and fractures."

Popov signaled him to approach Sasha. "Listen to her heart. She is not well."

When Max approached with his stethoscope, Sasha skittered away from him. She tossed her head as if to refuse his attention. Standing close to John, Caroline whispered, "I don't blame her. He makes me feel the same way."

Max tried again, but Sasha still wasn't having it. She wedged her swollen body into the corner of the stall and reared, kicking at him with her front legs. Max turned his back on the dappled horse and spoke to the owner. "Can you do anything to make her calm down?"

"I do not understand." Popov gave an expressive shrug. "She is never so anxious."

"We might need a tranquilizer," Max said.

Though John didn't wish misfortune on Sasha, he had secretly hoped the veterinary examination would get to this point. Because of his profession, Max was uniquely qualified to carry anesthetics and sedatives. Among the tranquilizers for large animals was ketamine, which was often used with Rohypnol to create a date-rape cocktail.

"I do not have medication," Popov said.

"No problem." Max preened. "I always carry tranquilizers with me."

"Why is that?" John asked.

"I never know when I'm going to run into a skittish horse or a nervous dog that needs sedation." He dug into his leather satchel and took out a hypodermic needle and a small vial. "There was a time on a plane when a woman's yappy little therapy dog would have bothered all the other passengers if I hadn't slipped the Chihuahua a ketamine trank."

Apparently, this jerk was oblivious to the implications. He had admitted to carrying ketamine, which solidified John's suspicion that Max had doped Caroline in Reno and talked her into an engagement with an eye to a marriage that would lead him to inherit big.

Max was, most likely, the bad guy. But his motives weren't clear. What caused him to attack Virgil now? And why kill Edie Valdez? There had to be a logical thread that tied the engagement, and their eventual marriage, to the murders.

John's cell phone rang, and he stepped out of the barn to talk to Agent Wright. The rumbling voice of the young agent called to mind his muscular physical appearance. John imagined him hunched over a computer in a cubicle, staring longingly through the windows at the sunlit day and the amazing spring weather.

"I came up with a link between Edie Valdez and Derek Everett," Wright said.

John had suspected as much. He offered a guess. "Was she Virgil's attorney at the trial when Everett was convicted?"

"Not exactly," Wright said. "The trial was almost twenty years ago, and Edie was a beginner lawyer who worked in her father's office. Her dad attended the trial to protect Virgil's interests. Since Edie specialized in finance, Virgil gravitated in her direction. He became more her client than her father's."

"But she was aware of Everett," John clarified. "I know Max Sherman is also her client. Is there any other connection between Valdez and Max? Or with Lola Powell?"

"As you requested, I did background work on the two of them," Wright said. "They're real boring. No criminal records to speak of. The therapist was sued by clients three times in the last eight years, all settled out of court. Max has been in financial trouble a couple of times, which kind of amazed me. Whenever I take my golden retriever to the vet, I can't believe how much it costs."

No surprise that Wright owned a golden. John easily imagined him jogging through the forest with his dog.

The lack of intersection between Edie Valdez and Max or Lola was disappointing. His murder investigation needed to concentrate on Edie's link with Virgil and, therefore, with Derek Everett. "Did you find anything more about Sylvia Cross?"

"After Everett was killed in prison, she moved with her two kids to Denver, where she worked as a librarian for four years before she died."

"What happened?" John asked.

"Suicide. She took pills. Her daughter found the body." Agent Wright cleared his throat. "A hell of a thing. Maggie Cross was only fourteen."

In the last report from Phillips, John had learned that the Cross children, a boy and a girl, had been placed in foster care. "How old are the kids today?"

"Early thirties. David has a car-repair business in Denver. Maggie went to the University of Colorado for a couple of years, got married and then divorced. Moved to California. For a while, she worked in libraries like her mother."

Sylvia's children might provide the link he was looking for. Though nobody named David or Maggie Cross had emerged in his investigation, that didn't mean much.

Changing names wasn't all that hard. "I'd appreciate photos of the Cross kids if possible."

"Do you think they could be involved in the Valdez murder?" Wright asked. "I'm not so sure. What's the motive? I mean, they might want revenge, but why go after a lawyer who was only marginally involved?"

"Don't know, but I've got to start somewhere."

Among his current suspects, he thought of Teresa Rosewood and her husband. It could be either of them. Both were the right age to be the Cross children. Then, there was the receptionist in the law office, Becky Cruz. A wider net could be cast if he considered men and women who were associates of Rafael Valdez.

"Let me know if you come up with more evidence," Wright said. "And I'll email you copies of the info I've gathered so far."

"Thanks." John turned back toward the barn. In the late-afternoon sun, the yellow building with white trim blended nicely with the emerging green leaves and grasses. "Another thing, Wright."

"Yeah?"

"Be sure you get away from the computer. It's a good time to be outdoors."

Which was what he hoped to do with Caroline. Take her outside into the mountains and allow nature to work its healing magic. It had been a long day that started with the discovery of Edie Valdez's bloody body. They deserved some alone time.

CAROLINE DIDN'T MIND when John took a detour. They left before Max had finished treating Sasha and didn't expect to meet with him and Lola for another hour or so. There was no need to rush. She settled into the passenger seat, rolled down her window and inhaled the mountain air. The approach of twilight turned the vast blue skies to a magenta hue and tinted the snow-capped peaks with a rosy glow while the sun reflected orange and gold off the underbellies of clouds. She sighed. “We don’t have sunsets like this where I live.”

“You’ve got Mount Hood outside Portland,” he said. “That’s a spectacular peak.”

She nodded in agreement. “But the coastal mountains and the Cascades don’t compare to the Rockies. On the other hand, Oregon’s beaches are rugged and wonderful.”

“Can’t argue with that. We don’t have an ocean in Colorado.”

Through the open window, she heard the rushing water of an unseen creek as he drove along a narrow gravel road that twisted through a forest of pine, spruce, cottonwood and aspen. John seemed to know where he was headed, and she was content to sit back and enjoy the fresh air.

Today had been stressful, but Caroline felt stronger and more capable of handling the threats and dangers that seemed to be part of her life in Colorado. Much of her newfound courage came from her association with the man sitting beside her. *I trust him.* When he wasn’t slapping on handcuffs, John encouraged her and believed in her.

She studied his chiseled profile and saw an outdoorsman who was stubborn and determined. When he lifted his aviator sunglasses off his nose and gazed at her with his silver eyes, she recognized his intelligence and sensitivity. Being with him was better for her outlook than hours of therapy. His kisses were a soothing balm. His touch cured her depression. *Really? Cured might be a bit much.* She pulled back a few mental paces. Her emotional well-being was certainly not based on John’s opinion or mood. Still, she enjoyed his influence.

She took off her cap, allowing the crisp, refreshing wind to weave through her hair and cool her cheeks. “I never appreciated Colorado when I was a kid. I wish my mom was here to enjoy it with me. And Virgil. I spent so much time being angry at him, and I wonder if there was ever a real reason. I still have Popsy, but it's not the same."

"Why do you call him Popsy?"

"Probably because his name is Popov." And she wasn't about to waste her limited recall on something so trivial. "Does it matter?"

"Do you think of him as family?"

"I guess so. I'm feeling more and more like I'm home in Colorado."

He parked the SUV in front of an A-frame cabin nestled against a pile of granite boulders that was almost artistic in its arrangement. His seat belt unfastened with a snap. "We're here," he announced.

She knew, without further explanation, that he'd brought her to his home. The triangular window at the peak faced west and probably displayed a great view of the sunset. The covered porch across the front spread into a wide deck on the side with a barbecue, several Adirondack chairs and a picnic table.

He led her up a few stairs to the deck, brought her to a railing and positioned her so she could see through a break in the trees. "This is the best spot to watch the sun slide behind the mountains."

She rested her hands on the wooden railing and leaned back, fitting herself against his broad, muscular chest. The crown of her head came barely to his chin. When his arms encircled her, she felt incredibly comfortable and calm. Tantalizing scents of pine and cedar—natural aromatherapy—wrapped around her as she watched the sunset deepen. "Beautiful."

"Wish I could say I built the house myself, but it was the second place the real-estate agent showed me. It was kind of a wreck but cleaned up real nice. And I added the deck. I wanted to come here before dark so you wouldn't be worried when I bring you back here tonight."

"Why would I worry? If you're thinking about my reputation, please don't. I'm a grown woman, and if I choose to spend the night at your house, that's nobody else's business."

"A grown, *engaged* woman," he reminded her.

"I've already told Max, several times, that we're never getting married. In my mind, I'm not engaged."

He dipped his head and nuzzled below her ear. "I wanted to reassure you. Even though I'm a bachelor, I lead a civilized life."

"Okay." She tried to pay attention to what he was saying, but his lips on the tender skin at her throat were a distraction that sent electrifying ripples throughout her body.

He nibbled at her earlobe. "You'll sleep in the loft at the top of the triangle. There's only one door that opens to that bedroom. You'll be safe there."

She arched her neck and gave a soft moan. Her knees went weak. She was ready to abandon all resistance.

His cell phone buzzed, and he adjusted his position to answer. "It's Agent Phillips. I have to take the call."

He stepped away from her, and she clung to the railing, needing that solid support to stay on her feet. Her gaze attached to the brilliant sunset. Later, she would return home with him and spend the night in his arms.

John disconnected his call. His expression told her it wasn't good news. "Preliminary autopsy results for Evie Valdez show the obvious. She was killed by being hit on the head with a rock or decorative pottery."

"What else?"

"Phillips doesn't have an address for David Cross, the kid who might be Derek Everett's son, but has tracked him to Colorado."

"He might be the killer."

"And could be nearby."

Chapter Eighteen

At Dolly's B and B, Caroline escorted Lola upstairs to her bedroom, which was, she hoped, soon to be her former bedroom after she moved to John's A-frame. Dolly's place was the best alternative for therapy because Caroline needed somewhere that felt safe. Obviously, Max's motel wasn't suitable. It was annoying enough that he'd insisted on driving Lola here and was waiting downstairs with John. She'd already turned down dinner plans that included him and refused to pretend they were engaged.

She closed the door behind Lola. "Thank you for agreeing to meet me here."

"Of course." She swept across the charming lavender-and-green room, putting her imprint on the hardwood floor and delicately patterned wallpaper. With a dramatic flourish, she unfurled her peacock-blue-and-green scarf and left it hanging loosely around her neck, revealing a thin gold chain necklace and a small lavalier. "Before we start your session, we need to make a few things clear. Much of today was wasted because we didn't have an agenda. We'll do a session now, another tomorrow morning and a final session tomorrow in the late afternoon."

"Agreed. One session should be about Derek Everett. He's a criminal my mother was involved with, and I hope to access memories, traumatic or otherwise, that I have of him."

Lola gave a brisk nod. "What else?"

"I need to talk about John Graystone and my relationship with him."

"May I remind you, Caroline, that you are engaged."

"Absolutely not." She confronted her therapist. "Max is the third thing I want to discuss. I need to recall what happened in Reno. Why can't I remember preparations for a marriage which, of course, never took place. He has photos so I know we got as far as an appointment with the Justice of the Peace. But how? Did I have a psychotic break?"

Skeptical, Lola raised an eyebrow. "Are you suggesting that we do a focused memory session on an event that happened only a few days ago?"

"Yes."

"An unorthodox approach. Usually, my clients can recall their immediate history."

"But I have amnesia. There are still chunks of my past that are blank. Gradually, the doctors said I'll regain almost everything. But I need an immediate reboot on what happened to me between Reno and finding Virgil's body."

On the drive here, John had talked to her about Max and his supply of ketamine. Being drugged gave a clear explanation of why she'd do something as wildly impulsive as getting engaged to Maxwell Sherman.

She didn't mention the ketamine to Lola, partly because it made her seem irrational. "There's one more thing." *Oh, damn, I hate to talk about this.* "I've been having paranoid incidents."

"Max told me about when you were certain someone was shooting at you."

I'm still certain. "Last night, I received a note—hidden under my pillow." An involuntary shudder twitched her shoulders. "The writing looked exactly like mine. Why would I send a threat to myself?"

Lola seated herself in one of the overstuffed chairs by the window, crossed her legs and ran her fingers down the length of the silk scarf. "We'll start with the paranoia, then do the focused memory session on Reno and we'll finish up with relationships."

"Nothing on Derek Everett?"

"We'll use our session tomorrow morning to explore your memories of the past."

"Popov knows something about Everett. Should I talk to him before our session?"

"I'd prefer for you to keep your memories untainted," Lola said. "Yuri Popov would see the past from his own perspective, which—if you don't mind me saying—is influenced by his affection for your mother."

Caroline wasn't surprised that her therapist had noticed Popsy's crush on Natalie. Lola was a perceptive woman... except when it came to Max. For some reason, she didn't see Max for the preening jerk that he was.

Stretched out on the bed in a relaxed position, Caroline stared up at the ceiling. "Getting back to the paranoia... Why am I feeling like this?"

"Are you sure these events didn't happen? I suspect that you and the deputy investigated. Correct?"

"Yes."

"Based on tangible evidence, did you conclude there wasn't a shooter?"

There hadn't been physical evidence—like shell casings, footprints, bullets or fingerprints—at the site of the shooting. "We're still exploring the possibilities."

"And the threatening note?"

"Agent Phillips is having the note analyzed by a handwriting expert. But we haven't heard back from him."

"After all you've been through, it's natural to feel threatened and to manifest those fears in symbolic visions. An imaginary shooter might indicate feelings that you aren't being well-protected. Or might be a cry for help. What did the threatening note say?"

"Basically, it told me to get out of town."

"How does that make you feel?"

Didn't Lola sound just like every shrink Caroline had ever had? "I see where you're going with this. I'd like to leave Sagebrush and put this tragedy behind me. Therefore, it's possible I wrote a note to myself, stating that very feeling."

"Now we're getting somewhere. Congratulations, Caroline."

She appreciated the praise from her therapist. Most of the time, Lola was like a rock. They weren't friendly, didn't go out for coffee or lunch. Lola made certain that Caroline was aware of the separation between a personal relationship and therapy. One time, they'd accidentally bumped into each other at a restaurant, and Lola pretended that they'd never met. And yet, she'd introduced Caroline to Max, almost setting up a blind date. If that wasn't meddling, what was?

"Suppose I wrote it," Caroline said. "Why wouldn't I remember putting pen to paper? And why was I compelled to show the phony note to John?"

Lola nodded. "I think you just answered your own question."

"I get it." *Well, duh.* "I wanted to use the note to get John's attention, which meant I had to write it to myself and wave it around like a flag. How pathetic!"

"Don't judge yourself. You must have erased your actions when you thought you were being targeted and when you wrote the note. Possibly because these issues are too difficult to face head-on. You don't want to think of yourself as being weak or a victim. Your subconscious mind really can't be blamed for protecting you."

"Is this what people call 'the lizard brain'?"

"Typically, lizard brain refers to a primitive neurological response based on reactions in the limbic system," Lola said.

"Like fight-or-flight. Or panic attacks." She kind of liked the idea. "It's an instinct, right? Something uncontrollable."

Lola didn't scoff outright, but her tone made it clear that she wasn't a fan of this theory. "A few years ago, the idea of lizard brain was trendy. To me, it seems like an over-simplification. But if it helps you to think of a green gecko inside your skull directing your actions, feel free to do so."

She recalled a more practical technique they'd used for dealing with panic attacks. "I can make notes of these events, like a journal or a diary. There's no right or wrong, just the experience. And no judgment."

"Exactly." Lola rewarded her with a smile. "Shall we start this session."

Caroline closed her eyes and went through the relaxation exercises that put her into a meditative state. After her breathing had regulated and she'd hummed all the verses to the Bunny Foo Foo song, her therapist gave her the prompt.

"Today is Friday," Lola said. "I want you to think back to yesterday. What happened?"

"I left the hospital. Went to Virgil's cabin. Somebody shot at me. Searched for Virgil's cache of jewelry. Came back here to Dolly's B and B. Took a nap. I was so tired. Maybe it was the injury."

"Stick to the events," Lola instructed. "What happened when you came here last night?"

"Ate dinner. Met the poker players. Went to bed. Found the note. Kissed John." She couldn't help smiling. "It was fantastic—definitely in my top five GOAT kisses—Greatest Of All Time."

"We'll get back to that later. The day before yesterday, what happened?"

"We were in Reno?" Events blurred in her mind as she mentally lost track of time. So much had happened so quickly. "I'm wrong. That happened on Tuesday."

"Yesterday was Wednesday."

"Woke up in Salt Lake City. Drove all day. Got to Colorado. I had a concussion." The inside of her head exploded with the sensation of the pain she must have experienced when she received the head wound. "Then I was running, running hard in the forest." Re-living the moment, she gasped for breath. "I was terrified. It felt like something or someone was coming after me."

"Did you see anyone?"

"Only shadows in the forest."

"Did you hear a voice?"

"Nothing but the cries from the coyotes and the screeches from owls."

Lola paused for a moment, then said, "But you determined nothing was there. No one was chasing you. That seems to be similar to your more recent paranoid events."

Caroline's pulse accelerated. Her muscles tensed as she remembered dashing through the trees, terrified. She'd been so sure that someone was coming after her.

Max. It was him. She had been escaping from him.

A sliver of memory inserted itself into her conscious mind. She and Max were in the Chevy Tahoe. He was driving in the mountains, and they were looking for Virgil's cabin. She'd been so tired and wanted to stop at a motel, but he insisted on pushing forward. A woozy feeling came over her. She felt ill. Her thoughts jumbled.

All she knew for certain was that she had to get away from Max. She'd flung open the car door and thrown herself out. That must have been when she hit her head.

"I must have been unconscious after I got the concussion but not for long." Just enough time for someone to steal her watch. "Splitting headache. It felt like my skull was breaking apart. I never knew what that meant before. Then Max was after me."

"He told me that he tried to find you. He was worried."

Caroline didn't believe his story. He put her in danger.

If he was really worried, it was because he feared the return of her memory. "He's lying."

"It sounds like you don't trust your fiancé," Lola said. "Why do you feel that way?"

"Not my fiancé," she said automatically.

"But he proposed. You said yes."

"If I don't remember, it doesn't count."

"Oh, Caroline. The work we've done with PTSD proves otherwise. Memory is too often ephemeral, unreliable. We'll leave that discussion for later, shall we?"

Anger crept through her, disrupting the meditative state. She didn't enjoy being treated like a child. "I'll take another step backward in time. On Tuesday, we arrived in Reno."

"Imagine the road signs, counting down the miles. And then, you're there. What did you feel? What did you hear?"

"It's not as flashy as Las Vegas, but Reno has plenty of spangles and bangles and neon. Slot machines make a lot of noise, and there was music. Golden oldies. I was feeling upbeat, proud of myself for taking this journey to confront Virgil."

She paused. Her concentration wasn't as focused as usual. Her mind seemed to be editing the experience rather than simply reporting it. She'd been so wrong about her great-uncle. Virgil hadn't traumatized her. He loved her.

"Caroline." Lola's soothing voice pulled her back. "You must have been glad to have a companion with you. Did you and Max celebrate?"

"Having fun. Laughing. We got a two-bedroom suite on the Lucky Seven floor of a fancy hotel. Two bedrooms." She held up two fingers. "Max and I have never slept together. Does that sound like a couple in love?"

"Maybe you ought to give him a chance."

Or maybe not. She didn't like the way Lola kept taking Max's side. Something had to change. Caroline realized that she didn't trust her therapist, either.

Chapter Nineteen

John paced the length of the wide veranda outside Dolly's B and B, listening to his second phone call from Agent Phillips. The first call—hours ago—had intruded at the moment when he and Caroline were about to become intimate at his A-frame. A well-timed interruption, as it turned out. They couldn't stay at his house and needed to be on their way. There hadn't been time for their closeness to expand to its full potential...whatever that was.

He'd only known her for a few days, and their time together had been filled with murder, injury and suspicion. But he was drawn to her in unexplainable ways. Physically, he was aroused, and hoped for something more than friendship. But he had no expectations.

Dusk had settled, replaced by nightfall as he listened to Agent Phillips complain about the tangled web of contacts that led to finally getting the right phone number for David Cross, son of Sylvia. "The young man claims to have no interest in his mother's relationship with Derek Everett the jailbird. David doesn't believe the guy was his father."

"Which means he has no motive for taking revenge against Virgil."

"He also has a rock-solid alibi for Wednesday night. Seems that Derek is a musician, a drummer in a rock band, and they had a gig at Sullivan's Saloon in Denver. At the time when Virgil was being murdered, David Cross was on stage."

"What about his sister?"

"Hasn't seen her for ten years, not since her marriage failed and she walked away with a big, juicy cash settlement. He thinks she moved to California."

"So they aren't close," John said.

"Not at all. I'll never understand how family can get so broken apart. I mean, they were brother and sister." Phillips sounded disgusted. "And now, David isn't even sure about her last name. She changed it to Thompson, her ex-husband's name, but she discarded that surname when they divorced. She hadn't been Cross for a long time. Little Miss Maggie is an independent type who likes to reinvent herself."

She was another dead end for a trail of evidence. "How about photos?"

"I'll send them to your phone," Phillips promised.

After John thanked him, he asked about the prior call. "You sent the preliminary autopsy information on Edie Valdez."

"Very preliminary," Phillips said. "The actual autopsy will take a few days, but the ME is willing to say that cause of death was homicide due to blunt-force trauma. He doesn't like to make assumptions but was fairly sure that Edie's cranial injuries were caused by a decorative rock in her outdoor cactus garden."

"No surprise," John said, remembering the blood smears at the crime scene.

"I've got more," Phillips said. "I convinced the ME to run a tox screen. Technically, he's supposed to wait for the autopsy, but so many drugs are difficult to trace if we have to wait and I had reason to suspect tranquilizers."

John hadn't discussed Max and his supply of animal tranquilizers with Agent Phillips. "Why tranks?"

"You," he said. "At the crime scene, you wondered why Edie didn't fight back. And you were right. Edie was physically active and strong. Certainly not meek."

"What did the tox screen show?"

"Her iced tea was dosed with a fentanyl derivative that would slow her reflexes."

Life would have been easier if traces of ketamine—Max's tranquilizer of choice—had appeared in the tox screen. From inside the B and B, he heard Max lecturing Dolly about a breed of cat, the Russian blue, that wasn't supposed to shed. His tone was gentle, almost friendly. Fondness for animals was his only positive trait. "Can fentanyl be used as an animal tranquilizer?"

"It's something a veterinarian would be familiar with."

"What are we waiting for?" John asked. "I can arrest Max Sherman right now."

"First, I need a warrant from a judge that allows me to go through his vet supplies and seize all drugs, which means I need enough solid evidence to suspect him. When we take him into custody, I want to make sure the charges stick."

"In the meantime, I'm worried about Caroline. She could be in danger." Max was too cowardly to hurt her, but John didn't want to take any chances. If anything happened to Caroline, he'd never forgive himself. "I'd feel better if Max was locked in a cage, where he couldn't cause any more trouble."

"I can take her into protective custody."

"We'll think about it." John was fairly sure that Caroline would reject that plan. "Thanks for the offer, Phillips."

He disconnected the call and stood quietly on the porch, staring at the blank screen on his phone. The progress they were making on the investigation should have gratified him, but the cost of justice was too high. Two good people had been murdered, and he couldn't imagine a solution that would make him smile.

All he wanted to do tonight was take Caroline to his home and watch over her. Actually, that wasn't the only thing he wanted, but he wasn't foolish enough to make half-baked plans. Their relationship depended mostly on her decisions.

When she and Lola came down the staircase together, he caught her gaze and saw a glow from her fascinating dark eyes. He could tell that she was glad to see him. He pulled her to one side. "We need to talk about the investigation. Phillips called again."

"Should we talk privately?" she asked.

"That would be best."

They weren't using code, but their words were meant only for each other. *We need to be alone.* They were on the same page, reading the same book, and the rest of the world was looking in the opposite direction.

Impatiently, he said their goodbyes to Lola and Max. While Caroline darted up the staircase to repack her suitcase, he thanked Dolly again for her hospitality.

"Caroline will be staying with me tonight," he told her. "She needs a bodyguard, and I need a full night's sleep."

"To tell you the truth," Dolly said, "I'm relieved. I heard you prowling around the house last night, even going outside. I just can't be responsible for any more dangerous incidents. You'll take good care of Caroline. That's what Virgil would have wanted."

"You knew him better than anybody."

She patted her long, curly blond hair into shape and gave him a sly smile. "Is there something going on with the two of you? Something deeper than friendship?"

"Could be," he admitted.

"Well, it's about time, Johnny boy. If you're going to be the next sheriff of Peregrine County, you ought to be settled down with a wife and kids."

"Whoa, Dolly. Caroline and I are only friends."

"Could be more," she said.

"And she lives in Portland."

"Tell you what, Johnny, I'll pay for the moving van."

Caroline descended the staircase, dropped her suitcase and gave Dolly a hug. "I'm glad that you and my great-uncle were close. From what I've learned about him, I think he would have been a hermit if it wasn't for people like you."

When Dolly hugged her back, there were tears in her eyes. She handed Caroline a large blue insulated cooler bag. "I made you some dinner. This way you and John don't have to stop in town. It's mostly healthy, but I had to make sure you had something sweet."

"Cookies?" Caroline asked.

"Brownies." Dolly guided the young couple toward the door. "If you're hungry for breakfast tomorrow, stop by."

"Lola and I want to do another session tomorrow morning. Can we use the master bedroom at ten o'clock?"

"Perfect."

As soon as Dolly mentioned food, John realized that he hadn't eaten since lunch. He had some groceries in the fridge at his cabin but would have been scraping to put together a decent meal. Dolly was a champ.

When they got settled in his SUV, he had the sense that they'd escaped potential disaster. Nobody had been murdered this afternoon. There had been no attacks. And they were on their way to his home. There was a possibility that everything would be all right. His upbeat mood reminded him of when he was a kid and his family took a trip to Disneyland. He and Caroline were in the midst of a murder investigation, but he felt like they were setting out on an adventure together. *Wishful thinking.*

She snapped her seat belt and glanced at him. "Okay, partner. What did Agent Phillips have to say?"

"Really? Do you want to get right down to business?"

"I could tell you about my therapy session, but you'd probably be bored to death."

He'd learned a lot when he listened to her memories of Baron the demon steed. "Is it okay for you to talk about it?"

"I don't usually discuss my deepest, darkest secrets. But as you know—" she reached across the console and caressed his arm with a feather-light touch "—I trust you, John."

Her instincts were correct. He'd never hurt her, and he'd destroy anybody who threatened this amazing woman. "I'm listening."

"Here goes." In the faint glow of moonlight through the windshield, he saw her smile. "Lola and I mostly talked about Max. Though I can't remember the exact moment or how he delivered the ketamine, I'm certain that he drugged me in Reno. But that's not as interesting as what came later."

While he drove away from Sagebrush and continued on the familiar route toward his A-frame, he listened to her report of the session, starting with Tuesday when they arrived in Colorado. She and Max had been driving her Tahoe, looking for Virgil's house, then she started to feel woozy. And scared. Again, she didn't know if he'd drugged her water or given her a surreptitious shot. She knew she had to escape from Max. Jumped from the moving vehicle.

"That must have been when I hit my head and got a concussion. Somehow, Max got my watch. Then I was running and running."

Anger shot through him. His fingers tensed on the steering wheel. "Was he chasing you?"

"I'm not sure. If he tried to catch me, I outmaneuvered him, which is no big surprise. I'm in pretty good shape. I work out all the time and jog almost every day." She exhaled a loud sigh. "I miss my daily run. Are there any trails near your house?"

He didn't want to discuss the roads and pathways near his house. "Don't leave me hanging, Caroline. Get back to your story."

"Nothing more to tell. I ran for a long time, then I stumbled across Virgil's cabin. And you know what happened next."

He had questions but only one really mattered. "Do you think Max tried to hurt you?"

"I really don't know what he had planned." She shook her head. "There are plenty of reasons to suspect him, but I just don't think he's a killer. If he shot Virgil, the murder happened after I got my concussion and before I found the cabin, which isn't a lot of time. And why would he drive around and pretend he didn't know where the cabin was?"

From the start, Max had been an obvious but problematic suspect. He wasn't clever enough to put this scheme together, and he lacked motive. "When he first talked about Virgil, he thought your great-uncle was broke."

"A lie," she said. "Max knew about the money."

"What did Lola say when you told her that you suspected Max of murder?"

"I didn't," Caroline admitted.

"Why not?"

"I don't know." She shrugged. "I don't trust her as much as I used to."

He was blown away. Consistently, she'd been adamant in her defense of Lola. Now…not so much.

At his A-frame, he pulled into a separate, double-wide garage and storage area to park. The overhead motion-detector light came on, illuminating the interior of his SUV. He focused on Caroline. Her features were relaxed, and her smile was calm. Her chin-length bob was smooth, not a hair out of place. She could have been talking about a movie she'd seen instead of recounting how Max had drugged her, threatened her and terrified her so much that she leaped from a moving vehicle.

"I don't know where to start," he said. "Are you quitting therapy?"

She pushed open her car door and climbed out. "It's not the first time I've thought about dropping Lola."

"What makes you think she's not trustworthy?"

"She doesn't back me up, doesn't support me. I can't stand the way she keeps hinting that I'm paranoid. She blames the symptoms and excuses my behavior."

"Give me an example."

"Suppose I went to the grocery store and threw a hissy fit because the checker rang up my order wrong." Caroline looked down her nose and lowered her voice to sound like Lola. "She'd say, 'It's not your fault. Your papa abandoned you, which means you have every right to demand perfection from others, including hapless clerks in grocery stores.'"

"Damn," he said.

"Damn, indeed. I'd rather figure out why I'm irritable and then deal with it."

That approach sounded mentally healthy to him. "Good decision."

"I have two sessions with Lola tomorrow. I made those appointments and will honor my verbal contract. After that…it's bye-bye time. There are plenty of other fish in the sea—therapists who are more in line with my way of thinking. I mean, she's protecting Max."

"Who could be a murderer." He worried about Lola's possible motives. Was she in love with Max? "Do you think they're a couple?"

"If they are, you can bet that Lola is the one in charge. Max is the brainless puppet, and she's pulling the strings."

At the time of Virgil's murder, Lola was all the way across the country in Portland. An air-tight alibi.

Chapter Twenty

The back door to John's A-frame opened into the kitchen. When Caroline stepped inside, she felt immediately comfortable. Unlike many bachelors she'd known, John kept a tidy house. His sink wasn't filled with dirty dishes, and his tile countertops were wiped clean. He must have had good training when he was a kid, which totally made sense. His mother was a cop, and his father was an officer in the military. Both occupations prized the ability to be organized and uncluttered. Oddly enough, Caroline was equally obsessive in her housekeeping for the opposite reason. Her mom was creative and messy. Since she didn't want to be like Natalie, Caroline reacted with extreme neatness.

He centered the insulated bag from Dolly on the kitchen counter and turned to her. "May I take your jacket?"

She peeled off her jean jacket, which, she hoped, was the first of many articles of clothing she would remove tonight. As soon as that thought popped into her head, she was embarrassed by it. She shouldn't assume that he was as interested in her *that* way.

While he hung her jacket and his thermal vest on hooks by the door, she explored the first floor, which was a mostly open design with a long counter separating the kitchen and living room. The only enclosed room was a small bathroom with a sink and shower. A handsome carved desk and oak file cabinets served as an office area. The front of the living room had a large window and sliding glass doors that opened onto the deck.

In the kitchen, John dropped his right hand to his belt holster. "Usually, this is when I disarm and put my weapon in the safe. But not today."

"Why not?"

"I brought you here to protect you. For that, I need the Glock."

She'd almost forgotten the stated reason for this night together. "We need to be careful."

"First, we need to eat." He unpacked the bag. "A container of potato salad, coleslaw and sandwiches. Great selection."

Caroline perched on a tall stool at the kitchen counter. "And what to drink?"

"Three choices. Tap water from a well, milk or beer."

She gave him a grin. "That sounds exactly right for a single guy. Your house is so clean that I was beginning to think you had a maid tucked away in a closet or elves who came out at night to tidy up and stock the fridge."

"I'm the housekeeper." He shrugged. "And the beer drinker. You'll like this one, it's from an Oregon brewery."

He took two longneck bottles from the fridge and twisted off the tops. When he poured her dark ale into a tall glass and did the same for himself, she was pleased to see that he served the beer properly with a frothy head. Again, Caroline sent mental kudos to his mother. Why, oh, why, was she thinking about his mother while, at the same time, she was admiring the snug fit of his jeans? Watching him in the kitchen, doing mundane tasks like taking plates from the cupboard and silverware from the drawer, she enjoyed his purposeful gestures. Not a single motion was wasted. She could have watched for hours.

Her mom would have explained her fascination in artistic terms, using the idea of proportion to analyze John's long, lean body. The breadth of his shoulders tapered to his waist and narrow hips in an inverted triangle. Mom would have wanted to sculpt him or paint him. Again? Why was she thinking about maternal influences?

Caroline held her beer aloft for a toast. "Here's to our investigation. Cheers."

"May we find the truth." He tapped the edge of his glass against hers. "And may we wrap it up. Soon."

She sipped the dark, Cascadian ale and savored the rich, sensual flavors of the Northwest. "Now, tell me about your phone call with Agent Phillips."

"The medical examiner won't complete an autopsy on Valdez for a couple of days, but he did run a tox screen. Her iced tea had been dosed with fentanyl, which can be used as an animal tranquilizer."

"Max," she said as she helped herself to one of the roast-beef sandwiches.

"Phillips wants more evidence before he makes an arrest. Tomorrow, he'll get a warrant to search Max's veterinarian bag."

She took a bite from the sandwich and chewed slowly. Max was greedy, self-centered and rude, but his motivation for murdering Edie Valdez and Virgil was confused. If he'd been after the inheritance, he should have waited until after they were married—which was never going to happen—to slaughter the golden geese.

While John discussed the findings of the medical examiner in Pueblo, she continued to nibble at the coleslaw and potato salad, both of which were excellent. She could smell the chocolate and nuts of the brownie and was anxious for dessert.

"Enough about medical stuff," he said. "Phillips also talked to David Cross who runs an auto repair shop in Denver. He claims to have zero connection with Derek Everett, and he hasn't seen his sister, Maggie, in years."

"Why are they estranged?" she asked.

"It sounded like they just drifted apart after she got divorced and moved to California." He paused with a forkful of potato salad held poised at his mouth. "Phillips was bothered about their separation. He didn't see how a brother and sister could turn their backs on each other."

"I understand them," she said. "I'll probably never know what severed the ties between Mom and Virgil, not that they're brother and sister. But that break was final."

He shoveled the potato salad into his mouth, lifted the ham-and-cheese sandwich to his lips and shifted his gaze away from her to the window. He seemed edgy. "Something bothering you, John?"

"Not really."

His mood was clear to her: he was hiding something. "If you have a reason to be upset, you have to tell me. I'm your partner, after all."

He chased down his mouthful of food with a swallow of beer. "I'm just thinking about David and Maggie. The guy who might have been their father was killed in prison, their mother committed suicide and who knows what kind of problems they had in foster care."

"A rough life."

She suspected that his sympathy for the Cross children wasn't the real cause for his concern, and she was determined to find out what detail struck discord in his mind. Luckily, she had all night to figure him out.

THE LOFT ON the third floor of John's A-frame felt different than the tidy first floor and the second floor, which had two bedrooms, an extra-large bath with a Jacuzzi and a television room. Those other spaces had utilitarian function and purpose. The first-floor desk was where John sat to pay bills and catch up on email. The second-floor master bedroom was, of course, where he slept.

When Caroline climbed the metal spiral staircase to the loft on the third floor, she discovered a playful, sensuous room bursting with rich colors and furnished mostly with pillows. The peak of the A-frame was barely a foot taller than John's standing height. If he took two strides in either direction, he'd bump his head against the exposed beams of the ceiling. Not so much of a problem for a shorty like her. She could walk several steps without having to stoop, not that the long, open loft invited pacing.

John had left her alone with her suitcase and duffel. While he went downstairs to his desk to call the other deputies and check in on further progress, she turned on a series of table lamps. There were only a few straight, direct pathways through the loft, so she slid around the rounded edges of coffee tables and cubes to a low-profile platform bed, queen-size, with a puffy duvet in brilliant shades of turquoise and magenta. Opening her suitcase, she found a soft cotton sleeveless nightgown which she draped across the foot of the bed. For a moment, she wondered if she should change into it before John returned.

Unable to decide, she wandered across the room to a futon with a zip-on cover of gold and ivory. A quick maneuver adjusted the futon position to flat. Though she could have popped onto the bed, this seemed more carefree and less presumptuous. She stretched out on her back and rested her head on a shaggy pillow with zebra stripes. She heard the loft door open and close.

John came toward her. "Sorry that took so long. We had a few minor crises at the courthouse. Miguel Ochoa says hi."

"I would never imagine you had a room like this with all these amazing jewel tone colors. They shouldn't go together, but they do." When she looked up, she found herself gazing through a skylight into a star-filled night. "There's even a view."

"You can see more from the balcony in the front." He removed his Glock, still in the holster, and placed the gun on a circular table. "The loft doesn't seem practical, but it is. There's only one door at the top of the spiral staircase. When it's locked, no one can get inside. You're as safe as Rapunzel in her tower."

"But I don't have long hair. And I want you, my prince, to stay here with me."

"I'm not going anywhere."

He lowered himself onto the futon beside her. Lying on his side, he propped his head on his hand and gazed down at her. The soft light from the table lamps reflected in his silver-gray eyes and highlighted his high cheekbones and firm jaw, which was covered in thick stubble. A stubborn hank of dark hair fell across his forehead. Reaching down, he traced the line of her face from her ear to her chin. A shiver of pleasure rippled through her.

She should have been content to accept this moment. They'd been leaning toward each other since their first meeting, when she was a suspect, and they had grown closer every hour, every day. Truly, he was one of the few people in the world that she trusted. But her feeling that he was keeping a secret wouldn't leave her. She needed to know.

"A little earlier, we were talking about David and Maggie Cross." Her voice became husky. Her throat tickled, and she almost abandoned these inquiries. But she cleared her throat and stuck to the topic. "I sensed that you weren't telling me everything."

"Photos." He reached into his back pocket and took out his cell phone. "Phillips said he'd send me pictures of the Cross kids."

She sat cross-legged on the futon and waited for him to scroll through the screens on his phone to find the photos. From the little she knew about the children of Sylvia

Cross, she supposed they were only a few years older than her. Maggie was the oldest. When John held the phone toward her, she studied the two kids, who were both towheaded and skinny. In another snapshot, they stood with their mother, a pretty blonde whose distinctive features—wide, well-shaped mouth and long nose—were dwarfed by huge sunglasses.

A recent driver's license photo of David showed a good-looking twentysomething with shaggy, light brown hair and a loose-lipped grin. The sort of guy who would fit in at the local tavern or watching a Broncos football game. "Do you have any pictures of Derek Everett so I can compare what they look like?"

"We thought of that." He skipped to another screen and held it toward her. "Here's Everett's mug shot."

There wasn't much in the way of a family resemblance. Everett had darker eyes and less rounded features. His thin lips were tense. Trying to think like a cop, she asked, "What about comparing their DNA?"

"No match," he said. "We found both of them quickly. David was in the army, so his DNA was on file. And, of course, we have Everett's from prison. They aren't related."

Which meant no real motive. She flipped to the next photo. The most recent picture of Maggie was a glamorous high-school-graduation picture with an over-the-shoulder glance and pale blond hair fastened on top of her head. She was young but wearing heavy eyeliner and fire-engine-red lipstick. "Does she look like her mom?"

"Somewhat," John said. "We don't have a current address or phone number, which makes me think she's changed her name and probably her social security number."

"Dropped off the grid." Searching for her would probably lead to another dead end, but Caroline was still curious. "What is Maggie short for?"

"I'm guessing Margaret, but I don't know for sure. I'll check with Phillips."

When she handed the phone back to him, their hands brushed, and she felt the heat from his body transfer to hers. "Is there anything else you haven't told me?"

He rose to his feet, bumping his head against the ceiling, and held out his hand to help her rise from the futon. "Have I mentioned how much I want to kiss you?"

He was avoiding her question, and she should have been irritated. Instead, she allowed herself to be pulled upright. Standing in front of him, she gazed into his magnetic eyes. The room seemed to contract around them, as though the colors and pillows were enclosing them in a soft embrace. "How much do you want that kiss?"

"I can show you."

His baritone voice, smooth as velvet, caressed her. When he held her, his male scent, flavored with cedarwood soap and minty toothpaste, overwhelmed her other senses. She needed to be part of him. Nothing else mattered. "Kiss me, John."

His mouth joined with hers. The light pressure became gradually firmer, more demanding. His tongue penetrated her lips and slid across the slick surface of her teeth. The sensation delighted and fascinated her. Having him inside her felt so right. The last time they'd kissed, she'd placed the experience in the top five. This was better, maybe even number one. Greatest kiss ever.

She clung to him. Her breasts flattened against his chest. Her heart hammered in time with his. They were becoming one. She couldn't tell if he lifted her off her feet or if she was floating, but they made their way across the loft to the low-profile bed with the puffy duvet. She sank onto the low bed and offered no resistance as he unbuttoned her blouse, pushed aside the fabric and trailed a burning line of kisses from her throat to her breasts.

She didn't remember removing his shirt but couldn't blame amnesia. Their intimacy was a perfectly choreographed dance that she'd been training for all her life. The taste of him and the feel of his hands stroking, fondling and pinching wakened familiar feelings that were, at the same time, thrilling and unique. The intensity was nearly unbearable.

After their clothing was gone and their naked bodies fitted against each other, he rose above her, supporting his weight on his elbows, and looked down at her. "You're beautiful, Caroline."

"Yeah?"

"Oh, yeah."

Though breathing hard, she couldn't resist teasing. "Maybe it's time to bring out those handcuffs."

"We'll save those for next time."

So glad, she was so glad there would be a next time. And maybe even a time or two or a thousand after that. She couldn't get enough of John Graystone.

Chapter Twenty-One

The dawn blush had chased away the night—a night that might possibly have been the best thing that ever happened to John. When they were in bed together, he felt like Caroline could read his mind. Every move she made, every word she spoke, every kiss and touch were exactly what he wanted.

They were good together, maybe too good because he didn't want his time with her to end. He almost wished it had been different.

Wearing only his jeans, he stood on the small, narrow balcony outside the triangle-shaped loft window and looked out at the sunlit forest, the rocky hills and the distant snow-covered peaks. This land fulfilled him. Sagebrush was his home—a major obstacle to their future relationship because Caroline would never move here. She had her own life in Portland, near the crashing waves of the dark, cold Pacific.

How could they be so different and yet fit together so perfectly? Not that it mattered. They had a deeper problem. She had asked him, point-blank, if he was keeping something from her. And he'd dodged her question. He hadn't been straight with her, and she prized honesty above all else. Starting with her father, every important person in her life had betrayed her. When she gave John her trust, it was more important, more special than love.

He didn't want to tell her that her mother had fallen for

a scumbag, thrown away an important family relationship and was too stubborn to apologize. Her beloved Mom had abused her. Much as that hurt, Caroline needed to know the truth.

He watched her tiptoe across the loft to the window that opened onto the balcony. She joined him. Her white cotton gown rippled in the dawn breezes as she stepped into his embrace. Her chin tilted up and her hair fell in a straight, sleek wing as she lightly kissed his cheek. "When I woke and saw you were gone, I thought I might have dreamed last night."

"It was real."

"All four times?" she teased.

"Lady, how much proof do you need?"

He snugged an arm around her slender waist and pulled her against him. Damn, this felt right. He hated to lose her. If he ignored Popov's story, would it go away?

She pointed up the hill. "Where does the road go from here?"

"Zigzags around to the top of the ridge, where it forks. If you go right, you'll eventually wind up on the highway. The left is a winding route that goes past Virgil's cabin."

"A good place for a morning run?"

"If you don't mind going uphill half the way."

"I told you before, I'm a runner. Athletic and flexible." She gave a slow, sensual grin. "After last night, I'd think you'd know that."

His body was already responding to her nearness. If he didn't tell her now, they'd wind up in bed together and he'd put off the conversation again…and she'd be even more ticked off when he finally got up the nerve. He exhaled a breath he wasn't aware he'd been holding. "I have something to tell you."

"Sure." She stepped away from him. "Let's go inside. It's nippy out here."

He followed her into the loft, where she went to the futon and crawled across it. Supple as a cat, she struck a sexy pose with her head propped up on the zebra pillow and her legs curled under her. John didn't trust himself to snuggle beside her. Instead, he stood at the edge of the futon and cleared his throat. "Here's the story Popov told me when he pulled me out of your bedroom at the B and B. It brings up some hard truths."

"Let me have it."

"Your mom and Derek Everett were having an affair."

"You hinted that there was something between them."

"Now I'm telling you, flat out, without a shred of uncertainty. They were lovers. On your visits to Colorado, she often left you with Virgil and took off with her boyfriend. And when she found out that Virgil intended to testify against Everett, she flew into a rage." He paused. "Is any of this ringing a bell?"

"Not a bit." She changed her position from sultry to alert, rising up on her knees and straightening her posture. "Please continue."

"It happened in the cabin. Natalie was yelling at Virgil. You were there with Popov, and he took you to another room. He went back in when he heard a crash. Natalie was threatening your great-uncle with a poker from the fireplace. You ran toward her, tried to stop her. And she shoved you to the floor. Popov helped you get away from her."

"I remember." Her dark eyes widened with remembered fear. "She threatened to kill him. That's not something you say in front of a child. I believed her."

"In the bedroom, Popov tried to console you, but you were hysterical. Natalie grabbed your arm, pushed you toward the door and into the car. Her last words to Virgil were a promise to never see him again."

"And she never did." Her fingers twisted in a knot. "This incident should have come up in therapy."

"Unless Lola didn't want you to remember."

"She always guided me to memories of Virgil being angry or hostile. The biggest trauma wasn't about him. It was my mother."

"I'm sorry, Caroline."

"You should be." Her hard gaze was like a slap across his face. "You didn't lie, but you hid the truth, which is almost as bad. How could you, John? I thought we were partners."

"We are."

She stood and pointed to the door. "I'd like to be alone."

Her outright rejection was pretty much what he expected, and he had no choice but to accept. On his way out of the loft, he picked up his gun. At least, he'd kept her safe.

CAROLINE HADN'T INTENDED to purposely evade John, but when she came down the stairs later that morning and went through the kitchen, he was nowhere in sight. The aroma of fresh-brewed coffee tickled her nose and enticed her to sit at the counter, wake up gradually and talk to him. *Not now. Too angry.* She took advantage of his absence and skipped out the back door. Since she hadn't been following her regular exercise regimen, it was especially important to stretch before she ran.

While she went through a series of warm-ups, a mountain wind swept across her cheeks and ruffled her hair. A thermal headband kept her ears warm, and her lightweight, breathable shirt and fitted pants were designed with enough stretch for running. She desperately needed this exercise.

Today, she hoped running would help her gain a new perspective on John's betrayal. He hadn't purposely set out to deceive her but was well-aware of her need to know what was going on in her past. *My past. My trauma.*

She bounced on her toes and jogged uphill on the steep, narrow road. It was after eight o'clock and morning light spread across the forest. She set an easy pace. Why hadn't

John told her? Had he been worried that she'd flip out? Surely, he knew better by now.

Maybe he'd wanted to spare her the knowledge that her mother placed the welfare of her criminal boyfriend above her love for her daughter. Caroline picked up the pace a bit. Many of her therapists had worked with her on "mother issues." No surprise. Her artistic, passionate mother wasn't a paragon of responsibility.

Usually, she listened to music while she was running, but she hadn't wanted the distraction today. Also, she needed to be able to hear a vehicle approaching so she could get out of the way. She heard a sound behind her. Another runner?

She halted and turned. "John?"

There was no one else on the road. The sound of footfalls had ended. Had she imagined someone chasing her? Was this another paranoid episode? She inhaled and exhaled in a mindful pattern until her pulse slowed to a reasonable pace.

They'd never heard back from Agent Phillips about the analysis from a handwriting expert on the threatening note. Maybe John hadn't bothered to tell her. She took her cell phone from the snug pocket in her running pants and sent the agent a text, asking him to get in touch with her.

A moment after she tapped "Send," Phillips called her back. "Caroline, what's up?"

"Thanks for getting back to me so quickly. This isn't urgent, but I was wondering if you ever heard back from the graphoanalyst."

"I did. In his opinion, there's an eighty-seven-percent chance that you did *not* write the note. Somebody copied your penmanship and did a credible forgery of your signature. He advises you to keep your checkbook away from this individual."

"That's a relief." She applauded every proof that she wasn't losing it. "Sorry to call so early."

"I was up, going over the case," he said. "While I have

you on the phone, here's a bit of information I want you to pass along to John. The full name for young Maggie Cross was Magnolia Emma Cross. See you later."

"Okay, I'll be sure to tell him." She repeated the name to herself. Magnolia. That was unusual.

She looked down the road and saw a man hiking toward her. He had a piece of paper in his hand, and he waved it as he called out. "Caroline, wait up. It's me. Rafael."

She didn't want to encounter him or anyone else on this lonely stretch of road. Since her phone was still in her hand, she hit the speed dial for John and listened to the buzz of ringing. *Pick up, pick up, John.* She left a voice mail telling him she was on the road outside his house and needed him.

Rafael came closer.

She held up her hand. "Stay back."

"I was hoping to run in to you."

Unbelievable! Did he expect her to believe he just happened to be in the neighborhood? "You tracked me down."

"It wasn't hard. I'm friends with Dolly, you know." He was only six feet away. "Anyway, I have to give you this photo. My Aunt Edie sent it to me before she died with the instruction that I should share the picture with you and John if anything happened to her."

She was intrigued by the idea of Edie Valdez reaching out beyond death with evidence, but she still didn't want Rafael to get too close. "Show it to me."

He stuck out his arm, holding the photo by the edges, and braced the other hand on his hip, posing like a model. She recognized the picture from one on John's phone—Sylvia Cross in sunglasses and her two children, David and Maggie. "Take it," he said.

"Fine."

"I was thinking," Rafael said. "Since you'll be receiving a huge inheritance, you might need the services of an investment counselor. My services."

"I have financial people. And I'm a CPA."

"Losing your great-uncle is a tragedy. Also, he was one of my best clients."

"Sorry." She craned her neck and looked downhill in the direction of the A-frame, hoping John had heard her voice mail and was on his way to rescue her. Not that she thought Rafacl would hurt her, but she didn't need to hear his business pitch.

A car crept around the last curve before the cabin and chugged toward them. Her Chevy Tahoe! Damn, now she'd have to deal with Max. Maybe she should have been relieved that she wasn't being left alone with Rafael. But Max?

Instead, Lola parked the Tahoe in the middle of the road, engaged the parking brake, got out and came toward them. "I thought I'd pick you up before our session at Dolly's. We can get some breakfast and go there together."

Caroline was puzzled. Lola didn't usually make friendly gestures. "I'm not dressed."

"Your running clothes are fine." She nodded a greeting to Rafael then returned her focus to Caroline. "Would you please drive? I'm not comfortable in the mountains."

"Okay." Something warned her that she shouldn't let Lola see the photograph. She passed it back to Rafael. "Please talk to John. Tell him that Lola picked me up, and we're going to Dolly's."

"I'll take care of it."

She dragged her feet as she went around to the driver's side and got behind the steering wheel. The unexpected appearance of Lola was weird…and suspicious.

Caroline adjusted the seat for her shorter legs, fastened her seat belt and started the Tahoe. "I'd really feel better if I changed clothes. We're very close to John's A-frame."

"I know."

"That's how you found me, right? Who told you I was

staying with him?" She released the parking brake and drove along a flat stretch of road before the final curving ascent to the top of the ridge. "Did you call Dolly? Or check in with one of John's deputies?"

"It doesn't matter."

"I'd like to know."

"Just drive." Her voice turned harsh. As Caroline glanced in her direction, Lola slipped on a pair of sunglasses. The resemblance to Sylvia Cross in the photo Rafael had shown her was apparent and shocking. Lola's hair color was darker, and she wore it in a more severe style, but they looked very much alike. This didn't make sense. Lola was part of her life in Portland, not Colorado. And yet, she saw the link. The two women weren't an exact match but were close.

Maggie. Magnolia. Lola.

Caroline heard a thumping noise from the cargo area in the rear of the Tahoe. "What's that?"

"It's Max." Lola's tone was ice cold. "You might say he'd all tied up."

"What are you telling me?"

Lola held a gun in her hand. "When you get to the top of the ridge, take a left. Until then, keep your mouth shut. I've heard enough from you to last a lifetime."

Chapter Twenty-Two

After he showered, shaved and got dressed, John went toward the loft, determined to fix the mess he'd made. He hadn't meant to deceive her, but she felt betrayed, and he couldn't blame her. She'd been hurt before by people omitting the truth. Somehow, he had to convince her to forgive him. He'd fight for her.

At the top of the spiral staircase, he raised his fist to knock on the door. It was open. When he entered the color-filled room, the space felt hollow. Empty.

He charged down the stairs to the first floor and searched. *Not here. Where the hell had she gone?* He snatched his phone off the counter. There were a couple of texts from Peregrine County deputies and a voice message from Caroline.

Her voice trembled. "John. I went for a run. I'm on the road up the hill. Rafael is out here. I need you."

He pivoted, snatched his fob for the SUV and yanked open the back door. As soon as he stepped outside, he sensed trouble in the air. His hand dropped to the butt of his gun, which he'd already holstered.

Rafael was standing on the deck and peeking around the edge of the house, making no attempt to hide. He held up both hands in surrender. "Don't shoot."

"Where is she?"

"She got into a car with Lola and drove off."

Lola? "Why?"

"Lola said something about picking her up before their session at Dolly's. She sounded reasonable, but…" He shook his head. "I could tell that she was stressed."

"Why should I believe you?"

Rafael gave a shrug that managed to be both elegant and apologetic at the same time. "I'm not going to plead my case, John. We've known each other long enough for you to figure out that I'm not a killer. My aunt was the second victim. Sure, Edie and I argued, but she was family, and I loved her." He held up a photograph. "She wanted me to give this to Caroline."

John studied the picture, a blowup of the snapshot of Sylvia Cross and her children that he had on his phone. In the photo, the focus was sharper and more distinct. Dismissively, he said, "I've already seen it."

"Look closer," Rafael urged. "Imagine Sylvia Cross with darker hair pulled back in a high bun on top of her head. Notice her long neck, the tilt of her chin and the way she doesn't show teeth when she smiles. Even with sunglasses, the resemblance is uncanny. It's Lola."

John saw it. Lola Powell was the daughter of Sylvia Cross. With that simple connection, so many pieces of the investigation fell into place. She had arranged for Caroline to come here and confront Virgil. She'd pushed for the marriage between Caroline and Max, and she was always there in the background, telling other people what to do.

Lola had a motive. She wanted Virgil dead to avenge her mother's lover. "Rafael, you said Edie gave you this photo?"

"Becky had it. In a note, Edie told me that you and Caroline should see it." His forehead pinched in a frown. "It's pretty damn clear what happened. Edie met Lola and recognized her. Lola couldn't let that identification stand. She had to kill my aunt."

"I'm sorry." His logic made sense. And now, Caroline

was with a woman who had already murdered two people to satisfy her sick need for vengeance. "Which way did they go?"

"Uphill," Rafael said. "Caroline was driving."

"You're coming with me." John ran from his house to the garage. Rafael wasn't his first choice for backup, but he needed to make something happen fast.

STARING INTENTLY THROUGH the windshield, Caroline flexed her fingers and renewed her white-knuckle grip on the steering wheel. *Concentrate.* Her mind skipped over many possible methods to get away from Lola. The most obvious escape route disappeared when Lola snatched her cell phone and threw it out the window of the car.

Caroline protested. "Why did you do that?"

"We can't have your deputy boyfriend tracking the signal from your phone, can we?"

Yes, we can. I want him to find me. I need him. John was her best, brightest hope. He was strong, brave and knew his way around these mountains better than anyone, surely better than Lola. John was a willing bodyguard, but she couldn't count on him coming to her rescue. Right now, her best bet was to get Lola talking. The more she said, the more information Caroline would have to stage her escape.

"Where are we going?" she asked.

"Didn't I tell you to shut up?"

With false bravado, she said, "You won't shoot me. Gunfire leaves behind too much forensic evidence. You want my death to look like an accident."

"Aren't you the clever little detective?"

There were more loud thumps from Max in the cargo area. She must have gagged him. "Is he all right back there?"

"Why do you care?"

"I don't want to be engaged to him, but I don't want him dead."

"I'm not going to kill Max. I need him as a witness to the tragic accident that will end you."

Caroline had succeeded in getting Lola talking. She wanted more information. "Are you planning to shove me off a cliff? I'll bet that's what Max was supposed to do to me on the night Virgil was killed."

"Wrong. He was supposed to drug you and meet me. We needed to fake your marriage before you took a fatal tumble."

"But you were late," Caroline said. "Too busy killing my great-uncle?"

"It was my great pleasure to watch him die. Virgil destroyed my father. Killing him was easy, almost too fast. I would have preferred to see him suffer. What took a long time was getting rid of correspondence that mentioned my name."

"Magnolia," Caroline said. "You were in Colorado all along."

"I couldn't very well leave this up to Max. He has his uses but isn't really competent."

"When did he steal my watch?"

"Earlier in the day. It made a nice clue for me to leave behind at Virgil's cabin. You surprised me by turning up there with a real case of amnesia."

"Sorry to mess with your plans," she said. "You must have been working out the details for a long time."

"My revenge took years to prepare. When I learned that you lived in Portland and were related to the same Virgil Hotchner who testified against my father, I started plotting." Still holding the gun, she loosened her long, silk scarf with a butterfly pattern in silver, black and royal blue. She proudly bared her throat. "Did you notice my necklace?

A gold cross that belonged to my mother. Do you get it? Sylvia *Cross*."

"You look a lot like her." Caroline wondered if Lola wore the cross necklace as a clue, taunting her victims with something they'd have noticed if they were paying attention. "You changed your name. I understand switching last names when you get married and divorced, but why your first name? Magnolia is unusual and interesting."

"Which is why I shortened it to Lola. After I settled in Portland and started practicing as a therapist, I didn't want any obvious connection with my past. No more Maggie."

"I have to ask about my therapy," Caroline said. "Are you qualified to practice?"

"I never claimed to be a graduate of anything. I went to two colleges, took seminars and read books. Then I developed my own combination of treatments. I do a good job with most of my clients." She tapped on the center console with the barrel of her handgun. "I helped you, didn't I?"

There was no way Caroline would risk criticizing a psychotic woman who was holding a gun on her, but this comment was partially true. "You did help."

"You were one of my success stories," she said smugly. "All you really needed was to have someone pay attention to you. I worked with a psychiatrist to get your meds adjusted and started you on the exercise program, which you adored. Then I took you to the stables to work through your fear of horses. And I listened to your endless stories about your past."

And she used that information to manipulate Caroline's feelings about her great-uncle. "I'm curious. Was Virgil ever really abusive to me?"

"What do you think?"

She thought Lola had twisted her memories to make Virgil look like a monster, but she didn't accuse Lola. Better to let the woman think she was in total control. "I had gone to several therapists before you. I've got to say, you were the best. When you proposed this trip to confront Virgil, I wasn't suspicious at all."

"Initially, I didn't intend to hurt you," Lola said. "This trip was supposed to end with Virgil dead and you eventually married to Max and inheriting Virgil's wealth, which Max would funnel to me."

Caroline swallowed her anger. She'd been nothing more than a pawn in Lola's revenge scheme. Her eyes had been blind to the ulterior motives. "I don't love Max, never have."

"I toyed with the idea of slanting your supposed therapy toward making the two of you into a believable couple. He's not bad-looking. You could do worse."

She fought the rage that surged through her veins. Instead of steering her Tahoe off the road and killing them both, Caroline used the mindful-breathing technique Lola had taught her to control panic attacks. The irony was horrifying. "Was the ketamine his idea or yours?"

"Mine. I knew he had easy access to tranquilizers, and it seemed logical to use what we had. Max isn't all that skillful at detailed planning. Are you, Max?"

The noise from the cargo hold got louder. It sounded like he was trying to speak.

"He didn't give you the right dose in Reno when you were supposed to get married. You were practically comatose."

"Were you there?"

"Every step of the way. I followed you and Max from Portland, driving behind your car, eating at the same roadside diners. For our phone session when you were at Dolly's B and B, I was parked at a rest stop off the highway in Durango."

How could she have missed the dark, evil presence of this woman? At some point, her instinct for self-preservation should have kicked in and warned her of the danger. "You encouraged my paranoia. You and Max gaslighted me."

"Indeed." She chuckled. "Take a left up here."

"Where are we going?"

"You'll find out soon enough. I must say, Caroline, that I enjoyed taking an active part in your deception. I disabled the camera at the B and B and forged the note in your handwriting. Remember when I asked you to write a journal? I had plenty of chances to study your penmanship. And I fired a gun at you behind the cabin. There was never any danger. The weapon was a stage prop that made a loud noise and emitted a flash like a real pistol."

"Which is why there were no shells or casings."

"You're catching on. Finally."

What about the gun Lola was holding right now? Another prop? Caroline made the left turn and shifted her gaze to focus on the weapon.

Lola waggled the gun at her. "This one is real."

"Why did you involve me?" Caroline asked. "Why not just drive to Sagebrush and shoot Virgil?"

"When I figured out who you were, the plan was too delicious. I could accomplish my primary goal of killing Virgil. And my secondary goal."

"What was that?"

"Max would wear you down and marry you. As your husband, he'd have access to your fortune and, when you died, he'd inherit it all."

"What does that have to do with you?"

"Max would pay me off. In return, I wouldn't testify against him. After I'd siphon off most of his cash, I could get rid of Max. Ultimately, Virgil's death would make me rich."

"That's an insane plot."

"Not me, Caroline. You're the lady with mental problems. After my gaslighting setup, everybody thinks you're unhinged. And that works well in this new scenario. They'll have no trouble believing that you committed suicide, especially not after Max and I explain how we tried to stop you before you took a swan dive off a high ledge."

A cold chill trickled down her spine. She might not make it out of this alive. "There's got to be another way."

"I'm not your therapist, not anymore." Her voice deepened. "I'm the woman who's going to kill you."

Caroline believed her.

"I DON'T HAVE a gun," Rafael said. "Do I need a weapon?"

"Just keep looking for the Tahoe. That's your only job."

"I could do more."

"Use the binoculars," John said.

At the fork in the road, John got out of the SUV and tried to track the imprints of tire treads on the gravel. He noticed the slight skew of a rear tire turning to the left, which made him think that Lola was headed toward Virgil's cabin. He had a fifty-fifty chance of being correct.

He got back behind the steering wheel. This terrain was familiar to him, but there were dozens of turnoffs and side roads. After switching his phone to hands-free, he contacted the dispatcher at the sheriff's office and told him to issue a BOLO for the green Chevy Tahoe, which he suspected was headed toward Virgil's cabin. He ordered backup from all deputies. "Tell them to approach the vehicle with caution. It's a possible hostage situation."

When he ended the call, Rafael spoke up. "If I can use your phone, I'll coordinate the deputies heading in this direction. That way you can keep watching for the Tahoe."

Though John wanted to handle every piece of the action himself, he knew the value of delegating, and Rafael was probably better at coordinating people than he was. He handed over the phone. Immediately, Rafael was juggling three different lines.

"You're good at this," John said.

Rafael nodded. "I want you to catch this bitch. She's going to pay for killing Edie."

John kept taking routes that ascended the forested, rocky hillside above Virgil's cabin. At the highest point, there was a jagged array of boulders called Cathedral Point. On a twisting road ahead of him, he spotted a small cloud of dust kicked up by another vehicle. It had to be Lola.

He feathered the brakes and made a gradual stop. His first instinct was to shoot out the tires and make sure they couldn't get away. But he wasn't sure how Lola would react. Would she hurt Caroline?

In the passenger seat, Rafael aimed the binoculars downhill. "I see the car," he said.

The road ahead had several hairpin turns, but the Tahoe wasn't far away as the crow flies. If John went straight downhill on foot, it was probably only a couple hundred yards. He needed to get closer.

"Rafael, get behind the steering wheel." He needed to keep his backup deputies out of the way until he needed them. "Stay here and direct the other guys. Nobody approaches until I give the signal."

John unholstered his Glock and jogged into the forest.

CAROLINE WAS AWARE that they weren't getting closer to the jagged spires of high boulders that she'd seen in the distance. They were going the opposite direction. The one-lane dirt road corkscrewed down the hillside.

"Can't you go any faster," Lola complained.

"If you want to drive, be my guest."

"We're going down instead of up. Turn this damn car around."

Caroline wasn't an expert when it came to mountain roads, but she knew the terrain was unpredictable. "There's no room for me to make a U-turn."

"Fine. Keep going."

Caroline had to go slow on the twisty road. If she could get out of her seat belt, this might be her best chance—her only chance—to slip out of the car and run…unless Lola shot her.

"You seem to be good at disappearing," Caroline said. "Maybe that's what you should do now. Let me go. Take the car and vanish."

"I've gone to a lot of trouble to get Virgil's money, and I'm not going to give up on it now. You're an obstacle—a hard woman to kill. Your deputy boyfriend kept you safe. When he wasn't watching over you, one of his deputies was standing guard."

She never should have left the A-frame. She should have trusted John, who had never intended to hurt her. The thought of losing their future together broke her heart. *Yeah, and what about losing my life? I won't let this happen.* Fighting off angry tears, Caroline kept driving. She needed a distraction, something that would divert Lola's attention.

"You're not really getting revenge," Caroline said. "When Agent Phillips talked to your brother, David told him that he did a DNA test. He's not related to Derek Everett."

"David isn't, but I am. We have different fathers, and mine is Everett. Of course, I did my own DNA research."

"I know you're not my therapist anymore." Every moment was fraught. She couldn't keep driving to her doom. "But I've got to tell someone."

"What?" Lola said impatiently.

"I'm in love with John Graystone."

Lola burst into harsh laughter, and Caroline made her move. With her left hand, she yanked the steering wheel and crashed the Tahoe into a fat granite boulder at the left side of the road. With her right, she unfastened her seat belt.

The Tahoe crumpled and twisted, throwing Lola off

balance. The passenger-side window shattered. The windshield cracked.

Caroline tried the driver-side door. It was stuck. She braced herself for a bullet she expected would be coming. When she looked toward Lola, she didn't see the gun. Instead, the therapist was holding a syringe. *Ketamine.*

Caroline threw her weight against the door, again and again. It creaked open, and she climbed out onto the road. Not fast enough. Lola had stabbed the needle into her thigh.

Caroline forced herself to stand. She had to run, had to make her escape before the therapist found her gun, before the drug took effect and she lost consciousness. She stumbled along the road and into the trees. Looking back over her shoulder, she saw Lola squeeze herself through the door.

Caroline's strength was fading. Her legs turned to rubber. Before she collapsed, John ran past her. His Glock was aimed at Lola.

"Drop your weapon," he ordered.

"Thank God, you're here." The therapist still held her gun. "Caroline is having a breakdown. We have to stop her."

"Drop it. Hands behind your back."

Before she lost consciousness, Caroline saw him take Lola's gun and cuff her. It was over.

WHEN THE DEPUTIES ARRIVED, John was happy to put Lola in their custody. He lifted Caroline off the ground and carried her to the nearest vehicle for a ride to the hospital.

And then, there was Max. He'd been released from the cargo space in the rear. His handcuffs were removed, and the duct tape on his ankles cut. The deputies also pulled off thc tape over his mouth, in the process ripping several hairs from his goatee.

He hadn't stopped talking, protesting his innocence and claiming that Lola was responsible for the murders and everything else that happened.

"What about drugging Caroline?" John asked.

Max rubbed his hand across his forehead. "Lola threatened me with a gun. She put on the handcuffs and made me get in the cargo space. It was horrible."

"You gave Caroline a dose of ketamine."

"I never meant to kill her," he said defiantly. "I just needed to lower her resistance so she'd agree to marry me. I'd never abuse her or hurt her."

When John thought of the gaslighting campaign, his stomach turned. In his mind, that counted as abuse. "You helped Lola commit two murders."

"It was all her idea. Her fault."

"Save your explanations for the judge, Max. You're under arrest."

While his deputies took Max into custody, he went to the car where Caroline was waiting. In the back seat, he held her, stroked her hair off her forehead. This rescue was too damn close. He never wanted her to be in such danger again.

She groaned. Her eyelids fluttered open, and she gazed up into his face. Her mouth stretched in a loopy smile as she said, "Have we met?"

"You don't remember."

"You look just like a guy who once told me he was sorry. Apology accepted."

He wasn't sure if she was goofing around or having another bout of amnesia. "What's my name? Tell me my name."

She cleared her throat. "I love you, John Graystone."

"Never do that again," he said. "I was scared that you had amnesia, again."

"Nope, that part of my life is over."

"Lola and Max have both been arrested. They'll pay for the murders, but there isn't a punishment for what they did to you."

"She encouraged me to believe that Virgil was an abuser, while I buried my negative memories of my mother." Her eyelids drooped, and she exhaled a sigh. "So tired."

He snuggled her close and dropped a kiss on her forehead. "Were you ever abused as a child."

"I'm not sure, and I don't want to think about it right now."

"Fair enough. What do you want to think about?"

Her eyes opened and she gazed up at him. "I told you that I loved you, and you didn't reply."

"My sweet Caroline, I love you so much."

"Prove it."

"How?"

"Move to Portland."

"How about if you move to Colorado?"

She shrugged. "Either way, it's fine with me."

He knew she was right on target. No matter what kind of challenges they faced, they were destined to be together for a very long time.

* * * * *

FINDING THE RANCHER'S SON

KAREN WHIDDON

To all the readers who have emailed me letting me know how much they enjoy the fictional town of Getaway, Texas. Thank you so much. Your kind words mean more than I can express.

Chapter One

The ranch wasn't difficult to find. In fact, having grown up in Getaway, Texas, Jackie Burkholdt remembered when it had belonged to one of her classmates' parents.

Now it belonged to a man who might have harmed her sister. A large handmade sign near the gate advertised riding lessons and horse boarding as well as training, while a smaller one proclaimed there were fresh eggs for sale.

She rang the bell, waiting impatiently for the faded oak front door to open. When it didn't, she pressed the bell again, and then tried knocking—several sharp raps of her knuckles. Still nothing. Since a brand-spanking-new Ford F-150 sat parked in the driveway, she figured Eli Pitts had to be home. Where else would he be at four in the morning?

Taking a deep breath, she tapped her foot, resisting the urge to kick at the still-closed door. Here in Texas, things moved much more slowly than they did in her adopted home of New York City, but this was ridiculous. How could any man be that difficult to wake up?

Finally, the door creaked open. A tall man, his dark

hair thoroughly mussed, peered out at her. "Do you have any idea what time it is?" he croaked. "The sun's not even up yet."

Damn. Looking at him felt like a punch to the gut, he was so ridiculously sexy. Whatever she'd expected upon meeting her sister's ex-husband, it wasn't this, a rugged specimen of pure male beauty.

"Hello?" he said, the annoyance in his tone reflected in his expression. "Would you please explain why you're pounding on my front door at this hour of the morning?"

Blinking and forcing her thoughts back on track, she waved her hand, dismissing his concern. "I just got in and drove straight here. Are you Eli Pitts?"

Suddenly, he appeared suspicious. "Look, lady. It's four a.m. on a Wednesday morning. I suggest you go somewhere and sober up and leave me the hell alone." He made a move to close the door.

"Oh no, you don't." As she'd seen people do in the movies, she stuck out her foot, just in time to prevent him from closing her out. "This is too important."

He tugged once more, slamming into her foot and making her wince. "Come back later."

"Wait," she practically screeched. "Just tell me where my sister is. That's all I want to know. What have you done with Charla?"

Hearing the name, he froze. "Charla? My ex-wife, Charla?"

She managed to bite back a retort and nodded.

"Sister?" He peered at her. "So you're the evil older sister?"

"Ouch." Despite knowing Charla's antagonism against her, hearing him put it like that hurt. "I am," she replied.

"You'd better come inside," he decided, opening the door wide and motioning her to go past him. "Then you can tell me what she's done now and why you'd even think she'd be here."

Jackie followed him inside, waiting quietly in the foyer while he flicked on more of the lights.

"This way," he grumbled, leading the way in his flannel pajama bottoms and faded sleeveless T-shirt. His feet were bare, more proof that she'd indeed dragged him out of bed with her insistent bell ringing and door pounding. She knew she should feel bad about doing that, but her worry over her baby sister superseded anything else.

When they reached the kitchen, he pressed a button, preheating his coffee maker. "Coffee?" he asked, rubbing at his eyes, clearly trying to wake himself up.

Though she'd already had two cups on the flight and a huge to-go cup on the drive here in her rental car, she nodded. "Thanks."

"Great," he said without any real enthusiasm. "Have a seat. Let me get some caffeine in my system before you tell me what my ex-wife has gotten herself into this time."

She nodded and sat, managing to throttle her impatience. "Judging by the text she sent me, it's pretty darn urgent."

Instead of looking surprised, Eli appeared resigned. "Everything is urgent with that woman." Then his gaze sharpened. "Unless this is about my son. Please tell me Theo is all right."

"I don't know," she answered truthfully. "Take a look at this text and then we'll talk."

"'I urgently need your help,'" he read. "'My life is in danger. Please come home.'" After handing her back her phone, he poured two tall mugs of steaming coffee. "What does that mean?"

"I was hoping you could tell me." She accepted her coffee and took a sip. Strong and black, just the way she liked it. Eyeing him over the rim of her mug, she waited for him to ask if she needed cream or sugar.

"I don't have anything to put in it," he said, correctly interpreting her look. "Maybe milk from the fridge, but that's about it."

"This is fine." She took another drink. "Now, why don't you tell me what's going on with my sister?"

Instead of pulling out a chair and taking a seat near her, he continued to stand on the other side of the room, almost as if he didn't want to get too close. "I would if I could," he replied. "But Charla and I aren't exactly on friendly terms. Though she did call me a couple nights ago and asked me to pick her up at the Rattlesnake Pub. Apparently, the guy she's been seeing found out she was also dating someone else on the side and they got into a huge drunken fight." He gave her an apologetic smile. "She got thrown out of the bar and had no way to get home."

Drunken fight, multiple boyfriends. Filing this info away for later, she focused on one thing he'd said. "That means you might have been the last one to see her."

He shrugged. "I doubt it. That was Saturday night, so it's been a couple of days."

Not buying his story, she pressed for more info. "Have you heard from her since then?"

"No, but again, that's not unusual. Charla and I aren't…buddies. We co-parent our son. Usually, if we talk at all, it's about Theo. I have visitation with him every other weekend."

Theo. The nephew Jackie had never met. Just like this man. Charla had met him, married him, had his child and then divorced him, all while Jackie was in New York. She couldn't help but wonder what had happened to end their marriage so quickly.

Though her mother had filled her in while Jackie waited at the airport to board her flight, Jackie wanted to hear it from Eli. "What happened with you two? One minute I hear you and Charla were engaged, then happily married. She got pregnant almost immediately and the two of you had the perfect baby. Then *bam.* Separated and divorced."

His expression hardened. He took a long, deliberate drink of coffee. "That's right. Of course you didn't know. I forgot that you and Charla weren't even on speaking terms. Mind telling me why?"

"Didn't Charla tell you?" She couldn't resist. In fact, she really wanted to hear what kind of twisted reasoning Charla had come up with to explain cutting off her older sister.

"Look, Miss…"

"Jackie," she said, realizing she hadn't even introduced herself. "Jackie Burkholdt."

He dipped his chin in acknowledgment. "Look, Jackie. Charla is…dramatic. She loves to stir things up and thrives on drama. Even if you and she haven't talked for a long time, I doubt that much has changed."

"It hasn't." She held up her phone. "But for Charla to break her own decision to not speak to me after three entire years makes me think she's serious this time."

Expression unchanged, he regarded her. "Did you call her back?"

"Yes, I did." After draining the last of her mug, she set it on the table and pushed to her feet. "She didn't answer. I want to ask you one more time and please, think very carefully about your answer. Where is my sister?"

Narrow eyed, he glared at her. "I've already told you. I don't know. Now, I'm going to have to ask you to leave. This is a working ranch and I have to be out in the fields in a few hours."

Stonewalling. If he knew anything, he wasn't letting on. Which would make sense, if he'd done something to hurt Charla.

But the love in his voice when he'd asked about his son… She shook her head. One could exist exclusive of the other.

Eyeing him, she reminded herself she had no proof he'd harmed her sister. Just because it turned out to be the spouse or ex-spouse something like 90 percent of the time didn't mean this man had done anything wrong.

Back stiff, he escorted her to the front door, standing aside while she swept past him, closing and locking it behind her.

As she walked to her car, she turned and eyed the low-slung ranch-style house. It was homey, in a west Texas type way. No matter how hard she tried, she couldn't picture Charla ever living in a place like this. The remote location would make going into town more difficult, not to mention the rustic air of borderline neglect the place gave off. The white frame house could certainly use a coat of paint, and the untrimmed hedges and crazy rose brambles didn't help with the ranch's appearance.

Eli Pitts had come in from somewhere outside Getaway, bought the place and devoted himself to trying to turn around a farm many had considered long past its prime. Jackie's mother, Delia, had been positively effusive in her praise for him, especially once he and Charla had started dating. They'd been happy, according to Delia, and over the moon when Charla had gotten pregnant right away. Jackie had called, gotten voice mail and left a heartfelt congratulatory message for her sister. All the while aching with hope that this time, Charla would reach out and patch things up.

She didn't. Jackie continued to get updates from Delia, truly pleased that her sister had found such happiness.

Everything had seemed to be going along just fine, until it wasn't.

When Delia had told Jackie about the split-up, Jackie had once again tried to reach out to her baby sister. And yet again, Charla had refused to take her call. This despite the fact that Jackie's only "crime" had been taking a job out of state and moving.

Worse, no one took Charla's text seriously. Not their mother and certainly not Eli Pitts. Meanwhile, Jackie had taken a leave of absence from her publishing job in Manhattan, where luckily she had an amazing boss who'd been understanding when Jackie had walked into her office first thing Tuesday morning, asking to take vacation due to a family emergency. After that Jackie had purchased plane tickets at far too high a price, gone home and packed, made numerous phone calls and then traveled across the country on the basis that her baby sister truly needed her.

Exhausted and numb, Jackie climbed back into her rental car and headed toward town. She could either get a room at the Landshark Motel or stay at her mother's house, assuming Delia would let her.

She chose the motel.

This late at night, or early in the morning, depending on how you looked at it, downtown appeared completely deserted. Main Street stretched into the horizon, flat and empty. When she pulled up at the Landshark, a structure that had been old back when Jackie had gone to high school, a light shone from the office window. At least she didn't have to worry about the hotel not having any vacancies. Not many people stopped in this small ranching town in the middle of nowhere west Texas.

After checking in with a bored and disinterested front desk clerk, Jackie got her room key, located her room and got ready for bed, even though the sun would be coming up soon. She'd start looking for Charla after she got a few hours of sleep.

The shrill sound of her phone ringing woke her. Unsure of the time, Jackie fumbled in the dark room, located her cell and barely managed to hit the accept call button.

"Good morning," Delia chirped. "I heard you paid Eli a visit at four a.m."

"I did." Stifling a yawn, Jackie turned on the bedside lamp and sat up. "What time is it now?"

"Nearly nine."

That meant she'd gotten a few hours of sleep at least. Even though she felt as if she'd been run over by a truck. "Did he call you?"

"He did. Eli couldn't understand why you showed up there," Delia prodded. "I confess, I don't get it, either. You know the two of them split up. Their divorce was just finalized, uncontested by either of them. Why would you even think Charla would be there?"

Jackie sighed. "Every single news story when something happens to a young wife and mother, it's almost always the husband or boyfriend who's..." She stopped short, not wanting to alarm her mother without any proof.

"Charla's fine." Delia sounded certain. "She must have finally decided she wants to fix things between the two of you and figured a dramatic message was the best way to do it. You know how your sister is."

"I do." Again, correct. Charla never had been able to understand the concept behind the little boy who cried wolf. "But Eli might have been the last person to see her."

"Because he gave her a ride home from the bar Saturday night? I talked to her after that, you know. Your sister has always been a free spirit. She was really upset that Leo caused such a scene."

"Leo." Though still groggy, Jackie pounced on that. "What's Leo's last name?"

"How should I know?" Delia sounded slightly defensive. "And before you ask, no, I don't have any idea who all else Charla might have been seeing. While she and I are extremely close, she doesn't tell me everything. Just promise me you don't plan on storming into the Pub and demanding names."

Since that was exactly what Jackie planned to do, she tried to be noncommittal. "We'll see." Pushing out of the bed, she looked around the room, hoping to spy one of those small, in-room coffee makers. "If you hear from her, will you call me immediately?"

"Yes, I will. I'm sure she'll call me soon. We rarely go more than a few days without speaking to each other."

Jackie managed to swallow back a comment on that. Her mother rarely called her, except on holidays. And when Jackie phoned home, Delia often let the call go to voice mail and then never bothered to call back. She'd long ago managed to pretend that didn't hurt her.

Then Delia surprised her. "Since you're in town, will you stop by for dinner tonight? Around six?"

Dinner. At her mother's. Would wonders never cease?

"Sure." Keeping it casual. "I'll see you then." After hanging up, Jackie took a long hot shower, then headed out in search of coffee and food, in that order. Then she planned to stop by Charla's job, pay a visit to the daycare center that Theo attended, and if neither of those places turned up anything, Charla's apartment.

Later, fortified by a large coffee and a breakfast

sandwich, Jackie drove to Levine's Jewelers. Charla had worked the counter since high school. She also took occasional part-time waitressing gigs at the Tumbleweed Café, mostly helping out friends who needed someone to cover their shifts. According to Delia, she'd also met her husband, Eli, there, too.

When she walked inside, Christopher Levine himself greeted her by name. Surprised that he remembered her, Jackie asked him when he'd last heard from her sister.

"I'm actually worried about her," Christopher said. "She called in sick four days ago, but I haven't heard from her since. I even took the liberty of going by her place to check on her, but she didn't answer the door. She's not picking up her phone, either, so I'm concerned she might be seriously ill."

Since Charla had worked for this man for years, Jackie showed him the text. "When I got that, I tried reached her, too. Since I couldn't, I took some vacation time at work and flew here. Now I'm trying to track her down."

Christopher shook his head and pushed his glasses up his narrow nose. "I don't know why she'd say she was in danger. I mean, we all know Charla could be a bit of a party girl, but she seemed to settle down now that she had a little one to look after." He sighed. "You might check at the Tumbleweed and see if any of her friends there know where to find her."

"Is she still picking up an occasional shift waitressing there?"

"Yes. She called it her fun money," he said. "I'm sorry I couldn't be of more help. But when you do get a hold of Charla, will you please ask her to call me? I need to know when she's planning on returning to work."

"I sure will." Feeling even more unsettled, Jackie got in her rental car and headed over to the Tumbleweed Café.

A wave of nostalgia swept over her as she stepped through the front door. With its same red vinyl booths and black-and-white linoleum floors, the place still looked exactly as it always had and probably always would.

"Jackie? Jackie Burkholdt?" an incredulous voice exclaimed. "It that really you?"

Looking up, Jackie spied Cassie Morgan, one of her best friends from her high school days. "Cassie!" They hugged, then pulled back to study each other. "You look great."

"So do you." Cassie cocked her head. She still wore her hair in long platinum waves, though she'd pulled that back into a ponytail for work. "What brings you to town?"

"I'm looking for Charla," Jackie said, keeping her tone light. No doubt all of Charla's friends knew that the two sisters no longer spoke. "Mr. Levine said she still picked up occasional shifts here."

"Oh. She does, but I don't know what's up with her," Cassie said. "She was supposed to cover for Julie the day before yesterday, but didn't show. And she'd agreed to open for Tabitha yesterday, but didn't." Cassie picked at her fingernail before looking up and meeting Jackie's gaze. "I'm a little worried. So are some of the others.

We've tried calling and even going by her place. It's like she just up and disappeared."

ELI PITTS TRIED to go back to sleep after the visit from Charla's sister, but once up, he couldn't shut his mind down enough to doze. He managed to wait until a semi-decent hour before dialing his ex-wife, aware she occasionally worked the breakfast shift at the Tumbleweed. But as it usually did these days, his call went unanswered. Just in case, he left a voice mail, saying that he wanted to discuss Theo's visit this weekend. Their son seemed to be the only subject Charla was willing to discuss with him.

Which in the end was fine. Life went much easier without the amped-up level of drama that Charla preferred.

Eli hated that he'd made such a colossal mistake. His and Charla's relationship had been a whirlwind thing, and he'd been blindsided when he finally understood that the woman she'd pretended to be did not actually exist. By then they were married with a baby on the way. Charla couldn't seem to understand why she needed to stop partying. She'd sulked and pouted the entire ninc months. As soon as Theo had been born, she'd insisted he be fed formula, so she could leave her newborn with Eli while she went out with her friends.

He'd taken it for a few weeks, hoping she'd get it out of her system and would come back and actually mother her infant. Instead, when he confronted her, she'd announced she'd met someone else and was leaving him.

Because he'd wanted full custody of Theo—after

all, she obviously had no interest in her son—she refused to grant that. Instead, she'd gotten custody while Eli got visitation. He'd worried nonstop about his boy for weeks and months after that. Eventually, the smoke had cleared, the mayhem and destruction stirred up in Charla's wake had subsided and Eli had realized Charla managed to be a decent mother to their son.

He thought of the woman—Charla's older sister, Jackie—who'd shown up on his doorstep in the predawn hours. She'd been dark where Charla was fair, serious instead of frothy and apparently willing to allow herself to be dragged into whatever unique form of drama Charla had going now.

More power to her, he supposed. As for himself, he wanted no part of it. As long as Charla brought Theo over at the agreed-upon time, he was good.

Due to lack of sleep, he found himself dragging as he went about his normal routine on the farm. He hadn't yet reached a financial point where he could afford to hire full-time workers, so he made do with paying a couple of teenage boys to work part-time after school and on weekends. He sold high-quality alfalfa hay and always had a full slate of standing preorders, so he had high hopes that next year he might be able to expand and add a second crop. He'd been doing a lot of research and had his eye on grain sorghum.

Lunchtime rolled around and he decided to head into town and grab a bite at the Tumbleweed Café. Even though normally when he knew Charla might be working, he tended to avoid the place, the text she'd sent her older sister had him curious. Actually, more than curious. A bit worried, too, especially because if Charla truly had gotten into some kind of trouble, would Theo be safe?

He arrived at the popular lunch place shortly after twelve. As usual, he had to circle the lot three times before he found a space to park.

Inside, he bypassed the people waiting for a table and headed toward the lunch counter. One spot remained open, sandwiched in between two burly truckers. Eli slid onto the stool, nodded a casual hello and began scanning the restaurant for a sight of his ex.

He didn't see her.

"Hey, Eli." Sheryl Jones, one of Charla's friends, came over to take his order. "What can I get you?"

"Bacon burger," he replied. "Have you seen Charla?"

"No." She frowned. "I'm not sure what's going on with her. She hasn't shown up to work any of the shifts she agreed to cover in the last four days." Sheryl shook her head, sending her long earrings swinging. "It's not like her."

That was true. Charla acted flighty most of the time. The only exceptions were her jobs. She'd worked at Levine's Jewelers and the Tumbleweed Café since she'd been in high school.

"Have you tried to reach her?" he asked.

"Yep." Sheryl's brightly painted lips turned down. "Several times. I've left several voice mails. She hasn't returned a single call. A couple of the other girls even went by her apartment, but they didn't have any luck, either."

Eli pushed back a prickle of unease. "That's weird."

"I know. Even weirder, her older sister is in town, asking around for her."

He grimaced, deciding not to comment. "You know what? Would you make my burger to go please?"

"Sure thing." She bustled off.

While he waited, he thought about the text message Charla had sent her sister. My life is in danger. Drama, though not the kind Charla usually dealt in. But why would she feel jeopardized in any way? And if so, by whom? Finally, why would she reach out to her estranged sister instead of her ex-husband? At least Eli was local, which would increase his chances of being able to help her.

Of course, he would have been skeptical. Who wouldn't, after all the lies and fabricated stories she'd told him? Oddly enough, Charla never spoke about her older sister. When pressed, she'd clamped her mouth tight and said she couldn't discuss a betrayal of such magnitude.

"Here you go, hon." Sheryl returned, carrying a bag with his to-go box. He paid, already knowing the exact total including tip, and headed back out to his truck. He'd eat while he drove. Next stop, Charla's apartment. He'd call Levine's Jewelers on the way.

When one of Charla's coworkers at the jewelry store answered, Eli went ahead and asked about Charla, even though he could already guess the answer. Sarah said she, too, was worried about Charla and found her disappearance problematic. She asked Eli to call her if he learned anything new. Eli agreed, ending the call just as he reached Charla's apartment building.

When he pulled up and parked, he wasn't surprised to see Jackie Burkholdt walking across the parking lot. He hopped out of his truck and waved. "Any luck?"

"No." Changing direction, she hurried over toward him. "I stopped by the jewelry store first, and then the Tumbleweed. She hasn't been in to work in four days, either place."

With her sleek dark hair pulled back into an elegant bun, she appeared as different as the cool, quiet shallows were from her sister's blazing-hot sun. Something about her drew him, a thought that he immediately discounted as foolishness.

"So I heard." He grimaced. "I stopped by the Tumbleweed, too, and just got off the phone with Sarah, who works at Levine's. I guess we had the same thoughts."

Her cool caramel gaze searched his face. "Does that mean you're concerned, too?"

Ah, how to answer that? "I wouldn't say *concerned*," he replied cautiously. "Charla can be a force of nature. I know you and she haven't spoken in quite a while. But I'm guessing her personality hasn't changed much. I'm not sure why she might have felt compelled to text you what she did, but in my experience, she always has her reasons."

Jackie exhaled, a sharp little puff of sound. "I know what you mean, but I'm still worried. Until I moved away, Charla always knew she could depend on me for anything and everything. Despite her…anger at me, I have to believe she still knows that. If she is in trouble, I'm the one person she can trust to help her out."

He noted the way her voice trembled, despite her obvious attempt to sound cool and collected. This actually made him like her just a little bit more.

"I know you're worried," he said. "But Charla and I have a son together. If something truly was wrong, I have to think she would have contacted me."

"To keep Theo safe?" she asked, frowning.

"Yes. Wouldn't that make sense? If Charla truly had some kind of trouble, why would she want to endanger her child?"

Her answer came slowly. "I guess." She looked around at the nondescript brick apartment building. "Then what now? I've checked her job and her home and came up with nothing."

"Let's check with the apartment manager. Bree knows me. I'm sure she'll let us take a peek inside Charla's apartment."

Though Jackie's frown deepened at this, she didn't protest.

A few minutes later, after explaining to Bree what was going on, they followed her back to unit 209. She unlocked the door and stepped inside. "Here we are," she said, glancing around. "Nothing seems out of place."

Eli stepped inside, thunderstruck. Theo's toys were strewn across the living room floor. Moving quickly, he hurried down the hall to his son's bedroom. That, too, appeared to be waiting for Theo and his mother to return home. If Charla had gone on the run, she hadn't packed anything.

This should have reassured him. Oddly enough, it didn't.

He turned to realize Jackie had followed him and

now stood in the doorway, gazing at the room's cheerful disorganization. When their gazes met, she swallowed. "What about day care?" she asked. "I'm assuming Charla took Theo to a day-care center."

"She did. It's right down the street from here." He took her arm. "We can take my truck."

Waiting while Bree locked everything up, he tried to get a grip on his emotions. Worry and fear could blind him if he let it.

Before they even went inside the day-care center, he suspected he already knew what they'd learn. "Theo hasn't been here in two days," the director told him. "We've reached out to his mother, but she hasn't returned our calls. Is everything all right?"

"I'm not sure." Eli scratched the back of his head. "Thank you. I'll be in touch if I find out anything."

Outside, he and Jackie trudged to his pickup and piled in.

"I'm getting worried," he admitted, starting up the engine. "I think it's time we talked to the sheriff."

The long, assessing glance she gave him made him wonder. "What?" he asked, slightly impatient. "I'm aware we don't know each other, but we both have the same concern."

"Do we?" Her cool gaze lingered. "Because from where I sit, you'd be the number-one suspect."

It actually took a minute for her insult to register. "Seriously? Please, enlighten me as to your reasoning."

"It's simple. Not only were you the last person to see her Saturday night, but if she went away for good, you would have the most to gain. My mom told me you tried to get full custody of Theo and lost. If Charla were out of the way, you could have your son with you a hundred percent of the time."

"That might be true," he replied, allowing some of his anger to show in his deep voice. "Except you're forgetting one very important thing. I would never hurt the mother of my child. And not only is Charla missing, if she truly is, then Theo is, too."

Staring out the window, she got quiet after that. He debated whether or not to simply drop her off at her car in Charla's apartment parking lot. Instead, he decided to bring her along with him to the sheriff's department. At least that way, maybe she could begin to understand that he wasn't the kind of person who would hurt any woman, for any reason.

Chapter Two

Remembering something about keeping your enemies close, Jackie forced herself to relax. She'd insulted Eli, she knew, but she couldn't bring herself to offer an apology. Not yet. She still wasn't sure about him. After all, abusers could be charming, too.

Even though she had no real reason not to trust him, she decided to keep herself aloof, at least until she knew more about what had happened to Charla and her son.

She knew her thoughts about him were irrational, to say the least. She didn't have one single valid reason to suspect him of causing harm to her sister. Everyone seemed to like and respect him, including her mother.

Now she'd see how the sheriff treated him.

While Jackie had never met Rayna Coombs personally, she'd heard a lot about her. Heck, Rayna had even made the national news, not once, but twice. Both times had involved serial killers. She appeared to be well respected by the townspeople and worked well with the federal law enforcement agencies. If anyone could help find Charla, Jackie suspected Rayna could.

After they parked, Jackie walked alongside Eli into

the sheriff's department. She noticed the town had spruced up the exterior of the cinderblock building with a fresh coat of paint and a new sign.

Rayna Coombs herself stood in the reception area, sorting through a stack of papers on the desk. She looked up when they entered, her pretty face breaking into a huge smile. "Eli Pitts!" she said. "What brings you to visit me today?"

"This is Jackie Burkholdt," Eli said. "Jackie, meet Rayna Coombs, our sheriff."

They shook hands. Rayna studied Jackie, her expression quizzical. "You look familiar, somehow," she said. "Have we met before?"

"No." Jackie shook her head. "But you may have met my sister, Charla."

"Oh." If Rayna's smile faltered slightly, it didn't last long. She looked from Jackie to Eli and then back again. "What's Charla done now?"

Jackie tried to summon up enough outrage to protest the sheriff's assumption, but she couldn't. She hadn't been around the past three years and had no way of knowing what kind of trouble her sister might have gotten involved in.

"May we talk in private?" Jackie asked.

"Of course." Rayna led the way through a set of double doors, across a large common work area and into a small corner office. "Here we are. Take a seat." She closed the door and then went to her own chair back behind the large desk. "Now, why don't you tell me what's going on?"

Jackie showed her the text message, explained how

she'd flown across the country to make sure her sister was okay. "But she hasn't shown up for work in two days, or taken Theo to day care. We went by her apartment, too. She's not answering her phone and some of her friends at the Tumbleweed are concerned."

"Even I'm a little bit freaked out," Eli agreed. "I know Charla does a lot of impulsive stuff, but she wouldn't involve Theo. Usually, she'd either drop him off at her mother's or leave him with me. This isn't like her."

"But she has done this before, right?" Rayna asked.

Eli nodded. "And I'm sure you've probably heard she and her latest man friend got into a drunken brawl at the Rattlesnake on Saturday night. Charla called me in tears and asked me to come get her, so I did. I dropped her off at her apartment. She said one of her friends was babysitting Theo."

"Which again, isn't unusual," Rayna pointed out.

"But she says her life is in danger," Jackie exclaimed. "I have to believe she's in very real trouble."

Listening, Rayna appeared to carefully consider her next words. "The problem we have here is that Charla is an adult. There's no evidence of foul play, so..."

"Does this mean you won't look for her until there is? Wouldn't that be far too late?" Jackie asked, keeping her tone calm and reasonable. "I want to find my sister now and protect her."

Eli and Rayna exchanged looks.

"What?" Jackie asked, pretty sure she already knew what the sheriff was about to say. "Look, even if Charla is a bit...dramatic, she and I haven't spoken to each other in three years. For her to actually text me, and with something like this, means I have to take it seriously. I'd appreciate if you would, too."

"I agree," Rayna replied, surprising her.

"Me, too," Eli seconded. "Charla's never involved Theo in any of her adventures before."

Which made Jackie wonder what kind of life her sister might have been leading. She decided she really didn't want to know. At least until her sister and nephew had turned up safe.

"What about your mother?" Rayna asked Jackie. "She and your sister appear to have a very close relationship. What are her thoughts on all of this?"

"She doesn't seem too concerned," Jackie admitted. "I'm going over there for dinner tonight and we'll talk more. But she's always been super indulgent of Charla's quirks, so it's hard to tell with her."

Eli shook his head, eyeing Jackie. "From my perspective, Delia acts more like Charla's friend than her mother sometimes. If Charla would have told anyone what's going on with her, she'd have told your mother."

"Good. Then maybe I'll find something out tonight." She considered, a thought occurring to her. "Why don't you come along? I'm sure you and Delia have a lot to catch up on."

Though his gaze narrowed, Eli didn't refuse. Instead, he muttered something noncommittal, which made Rayna grin.

"I'll start asking around," Rayna said. "And I'll let you know if I hear anything."

"Thank you." Jackie pushed to her feet. "And if I

learn anything new at my mother's tonight, I'll give you a call."

"Perfect. Here's my card." Rayna stood, too. "We'll be in touch."

Eli opened the door and led the way. As they got back into his truck, he gave her a quizzical look. "Do you really think I should have dinner tonight with you and Delia? Don't you think she might find that a little weird?"

"Maybe." Jackie shrugged. "But what does it matter in the scheme of things? I'm hoping once she sees that you're also concerned, she might take this all a bit more seriously. Especially since her grandson is involved."

"I agree." He pushed the button to start the ignition. "But whatever else she might be, Charla loves Theo in her own way. I'm having trouble thinking she'd allow him to be in danger for even a second."

In her own way. Jackie filed that statement away for later. She had to admit, she found Eli Pitts attractive. But she couldn't let that blind her to the possibility that he might have somehow been involved in her sister's disappearance. He still might have been the last person to see Charla.

"Please come with me tonight," Jackie asked. "To be honest, having you there might make my mother open up more. She's always been defensive of Charla around me."

Though he shook his head, Eli didn't outright refuse. He drove her back to the apartment parking lot, pulling up right behind her rental car. "I'll go," he said quietly. "But only if we ride together."

"That sounds good," she replied, amazed at the way her stomach did a quick somersault.

"Are you staying at the Landshark?"

She nodded.

"I'll pick you up there. What time?" he asked.

"She wants to eat around six," Jackie replied. "So five thirty?"

"Perfect." He kept the truck running while she opened her door and climbed out. "I'll see you then."

Nodding, she watched him drive away. She told herself his words sounded more like a promise than a threat. While she honestly didn't think Eli Pitts was dangerous, she knew better than to let her guard down. Until her sister stood right in front of her and vouched for her ex-husband's character, she had no choice but to consider him a possible dangerous suspect.

Despite all of that, as she got ready for dinner, she found herself a bundle of nerves. Part of that would be because she hadn't seen her mother in three years. Delia had made it very clear on which side she stood when the rift had opened up between sisters. Despite Jackie's pleas for their mother to help mend things, Delia had steadfastly refused. Part of Jackie had trouble forgiving her for that. She probably always would. Parents weren't supposed to choose one child over another.

Once she set up her laptop and logged in to the motel's Wi-Fi, Jackie spent the next couple hours catching up on work. She could still do editing remotely, along with several other tasks that didn't require a physical presence in the office.

Finally, her stomach growled, reminding her she

hadn't eaten anything since breakfast. Checking the time, she realized she'd have no choice but to wait until dinner now.

Dinner at her mother's. Which, if she was completely honest with herself, she dreaded. Part of the reason she'd asked Eli Pitts to accompany her was to act as a buffer between her and Delia.

After touching up her makeup, she brushed her hair and decided she was as ready as she was going to be.

She heard his truck pull up outside and swallowed back a sudden spate of nerves. This irritated her, because of all the reactions she might choose to have to her sister's ex-husband, sexual attraction wouldn't be one of them.

Instead of waiting for him to knock on her door, she let herself out, giving him a cheery wave as she walked to his truck. She'd decided on jeans and a T-shirt, with her feet in flip-flops.

When she climbed into Eli's truck, she noted he'd changed into a pair of well-worn khakis and a T-shirt that showed off his muscular chest and arms. He looked damn good. Eyeing him, she pretended her mouth hadn't gone dry and her heart hadn't skipped a beat.

"Hey there," he said, his warm smile friendly rather than flirtatious. Once she'd buckled herself in, he put the truck in Drive and pulled away. "Did you let Delia know I was coming?"

Crud. She grimaced. "I forgot. But honestly, she won't mind. She always speaks so highly of you."

He considered her words for a moment. "That's good to know. Hopefully, she'll have made enough food."

This had Jackie laughing. "I take it you and Charla didn't go over there for dinner very often?"

"No. We mostly met at restaurants or she came by the ranch." He gave her a curious glance. "Why?"

"Because Delia doesn't cook. She'll either have ordered to have something delivered or she'll have picked up tacos or fried chicken. And she always gets way too much. It'll be fine."

"I'll take your word for it."

He had his radio on low, tuned to the local country music station. A Garth Brooks song came on, one of her old favorites. She sang along under her breath. He glanced at her, noticing, and turned the volume up. Together, they sang along in a kind of clumsy camaraderie.

When the song finished, he turned the volume down and grinned at her. Flushed with pleasure, she grinned back.

"Here we are." He pulled over and parked at the curb in front of her mother's house.

Jackie stared at the small bungalow, still painted the same shade of pale yellow that she and her sister had hated. The manicured landscaping had grown out a bit, but overall it appeared time had stood still.

Slowly, she got out of the truck, stunned by the surprise rush of emotion closing her throat. Dimly aware of Eli moving to her side, she continued up the pathway to the front entrance. As she reached out to press the bell, the door flew open. Delia squealed, wrapping Jackie up in a tight, and unexpected, bear hug.

"I can't believe you're finally here," Delia said, acting as if Jackie had voluntarily stayed away. Then Delia's eyes widened as she spotted Eli standing on the front porch behind Jackie. "Eli? What are you doing here?"

"I'm sorry, Mom. I forgot to tell you I was bringing him," Jackie said. "He's been helping me try and figure out how to find Charla."

Delia frowned. "I told you to quit worrying. Your sister will turn up when she's ready to. I'm sure she's fine." She stepped back, motioning them to go past her into the house.

Jackie headed straight for the kitchen, unsurprised to see a huge bucket of fried chicken on the table. Eli followed a bit more slowly, clearly not sure how to respond to Delia's complete lack of concern for her missing daughter.

Once Delia reached the kitchen, she rounded on them. "Jackie, why are you so determined to make it seem as if something has happened to Charla?" she demanded. "Eli, you know her better than anyone besides me. It's not like Charla hasn't taken off before. She'll be back once she's had her fun."

Eli straightened and met her gaze directly. "While it's true Charla has done this before, this time she's involved Theo. She hasn't been in to work at either the jewelry store or the café, and Theo hasn't been to the day care in two days. She's not responded to anyone's phone calls or texts."

"That, combined with the text message she sent me saying she was in danger, seem to be a clear reason to be concerned," Jackie put in. She hated that her mother always seemed so blind to Charla's shortcomings, but right now Delia needed to open up her eyes.

Instead, Delia looked from Jackie to Eli with suspicion plain upon her face. "What are you two doing together anyway?" she asked. "Eli, I wouldn't have taken you for the sort of man who'd gang up on the mother of his child."

"Gang up?" Try as she might, Jackie couldn't keep her voice from rising. "Mom, I'm not the enemy here. Charla texted and asked for my help, remember? I took vacation time and flew the red eye across the country, for her. Because she needs me."

Uncertainty crossed Delia's face. Clearly, she didn't know how to deal with a reality where her two daughters weren't enemies. "Well," she said briskly. "How about we eat? Eli, I haven't seen you in a long time. I'm sure we have some catching up to do."

ELI WASN'T SURE what to make of the charged atmosphere between his former mother-in-law and her other daughter, but he suddenly understood why Jackie had asked him to come. During his brief marriage to Charla, he'd noticed how close she and her mother were, but he hadn't realized the full extent of Delia's willingness to turn a blind eye to her daughter's faults.

While clearly, Jackie could do nothing right in her mother's eyes. He didn't want any part of the strange dynamics and he resolved to try and make a graceful escape as soon as humanly possible. Somehow, he suspected Jackie wouldn't be averse to cutting short the visit.

Delia got out paper plates and napkins, along with plastic utensils. “I got extra crispy,” she said. “And there’s coleslaw, mashed potatoes and beans. Dig in.”

Taking care to avoid making direct eye contact with Jackie, Eli sat. He hadn’t had fried chicken in a while, and figured at least while everyone was eating, the thick tension might dissipate somewhat.

He dug in. Sitting across from him, Jackie did the same. Meanwhile, Delia nibbled on a drumstick, her gaze alternating between her daughter and Eli.

“How do you two know each other?” Delia asked suddenly. “Eli, were you acquainted before you met Charla?”

He hastily swallowed what he was chewing. “No. I first met Jackie yesterday, when she came pounding on my front door in the middle of the night.”

“I heard,” Delia drawled, glancing at her daughter. “What you didn’t tell me is why would you do such a thing?”

Jackie sighed. “I was looking for Charla. I’m *still* looking for her. I know you don’t think anything is wrong—and I really hope you’re right. But until I actually see Charla and hear her tell me that she’s okay, I’m not going to rest.”

Delia shook her head. “Aren’t you worried she’s going to be upset to see you hanging around her ex?”

Outwardly, Jackie didn’t react. Eli saw her hands tense on the table, but she picked at her piece of chicken with a single-minded intensity that matched her clenched jaw.

“Delia?” Eli cleared his throat. “I’m worried about

my son. I know you and Charla are close. Do you have any idea where she might be?"

Delia considered him. Meanwhile, Jackie shot him a grateful look, abandoning any attempt to eat.

"Actually, I haven't heard from Charla in about a week," Delia admitted. "She's been busy, between trying to be a single mother and working two jobs." Somehow, despite the fact that Charla had been the one to end the marriage, Eli detected a note of accusation in her mother's voice.

He ignored this. Delia Burkholdt was no longer his problem. Finding his son was. "If you hear from her, will you let me know? She's supposed to bring Theo on Friday. It's my weekend to have him. I hope to hell she shows up."

Pushing to his feet, he found Jackie's gaze. "Are you ready to go?" he asked. If she wasn't, he figured he'd offer to return and pick her up.

But judging by the relief that flashed in her expressive eyes, and the way she jumped to her feet, she was just as ready to get out of there as he. "Yes," she said.

"But you've hardly eaten anything," Delia protested halfheartedly. Eli suspected she'd be glad to get them out of her house.

"I'm not very hungry," Eli lied.

"Me neither," Jackie seconded.

"Oh. Well, then..." Delia waved them away. "I'll let you two show yourselves out."

Marveling at the difference between this Delia and the one who'd been practically giddy with happiness hanging on his ex-wife, Eli strode for the front door.

He opened it and stepped back so that Jackie could go ahead of him.

They rushed to his truck. Inside the cab he couldn't press the ignition button quickly enough.

"I'm not sure whether to laugh or cry," Jackie admitted, her mouth trembling and her eyes shiny, though she didn't shed a tear. "The bad thing is, I'm starving."

"Me, too." He made a snap decision. "How about we stop by the Rattlesnake for a burger and a beer."

"That would be awesome."

Her phone pinged. She glanced at it and shook her head. "She's still at it. Now you see why I was so eager to move to the other side of the country."

"I get that." He glanced at her, considering. "I've definitely seen a different side of her tonight. In fact, I'm still in shock."

With a weary sigh, she shrugged. "I wish I could say I was used to it, but I foolishly hoped after three years away, things might have changed. She's always doted on Charla and treated me like an afterthought."

"I'm sorry."

"Me, too. But in a way I guess it was a good thing. Gave me the drive to do something different with my life. I worked my way through college, graduated with honors and landed my dream job in publishing in New York." She smiled a little sadly. "Though Charla never forgave me for abandoning her, as she put it."

Incredulous, he stared. He'd known Charla was self-centered, but from the way she'd talked about her older sister's betrayal, he'd thought it had to have been something awful. "You're sure that's the entire reason?" he asked, letting his disbelief show.

"That's what she told me," she replied. "Though if she mentioned something else, I'd appreciate you letting me know."

"She was always deliberately vague," he said. "And now I understand why."

This made her laugh, a genuine sound of amusement that also succeeded in chasing the shadows from her eyes.

He pulled into the Rattlesnake Pub's half-full lot and scored a spot near the door. She jumped out and waited for him to join her. "It's been years since I had their Swiss-mushroom burger," she said. "I hope it still tastes as good as I remember."

Inside they were shown to a small booth near the back. When the waitress tried to bring menus, they both waved them away. "We already know what we want," Eli said, grinning. He ordered them both burgers. "What do you want to drink?" he asked Jackie.

"You mentioned beer," she said. "I'll have a Shiner please."

"Make that two." Since that happened to be his favorite beer. As the waitress moved away, he leaned back in the booth and studied the dark-haired woman sitting across from him. He refused to examine or even think about the strong attraction he felt toward her, which would be too weird since she was his ex's sister.

Thinking of Charla, he pulled out his phone and double-checked to make sure she hadn't texted or left a voice mail. Nothing. Looking up, he saw Jackie doing the same.

"You're really worried about her, aren't you?" he asked.

"Yes." She let out a puff of air in frustration. "I just don't understand why no one else is."

Their beers arrived and he took that moment as an opportunity to sip, and considered whether or not to say anything. Finally, he decided she deserved to know the truth about her sister. He'd try to be as tactful as possible.

"Maybe because Charla's done this before." He kept his tone mild, watching closely for her reaction.

"You and Rayna mentioned that before," she replied, a slight frown creasing her brows. "As did my mother. I was sort of afraid to ask. You mean she randomly disappears?"

"Yes. She takes off on a regular basis." He took another sip of his beer. "Though usually she doesn't take Theo with her. Saturday she claimed she'd left him with one of her friends. Usually, by now said friend would have shown up with Theo in tow. The fact that she hasn't is something that's got me concerned." He shrugged, refusing to give in to his early feelings of panic. "It's only Wednesday. I imagine Charla will pick him up and show up before Friday, since that's when she's supposed to drop Theo off at my house."

Though Jackie nodded, her expression remained troubled. "At the risk of sounding redundant, what about the text she sent me?"

"I don't know. Maybe that's her way of trying to reconcile with you."

Whatever response she'd been about to make, she didn't because their burgers arrived. Eli watched her as she accepted her plate from the waitress, enjoying the way she eyed her meal with a rapt, intent expression, as if she hadn't eaten for days.

He took another long pull on his beer before picking up his burger. Jackie had already taken a huge bite out of hers, no messing around and cutting it in half like some women did. He liked the way she went all in, then mentally chastised himself for even noticing.

They ate in a sort of companionable silence, she intent on devouring her meal, and he intent on trying not to watch her. He knew she didn't entirely trust him, and he supposed he couldn't blame her. She'd been away for three years and had missed out on a huge chunk of her sister's life.

Finally, she finished her burger and started on her fries. When she looked up and caught him watching her, she nodded. "Are you ever going to tell me what happened between you and Charla?" she asked.

The question was a reasonable one. Even if answering it truthfully—the only way he could—revealed him to be a complete and utter fool.

"Charla came into my life like a cyclone," he said, allowing himself to smile slightly at the memory. "You know how she is. So full of herself, brimming over with life. She waited on me at the Tumbleweed and when her shift was over, she drove herself out to my farm."

Jackie nodded, watching him closely. "I can see her

doing that. Once Charla decided she wants something, she goes after it with everything she's got."

"Which is exactly what she did," he agreed. "It was crazy and beautiful and we were happy." He thought for a moment, and then amended that. "Or at least, I was. I didn't realize at the time that Charla lived her life kind of like a butterfly, flitting from one thing to another. I asked her to marry me. She asked to think about it. And then she discovered she was pregnant, so she said yes."

"That's the part of the story my mother left out," she said quietly, pushing her nearly empty plate away. "I'd thought—I'd hoped—Charla might have grown out of that sort of behavior."

He shrugged. "It's okay. The person I thought I was marrying didn't exist. Part of the fault of that is on me." And part was on Charla, for pretending to be something she never could have been, though he didn't voice that. He was pretty sure Jackie understood.

"Charla seemed to enjoy being pregnant," he continued. "She thrived on all the attention, though she didn't like that she had to stop partying."

Jackie rubbed her temples, as if trying to ward off a headache. "But she did stop, right?"

"Yes. As far as I know."

She grimaced. "Tell me about when Theo was born. It's so hard to know I have a nephew and I've never even met him."

Impulsively, he reached across the table and lightly touched the back of her hand. "We'll make sure that changes."

"Thank you. I'd like that."

The waitress reappeared and collected their plates. He ordered another beer. Jackie declined, since hers was still half-full.

Once the waitress had gone, Jackie leaned forward. "I know all of this is incredibly personal, and I really appreciate you sharing it with me. Do you mind telling me what happened to end your marriage?"

Did he mind? Flashback of anger and tears, memories of him trying desperately to hold on to their little family, of Charla's scornful laughter and the way she'd called him a fool. Her partying, not coming home or spending time with her son for days. Eli had known the entire town saw and gossiped about it, especially since several people had taken it upon themselves to call him, informing him of his wife's every move. One older rancher had even gone so far as to advise Eli that he needed to get his wife in line. The man hadn't appreciated or understood Eli's laughter.

The end of Eli and Charla's marriage had been a time of great pain. Only Theo—and their love for him—had been a bright light shining in the murky darkness.

"It wasn't working out," he simply said. "Charla wasn't happy. She found someone else and asked for a divorce. I gave her one."

The waitress delivered his second beer, along with the check. "No hurry," she said. "Just let me know when you're ready."

He thanked her, returning his attention to Jackie. "She has custody of Theo, while I have visitation every other week. I also get him for two weeks every summer, and we alternate major holidays."

This schedule had been, to him, the worst of all of it. He loved his son and would have done anything for him. So did Charla, he knew, but as far as he could tell, Charla treated Theo more like an afterthought than the center of her existence.

Jackie watched him, the sympathetic expression in her dark eyes telling him she understood much of what went unsaid.

"Yet you still pick her up from a bar when she calls and asks?" she questioned, drumming her fingers on the table.

He winced, aware she had a point. "What else could I do? She and I might not have worked out as a couple, but she's still my son's mother."

"And you have no idea where she left Theo that night?"

"No. I'd made her a standing offer to babysit when Charla felt the need to go out, but she claimed she didn't like me being that deeply involved in her life, so she got various friends to do it."

Out of habit, he pulled out his phone and checked it. "She still hasn't responded to my texts," he mused, scrolling over to various social media apps and checking the feed. "And she hasn't been active on Facebook, Twitter, Instagram or Snapchat. That's unusual for her."

Jackie leaned forward. "Does this mean you're starting to get worried?"

"Not yet," he answered truthfully. "But if she doesn't bring Theo on Friday, that will definitely change."

Reaching into his shirt pocket, Eli pulled out a business card and handed it to Jackie. "My number," he said. "Call me if you need anything."

"Thanks," she replied, accepting it. "I'll text you so you have mine."

"Sounds good. I'll let you know if I hear anything before Friday."

Promising to do the same, she got up and headed toward the door. He put enough cash on the table to cover both the meal and a nice tip, and followed her. Walking behind her, he couldn't help but admire the sway of her hips as she made her way through the room, or the way several other men eyed her. He had the strangest urge to catch up to her and put his arm around her shoulders, the classic gesture to show she was his.

Except she wasn't. Nor would she ever be. She was his ex-wife's sister, nothing more. Once Charla turned up, and he had no doubt she would as soon as she was good and ready, Jackie would head back to her life up north. Eli would continue to farm and raise his son, and Charla would continue sowing her wild oats.

On the surface it would appear that nothing had changed. Eli suspected that everything had.

Chapter Three

After leaving the Pub with Eli walking strong and silent behind her, Jackie once again climbed into the cab of his truck. She hadn't expected to like the man, but she did. She'd watched the hurt chase across his rugged face as he talked, saw him struggle not to say anything totally negative about Charla to her sister, and respected him for that.

He was easy on the eyes, too, she had to admit. However, she understood that the insistent tug of attraction she felt would be nothing but trouble for both of them were she to give in. So she wouldn't. After all, she was only in town to find her sister, make certain Charla was all right and meet her nephew. Bonus points for having time to catch up on everything she'd missed for the past three years. She might be worried, but she was glad Charla had finally reached out, whatever the reason. She could only hope her sister was, as everyone seemed to think, simply being dramatic.

Onc more day. Friday would roll around and Charla would either show up at Eli's farm with Theo, or she wouldn't. With all of her heart, Jackie hoped it was the former.

Eli dropped her off at Charla's apartments where she'd left her rental car. Thanking him, she got out of his truck and walked toward her vehicle, resisting the urge to glance back over her shoulder at him.

She unlocked the doors and got inside. Only then did Eli leave. After he'd driven off, Jackie got out and tried Charla's apartment one final time, unsurprised when she didn't get an answer. Wherever her sister might be, Jackie could only hope she was safe.

One more day, she reminded herself yet again. One. More. Day. Yet knowing that didn't help the roiling worry inside her. It made everything worse knowing she was alone in this. Even her own mother acted as if Jackie was a fool to worry about Charla.

Strange as it might be to understand, it seemed no one but she was truly afraid for her sister. Charla's friends had expressed concern, but mainly because she hadn't shown up at work to cover her shift. That seemed odd to her. Did Charla actually not have any real friends? As a child and a teenager, Charla had been popular. Everyone had wanted to hang out with her.

Clearly, not anymore. But then again, Jackie had been gone for three years. Everyone else had been here while Charla apparently burned a lot of bridges. To Jackie, Charla would always be her baby sister. Spoiled, true. But deeply loved.

Driving back to the Landshark Motel, she made a detour for nostalgia's sake and drove past her old high school. The two-story tan brick structure looked exactly the same, just older. Getaway High, home of the Fighting Hornets. Jackie slowed, gazing at the imposing building, wishing she had better memories. She'd spent her entire time here studying hard, working toward her goal of coming out at the top of her class. She'd achieved this goal, despite her mother's baffling lack of support.

After graduating as class valedictorian, she'd been offered a scholarship to Texas Tech, enough to cover almost everything. Charla had been furious, accusing Jackie of leaving her to rot in a dying little town, as she'd put it. Only Jackie's promises to come home most weekends had mollified her.

Jackie had hoped her younger sister would study and work hard and follow in her footsteps. Instead, Charla had seemed determined to do the opposite. She'd partied hard and often, her grades falling so low that she almost didn't graduate.

So many memories here. Not all of them were good.

After leaving the high school, Jackie stopped by a small beer and wine store and picked up a bottle of Pinot Grigio and a few snacks. She had her e-reader loaded with manuscripts for work and planned to spend a quiet evening sipping wine and reading. It never hurt to get a jump ahead on the work that always seemed to pile up.

Back at the Landshark Motel, which took on a sad appearance in the waning sunlight, she let herself into her room. Then she changed into her pajamas, poured a generous glass of wine, using one of the motel plastic water glasses, and climbed into the bed. Propping her back up with pillows, she got under the covers, took a sip of wine and began to read. These were from the slush pile, the unsolicited manuscripts aspiring authors sent in. There were always tons of them and Jackie enjoyed wading through them, aware that somewhere she might find a rare gem.

Of course, almost immediately her cell phone rang. Seeing her mother's name come up on the caller ID, Jackie was sorely tempted to let the call go to voice mail. Only the possibility that Delia might have finally heard from Charla forced Jackie to accept the call.

"Hey, Mom, what's up?" Jackie asked.

"I know you've been gone three years, but how could you have forgotten about the gossip in this town?" Delia demanded, her tone peeved. "I've already gotten three phone calls from people who saw you and Eli at the Pub."

"So?" Jackie asked, not bothering to conceal her impatience. "Are we not allowed to have a meal together?"

"People are saying you're poaching your sister's ex-husband."

"But I'm not," Jackie pointed out, rolling her eyes. "You know that, I know that and he knows that. What's the problem? Why are you even listening to gossip anyway?"

Delia sighed, a loud, dramatic sound that reminded Jackie of Charla. "Imagine what Charla is going to think once she gets home. She reached out to you in hopes of mending the rift between you and this is how you repay her?"

Jackie struggled to find the right words. Any words, actually, that wouldn't escalate the tension between her and her mother. Since the *rift*, as her mother put it, had been entirely Charla's doing, she wasn't sure what to say. In addition to that, while it was true Charla had reached out, she'd only done so because she needed help. Badly. No matter what anyone else thought, no matter how fickle her sister might be, in that moment when she'd sent Jackie the text, she'd honestly felt her life was in danger. Jackie believed that with every fiber of her being. It was why she'd put in an emergency request for vacation, bought an overpriced plane ticket, flown here and not only rented a car, but also paid for a hotel room. All of the money she'd saved for a trip to Key West with a couple of work friends would be depleted by the time she returned home.

Jackie had always been the one who saved her sister. Despite a three-year-long absence, she'd do whatever it took to save her now. Despite a lack of evidence, she would bring Charla home safely. If Charla's life truly was in danger, Jackie would stop the threat and protect her sister.

Meanwhile, Jackie could only cling to the hope that Charla had been wrong and that she wasn't too late.

On the phone Delia continued to worry about irrelevant nonsense. When she finally paused for air, Jackie jumped in. "Are you finished, Mom?" Jackie asked softly. "Because tomorrow is when we find out if Charla is actually missing. I'm trying to catch up on work and after that, I'd like to get some rest so I can be ready to see my sister again." As if there wasn't a doubt. Always thc optimist, Jackie thought.

"There's more," Delia continued, her voice reluctant.

"People apparently are taking bets on where Charla is and with whom."

This had Jackie sitting up straight. "People? What people?"

"I don't know." Delia sounded miserable. "She's not really well liked in town these days. Mostly because she can be a bit…careless. But Charla's a good person, a wonderful daughter and an amazing mother. I don't know why all these others can't see that. Instead, they chose to focus on her faults. Who cares if she likes to have a good time? She's young. She'll outgrow that eventually, like I did."

Jackie winced, glad her mother couldn't see her. When she and Charla had been younger, Delia had spent a lot of time hanging out in bars, too, leaving Jackie to watch over her baby sister. Delia had often come home drunk and passed out on the couch. Though Jackie had hated when that happened, it had been infinitely preferable to those nights when her mother hadn't come home at all.

Again, she wisely refrained from commenting. Delia had rewritten the past in her own mind and if her version of the truth bore no resemblance to reality, nothing Jackie could say would change that.

"I do have some better news, though," Delia said, her tone brightening. "I called a few of Charla's girlfriends and found out the names of Charla's latest two boyfriends."

"The ones who got into a fight at the Pub over her?"

"Yes. Wasn't that something?"

Unbelievably, Jackie heard an undercurrent of pride

in her mother's voice. Grimacing, she poured herself a second glass of wine. "Yes, Mom, that was something. Did you pass that information along to the authorities?"

"Yes, I did." Delia's voice rang with triumph. "I called Rayna and passed both names along to her, just in case. She promised to talk to them. Which means if they know anything about where Charla might be, Rayna will get that information."

"Thanks," Jackie replied, impressed despite herself. "Does this mean that you're also beginning to worry about Charla?"

"A little," Delia admitted. "I'm worried about my grandson, as well. I usually see Theo several times a week, and it's not like Charla to keep him away from me for so long. But like you said, tomorrow is when she's supposed to bring Theo to Eli. If she doesn't show up, I know we'll all worry." She took a deep breath. "A lot. Is Eli going to let you know?"

"I hope so. Though what I'd really like is for Charla to call me first." She closed her eyes, allowing herself to picture it. Charla would be laughing, not even slightly apologetic for worrying anyone. They'd meet at Tres Corazons for dinner, have a margarita with their enchiladas and catch up on the past three years. Sisters once again.

"Well, call me the instant you hear anything," Delia ordered. "And if I hear from Charla first, I promise to do the same."

After ending the call with her mother, Jackie settled back against the pillows with her wine and her work, but she couldn't concentrate. She finally dug in her bag for a pad of paper and a pen and began making a list of what she knew about Charla and her disappearance.

She began with receiving the text. That had been late Monday night—actually, early Tuesday morning. Jackie hadn't seen the text until she'd gotten up around 8:00 a.m. Either way, the text had evidently been sent sometime after Eli had given Charla a ride home from the Pub.

Over to the side she listed the events that had occurred before Eli picked her sister up. A bar fight between two men.

She also listed how her sister hadn't shown up for work, four days at the jewelry store, which would have been Saturday, Monday, Tuesday and Wednesday, the day Jackie had arrived in town.

Two days. She'd only been back in Getaway for two days and it already felt like an eternity. She shook her head, half-relieved and half-worried that tomorrow they'd finally know something for sure.

And unless Charla called her, she still had to kill time Friday during the day. Eli had said Charla always brought Theo to the farm after five. After work. Where she hadn't been all week.

Pushing away the chill that ran down her spine, she decided to stop by the sheriff's office in the morning and chat with Rayna. Even though right now the general consensus seemed to be that Charla had taken off on some kind of lark and no one took her seriously. But if that actually was the case, what had she done with her toddler son? More than anything, Jackie hoped Charla showed up at Eli's farm tomorrow afternoon.

Somehow, Jackie didn't think she would.

Pulling out her phone, Jackie tried calling Charla again. The call once more went directly to voice mail. She also sent another text but got no response. Though almost everyone acted as if she was overreacting, she couldn't shake the feeling that this time something really was wrong.

If her sister showed up tomorrow—no, *when* her sister showed up tomorrow—Jackie vowed she'd suppress the urge to chew her out for all the worry she'd put her through. She'd hug her instead, she thought. They'd spend some time catching up, and then Jackie would bring up how worried she'd been. Since she'd taken a two-week impromptu vacation, she allowed herself to picture some of the things she and Charla might do. Girls' night out, maybe catch a movie or two. Heck, if Charla wanted, Jackie could even arrange for them both to fly back to New York, and she'd spend the rest of her time off showing her sister around the city.

Thinking such happy thoughts helped lighten the stressful uncertainty that had plagued her ever since arriving back home and not being able to locate her sister.

What if something really had happened to Charla and Theo, the nephew Jackie had never met? If so, Jackie knew she'd move heaven and earth to find them, as well as whoever meant to do her sister harm.

She thought about Eli, who should still be her number-one suspect if anything truly had happened to her sister, and wished she'd managed to put a bit more distance between them. Instead, after a mere two days, she felt as if he was her friend. She berated herself for being seduced by his earnest friendliness and handsome face. Still, all her life she'd been good at judging character, and she truly believed Eli was exactly as down-to-earth and real as he appeared to be. Someone like him would have been a steadying influence on her sister, though she could also see Charla deciding he was boring. Hopefully, Jackie would get a chance to hear everything directly from Charla's mouth tomorrow.

Hopefully. Definitely.

FRIDAY MORNING. FINALLY. Eli opened his eyes, as usual well before his alarm clock went off, aware of a sense of both anticipation and of a niggling worry that he couldn't shake. Would Charla show? He had to believe she would. But then why hadn't she answered any of his texts or voice mails? They might not be able to talk about anything else, but they'd had an agreement to always stay in touch whenever it concerned their son.

Theo. Due to Charla's party-girl attitude, he'd asked for joint custody of their boy. Charla had laughed at him and the judge had apparently agreed with her that a child belongs with his mother. Instead of equal parenting rights, Eli received visitation, a standard schedule worked out by the judge that he'd apparently been using for over thirty years. Alternate weekends, two weeks every summer and switching holidays every year with Charla.

With no choice but to accept the ruling, Eli tried not to worry about his young son. At first, fears for his boy's safety had kept him up at night, but as time passed and Charla proved to be a fairly capable mother, some of his foreboding abated. At least when she went out partying, she always made sure Theo had a babysitter, sometimes her mother, sometimes Eli, mostly one or two of her friends.

Though missing Theo was a constant ache, Eli eventually got accustomed to his new reality. It wasn't what he wanted or hoped for, but it was what he got. He had no choice but to learn to live with it. He'd wanted to be present when Theo spoke his first words, began to crawl, took his first steps. Instead, he'd missed most of the major developments of his boy's life, though he made a big deal out of each new thing when he finally saw it.

His weekends with Theo were the best part of his life. Eli spent all the time in between them waiting for the next one to roll back around. So far Charla had never missed one or even been late. Eli always spent the entire day working to kill the hours until he got to see his son.

Today, though, with no response from Charla to his texts or phone calls, he wasn't entirely sure whether or not she would show. Even the thought had his stomach churning. He had no idea why she would do something like this, why now, unless she'd engineered all of this to make some sort of point to her older sister, Jackie.

He allowed himself to feel a flash of anger. Just a small one, quickly tamped down. He'd learned long ago not to allow himself to react emotionally to Charla and her drama. It wore him out. How like her this was. Charla had never cared about inconveniencing others; as long as she got what she wanted, the world was a bright and shiny place.

He knew Jackie was worried, but she hadn't been around her sister in a long time. She had no idea that acting like this—getting people riled up, disappearing for days without making contact—was normal behavior for Charla.

As far as Eli was concerned, Charla could live her pursuit of narcissistic bliss all she wanted, as long as Theo was safe. He had to be safe. The alternative simply wasn't acceptable.

Except he couldn't shake the unwelcome sense that something really had gone wrong.

Where was Theo? Why hadn't he been in day care? The only thing he could think of was that Charla must have gone on a trip and taken Theo with her. Even though to do such a thing was highly unlike her.

Worry over his son was the one aspect of all this that concerned him. To be fair, he knew Charla had a lot of close female friends, many of whom enjoyed looking after her toddler. This and only this knowledge is what staved off the pending frantic concern. He had to believe that whatever else Charla might have become, she would still make sure their son came to no harm.

But would she bring Theo tonight?

He worked hard all through the morning, throwing himself into the plowing, doing twice as many rows as he normally did. When he broke for lunch, he wolfed down a cold meatball sandwich, toyed with the idea of calling Jackie just to hear her voice and rejected the thought for the same reason.

Back at it, he worked right up until four thirty, then hurried back to the house to take a quick shower. Charla always dropped Theo off between five thirty and six, as stipulated in the custody agreement. He made a big pot of macaroni and cheese, Theo's favorite, and parked himself on a chair with a clear view of the road and driveway. Any minute now he hoped to see that telltale plume of dust kicked up by a car coming down the gravel road.

While waiting, he checked his phone, just in case she decided to text that she was on her way, as she sometimes did. Instead, there was nothing. A vague sense of unease settled around him, but he refused to give up hope. Theo would be here. He had to be.

Five thirty came with no sign of her and Theo. Pacing now, he fought the urge to check the clock every two minutes. But at 6:05 p.m. he'd begun to understand they weren't coming. Which meant Jackie might have been right all along. Charla could actually be in some sort of danger. If this was true, what about his son?

His phone rang, startling him. He snatched it up, his stomach twisting when he realized it wasn't Charla. Instead, Jackie was calling him, no doubt to confirm her sister's appearance. Or lack of.

He froze, not ready to actually say the words out loud. But realizing the ridiculousness of this reluctance, he answered the phone. "She didn't show," he said, his voice tight, just like the leash he had on his emotion. "Not yet, at least."

Silence, broken only by Jackie's harsh intake of breath. "No calls or texts, either?" Her voice shook, most likely because she already knew the answer.

"No." Finally, he allowed himself to say the unthinkable. "I'm worried about the safety of my son."

"And my sister," she added. "Both of them." She took a deep breath. "I think you need to call Rayna. Better yet, go see her in person. I can meet you there."

Feeling queasy, he agreed. "I want to wait just a few more minutes," he said. "Just in case they're running late."

Though she knew just as well as he that this was unlikely, she agreed. "Half an hour," she said, and ended the call.

While he waited, Eli paced. Front door hallway to back door. Around the living room coffee table, making periodic stops by the front window. Outside, nothing stirred up the dust on the gravel road. The late-afternoon sun continued to beat down, relentless in its brightness. Everything outside looked like a normal late-spring day. But it wasn't. Not even close. His son was truly missing.

He made it for twenty minutes before he snatched up his truck key fob and slammed from the house. He drove faster than usual but despite that, Jackie was already waiting for him in the sheriff's department parking lot. She took one look at his face and nodded, her expression grim. Side by side they walked in and asked to see Rayna.

The sheriff took one look at their unsmiling faces and motioned for them to follow her back to her office. Waving her hand at the guest chairs, she closed the door before turning to face them. "I'm guessing that Charla didn't show."

"No." This time Eli didn't even try to hide his worry. "What if something has happened to my son?"

"And what if something has not?" Rayna countered. "Let's think positive. While not showing up for the agreed-upon visitation isn't something Charla has ever done, that doesn't necessarily mean she and your boy have come to any harm."

While he appreciated her attempt to calm him down, Eli wasn't having it. "How about we find her?" he asked, a definite edge to his voice. "And my son."

Jackie squeezed his arm, which made him feel as if she offered her support.

"I know my mom gave you the name of Charla's two boyfriends," Jackie said.

"Yes, and we've already spoken to them," Rayna replied. "Neither of them claims to have heard from Charla since that night in the Pub."

"Other than Eli, I might be the only person who heard from her after that," Jackie interjected. "She sent her text to me early Tuesday morning."

Rayna nodded. "Then where has she been all this time?" Her steely gaze drifted over to meet Eli's. "It appears you might have been the last person to see her before she disappeared."

The words chilled him. Back to that again. "As if I would ever hurt her," he said, conscious of the way Jackie narrowed her eyes as she watched him. "Or my son. Come on, Rayna. You've got to do better than that."

Her curt nod didn't reassure him. "We're going to need to get the word out in town. I know people are already talking about this. Most of them assume it's simply Charla being Charla. I've spoken to Christopher Levine, too, and he said if Charla didn't turn up by tonight, he'd be willing to offer a thousand-dollar reward for information leading to her safe return."

"That's impressive," Jackie said. "When I talked with him, he seemed to think very highly of my sister."

Eli decided not to mention that Charla had claimed to have had an affair with her boss shortly after Theo had been born, confiding they'd also been together before she and Eli had met, though that had ended. The two of them had only picked up their relationship after she'd had her son. She'd then proudly shown Eli a large diamond ring the man had given her. Since Christopher already had a wife, it wasn't an engagement ring. Just a pretty and very expensive trinket, the kind a rich man might give his mistress.

If Rayna knew about the affair, she didn't say anything about it, either.

"What can we do?" Jackie asked, leaning forward. "Surely, there's some way we can help."

Rayna perched on the edge of her desk, her expression solemn. "I've already asked Delia for a list of Charla's friends—both male and female. Eli, if you can provide whatever information you might have, that would be helpful."

He nodded. Jackie, who now sat up straight at full attention, clearly waited for Rayna to say something to her.

"Jackie," Rayna finally said. "I know you've been away for a while and that you weren't involved in your sister's life recently. I'd ask you to help Eli here as much as you can. Also, I'm guessing your mother might need your support."

Eli could imagine how distraught Delia would be once she learned Charla truly was missing. She loved her younger daughter more than anything. In fact, he believed Charla had received her love of drama from her overly excitable mother.

"I will," Jackie agreed. "I'd like to ask you exactly what your plan is. Where do you go from here?"

Rayna nodded, her sharp gaze going from Jackie to Eli and back again. "Excellent question. I'm going to start with talking with all of her friends. I'd like to find out if she might have mentioned anything about taking a trip. We'll be checking the bus station and security logs out at the airport. I've put out an APB for her car, so if that shows up we might have a bit more info."

"I like that. Very thorough." Still, Jackie held up her phone. "And since she sent me the text message, can you ping her phone or check her GPS?"

"We already have." Rayna paused. "Her phone is not turned on."

This news hit Eli like a blow to the stomach. Charla and her phone were inseparable. She was always on the damn thing, either checking social media or one of her dating accounts.

"Dating accounts," he said out loud. "Charla had joined multiple dating websites. She claimed there weren't enough decent men in Getaway."

"We'll check those out, too," Rayna agreed. "Hopefully, Delia will have a bit more specific information for us about that." She cocked her head. "Unless you have more specifics."

"I'll make you a list of the ones I know she was on," he replied, and then took a deep breath. "What about an Amber alert for Theo? Can we do that? It might help him get spotted faster."

"I wish we could," Rayna replied. "Unfortunately, since Charla is the custodial parent and has never been a danger to Theo, this doesn't meet the criteria of an Amber alert. I'm sorry."

For one second he allowed his desperation to show. "We've got to find them. We have to find my son."

"We will," Rayna soothed. "I'm putting all my best people on the case."

Chapter Four

Now that what Jackie had feared all along had come to pass, she refused to let go of that last shred of hope, despite the chill that had settled deep into her bones. Her sister and nephew would be all right. They had to be.

Meanwhile, Charla and Theo were officially missing.

Though she dreaded calling her mother, she figured it would be best to get it out of the way now. Excusing herself from Rayna's office, she crossed through the large work area, spied an empty conference room and slipped inside. Once she'd closed the door, she quickly pulled up her mother's contact info and took a deep breath before pressing Call Now.

Delia answered on the second ring. As soon as Jackie filled her in, her mother let out a bloodcurdling scream, so loud Jackie had to hold the phone away from her ear. She waited silently while her mother railed and cursed and sobbed, aware that there was nothing she could say to make things any better.

"I knew it," Delia declared after she'd finished her theatrics. "I just had this feeling something was wrong. All along, I knew."

Somehow, Jackie managed to refrain from reminding her mother that in fact, the opposite had been true. None of that mattered right now. "I'm at the sheriff's office now with Eli," she said. "Rayna is getting a plan put in motion. She's going to need a list of all Charla's close friends."

"Why would you think I'd have that?" Delia sounded both angry and frantic. "I'll do the best I can, but Charla didn't involve me in every aspect of her life."

Jackie blinked. Up until right this moment, her mother had talked as if she and Charla were super close, living practically in each other's back pocket. "Okay, Mom. I'm going to let you go now. I want to get back in there so I don't miss anything." She ended the call without giving Delia a chance to protest.

As expected, Delia immediately called back. Jackie declined to accept the call, sending it to voice mail, and left the conference room, heading back to Rayna's corner office. She opened the door quietly and slipped inside.

"There you are," Rayna exclaimed. "Why don't you and Eli keep each other company for a bit. I'm afraid I have to shoo you both off. I need to get to work." She glanced back at a stack of papers on her desk. "I promise I'll keep you informed."

Glancing at Eli, Jackie realized he was barely keeping it together. The thinly veiled, stark fear in his eyes had her taking his arm and leading him out of Rayna's office. "Let's go get a cup of coffee or something," she suggested. "I think it'll be better if we stay out of everyone's way and let them do their job."

He nodded and allowed her to steer him toward the exit. Once outside he glanced at her, his expression now carefully blank. "Where to?" he asked, the lack of inflection in his voice letting her know he definitely needed some time to process everything.

"How about we go for a drive?" Snap decision. Inside his truck he could rant and rave, if he wanted. Ask tough questions—and possibly answer them. Much better than in a crowded restaurant, where others would no doubt want to talk to him.

He shrugged, glancing at her. "I thought you wanted to get coffee."

"We can pick up some in a drive-through," she replied. "I think a ride might do us both some good."

Posture uncharacteristically stiff, he nodded and used his remote to unlock his truck. "If you say so. Let's go."

As she climbed into the passenger seat, her heart went out to him. She couldn't help it. Even though she knew she should consider him a suspect, especially since she didn't know him all that well. While his fear for Theo was palpable, he might be a damn good actor for all she knew. Without Charla there to tell her, she had no idea if she and Eli had been fighting. Maybe even over Theo.

Still, when someone needed comfort as badly as he did, she had to offer it. Especially since she knew doing so would help her find a bit of solace as well. "They'll be found soon," she said, injecting a note of certainty into her voice. "I'm sure they're both fine."

"Are you?" A thread of bitterness seeped into his

voice. "Because I'm beginning to wonder. What the hell did Charla get mixed up in this time? And how could she not take Theo's safety into consideration?"

Since she had no answer, she didn't reply. Instead, she looked out the window as he pulled onto Main Street.

"Where to?" he asked, barely glancing at her. "I'm assuming you have some destination in mind."

"You decide. Let's just drive around. Maybe out on the Farm to Market roads. If you want coffee, we can pick some up on the way."

"I think I'll pass on the coffee," he replied. "I'm already too agitated without adding caffeine. But we can pick some up for you if you want."

She shrugged. "That's okay. Let's go. Somewhere outside of town."

In response, he turned off Main Street and headed west. But instead of driving toward the highway, he stuck to the back roads, the ones that meandered through wheat fields and by cattle pastures, with numerous four-way stop signs.

Eyeing the passing scenery with interest, Jackie realized the last time she'd been this way had been as a young college student, home on break, with a group of friends looking for a pasture to have a bonfire and party.

Glancing at Eli, she wanted to ask him where he'd grown up. Had it been in a small town like Getaway, or somewhere else? Was he even a native Texan?

But small talk not only seemed like too much effort, but also would have felt wrong. She'd suspected all along that Charla wasn't simply off on a lark. Eli, along with nearly everyone else, had just now come to the realization. He'd need time to grapple with the knowledge. While she needed to figure out what to do next.

The paved road gave way to gravel, and Eli slowed down some. On all sides of them the horizon seemed to stretch out forever. West Texas with its wide-open spaces and endless sky always made her feel a sense of peace. When she'd first arrived in New York, with skyscrapers blocking the sun and people hurrying everywhere, she'd battled claustrophobia. Eventually, she'd found her own pace and had managed to get used to the city. Having a place like Central Park to visit had helped a lot, too.

Eli slowed, swinging the truck to the left of the road to avoid a series of ruts. As he drove, some of the tension he carried seemed to dissipate. He sighed, fiddled with the radio and finally snapped it off.

"I just don't understand," he said, glancing sideways at her. "I get that Charla might have taken off. As you know, her doing so wouldn't actually be anything new. But Theo...my boy. She knows how much I love him. And he loves me, too. Why would she take my son away from me?"

The very real anguish in his voice made her eyes sting and her throat close. She hadn't expected to feel this sense of kinship with him, the man who still could be the one who'd actually threatened her sister. "I don't know," she answered quietly. "Maybe she had no choice."

"There's always a choice. Always." He looked straight ahead, his rugged jaw tight. "I don't know what to think. The one thing Charla and I always agreed on was that our son would grow up with two parents who got along no matter what."

"I respect that," she said, meaning it. "But if someone was threatening Charla for whatever reason and she had to disappear fast, she'd have no choice but to take Theo with her. If that's the case, it won't be permanent. We just have to find out who's after her and why. Once she's safe, she'll be able to come back home."

"You really believe that?" he asked, his tone indicating he did not. "Since you've been back in town, you've learned a little bit about what kind of person your sister has become."

His cell phone chimed. Pushing a button on his dashboard, he had the vehicle read the text aloud. "Are we still on for tomorrow? Sasha Yacos."

Jackie glanced at him, her stomach in knots. "Girlfriend?" she asked.

"No." Turning left onto an even rougher road, he hardly glanced at her. "One of my students. I give group riding lessons to kids on Saturdays. I'm guessing news of Charla and Theo's disappearance is making the rounds. Sasha is wondering if we're still having the class. She'll probably be the first of many, now that word has gotten out."

More relieved than she should have been, she nodded. "How many groups do you have?"

"I usually have four," he answered, still seemingly distracted. "I teach the youngest kids, the beginners, in the morning. After lunch I have two groups of older kids, one intermediate and the other advanced."

"Are you still going to have them?"

He thought for a moment. "I don't know. Actually, until that text, I'd completely forgotten about them." He turned again, this time onto a very narrow, very rugged road. Jackie realized he clearly had a destination in mind.

A shiver snaked up her spine. What if he was taking her to where he'd killed Charla and Theo, to show her the bodies before he murdered her, too?

Chiding herself for her foolishness, nevertheless, Jackie resolved not to let him catch her unawares. She might not be good at fighting, especially if he had a gun, but she'd recently taken up running. She was fast and she had endurance going for her.

"What do you think?" he asked, still talking about the riding classes. "Should I cancel them?"

"No." Despite her trepidation, she managed to speak calmly. "What purpose would doing that serve? In fact, if you don't mind, I'd like to come watch one or two of the classes. It might help take my mind off things."

"I don't know. I feel like I should be doing more. Out searching or something. Though I know Rayna's a professional, and a damned good one, it feels weird to do nothing when my son and his mother are missing."

Absurdly grateful that he'd included her sister, she nodded. "I know that feeling very well." They hit a deep rut, sending both of them bouncing. "By the way, where are we going?"

"There's an overlook," he said. "Notice how we're going slightly uphill? When I first moved here, I discovered this place on one of my Sunday drives."

"What does it overlook?" she asked.

"You'll see," he replied.

At least he hadn't said something sinister, she thought. Still, she tried to remain alert, alternating between watching him and trying to notice landmarks in case she had to go on foot. Even though she knew her entire line of thought might be ridiculous, better safe than sorry.

"You still don't trust me, do you?" he asked, his voice casual.

Briefly, she debated how to respond, deciding to parry his question with one of her own. "Should I?"

"I didn't harm your sister," he replied. "Or my son."

An answer that really wasn't an answer.

One more turn, this time up a bit of an embankment, and he parked. Below them thousands of acres of farmland spread out. Along with a massive herd of longhorn cattle, roaming almost directly underneath.

Awestruck despite herself, she slowly got out of the truck and walked toward the highest point—a large, flat rock that made the perfect natural observation deck. He came up behind her and she tensed, remembering her earlier concerns.

"It's okay," he said quietly, a slight thread of humor in his voice. "I'm seriously not a murderer."

If her laugh sounded a bit nervous, he pretended not to notice.

He stood beside her, gazing at the majestic herd below. "If you're really that nervous, I can take you back to town."

With a sigh, she turned and looked at him. "I don't

know what to think about you, Eli Pitts. Statistically, when women disappear, it's usually the husband or boyfriend who caused them harm."

"I'm neither of those things," he pointed out.

"That's splitting hairs. Ex-husbands, too, I think."

He considered her, his cowboy hat putting his face into shadow. "You're forgetting that Charla had several boyfriends. And while your theory makes sense, I also find it terrifying that you think Charla—and Theo—might have come to harm."

"I don't think that," she protested, swinging around to face him. "It's just one of many possibilities. More than anything, I hope Rayna locates them safe and sound."

He nodded, averting his face from hers. She watched him, aware he could see her intense scrutiny, her thoughts in turmoil. The slightest movement of his shoulders, the way he swallowed hard, not once, not twice, but three times, made her freeze.

Was he...crying?

Surely not. But then again...she knew enough to give him privacy, pretend not to see. But she couldn't seem to make herself move. Instead, she fought the strangest urge to wrap her arms around him and offer comfort the only way she could—through touch.

Would he rebuff her clumsy attempt if she did? Would it be better if she turned away and went back to the truck? While her internal debate raged, Eli continued to keep his profile averted, his entire body rigid, a testament to his attempt at maintaining self-control.

She had to see, to know the truth. Reaching out,

she touched his arm, making him instinctively turn to look at her.

Silent tears made silver paths down his rugged cheeks, spilling from his eyes, though he'd compressed his mouth in a tight line to keep from crying out in his pain.

"Eli…" She went to him, meaning only to hug him, but somehow his mouth, salty with tears, ended up pressed against hers. Need, raw and urgent, blossomed, and she kissed him instead. Part of her wished she had the power to kiss away his pain; the other, more primal part, only wanted to deepen the kiss, to turn it into more. This man, who'd once loved her sister and undoubtedly loved his son, had inadvertently borne his soul to hers.

Aching for them both, she could only offer this small touch, and hope they could somehow find a temporary respite.

TURNING AWAY, ELI BLINKED, trying to figure out what exactly had just happened.

Damn it all to hell. Not only had he cried, something he'd only done one other time, at his father's funeral, but gorgeous Jackie Burkholdt, his ex-sister-in-law, had kissed him out of pity, too. Pity. Even worse, at a time when physical attraction should have been the last thing on his mind, he'd found himself wanting to deepen the kiss, aching for *more*.

Clearly, Jackie hadn't felt the same. In fact, he couldn't actually blame her if she thought less of him.

"I'm…" He struggled to find the right words. An

apology might be in order, but damned if he wanted to apologize for something that had felt so right.

"It's okay," she murmured, her color still high. "I understand how easy it is to get carried away by a distraction like that."

A distraction. Odd choice of words, but maybe actually accurate. Because she'd wanted him, too, if only for that brief moment in time.

"Let's go back," he said. "It'll be dark soon and I'd like to be back in town." Instinctively, he checked his phone, just in case Rayna might have texted something. The screen remained blank.

Jackie nodded, her gaze still averted. "I agree." She checked her own phone, frowning. "Great. Just great. Delia has texted six times and left two messages. All the texts are her demanding to know what's going on, so I'm sure the voice mails will be the same."

He grimaced, climbing back into the driver's seat and waiting while she got in and buckled herself in. Several times on the way back he almost mentioned the kiss, but decided in the end it would be simpler to pretend it had never happened.

They made it to the outskirts of town before she spoke. "We have to believe that Charla and Theo are all right."

He nodded. "I agree. Because the alternative is unthinkable." And unbearable. He thought of his son, the bright spark of joy in Theo's clear blue eyes, his unruly shock of blond hair, his ready smile and infectious laughter. This time he managed to swallow past the huge lump in his throat. Damned if he'd cry again in front of Jackie. "I just want my boy back."

"I'm with you on that," she replied. "The sooner, the better."

After dropping her off, Eli made his way home. Knowing Theo was supposed to be here made his house feel emptier than usual. He turned on the TV, but couldn't settle on anything to watch so he turned it off. He went outside, making his usual rounds to check on the livestock, making sure the chickens were all penned up in the coop and closing all the barn doors. Because it was spring, darkness came later and later, but by the time he'd finished, the moon had risen in the starry sky.

Back inside he ended up going for a run on his treadmill, something he hadn't felt the need to do in a good while since the ranch kept him so busy. Forty-five minutes later, drenched in sweat, he stopped. A huge glass of water, a quick cold shower, and he felt as if he might be able to get some sleep after all.

Saturday morning Eli managed to get out of bed at his usual time, took a hot shower and made himself a large mug of strong coffee. The first group of kids and their parents would be there soon for the first riding class and he needed to be both awake and alert. Some of them trailered in their own horses, while others rode several of his.

After scarfing down a bowl of instant oatmeal, Eli made a second cup of coffee and headed outside. He raked the arena, using his tractor and a specific blade, before going over to the barn. He had four young riders who'd be needing horses, so he gathered up his calmest, most reliable ones—two mares and two geldings—and got them saddled and ready, tying them to the post just outside the riding arena. Staying busy was one way of keeping his mind off worrying about Charla and Theo. Since he hadn't heard from Rayna, he figured he'd call in between the first riding class and the second, just to see of there'd been any new developments.

He checked his watch. People should start arriving any moment. In fact, squinting into the sunlight, he swore he saw a plume of dust making its way up his road.

As the car drew closer, he realized that instead of one of his students, Jackie had arrived.

Despite everything, his heart stuttered in his chest at the sight of her long jeans-clad legs swinging out of her car. She wore Western boots, he noticed, and had tied her long, dark hair up into a jaunty ponytail.

Stunning and sexy, he mused, before shutting that train of thought down. "Good morning," he called out, using the same pleasant tone he used with his young students and their parents.

"Mornin'." She smiled and waved, looking around at his tied-up, well-fed horses and the freshly raked arena. "This is really interesting to me. I can't wait to watch the lessons."

"Thanks." He managed a hopefully impersonal smile. "Do you ride?"

"No. I never learned. I always wanted to as a kid, but Mom was a single parent and money was too tight."

On the verge of offering to teach her, he made himself close his mouth. Once Charla and Theo were found, Jackie would be going back to New York.

Luckily, more of his students began to arrive. At 8:55 a.m., his entire class of eight-and nine-year-olds had assembled, along with their parents. As usual, the adults all clustered together alongside the arena rail. He couldn't help but notice the way they all glanced at Jackie, who stood slightly apart.

Not his problem, he told himself, beginning the lesson by having everyone ride at a brisk walk around the arena. He made gentle corrections on body position, urging one boy to loosen his grip on the reins, another girl to sit up straight with her shoulders back and her heels pointed down.

From the walk to a jog, also known as a trot. Some kids had been born with a natural seat, able to adjust comfortably to the horse's pace. Others, too stiff or rigid, bounced, their elbows flailing. He corrected those, too, taking care to toss out an equal number of compliments.

Finally, the lope. A controlled canter. Their glee palpable, the kids grinned. Some outright laughed. They loved this.

Eli grinned back. The hour was nearly over. He clapped his hands, ordering them all back to a walk. "Line up," he said.

Once they'd all ridden into the center and formed a line, he gave them all a short pep talk, complimenting their skills, before urging them to take their horses for a walk to cool down.

After the students had ridden off, as usual all the

parents surrounded him. Eli talked and joked around with them, ignoring one of the women's blatant flirtation attempts. All through this Jackie held herself apart, observing but not participating. More than one of the parents glanced her way, offering her a friendly smile, which she returned.

Eventually, the kids made their way back. Eli supervised the unsaddling of his horses and made sure the kids brushed out any sweat. Those who had brought their own mounts brushed out their horses, too. One thing Eli refused to allow was anyone who thought they could rush through taking care of the horses.

One of the women broke apart from the group and walked over to Jackie. Trying not to be too obvious, Eli kept an eye on them, just in case. The other woman hugged her and rejoined the group of other parents.

Right on time, everyone loaded up and left. He checked his watch, walking over to where Jackie still stood, her expression unreadable. "Well?" he asked. "What'd you think?"

"Pretty cool," she responded, raising her hand to smooth her hair. "Turns out one of the women I went to school with has a kid in your class." She grimaced. "That kind of makes me feel old."

This made him laugh. "Right."

She shook her head. "How long until your next class?"

"Just under an hour. I have to grab a couple of different horses for the kids who don't have their own. I don't like to use the same ones twice." He caught himself staring at her mouth, aching to kiss her again.

Talk about having absolutely no common sense. To cover, he checked his phone again. "Still no word from Rayna," he said.

Pressing her mouth into a straight line, she nodded. "I know. I can't seem to stop pulling out my phone. This waiting is driving me crazy. Even though it's been more than a few days..." She let her words trail off.

He understood exactly what she meant. Before, the worry had been only speculation. Now it was something more.

"Would you like some coffee?" he asked. She accepted his offer. They walked back to the house together. He grabbed yet another cup before telling her he had to get the horses ready. "But you're welcome to hang out here in the house if you want."

"If you don't mind, I'd like to come with you to the barn," she said, surprising him. "I haven't really spent a lot of time around horses, but I'd like to. Plus, I've got to keep busy or I think I might lose my mind."

"That I get," he said. "Follow me."

To his surprise, she stayed for the entire next hour of lessons, as well, continuing to keep herself apart from the group of parents, but watching everything intently. He couldn't help but notice every time she pulled out her phone and actually took a weird kind of comfort in knowing she'd let him know if anything changed.

This time, one or two of the parents asked him directly about Charla, since word had already traveled around the town. He deflected, keeping his answers vague, relying on saying mostly he felt sure Rayna would find her.

All the while, he kept the terror at bay, well aware if he let it get past his shield, it would kill him. Every thought of his son, the bright and beautiful boy, brought a physical pain that he simply couldn't allow. He couldn't speculate, refused to think the worst and told himself he had no choice but to believe Theo would be found safe and whole.

When the second class was nearly over, Jackie turned and walked off, disappearing inside his house. Several of the parents watched her go, their expressions ranging from curious to speculative.

Again, after class he sent the kids down the road to cool the horses off, bracing himself for the chat with the parents.

This time several asked about Jackie, one in particular a single dad named Jared. "New girlfriend?" he drawled. "She's a looker, that's for sure."

"She is," Eli agreed. "She's also Charla's sister, Jackie. Jackie's in town to help look for Charla."

Jared winced. "Sorry, man," he mumbled. "I completely forgot." Expression sheepish, he moved away, ostensibly to check on his daughter.

Finally, all the students and their parents left and he made his way back to his house, his stomach churning, making him realize he needed to eat something. As he let himself into his house, he spied Jackie in his kitchen.

"I hope you don't mind, but I made us some lunch," she said, her smile not matching the grim look in her eyes. "Just sandwiches, but I'm thinking we need to keep our strength up. For when, you know, Rayna calls."

He nodded. "Thanks, I appreciate that." He dropped

heavily into a chair at the table, eyeing the plate with a sandwich and chips that she slid in front of him.

Once she sat down across from him, they ate in a kind of bleak silence. He couldn't taste his food, but he managed to choke down the sandwich and most of the chips. "Thank you," he told her, noting she picked at her food. "I'm thinking about calling Rayna to check on things."

"I've been fighting the urge to do exactly that," she admitted. "But I've been...afraid."

He got that. "Because she said she'd call us and she hasn't. Which means she hasn't found out anything yet."

She nodded, her expression miserable. "It's Saturday. How much work does the sheriff do on the weekend?"

"You'd be surprised," he responded. "Especially in a situation like this with missing people. Rayna is really good at her job and takes everything very seriously. I imagine she and her people are out canvassing the town. Most people are home instead of at work, which makes it easier to ask questions."

"That makes sense," she admitted. "But even knowing this doesn't make my anxiety any less."

"Me neither," he admitted. He didn't tell her the various scenarios that had gone through his mind, each one worse than the next. All he could hope for was that none of them would turn out to be true. Charla had been known to be flighty. Maybe she'd taken Theo with her on some sort of vacation and had lost track of time.

Of course, that thought brought to mind images of Charla passed out drunk and some stranger taking off with his son. Better not to go that route at all. "I just hope they show up soon."

"Me, too," Jackie agreed. "Me, too."

Chapter Five

After watching Eli drive away, Jackie turned to go back to her motel room. But after a few steps, she stopped and reconsidered. She hadn't come all this way to sit around and do nothing. While she didn't want to interfere with Rayna's investigation, surely asking a few questions around town couldn't hurt.

With her decision made, she retraced her steps across the parking lot. Getaway had two main bars—the Rattlesnake Pub, where most of the older locals went, and The Bar, an ultra-modern drinking establishment specializing in craft beers and elaborate cocktails. While she figured her sister hung out mostly in the Pub, it wouldn't hurt to make a stop by The Bar and see if anyone there might know her.

Though she wasn't dressed stylishly enough, she figured her T-shirt, skinny jeans and boots would be okay enough to get her in the door at either place. Since so far all she'd heard about Charla's reputation had been worrisome, to say the least, she hoped she could find someone with a slightly different perspective.

Even though it was still relatively early, too early for

the evening crowd, the parking lot at The Bar had very few empty spots. It must be happy hour. She found one and parked, taking a deep breath before getting out of her car. Since The Bar had opened after she'd moved away, she'd never been inside this place. She'd only learned about it because she kept up an online subscription to the Getaway newspaper.

Once inside, she stopped for a minute to let her eyes adjust to the dim lighting. The minimalistic decor managed to be both chic and inviting, not an easy task. Turning in a slow circle, she realized with a sense of surprise that she felt as if she'd stepped into one of the trendy bars back in Manhattan.

Though most of the tables and booths were occupied, there were still a few empty bar stools, so she made her way to the dark wood-and-granite bar and slid up on one. She didn't see anyone she recognized. Most of the patrons appeared to be barely over legal drinking age.

A smiling bartender with a man bun came to take her order. She asked for a draft wheat beer, whatever kind they kept on tap. When he requested her ID, she smiled and passed her still-valid Texas driver's license over. Since she didn't drive in New York, she'd kept it.

One brow rose as he studied it, but he handed it back to her with a nod and went to get her beer. When he returned and slid a tall frosted glass across the bar to her, she showed him a screenshot she'd made from Charla's Instagram account. "Do you happen to know this woman?" she asked.

"Charla?" He grinned, which made him look even younger. "Sure. She's a regular, though she hasn't been around in a few weeks. She mostly liked to stop by after her shift at the jewelry store. She also works part-time at the Tumbleweed Café, so you might check there."

A few weeks. Disappointed, she took a sip of her beer. "I already tried that. I'm her sister and I'm just in town for a short time. I was hoping to see her while I'm here."

"Bummer." Looking past her, he scanned the room. "You might talk to that table over there, the six-top. Your sister hung out with them sometimes."

"Thank you." Grateful, she picked up her beer and headed over. The table of six had four men and two women. One of the men, a burly guy wearing a knit beanie and sporting a nose ring, watched her approach.

"Hi," she said, refusing to allow herself to feel awkward. "I'm looking for my sister, Charla, and the bartender mentioned y'all were her friends."

One of the women snorted. "I wouldn't say *friends*, exactly," she said. "Maybe more like frenemies."

"Speak for yourself," a man wearing round, wire-rimmed eyeglasses and a cotton shirt buttoned all the way to his collar reprimanded. "Charla is good people." He eyed Jackie, appearing to consider his next words. "But as I'm sure you know, Charla is missing. Everyone in town is talking about it. And Rayna—that's our sheriff—has already been by here asking if anyone knew anything."

"She has?" Impressed that Rayna clearly was on top of things, Jackie thanked them and turned to head back to the bar.

"Wait." The other woman, a slender waif with short,

wavy blond hair, stopped her. "Have you talked to Serenity? It might sound weird, but she knows things other people don't."

"I haven't, but that's a great idea." Serenity Rune, a self-styled psychic, ran a combination floral/metaphysical shop downtown. Jackie would try to swing by there soon, since she knew Serenity wasn't open on Sunday.

Back at the bar, Jackie asked for her tab. Once she'd settled that, leaving a few dollars for the bartender, she took one final sip of her beer and left.

Next stop, the Rattlesnake Pub. From experience, the Pub would be much louder, more raucous and likely full of people Jackie and Charla both had gone to school with.

There, with the lot already full, she had to park down the street. Getting out of the car, the loud thump of music escaped the building, making her realize it must be late enough that the live band the Pub always hired on Friday or Saturday night had already started.

Pushing through the door, she stepped inside. Just inside the door, a bouncer wearing a black cowboy hat, leather vest and boots stopped her, asking for her ID and a three-dollar cover charge.

"It's not even seven," she protested. "I'd think charging cover would start around nine. When did y'all start charging a cover charge, anyway?"

"We only do on Friday, Saturday and lately Sunday nights. That's when we have live music," he responded.

"That's new," she said, handing both over.

"Not really." He passed back her license and studied her face. "Your name sounds vaguely familiar, but I don't recognize your face."

"I've been away from town for a while," she admitted. "I'm Charla Burkholdt's older sister, Jackie."

He did a double take at that. "Wow. You two look nothing alike."

Jackie had heard this her entire life. Not only was Charla blonde and Jackie brunette, but Jackie was tall and lean while Charla short and curvy. "True. Anyway, I'm trying to find my sister. I was hoping maybe some of her friends here might have an idea where she might have gone."

He shook his head. "Everyone in town is wondering where she up and disappeared to. Rumors are flying like crazy. Anyway, the sheriff was here earlier asking around. You might talk to her and save yourself some time."

Wow. Rayna continued to impress her. Jackie nodded. "Thanks. That makes a lot of sense. Since I'm already here, I might as well have a drink and look around."

"Knock yourself out." A group of people came through the door and he turned his attention on them, leaving Jackie to make her way inside.

Inside, everything looked just the way she remembered it. In keeping with its name, the Rattlesnake Pub had been decorated in a Western theme. Old black-and-white photos of popular country music artists adorned the walls. It had occupied this building for as long as Jackie could remember.

The main part of the Pub had zero empty tables

and a lot of people milling around with drinks in their hands. Jackie headed straight for the long bar on the right side, even though she could see there were no bar stools available and people stood three deep in line waiting to order drinks. If it got this crowded so early on a Sunday night, Jackie didn't like to think about what it must be like on Friday or Saturday.

Then she caught sight of a poster advertising the musical act tonight and understood. A very famous and very popular country music singer would be performing tonight. Often some of the greats liked to make pit stops in small Texas towns, and Getaway often made that list. In view of this, three dollars as a cover charge wasn't nearly enough. This crowd must have come from Abilene and all the small towns in between.

Well, Jackie thought, maybe someone in this crowd might have more insight as to where Charla could be.

Deciding to circulate instead of getting a drink, Jackie wove her way through throngs of people, searching for a familiar face. If she was completely honest with herself, she inexplicably hoped to find Charla here, beer in hand, laughing with her friends over some stupid joke. Which made no sense, but she couldn't shake the feeling.

Though she had to have grown up with at least some of these people, Jackie didn't see anyone she recognized. Then a woman at one of the tables glanced up and did a double take while Jackie tried to place her. The woman pushed to her feet and hurried over, walking confidently despite wearing what had to be at least four-inch heels. "Jackie Burkholdt? Wow! Long time, no see."

Staring, Jackie scrambled to remember the woman's name. Finally, it came to her. "Pam Milan?" Jackie had been off-and-on friends with her in high school. They embraced, Pam's strong perfume almost making Jackie sneeze.

"I heard you were in town," Pam exclaimed, tugging at her arm. "Come sit with us. Have you had any luck locating your sister?"

"Not yet." Having to lean close to be heard over the noise, Jackie's nose twitched at the strong perfume.

"Come on, come on," Pam insisted. Jackie followed the other woman over to the already crowded table. Someone grabbed a spare chair and pulled it up. "Sit, sit."

"Thanks." Now Jackie recognized a couple of the others, one or two of them former classmates. If she remembered right, the stocky man with the receding hairline had also gone to Tech, where he'd played football. She didn't remember much about him other than that. And the woman with the super-short chic hairstyle had been on the drill team.

Pam performed introductions. A few of the others were several years younger, which explained why Jackie hadn't recognized them. Two people were from the next town over. When Jackie asked, she learned none of them had even talked to Charla lately and most of them didn't even know her. Most of the conversation centered on the country music star performing tonight.

After a couple of minutes, Jackie pushed to her feet

and excused herself, saying she really needed to ask around about her sister. Pam waved goodbye, hollering at her to stay in touch. Jackie responded with a vague wave of her hand, moving back into the even more crowded room.

This time, instead of waiting in line at the bar for a drink that she didn't really want, Jackie decided to make her way through the room and look for people she might recognize as friends of her sister's. At first, she didn't see anyone, but then as she neared the dance floor area, she spotted Bobbi Jo Fleming, who'd once been one of Charla's closest friends. Bobbi Jo kept her straight, shoulder-length hair platinum and favored large, gaudy jewelry and short, tight skirts.

Laughing with a drink in one hand, Bobbi Jo's expression changed when Jackie made eye contact with her. She blinked her obviously false eyelashes and set her drink down on the table as she stood. "Jackie? Is that really you?"

"Yes, it is. It's great to see you." Jackie moved closer and they made small talk as best as they could over the noise. Unfortunately, that meant they had to stand uncomfortably close, and like Pam, Bobbi Jo also applied her perfume liberally. Though Jackie tried not to inhale, her eyes began to water. Quickly, she asked about her sister.

"I heard you were here looking for Charla," Bobbi Jo drawled. "I'll tell you up front I don't have any idea where that girl got off to. She seemed to have finally gotten her act together, being a mom and all. Until last Saturday night, when both her boyfriends showed up here at the same time and got into a huge fight." She rolled her heavily made-up eyes. "It got so bad they were all kicked out. Charla took that hard. This is her bar, you know. She loves this place, calls it her home away from home. Her ex had to come pick her up. After that, no one has seen or heard from her."

Her ex. Eli. Once again, he appeared to have been the last person to see her sister.

Jackie chatted with Bobbi Jo a few more minutes before excusing herself and moving on. After three complete circles around the room, weaving in between groups of people, she decided to leave the Pub and go back to her motel room to get some sleep. She planned to be up bright and early in the morning to keep trying to locate her sister, though she hadn't been able to make an actual plan. In a town as small at Getaway, there were only a few options. Once those had been exhausted, she wasn't sure where else she could look or what else she could do. She tried to take some comfort from the fact that Rayna appeared to be on top of things.

Her thoughts kept returning to Eli. On the way back to the motel, she stopped and got a salad at the burger place, since she couldn't remember when she'd last eaten. It tasted surprisingly good, and she devoured it, along with another cup of her wine. She wondered how Eli was coping and reached for her phone half a dozen times to call him. In the end, she decided not to disturb him, just in case he'd actually managed to get some rest.

That night, she slept poorly, her sleep interrupted by horrible dreams featuring her sister and the nephew she hadn't even met yet.

Finally, sometime after midnight and two hours of tossing and turning, she fell into a deeper sleep. When she opened her eyes again, sunlight beamed through the space in between the curtains, and a quick glance at her phone revealed it was nearly seven. She rushed through her shower, applying minimal makeup and putting her hair in a ponytail before dressing in a comfy pair of jeans and a T-shirt. She slipped on her favorite running shoes, since she figured she'd spend most of the day on her feet.

Her phone chirped just as she'd grabbed her car keys to head out. A text from Eli.

I'm headed to the sheriff's office, it said. In case you want to meet me there.

Yes, she sent back. On my way.

She arrived at the sheriff's office just before he did. She'd gotten out of her car when she saw his truck pull into the lot. Waiting while he parked, she felt her heart jolt a little at the sight of him striding toward her, well-worn jeans slung low on his narrow hips, a gray cowboy hat on top of his head.

"Mornin'," he greeted her, his gaze weary. "I hope you slept better than I did."

"Probably not. I'm really worried," she confessed. "As I'm sure you must be. I stopped by both The Bar and the Rattlesnake Pub last night and asked around about Charla. Rayna had already been there, so she's definitely doing due diligence."

After removing his hat, he used his fingers to comb out his hair. "That's good. Let's see if she has time to talk to us and tell us what she's learned, if anything."

Inside, they once again found Rayna digging through paperwork on the front desk. She looked up when they entered, smoothing away her frown when she saw them. "Hey, you two," she said. "Come on back to my office."

As they followed her through the main area, Jackie couldn't help but hope this meant she had something substantive to tell them. A quick glance at Eli revealed a similar hopeful expression.

Once they were all in, she closed the door and walked around behind her desk. "Take a seat," she said, though she remained standing behind her desk. "I'm afraid I have some bad news."

Jackie gasped. Eli gave her a stricken look, before swallowing hard. "What is it?" he asked. "Did you find Charla?"

"No." Rayna looked from one to the other, wincing. "I'm sorry. I should have been more careful with my choice of words. I've gotten some more information that might explain why Charla took off."

"Do you really think that's what she's done?" Jackie asked, still trying to regain her equilibrium. "Taken off?"

"It's possible. Christopher Levine was already in to see me," Rayna said, the downward turn of her mouth letting them know it hadn't been pleasant. "He says his books are off. Way, way off. As you may know, Charla acted as his bookkeeper."

To Jackie's shock, Eli rolled his eyes and made a dismissive sound. "The two of them were also having an affair. If his books are off, I guarantee he had something to do with it."

"An affair?" Jackie couldn't believe it. "Charla has known Christopher Levine since she was a senior in high school. Not only is he a lot older than her, but he's married." Even as she spoke, she remembered her sister showing off diamond earrings and necklaces, jewelry she'd supposedly purchased using her employee discount. Now she had to wonder if they'd been gifts from the jewelry store owner.

Rayna said nothing, her gaze alternating between Eli and Jackie, clearly waiting to hear them out.

"Yes, an affair." Eli shrugged. "Apparently, it was going on before she met me, though Charla claimed it was over a few months before we started dating. Strictly platonic, she said. Until it wasn't. She said they resumed the relationship sometime shortly after our son was born." He glanced at Jackie. "I didn't find out until after she asked for a divorce, just in case you're wondering."

Swallowing, Jackie nodded. She felt numb. If this was true, then she had to wonder if Charla had really been embezzling from Levine's. She had to wonder why. What the heck was wrong with her sister?

"Do you have proof?" Rayna finally asked. "I'm talking about your theory on the books. Because if you do, I need it quickly. Christopher wants to press charges."

"Against Charla?" Still reeling from the accusations of Charla having a long affair with a much older man, Jackie struggled to keep up. "I don't understand."

"Embezzling." Rayna's crisp reply. "According to Mr. Levine, your sister may have made off with a large sum of money over time. Not to mention various items out of his storeroom stock."

"In other words, stealing money and jewelry," Eli said, his expression impassive.

"Why? Why would Charla do something like that?" Jackie asked, feeling sick. "She's worked at Levine's since high school. She was very proud of that. She also worked at the café, and took care of her son. Why on earth would she jeopardize her entire life like that?"

"Maybe she felt like Christopher Levine owed her for something?" The ache in Eli's tired voice made Jackie want to slip her hand into his. "Anyway, isn't the burden of proof on him?"

"It is," Rayna agreed. "Though honestly, from the way he was talking, he's got quite a bit of evidence proving his claim. He's getting all of that together and bringing it by in about an hour."

"Meanwhile," Jackie said, "Charla's still missing."

"And Theo," Eli added.

Rayna nodded, tapping her pencil on a manila folder. "I think at this point we have to consider the possibility that she might have left of her own accord."

Not again. Despite beginning to feel as if she might never have known her sister, Jackie felt obligated to mention the text. "Remember, she said she felt as if her life was in danger. Maybe that had something to do with this." She took a deep breath. "I have to think only pure desperation would make her steal from Levine's."

Eli gave her a skeptical look, but didn't comment.

Rayna considered her words for a moment. "Whatever her motive might have been, that wouldn't make this any less of a crime. If Mr. Levine's claims turn out to be true, once we find Charla, we'll have no choice but to arrest her."

Though Jackie nodded, hearing this hit her hard. "I'll have to tell my mother," she said, wincing as she imagined Delia's reaction.

"I'm sorry." Rayna reached across her desk and touched Jackie's arm. "I wish Charla would come back and help clear all this up. But she won't—or can't—so there's that."

"Can you search her apartment?" Jackie asked. "Maybe if she left a laptop behind, or has a computer, you could find some hint on it."

"We can't do anything without a warrant," Rayna replied. "Once Mr. Levine presses charges, we shouldn't have any difficulty obtaining one."

"A warrant," Jackie echoed, hardly able to believe what she was hearing.

Shaking his head, Eli looked from one woman to the other. "If Charla did take off on her own accord, and I agree that now it's entirely possible she did, she would never be that careless. But most importantly, what about my son? I'm still worried about him, and I consider him to be in danger, no matter what the reason for their disappearance."

"I understand." Rayna stood. "And I promise to keep you both posted if anything new develops. Now, if you'll excuse me, I have to get ready to meet with Christopher Levine."

Jackie pushed to her feet. Next to her, Eli did the

same. "Thank you," she said. "Please continue to keep me informed."

"Us," Eli corrected. He took Jackie's arm and rather than make a scene, she let him. At least until they cleared the doorway, when she gently tugged herself free, walking ahead of him all the way outside. He walked her to her car, waiting to speak until she'd pressed the key fob to unlock the doors.

"What, are we enemies now?" he asked.

Coolly, she turned. "I'm not sure what you mean. We barely know each other." Truth, even though when they were together she honestly felt as if she'd known him forever.

Evidently, he shared that sentiment. "Come on, Jackie. It's just me. What's going on?"

Fine. "You appeared awfully ready to believe that Charla could be a criminal."

"You don't?"

Staring at him, she struggled to find the right way to respond. In the end, she settled on truth. "I don't know. But ever since I've been back in town, I've learned one bad thing after another about Charla. I mean, I always knew Mom spoiled her—I did, too—but she wasn't an awful person."

"I know," he agreed. "We're all complicated."

Was that a warning? She narrowed her eyes, unsure how to respond.

Before she could, he leaned in and kissed her. A hard press of his mouth against hers, sending liquid fire right through her veins. Her gasp had her opening her mouth to him, and she mentally said the hell with it and kissed him back, right there in the sheriff's department parking lot, for all the world to see.

ELI WASN'T SURE WHY—maybe it was the vulnerability in Jackie's amber eyes—but he leaned in for what he intended to be a quick kiss. Just a press of his lips on hers, maybe for reassurance or some other reason he didn't want to think too deeply about.

However, the instant their mouths touched, all self-control went up in a blaze of heat. To his stunned shock, she yanked him closer, until he pinned her with her back pressed up against her car, and kissed him as if she wanted much, much more.

Only the sound of a car honking its horn in the street made him come to his senses and break away.

They stared at each other for a moment, both breathing heavily, her mouth slightly puffy, making him ache to kiss her again.

He started to apologize but realized he would never be sorry for a kiss like that, so he settled for quick nod and turned away. So aroused he could barely walk, he felt her gaze on him the entire time he made his way back to his truck.

Damn.

Only once he'd driven off did he allow himself to think about what had just happened. If he knew this town—and he did—news of his and Jackie's kiss would be all over Getaway by dinnertime. For himself, he didn't worry too much, but he could imagine Delia's reaction to learning her daughter had been kissing her favorite other daughter's ex. It wouldn't be good. In fact, he imagined it would be spectacularly awful.

For him, that kiss had been worth it. For her… He wondered what Jackie thought. Even though they barely knew each other, he wanted her. From her sensual reaction, he believed she felt the same way. However, even he understood what a huge mistake giving in to that desire would be in the middle of all this. Now was definitely not the time to be worrying about his libido. His focus needed to be on finding his son and bringing him home safe. End of subject. Since the monumental mistake he'd made with Charla, he'd prided himself on his self-control. He needed to call upon every ounce of it now.

Thus fortified, he drove home. Rayna had seemed quite certain that Christopher Levine had a good case that Charla had not only embezzled from his store, but had stolen precious gems, too. Shockingly, the idea that Charla could have stolen from her employer barely surprised him. He'd realized some time ago that he'd never really known her. The things she'd done since the moment he'd met her, and her complete and utter lack of remorse, meant anything was possible.

In fact, if she'd gotten away with a significant amount of money, he'd bet she'd taken Theo and escaped to some tropical beach. She'd always talked about living in the Caribbean. If he had even the slightest idea what island she'd gone to, he'd hop a plane himself and hunt her down.

The only thing that gave him pause was the weird text she'd sent Jackie. She hadn't contacted him or

Delia, but her estranged sister. He didn't understand the logic behind that, but since Charla never did anything without a reason, he knew there had to be one. He just had to figure out what it might be.

Now once again his thoughts had circled right back around to Jackie. She truly worried over her sister and appeared to be having a difficult time adapting to hearing the truth about her. Had Charla really changed that much in three short years? Somehow, he doubted that.

Since he had plenty of work to do on the farm, he drove back there. Recently, he'd taken in two young geldings to train, one as a cutting horse, the other for the client's daughter to show in stock seat equitation. He knew if he could train even one successful cutting horse, his reputation would be made and he'd have a waiting list of people wanting to bring their horses to him. His current financial woes would be over.

Working with the first horse, a flashy sorrel quarter horse called Ro, he let himself get lost in the movements. Focusing on the animal drove everything else out of his mind. When he made the connection with a horse, magic happened. This, a gift he'd recognized ever since he'd been a young boy, had made him realize what direction his life had to take. Other people found magic in numbers and became accountants; those with a gift of words, authors. He'd been born to train horses and had worked his fingers to the bone in his corporate job in Houston to save enough money to buy the small ranch here in rural west Texas, where property sold for much less than it did in areas near big cities.

As soon as Theo was old enough, he planned to teach

his son to ride. He wanted to see if his boy had inherited his gift with horses.

Theo. Mingled anger, worry and sorrow filled him, which he quickly pushed away. Still, the horse underneath him faltered in his stride, clearly sensing some of his rider's unrest.

Eli got his mind back on track and finished the training session. As he unsaddled the gelding, he put him on the hot walker to cool him down while he went to get the other horse.

By the time he finished with both horses, after brushing them out and returning them to their stalls, he realized he'd managed to skip lunch. He returned to the house, made himself a quick sandwich and checked his phone. A text from Rayna confirmed what he'd already guessed to be true. Charla was a thief and had most likely gone on the run.

With his son.

He supposed he should be glad that would mean Theo wasn't in any danger, but Charla had single-handedly wrecked his entire world in one fell swoop. The worst of it was that he still didn't entirely understand why she would do such a thing. They hadn't been good married, but he believed they got along just fine as co-parents.

He saw a notification for a missed call. Jackie's number. She'd also left him a voice mail. After hesitating, he finally played it back. She'd simply asked him to call her. No doubt because she'd received the same text from Rayna.

Leaving his phone in the kitchen, he walked down

the hallway to Theo's room, with its race-car bed and football-shaped toy box full of toys. The room sat untouched between visits, though Eli kept fresh sheets on the bed.

Eli stood in the doorway, finally allowing anger to fill him. Only once before in his life had he felt this furious sort of helplessness—when he'd lost his bid for joint custody of his son. This situation, while in its own way worse, brought about the same urge to do something, *anything*, but he was unsure of what. He needed to find his son. But he had no idea where to start looking.

Chapter Six

Jackie read the message again and again. Rayna's text had been short and to the point.

After reviewing the evidence provided by Mr. Levine, we have issued a warrant for Charla's arrest.

She'd sent it to both Jackie and to Eli.

Which meant Charla was a thief. Jackie sat for a moment, staring at her phone with a lump in her throat and a knot in her chest. She couldn't help but wonder how Eli had reacted when he'd received it. Because this new information made it likely that Charla had taken off on her own with Theo.

The only anomaly had been the text Charla had sent Jackie. Why claim to be in danger? And why involve Jackie at all? Though bringing it up so often made Jackie feel as if she was beating an already dead horse, she couldn't let go of the very real fear she'd sensed in her sister's message.

Had Christopher Levine found out about her embezzling and gone after her? Or had she been using someone—one of her other boyfriends perhaps—to fence the stolen jewelry and things had gone sideways?

Jackie sighed. Either way, now Charla had a warrant for her arrest. Time to call her mother. She'd put it off as long as she could. While she knew news like this should probably be delivered in person, she felt safer talking to Delia on the phone. She had an idea her mother's reaction wouldn't be pretty.

Taking a deep breath, she figured she might as well get it over with. Otherwise, if Delia heard from the Getaway grapevine before Jackie got a chance to tell her, there'd be even more hell to pay.

Delia answered on the second ring. "Do you have news of your sister?" she demanded, forgoing any type of greeting or pleasantries at all.

"Sort of." Speaking quickly, she filled her mother in on everything Rayna had said, including her recent text.

When she'd finished, Delia's unusual silence felt unnerving.

"Oh, no," Delia finally said, her voice quivering. "That would certainly explain how she could afford all the extravagant jewelry gifts she gave me over the years. She told me she had a huge employee discount."

Stunned, Jackie wasn't sure how to respond.

"I wonder if I take everything and return it to Levine's, if Christopher will drop the charges," Delia continued. "It's worth a shot."

"Mom, I think there was a lot more involved than just a few pieces of jewelry," Jackie said, still cautious. "While Rayna didn't give an amount, it appears Charla has been embezzling money from the store for years."

Again, Delia went quiet. When she finally spoke, her response lacked conviction. "She wouldn't do that. Would she?"

Jackie didn't have an answer for that. But she did have a few questions. "Mom, if Charla were to escape somewhere, to some tropical island or something, where do you think she'd go?"

"How would I know?" Now Delia let her frustration show. "She was always talking about taking a beach vacation. Maybe the Bahamas or Jamaica. But I refuse to believe she'd run away without at least saying goodbye to me."

Before Jackie could say anything else, Delia said a quick goodbye and ended the call. At least her mother hadn't yet heard any gossip about Eli and Jackie kissing. When that happened, and it would, Jackie figured there'd be hell to pay.

Before she could think too much about it, Jackie called Eli. The call went to voice mail, making her wonder if he'd be avoiding her now. Ignoring the pang in her heart at the thought, she left a brief message, asking him to call her. She couldn't stop thinking about him, not only about that kiss, but about the raw vulnerability he'd allowed her to see.

Restless, tired of being confined to a small hotel room, Jackie decided to go out instead of turning in for the night. While mostly to keep from letting boredom drive her up a wall, she also figured she could see if there were any other people there who might know Charla.

Decision made, she quickly applied her makeup and

then grabbed her favorite pair of trendy torn jeans, high-heeled shoes and a low-cut blouse. Since this outfit was one of her standard choices, she'd brought the jewelry she always wore with it—black dangly earrings shaped to look like feathers, a silver necklace that nestled perfectly in her cleavage and several bracelets on one arm. Satisfied after checking her appearance in the mirror, she got into her car and drove to the Rattlesnake.

As she pulled into the packed parking lot, she could hear the steady thump of the band's bass. At nearly ten, the Pub's crowd appeared to be partying in full swing and she only found a spot because someone else happened to back out.

She paid her cover charge and allowed them to stamp the back of her hand. Once inside she could barely squeeze past a large group of people who had apparently been unable to find seats, so had decided to stand close to the exit.

Immediately, Jackie headed for the bar and got in line. When her turn finally came to order, instead of her usual beer or wine, she asked for a large margarita. If she remembered right, they were good here.

Then, drink in hand, she began to circulate the room.

A woman eyed her as she walked past. "Wait," she said, touching Jackie's arm. "Aren't you Charla's older sister?"

Wondering if she'd ever get used to the efficiency of the gossip in Getaway, Jackie nodded. "I am."

"I'm Marissa, one of Charla's friends," Marissa explained. She wore her jet-black hair in a short, trendy cut and used heavy black eyeliner to outline her eyes. "I heard you were in town looking for her."

"I don't suppose you've talked to her or seen her lately?"

"No." Marissa took a long drink of her wine. "Rayna has already been around, asking questions. Maybe you should talk to her."

"I have. I just feel like there's no harm in talking to people myself. Plus, I needed to get out of that hotel room," Jackie admitted.

"The Landshark?" Horror echoed in the other woman's voice.

"Yep."

"I feel ya. Anyway, check out that guy over there playing pool." Marissa jerked her head to indicate. "He was one of the guys Charla dated."

Eyeing the burly man wearing biker's leathers, Jackie's eyes widened. "Was he one of the guys who got into a fight over her?"

"I think so." Marissa went back to sipping her drink. "Though if he was, they kicked him out. I'm not sure how he managed to get back in."

"Different bouncer, no doubt," Jackie said absently. "I'm going to go talk to him."

"Are you sure that's wise?" Though a stranger, concern echoed in Marissa's voice. One of her friends, who'd been silently observing the conversation, voiced her agreement.

"Normally, I'd be a bit apprehensive," Jackie admitted. "But this is a crowded bar. I should be safe here."

Marissa shrugged and turned away.

Jackie took a deep sip of her margarita and strode over to the pool table. She watched while the man took his shot. When he'd finished, she summoned up a smile and asked him if she could talk to him a minute.

"Honey, I can do more than that." He moved closer, too close. When Jackie took a step back to get away from him, she bumped into another man. Apologizing, she managed to maneuver herself into what looked like a safe spot.

Unfortunately, the band chose that moment to launch into a loud, raunchy song that had most of the bar singing along. Aware there was no way this man would be able to hear her from any sort of distance, Jackie moved a tiny bit closer than she felt was wise. "I'm Charla's sister," she said, looking up to find him staring down her shirt.

He smirked as he let his gaze travel slowly back up to her face. "You don't look like her."

"I know. I get that a lot." Hoping the band would soon settle down, she indicated the pool table. "I think it's your turn."

To her relief, he took his cue and went back to studying the table. He made several shots in rapid succession, clearing all of the solids from the table. "Pay up, Joe," he ordered, holding out his hand. His opponent, the hapless Joe, who looked as if he was three sheets to the wind, dug out a twenty from his pocket and handed it over.

"Now, where were we?" big biker dude asked her. As he leaned in close, she got a whiff of strong whiskey and cigarettes. "I'm Scott, by the way. Oh, I know.

You were about to show me if you can kiss as good as your sister."

"No, no, I wasn't," Jackie replied emphatically. "I just wanted to ask you if you happened to have any idea where Charla might be."

Ignoring both her refusal and her question, Scott lunged for her, hauling her up against him and pressing the full length of his large body against her. Furious and scared, she tossed the contents of her glass on him, coating the front of him with margarita.

Instead of deterring him, if anything, this appeared to spur him on. "Oh, so you like it rough, do you?" He pushed her hard, slamming her back into the wall.

Disbelieving, she looked around for help. To her shock, no one seemed to be paying them the slightest attention.

"Get. Away. From. Me," she ordered, teeth clenched. "I mean it. Don't touch me!" This last, she shouted. But with the band playing the raucous chorus, they drowned her out.

Except he heard. He had to. Because the glint in his bloodshot eyes turned mean. He used his big hands to pin her shoulders against the wall.

Desperate, she brought her knee up, hard. But somehow, he managed to block her. He swooped in, about to plant his wet lips on hers, when suddenly someone jerked him off her.

"Leave her alone."

Eli. Grateful, Jackie moved away from Scott, who turned unsteadily to face Eli.

"Mind your own damn business," Scott snarled, bringing up his fists.

Eli stood his ground. "Jackie," he said without taking his eyes off the larger man. "Go ahead and move away. There are bouncers near the door. Go get one of them and send him over here."

Heart pounding, Jackie hurried away to do as he'd requested. She spotted a man who looked as if he might be a bouncer and tugged on his arm. He bent down so he could hear her. Quickly, she told him what was going on. "Over by the pool tables."

With him leading the way, they pushed through the crowd, arriving just in time to see Eli sidestep as Scott swung at him, before landing his own punch on Scott's chin.

Though Scott staggered, he didn't go down. Instead, he hauled off and managed to get a blow in on Eli's eye. Eli staggered backward, but launched himself at Scott again, shoving the larger man backward into the pool table, sending balls flying.

By now, people had begun to notice and a crowd had formed.

"Break it up," the bouncer ordered, pushing his way through and grabbing a hold of Scott. Unwisely, Scott swung at him, and the bouncer clocked him hard, knocking him down. But not out. He lurched back up to his feet.

The band, apparently catching wind of all this, stopped playing. By now, the entire bar seemed to be craning their necks to see what was going on.

Meanwhile, Scott continued to curse and swing

wildly, his eyes bulging, looking for all the world like an enraged grizzly bear.

A second bouncer joined the first and together, they managed to subdue Scott, who continued cursing at them. Jackie rushed over to Eli. His eye had already started swelling. With a muscle working in his jaw, he seemed furious.

"The police are on their way," someone said. "And probably an ambulance."

"He started it," Scott shouted, struggling to break free of the two bouncers. "I want to press charges for assault."

Jackie spun around. "You tried to feel me up and kiss me, despite me telling you no. He *defended* me from you. And if anyone is going to press charges, it will be me."

"Come on," one of the bouncers said, herding Scott away. "You can tell it all to the police."

The second bouncer stayed with Jackie and Eli. "Don't worry," he said. "That guy Scott is a known troublemaker. Plus, we have cameras on the pool area, so I'm sure we have everything on film."

Jackie nodded. "Can I get some ice for his eye?" she asked. One of the waitresses, hearing her request, went to the bartender and returned with some wrapped up in a dish towel.

When Jackie pressed it to his eye, Eli winced. "I've seen that guy before," he said. "I think he might have dated Charla."

"He did, or so I was told," Jackie replied. "That's why I tried to talk to him in the first place."

The band started up again and everyone returned to what they'd been doing.

"Come on back with me," the bouncer ordered. "The police will come and talk to you there. It's much quieter."

A few minutes later two police officers entered the back room with an EMT in tow. "Go ahead and check him out," one of the officers gestured to the EMT before turning to Jackie. "We'll go ahead and take your statement, ma'am."

Jackie told them exactly what had happened and why. When she'd finished, he nodded.

The EMT finished taking Eli's blood pressure.

"And you, sir?" the officer asked Eli. "Do you concur with her version of events?"

"Yes." Eli met Jackie's gaze. "I'm not a violent man," he muttered. "But I will fight to defend someone I—" he glanced at Jackie and swallowed "—care about."

Jackie's heart stuttered. Had he been about to say *loved*?

Meanwhile, the EMT nodded, using a penlight to check Eli's pupils. "I get it." He wrote something down and then stood. "Looks like you're okay to go. Put some ice on that eye and take ibuprofen every six hours."

Eli nodded, wincing slightly at the movement.

"I'll take care of him," Jackie volunteered. Eli shot her a grateful look.

"Good. You do that," the EMT said and walked off.

"We'll be in touch." The police officer nodded to his partner. "You are free to go."

"Let's get you home." Jackie took his arm. "We can pick up your truck tomorrow."

He let her lead him to her car and help him into the passenger seat. "You know, I can probably drive my truck."

"Maybe." She gave him a soft smile. "But let's not take any chances. I'm sure your truck will be fine until the morning. I'll drive you back over to pick it up."

Finally, he gave a weary nod. "Okay."

"What were you doing in the Rattlesnake anyway?" she asked, pulling out onto Main Street.

"Probably the same thing as you," he replied, eyes closed. "I couldn't sleep and thought it might be nice to get out and have a drink. I got your message and thought I'd call you back in the morning. If I'd known you were awake, I would have asked you to join me. Next time, I'll ask."

Next time. The simple statement gave her a visceral thrill. Foolish, she told herself. But still, she couldn't keep from smiling. "I assume you got Rayna's text," she began, but a quick glance over at Eli revealed he'd fallen asleep. Or was, like her mother used to say, just resting his eyes. She couldn't tell very well in the dim light, but she'd bet he'd have a hell of a shiner in the morning.

As she pulled up in front of his ranch, he woke, his hand instinctively going to touch his eye. "Ouch," he said.

"We'll put some ice on it as soon as we get inside." After turning off the engine, she got out and went around to his side, intending to open the door for him. But by the time she got there, he was already out.

"Thanks, but I'm okay," he said when she held out her arm just in case he needed the support. Figuring his male pride might be stung, she nodded and simply fell into step beside him.

As he unlocked the front door, she wondered if he would ask her in or send her away.

ELI HURT FAR more than he wanted Jackie to know. Not just his eye, but his pride. When he'd seen that drunk jerk pin her up against the wall, he'd seen red. He'd rushed over, his only thought the need to get that guy off her. The fact that the other man outweighed him by at least seventy-five pounds hadn't mattered.

Instead, it had taken two bouncers to bring the guy down. No shame in that, he told himself. Yet, he still felt as if he'd somehow failed her. And the way she hovered over him, as if she thought he'd collapse at any moment, didn't make him feel any better.

Five steps inside his house and he turned to face her. Silhouetted by the front porch light, she appeared achingly beautiful and fragile. "I'm sorry," he said. "I should have been able to protect you."

"That's what you're worried about?" she asked, slipping inside and bumping the front door closed. She wrapped her arms around him, holding on tight. "If you only knew how it felt, having you rush to my aid. No one has ever done that for me."

No one. Not just no man, but no one. This made him wonder what her childhood must have been like, living with two narcissists like Delia and Charla.

Unable to resist the soft shape of her body pressed

against him, he held her, breathing in the sweet scent of her hair. He ached to tell her how he'd begun to feel about her, but he knew the timing wasn't right. He didn't know if it ever would be.

Finally, she released him. "Let's get some ice on that eye," she said, her voice brisk.

In the kitchen, she pulled a bag of peas from the freezer and handed it to him.

Accepting it, he sank into one of the kitchen chairs and pressed it to his eye. "You don't have to stay if you don't want to," he said.

Hands on hips, she regarded him, her dark eyes shadowed. "Are you asking me to leave?"

He decided to be honest. "No. I'm only giving you your options. Don't feel you have to watch over me out of pity."

"Pity? Is that truly what you think I feel?"

Now he felt like a jerk. "I'm not sure of anything at this point," he said softly. "Everything is off kilter. Just pretend I didn't say that, okay?"

Instead of responding, she crossed the room and gently took the frozen peas away from his face, placing them on the table. Then, straddling him, she leaned in close. "Let me show you exactly how I feel."

Then she kissed him. It wasn't a gentle press of her mouth on his, but instead, a fierce, raw claim of possession. His body instantly responded as they opened their mouths to each other. She laughed when she felt the strength of his arousal pressing against her. Then, gaze locked on his, she began to move against him, still fully clothed. The friction, unbelievably sensuous, nearly had him losing all control.

"We can't," he gasped, though damned if he could think of a good reason why. Then he remembered. "No condoms. I, er, haven't exactly had a reason to buy any."

"That's okay," she breathed. "We can still have fun with our clothes on." And she proceeded to show him exactly how.

After, with her body still trembling, she stayed where she was, just hanging on to him. He couldn't believe it—he hadn't done anything like this since he'd been a teenager—and even then the release hadn't been nearly as powerful.

This woman. He smoothed her hair away from her face, placing a soft kiss on her temple, which made her smile. "Come on," he finally said. "Let's get cleaned up and get some rest. We can talk about Rayna's text in the morning."

"I should go." Moving awkwardly, she climbed off him and disappeared into the bathroom.

While she was gone, he grabbed the frozen peas and put them back on his eye. Damn, she confused and delighted him. He'd never met a woman like her and doubted he would again.

A moment later she returned. She'd smoothed down her formerly disheveled hair, though her swollen lips revealed her to be someone who'd just been thoroughly kissed. "We'll talk tomorrow. I'll come by and take you to get your truck. How about nine?"

Distracted, he managed to nod.

"I'll let myself out," she told him, and left as quickly

as if she thought he might chase after her and beg her to stay.

Bemused, he locked up and jumped into the shower to clean up.

The next morning he woke up and winced when he touched his eye. A quick glance in the mirror proved Jackie's prediction had come true. He looked like he'd gone ten rounds with an enraged grizzly and lost.

Jackie pulled up at five minutes until nine. She sent him a text, letting him know she was out front.

Just the thought of seeing her again sent his pulse racing. He felt like a besotted kid, aching for her when she wasn't around. Slugging down the last of his coffee, he went outside to meet her.

"Good morning," she said as he got into her car. "That eye looks like it must hurt. Did you manage to get any sleep?"

Back to impersonal yet friendly.

"I did. How about you?" he asked politely, taking his cues from her. With her aviator sunglasses on, he couldn't see her eyes.

"As best as could be expected after learning my sister now has a warrant out for her arrest."

Aware they might be treading on dangerous ground, he nodded. "It's surreal. But then again, this entire situation with Charla and Theo defies belief."

She drove, quietly competent, clearly lost in her own thoughts. As they pulled up to the Rattlesnake Pub where his truck sat alone in the empty lot, she sighed. "I'm sorry about last night."

"Don't be." He waited until she'd parked to plant a quick kiss on his cheek. "I'm not."

Leaving that there, he smiled and got out of her car. "Talk to you later, I hope."

Absently, she nodded, her color high. "I'm sure we will."

He stood next to his truck and watched as she drove off. Damn, he had it bad. He didn't know what he was going to do when she took off back for the east coast.

Hopefully, the rest of the world would have settled down by then. Somehow, with Charla wanted for theft and embezzlement, he knew things would change. But at least he'd have Theo back, and the constant worry that lurked in the back of his mind would be gone.

Chapter Seven

Her phone rang, the caller ID displaying a number she didn't recognize. Though Jackie usually let calls like that go to voice mail, Charla's having gone missing changed everything. She answered it, hoping against hope it would be her sister. Maybe Charla had to use another phone.

"Is this Charla's sister?" a feminine voice asked. Once Jackie answered in the affirmative, the woman identified herself as Melanie. "I think my boyfriend might have spotted Charla. I called you instead of the sheriff," she said, "because Charla is my friend and I don't want her to get in any more trouble. I heard about the jewelry store thing."

Already? Shaking her head at how fast gossip traveled in this town, Jackie thanked her before she asked where.

"Big Bend National Park. He and a friend went camping there. He swears he saw someone who looked just like her ahead of him on one of the hiking trails. He says he called out to her, but she kept going. He tried to catch up with her, but says she was gone."

As far as Jackie knew, Charla had never gone hiking. She was more of a Zumba or yoga in the gym–type person as far as exercise. "How sure is he?" she asked. "As far as I know, Charla doesn't hike."

"Zach got her into it," Melanie replied. "He was one of her boyfriends. He's a personal trainer at the gym. You might check with him and see if he's been hiking with her lately."

"Thank you," Jackie replied. She ended the call.

More than anything, she needed to talk to Eli. Even though she'd just dropped him off and calling him again sort of felt like stalking. Still, this was too important to simply let slide. She punched in his number again.

He answered immediately. "Missing me already?" he teased.

Despite herself, she blushed. "I am, but that's not the only reason I wanted to talk to you." She filled him in on what Melanie had said.

"I know Zach," he replied. "I know he and Charla went out a few times, but they both liked to play the field. From what I know of Charla, she's not much into outdoor activities."

"I think we need to go talk to him," she said. "Just in case that really was Charla up in Big Bend." Then, realizing she'd said *we*, she walked back her words a little. "Or I can go talk to him, if you're busy. I'll report back to you what he says."

"How about you pass the info along to Rayna and let her investigate?" he suggested.

Exhaling, she struggled to find the right words to convey her feelings. "I'd like to check this out myself," she finally said. "I don't expect you to understand, but I'd really like to talk to Charla before she gets arrested."

He sighed. "I know what you mean. She's your sister. I get that. But if she really did embezzle and steal, she needs to pay for her crimes."

"I agree. But I still can't get past her text to me. She said she was in danger. What if she still is?"

"I'll go with you," he finally said. "We'll talk to Zach and then decide if we want to drive out to Big Bend. I'll have to get one of my part-time workers to come stay at my ranch and take care of the livestock since it will be an overnight trip. You know how long that drive is."

"I do." It had always been one of her favorite road trips. "My friends and I used to go out there on spring break and hike when I was in college." She wished she'd kept her old hiking boots. "If we end up going, we'll need to stop somewhere and pick up supplies. Have you ever been hiking?"

He laughed, the low, husky sound giving her goose bumps on her skin. "Only on horseback, and I have a feeling that doesn't count."

"Are you up for it?" she asked, ready to go alone if he wasn't.

"Sure. But I'll need to stop by my place to arrange the care of the ranch and to pack a few things. So let's talk to Zach and then we can make our decision."

Though she already knew she'd be going no matter what Zach had to say, she agreed.

"I'll pick you up in fifteen minutes," Eli continued. "I need to make a quick stop at the drugstore first. The gym is right off Main Street, so not too far."

"Sounds good. Since the weather is nice, I'm just going to wait for you outside. I'll sit by the pool."

As usual, when she caught sight of Eli's pickup, her heart did a funny little skip. Shaking her head at herself for acting like a teenager with a crush, she hurried over and climbed inside.

"Hey there." His slow smile had her inwardly melting. "Let's see what Zach has to say."

Though the gym seemed on the smaller side, there were quite a few people working out, several on the line of treadmills or elliptical machines. Eli waved at the receptionist as they walked past, heading toward the free weight area.

"There he is." Eli pointed to an extremely muscular man helping a woman do push-ups.

When Zach turned, his piercing blue eyes meeting hers, Jackie caught her breath. She hadn't expected such patrician features along with the superhero build. But—she looked again—there was a certain kind of self-assured smugness in his expression. As if he knew exactly how she or any other woman would react at the first sight of him.

Apparently hearing her reaction to Zach, Eli glanced at her and rolled his eyes. "Charla's type," he said. "Poor Christopher Levine didn't stand a chance."

The comment made her grin because he was right. In high school, Charla had valued appearance over everything else. Despite that, as far as Jackie was concerned, Zach couldn't hold a candle to Eli's easy confidence.

"Eli, man." Zach clapped Eli on the back. "Long time, no see." He squinted, taking in Eli's black eye.

"Wow. I heard about the bar fight, but that looks bad. I'm just about finished up with Madeline here, so I can talk to you then."

Eli nodded.

Jackie struggled to keep her expression neutral. Once again, the speed at which gossip traveled in this town surprised her. Zach sauntered away. Slowly, Jackie let her gaze follow him. "How long did Charla and Zach date?" she asked.

"Not too long." Eli shrugged. "Zach is Charla's twin, personality wise. And as you can imagine, he's really popular with the ladies."

"I can see that," she said. "He seems awfully sure of himself."

"I can't blame him. He's really a nice guy, despite the fact that every single woman falls all over herself the first time she sees him." He eyed her. "Speaking of that, are you feeling okay? Or do you need to sit down?"

She laughed. "I'm fine. Zach is rather startling, but he's definitely not my type."

"Really?" He sounded skeptical. "What is your type, then?"

Heart pounding, she locked gazes with him. If she told him the truth, that he was her type, it would sound as if she was flirting or trying to get a reaction. She swallowed hard and managed a shrug. "I don't really know." That part was definitely true. She'd simply left out the part about the zing of physical attraction she felt just being in the same proximity as Eli.

With a slow nod, Eli appeared to accept her answer. "Here he comes," he said.

"Eli, what can I do for you today?" Zach asked, his gaze sliding past to Jackie. "And who's your friend?"

Jackie held out her hand, introducing herself before Eli could. "I'm Jackie Burkholdt. Charla's sister."

He shook her hand, a slight frown creasing his brow. Though his smile remained in place, something flickered in his eyes.

"I heard about Charla taking off," he said. "I'm guessing that's why you're in town?"

"It is," Jackie replied. "But Eli and I wanted to come see you to ask about hiking."

"Hiking?" Voice puzzled, Zach looked from her to Eli.

"Someone reported that they thought they saw Charla hiking out in Big Bend," Eli interjected. "Since we heard you got Charla into it, we thought we'd ask if you might have known anything about this."

"Once," Zach said. "I took Charla hiking one time. We went to Palo Duro and took easy trails. She hated it. Complained the entire time. I seriously doubt she would have gone hiking anywhere, never mind Big Bend."

"That's kind of what I thought." Eli stuck out his hand. "Thanks, man."

"No problem." Someone called Zach's name. "Gotta go. My next client is here."

A petite blonde woman waved at him, eyeing him as if she'd like to eat him up.

"Come on." Eli took Jackie's arm. "I think we've found out what we came for."

Following him outside, she waited until they were in the truck before telling him. "I'm going out there anyway. You don't have to go with me, though you're certainly welcome to if you want."

About to start the engine, he turned and looked at her. "You realize there's, like, a ninety-nine percent chance she won't be there, right?"

"I do." She lifted her chin. "But because there's even a one percent possibility that she will, I have to go. I can't let the chance that I might find her slip out of my hands."

For one heart-stopping moment, she thought he might kiss her again. Instead, he shook his head and pressed the button to turn the motor on. "I get that. And because I do, I'm going with you. Though honestly, I'd feel better if someone had mentioned seeing a toddler, too."

He dropped her off at the motel to pack, telling her he'd text when he was on his way back. "It'll be at least an hour," he said. "I've done my horse training for the day, but I've still got to line up someone to come stay at the ranch. Plus, I need to dig out my old camping gear and see if I can drum up a pair of hiking boots."

"I'm going to have to stop and buy some," she said. "And unless you have an extra sleeping bag, I'll have to purchase one of those, too."

"I'll let you know."

Nodding, she slipped out of his truck, telling herself she was imagining the way she felt his gaze on her back as she walked away.

AFTER WAITING TO make sure Jackie got into her motel room safely, Eli exhaled before putting the truck in Drive and pulling out into the street.

While he seriously doubted they'd find Charla anywhere near a hiking trail, there wasn't any way he could bring himself to stay here while Jackie took off on her own. Though she hadn't asked, he wanted to protect her. There were too many potential mishaps that could happen to a woman alone in the wilderness. At least if he went with her, she'd have backup.

Now he only had to figure out a way to protect her from himself.

Back at the ranch he called Jimmy Stephens, one of the teenagers who worked for him part-time. Jimmy seemed thrilled to come stay at the ranch and earn extra cash, so Eli asked him to come by now.

With that taken care of, Eli went out into his garage to locate his camping gear. When he'd lived in Houston, he'd frequently taken solo camping trips on the weekends, though he'd packed everything away when he'd purchased the ranch.

He located the tent without too much trouble, and a sleeping bag. He knew he had another one somewhere, because at one point he'd talked the woman who'd been his girlfriend at the time into going camping. She hadn't even lasted the entire night, asking him to take her home when she'd learned she'd have to walk to the public restroom.

In addition to the tent, he loaded up all his other supplies. The portable stove, the lantern, a coffeepot and some cooking pots and eating utensils and plates. Everything he'd once enjoyed using. He even managed to locate his battered old hiking boots, a little stiff from disuse, but he figured they'd loosen with use.

He threw a few clothing items into a small duffel bag, including a coat since he knew the nights might get chilly.

While he knew they'd only be gone one night at the most, he couldn't help but wonder how Jackie would take to the primitive conditions. She'd said she'd done hiking trips in the past, but hadn't mentioned anything about staying in the wilderness. He guessed he'd be finding out soon.

Once he'd stowed all the gear in his truck, he grabbed his ice chest and set about loading it up with provisions. He also packed dry goods, figuring the more he brought, the less they'd have to buy when they got to the national park.

Right before he left, he sent Jackie a text to let her know he was on his way. When he pulled up to the Landshark, he spotted her sitting in one of the chairs near the pool. She stood and grabbed her bag, a carry-on size, and hurried over to his truck.

As she climbed into the passenger seat, her silky long brown hair swirling around her, he was struck by a mental image of that hair spread underneath her on a pillow, her body naked and welcoming his.

Damn. Instant arousal. He shifted in his seat to hide it and managed a hopefully banal smile. "We can stop at the sporting goods store on the way out of town."

"Perfect." Her warm smile stirred his body again. What the hell?

Looking away, he shifted into Drive and pulled out into the street.

After stopping at Ramos's Sporting Goods, where

Jackie purchased a pair of hiking boots, they hit the road in earnest.

She'd been happy to hear he'd brought an extra sleeping bag and camping gear.

"What if she crossed the border into Mexico?" she asked. "I mean, if she really did embezzle from Levine's, maybe she's going to try and hide out there. I can see her in one of the resort towns, hanging out in a bar on the beach."

Suppressing a twinge of panic at the idea of Charla spiriting his young son across the border, Eli sighed. "Maybe, but I still think she would have flown, maybe under an assumed identity. Charla wouldn't do it the difficult way, which is why I truly don't think we're going to find her hiking in the Guadalupe Mountains. Are you sure you want to make that drive?"

She studied him for a moment before replying, her expression thoughtful. "Seriously, you don't have to go with me. I know this trip probably won't turn up anything, but while Rayna is doing everything she can to find Charla and Theo around here, what can it hurt? Maybe there will be some clues."

"Maybe." But he wasn't hopeful. "I left a message for Rayna, letting her know where we're going and why."

Glancing at him sideways, one corner of her lush mouth kicked up. "Me, too," she said. "Though I didn't mention it to my mother. It's already bad enough that she's accused me of trying to *poach* my sister's ex, as she put it. Even though I explained to her that we are both just trying to find Charla and Theo, I could tell she didn't believe me."

This so boggled his mind, he could only shake his head in disbelief.

According to his phone, the drive would take a little over six to seven hours. When he passed this information on to Jackie, she grinned. "That's about right," she said. "Depending which route you chose. I'm assuming you're taking I20 west to 385 south?"

"I am." He paused. "Unless you prefer another way."

"I'll leave that up to you since you're driving." She stretched, the seat belt tugging at her shirt and drawing his gaze to her torso. Instantly, he forced his attention back to the road.

"And though some people might find the scenery boring," she continued, apparently oblivious to the direction his thoughts had taken, "I think it's beautiful."

"Me, too," he admitted. "I grew up in Houston. The first time I made a trip to west Texas, I knew that's where I belonged. Something about the wide-open spaces and the unbelievable skies got to me. Plus," he added drily, "I really enjoy the noticeable difference in humidity."

This earned a laugh. "I've been through parts of Houston when I went to Galveston," she said. "I agree with you there. What did you do in Houston before you came to Getaway and became a ranch owner?"

"I worked as a financial analyst for a huge corporation," he answered, somewhat reluctantly. "Though I hated every minute of it, I knew what I wanted to do. I saved as much as possible so I could buy my place." He'd also made several lucrative investments that continued to pay small dividends.

"But the horse training, the riding lessons. How did you learn those skills?"

He shrugged. "My uncle is a big-time cutting horse trainer. He owns his own place up near Conroe. From the time I was eight years old, I spent every summer up there. Plus a lot of weekends during the school year. He taught me everything I know. And he gave me my lifelong love of horses."

"Wow. I'm impressed."

"What about you?" he asked. "I know you work in New York City, but what do you do? And how did you choose your career?"

"I've always loved to read," she said. "Neither my mother nor my sister could understand why, but I did. I discovered romance novels in high school. I studied hard so I could graduate at the top of my class and get financial assistance to college. I went to Tech." Her voice rang with pride. "I majored in English. As soon as I had my degree, I began applying for my dream job, working for the largest publisher of romance in the world."

"And is that where you work now?"

She beamed. "It is. I love my job and my life. Life in New York City took a little getting used to and I was lonely at first, but now that I've been there three years, I love it."

Though he nodded, his heart sank just a little. Honestly, he knew he should be glad to hear her say that. Maybe now he could stop himself from occasionally imagining a future together with her.

About halfway through the drive, they stopped and grabbed some tacos at a little hole-in-the-wall place.

They made it to the Rio Grande Village Campground before nightfall. Since they'd planned to go hiking first thing in the morning, this meant he'd have plenty of time to set up camp, build a fire and make them a hot meal.

The tent seemed a lot smaller than he remembered, but he managed to fit both sleeping bags in, side to side. There wasn't a whole lot of wiggle room. And yet he wouldn't have been able to account for his body's reaction if he and Jackie had been forced to share one bag. In fact, just thinking about what such a thing would be like had him semi-aroused.

"Should we make a campfire?" she asked, rubbing her hands together against the chilly night air. The mountainous desert could be hot as Hades during the day, but as soon as the sun went down, a chill crept over the landscape, deepening with the darkness.

"Sure," he said, noticing she'd already assembled a nice stack of twigs and sticks, using crumpled newspaper as a base. He rummaged in his supply box and located the long-handled lighter and used it to catch part of the newspaper on fire. It wasn't long before they had a decent-size fire going.

"I can heat us up some canned meat and beans, if you're hungry."

At that, she made a face. "No, thanks. Though I do wish we had some marshmallows," she said, grinning at him. The flickering fire made copper highlights dance in her dark hair, making he appear earthy and mysterious and sexy as hell.

Abruptly, he pushed to his feet. "I'll be back in a few," he rasped, heading toward the campground restrooms, when in fact, he needed to go for a walk in the darkness and get his head back on straight.

Right now, with everything going on in his life, he had no reason or right to crave a woman this much. But he did. And he wasn't entirely sure how to turn that need off. All he could hope for was to try and resist it.

He made one complete circle, almost back at their spot before turning around and going back the way he'd come. As he approached, he saw Jackie still seated by the fire, gazing pensively off into the darkness.

His reappearance seemed to briefly startle her.

"Nice night," he said, dropping to a seat on the wooden picnic table bench. "And yeah, marshmallows or s'mores would really taste good right now."

This made her laugh. "You definitely took the snack craving up a notch."

"I have a box of protein bars if you want one," he told her. "Assorted flavors, so there might be something you like."

"No, thanks." Turning her attention back to the fire, she lapsed into quiet, once again giving him the opportunity to study her.

Instead, he tore his gaze away, trying to stare at the flames, as she did. The silence should have felt companionable, but this kind of silence led to self-examination, and right now that was the last thing he wanted. Better to get up and find busywork instead.

Since he'd already set up the tent and the sleeping bags, he began going through the supplies he'd packed, sorting them. He knew better than to let them remain outside while they slept, but he could at least see what they had by meal.

"I thought we could set out on our hike right after sunrise," she said softly. "It'll still be relatively cool. We can ask about Charla when we meet up with other hikers. I'd also like to try and find some park rangers. What do you think?"

As a plan, it lacked structure, but since he still believed this entire trip would turn out to be pointless, he agreed. "We might also show her picture to the other campers."

She nodded. "I'm thinking I'll turn in early."

His heart skipped a beat. Maybe that would be the best way to deal with their enforced closeness. If Jackie went into the tent first and fell soundly asleep, he might have a lot less trouble sliding into a sleeping bag next to her and nodding off.

"Worth a shot," he said out loud, earning a quizzical look from her. "I mean, you go ahead. I'm going to finish going through our provisions and get them stored in the truck cab for the night. No sense in attracting any hungry wildlife."

Her eyes widened at that comment, but she only nodded, stifling a yawn. Her sinuous stretch drew his gaze to her slender body, sending such a strong bolt of desire through him that he shuddered. How the hell was he going to be able to sleep inches away from her for an entire night?

Clearly, she had no such worries. "Good night, then," she murmured, climbing to her feet and disappearing into the dark tent. A moment later she used her flashlight to see, illuminating her silhouette. He stared at her across the flickering firelight, hoping against hope that she wouldn't undress, though honestly, he prayed she would.

But of course, like him, she'd be sleeping in her clothes. She simply used the flashlight to adjust her sleeping bag and climb into it. Then the light went out, leaving him alone with the campfire and his aching body.

Again, he decided it might be best to find busywork, as if by doing that he might wear himself down enough to be able to find sleep. He stowed their provisions, dumped dirt on the campfire to extinguish it and stood facing the tent. He could do this. By now, Jackie should be deeply asleep. He just needed to slip inside, get into his sleeping bag and close his eyes.

Like Jackie, he carried a small flashlight, which he used to find his way to his side of the tent. Standing quietly for a moment, listening to the deep, even sound of her breathing, he pushed away the ever-present ache of wanting her. Moving slowly and deliberately, he took care not to shine the light on her, not wanting to risk causing her to wake.

After removing his shoes, he went to crawl over Jackie to get to his sleeping bag, hoping he could do so without disturbing her. Halfway there, he honestly believed he was going to make it when she sat up abruptly, her forehead colliding with his midsection.

"Eli?" The husky note in her voice made him swallow hard.

Before he could reply, she reached for him and pulled him over to her. "Come here," she said. "It's too cold not to share."

Chapter Eight

Jackie had been trying to stay awake until Eli joined her, though he took so long she found herself dozing, despite the occasional bouts of shivering. She swore cold seeped in from the hard ground underneath the tent and her sleeping bag. Though she'd kept her jeans and sweatshirt on, she'd begun to rethink shucking her jacket. When she woke up with her teeth chattering, she crawled out from her sleeping bag and retrieved it. The jacket helped somewhat, though her legs and feet were still cold.

If only Eli would turn in for the night, she suspected the two of them could generate enough heat to banish this awful chill. Because despite the fact that he'd laid out two separate sleeping bags, she fully intended that they share one.

Just the thought brought a surge of warmth. She was going to do this; she'd known that ever since they'd started discussing this trip. She craved him with a fierceness that consumed her. She knew he wanted her, too—heat blazed from his gaze every time he looked at her. He might be her sister's ex, he might be someone she'd never see again once she got on that plane to fly back to New York, but damned if she was going to let this opportunity to experience making love with him slip past. Somewhere deep inside she suspected she'd never meet another man like him. A man's man, rugged and tough and independent, yet also generous and kind and giving. And sexy, too. Sexy as hell. And apparently avoiding her.

Finally, the flickering glow from the campfire went out. Which meant Eli was about to come inside the tent. While she'd been waiting, she'd run through several different scenarios to tempt him, most of them involving her being totally naked, and discarding them all due to the cold. They'd undress each other, she thought, and make their own warmth, skin to skin.

The tent flap opened. Though he kept his flashlight pointed away from her, it provided enough light for her to view his outline. She tried to keep her breathing slow and steady, mimicking sleep, though she wasn't sure why.

As Eli began to clumsily attempt to crawl over her without touching her, she sat upright, hoping he'd think he'd awakened her. Acting on instinct, she reached out and tugged him close to her, letting him know she was cold.

She wanted to say she needed his warmth, but what came out was a simple declaration. "I need you," she said, seconds before his mouth covered hers in a fierce, intense kiss.

He kissed her as though he'd been starving for this, and the way she returned the kiss had to let him know she felt the same. Somehow, he managed to fit inside her sleeping bag, zipping it up to create a tight cocoon of warmth.

His hands slid over her body in ways she'd only dreamed of until now, her clothing an unwanted barrier. She touched him, too, sliding her hand up under his shirt, feeling his muscular stomach contract at her touch.

She needed more. All of him, nothing between their bodies.

Unfortunately, there was no way they could manage to remove their clothes in the narrow confinement of her sleeping bag.

Eli must have realized this about the same time she did. He broke away, his breathing jagged. "Before we go any further," he rasped. "Are you sure you want—?"

"Yes." Interrupting him, she pulled him in for one more long, deep kiss. By the time he lifted his head, she figured he had no doubt what she wanted. "Now, let's unzip this thing so we can undress."

They made quick work of shedding their clothes, urged on by both desire and the chilly night air on their bare skin.

"Go," he ordered. Laughing, she dove back for the still-warm sleeping bag. He didn't move. "I've got a condom," he said. "I bought some. I just need to get it out of my wallet."

Eyeing his muscular body silhouetted in the darkness, she managed a nod.

He made a sound in between a grunt and a groan and moved over to the clothes he'd just shed. A moment later he clicked on his flashlight and located his jeans, pulling out his wallet and the condom he now apparently kept stashed there.

Breathless, she watched as he opened the wrapper and tugged it over his huge, swollen arousal. He looked up, flashed a grin and then turned the flashlight on her. "I want to see you," he rasped. "You're even more beautiful than I imagined."

In response, she moved aside the sleeping bag and opened her arms. "Get over here, you."

A moment later he covered her body with his, the proof of his desire pressing hard against her belly. Moving against him, this time she opened her legs, arching her back in a silent plea.

"Not yet," he rasped, but she already knew he was lost. She shimmied, he groaned and then he buried himself deep inside her.

"Oh," she managed, loving the way he completely filled her. And then he began to move.

Deep and hard and fast, then slowing, until she thought she might lose her mind. She begged, she pleaded, she tried to urge him on with her body, but he kissed her instead.

Finally, just when she thought she might shatter into jagged little pieces, he groaned and finally released his iron control. *This* was what she wanted, needed, and she felt her body start to dissolve as she found her release.

At the moment her body clenched around him, he shuddered with his own release. They clutched each other tight, riding the waves together.

Finally, she stopped shuddering, depleted and fulfilled and in a dazed sort of awe at what had just happened. He continued to hold her, still buried inside her.

"That was..." he began. She silenced him with a quick press of her finger against his lips. Right now, in the aftermath of what had been the most intense lovemaking she'd ever experienced, she didn't want to talk or analyze; she simply wanted to be still and let the moment wash over her.

As if he understood, he didn't speak again, though he finally rolled away from her and rummaged in his pack for something to use to clean himself up.

"Do you want your clothes?" he asked. "It's getting colder."

She opened one eye, looking up at him illuminated by his flashlight. "No. I'm betting between you and me, we can manage to keep each other warm."

This made him chuckle, even as he made his way back to her. Once he'd crawled in beside her, he zipped the bag closed and then gathered her in his arms.

She let herself drift off with her face against his broad chest. Pure happiness, she thought, the last thing that went through her mind before she gave in to sleep.

When he woke her the next morning, she could tell by the absence of darkness inside the tent that the sky had begun to lighten, even though the sun had barely skimmed the edge of the horizon.

"Mornin'," he murmured, nuzzling her neck before his mouth found hers. Already wearing protection, he nudged her with his aroused body, making her laugh and pull him close. They made love again, less frantically this time, slow and unhurried, though he soon had her arching her back and urging him to go deeper, faster.

Again, they climaxed together, and he held her until her body stopped shaking. She could get used to this, she thought.

"Great way to start a morning," he muttered, stroking her shoulder.

"It is," she agreed, unable to keep from smiling. "So how many condoms do you keep in your wallet?" she asked, only half teasing.

"I had three," he replied. "That means we have one more left in case we want to do this again."

This had her smiling, even though she ached inside. This man, this amazing, sexy, rugged man, was something she'd never thought she'd find. Not here, not in New York, not ever. The fact that he'd once been married to her sister mattered less than knowing she would soon have to leave him forever. He didn't belong in New York any more than she belonged in Getaway. Heart both full and heavy, she got dressed, grabbed her bag with its change of clothes and toiletries and accompanied him to the campground showers.

The morning air still carried a chill leftover from the darkness, though she could tell the day would heat up with the sun. At the facility she and Eli went their separate ways. While she dreaded the icy shower, she figured if she rushed it might not be too bad.

She was wrong.

Teeth chattering, she got herself clean in record time. Glad Eli'd had the foresight to bring towels, she dried herself off and pulled on clean clothes, dressing in layers. Her hair was another story. Since there was only so much drying she could do with a towel, she had no choice but to let it mostly air dry before putting it into a braid.

Walking outside, she saw Eli waiting. The sight of him, so tall and muscular and handsome, brought on another rush of longing. To cover, she made a show of studying her new hiking boots. "They're not broken in," she told him, lifting one foot so he could see. "Here's hoping I don't have blisters a couple of hours in."

He shook his head but didn't comment. Once she reached him, he walked with her all the way back to their tent.

"Canned meat and beans or protein bars?" he asked, his eyes crinkling at the corners. "Sorry, but I didn't bring anything perishable like eggs or bacon."

"Protein bar, please," she said instantly. "The idea of eating canned meat makes me feel nauseated. I tried it once in college. While I'm not sure if it was that or the peppermint schnapps, I've never been so sick in my life."

Still smiling, he made a face. "Sounds like it might have been both. That's a bad combo right there." Handing her a box of protein bars, he shrugged. "Help yourself. They're assorted."

She chose a blueberry and almond bar plus an apple cinnamon nut combo and passed the box back to him. "I grabbed an extra for my backpack," she said.

"Good idea." He did the same. "Let me make a small campfire and brew us some coffee."

Grateful, she nodded. "That would be heavenly."

She sat on the wooden picnic table bench and watched while he brought a small fire to life, expertly handling a battered metal coffeepot. He'd brought stainless steel mugs and once the brew had finished, filled two and handed one to her.

After taking a cautious sip, she made a sound of approval low in her throat. "This is really good."

Her comment made him grin. "Not what you were expecting, I take it?"

Instead of answering, she drank again.

They allowed themselves a few minutes to drink their coffee before disassembling the tent and stowing all their gear back in the pickup. When they'd finished, he turned to her. "As I'm sure you know, there are a lot of trails out here. Do you want to try beginner hikes or something more challenging?"

She considered. "What do you think Charla would be most likely to do?"

"None of this," he responded. When she made a face at him, he sighed. "I don't know." He pointed to a sign. "Since we're already in the Rio Grande Village Campground, let's take this nature trail. It's only three quarters of a mile and since it's relatively easy, probably something Charla might have done."

"Then after this, I'd like to see if we can try the Santa Elena Canyon Trail," she said. "Though I'm not sure how far it is from here."

"We can ask."

Side by side, they set off on the trail. This early in the morning, they only encountered two other hikers.

Jackie showed them a photo of her sister, but neither had seen her.

The short hike didn't take long, but by the time they'd returned to the trailhead entrance, she could feel soreness at the back of her heels.

"Are you okay?" He must have noticed her limping.

"New boots." Grimacing, she waited while he unlocked the truck. "I'll survive."

"I thought we'd stop at the visitor center next. Show Charla's picture around and see if they've seen her. Usually, you can find a park ranger there, too."

She nodded and buckled her seat belt. "Two for one. I like it."

Unfortunately, Charla hadn't been by the visitor center, and the park ranger they talked to hadn't seen her, either. Jackie's spirits sank. With Charla's blond prettiness and vivacious personality, people tended to remember her.

"Maybe you're right," Jackie admitted as they climbed back into the truck. "This trip might have been a complete waste of time."

"Maybe," he allowed, starting the engine and backing from their spot. "At least as far as finding Charla and Theo are concerned." He met her gaze, his own intense. "But I want you to know that I wouldn't trade last night or this morning for anything."

Blushing, she looked away, making a show out of watching the scenery go past.

"Do you still want to go on that other hike?" he asked. "We can if you want. Your choice."

She thought for a moment and sighed. "The likelihood of us finding anyone who's seen Charla is slim to nothing. I guess we might as well head back home."

Home. The instant she finished speaking, she regretted her word choice. Getaway wasn't her home, not anymore. She could only hope Eli hadn't noticed and drawn the wrong conclusion.

HOME. ELI WONDERED if Jackie realized what she'd said. If she meant what she'd said. Probably not, he decided. After all, lots of people referred to the place they'd grown up as home, even if they resided elsewhere. That was most likely all she'd meant. Not a reason for his heart to skip a beat and hope to make his chest tight.

"I'm sorry," he said. "I wish we could have had better luck."

"Me, too."

They stopped for more coffee at a gas station. After the restless night he'd had, Eli knew he'd need the caffeine for the long drive home. He knew he needed to address the elephant in the room, but wasn't sure of the best way how.

"I'm thinking we need to talk," he finally began as they drove down a two-lane highway in what seemed to be the middle of nowhere.

Though she'd been dozing, his statement had her blinking and sitting up straight. "About last night?" she asked, her tone cautious.

"Yes." He glanced her way, trying to read her expression but couldn't. "That was—"

"A mistake?" she interrupted. "Because so help me, if that's what you're going to call it, you'd better think carefully. We still have several hours remaining on this drive."

Not quite sure how to take that, he considered. "What would you call it, then?" he asked. "And for the record, I was going to say it was amazing."

She flashed him a quick smile. "Good save. And yes, it was amazing. But that's all it can be. No strings, no emotions. Just a onetime thing. You're my sister's ex-husband after all."

"Two-time thing," he corrected, watching her smile broaden.

"And yes, I know you're going to be returning to New York," he finished. "I get it. But I wanted to make sure what happened doesn't make things weird between us for however long you're here."

Her brows rose. "Definitely not. We're both adults, Eli. It doesn't have to mean anything."

But what if he wanted it to mean something? Wisely, he bit back those words. He realized he had begun to fall for Jackie, though clearly, she didn't feel the same way.

Of course she didn't. It seemed he was eternally doomed to be a fool for love.

"Good," he managed. "You're in agreement, then? What happened changes nothing between us."

"Maybe one thing," she drawled, reaching over and placing her hand on his arm. "Sex is a great defuser of tension. So I recommend whenever things get too intense, we help each other out."

With her touch burning his skin, her sultry tone had his body stirring. He swallowed hard, working on concentrating on the road. "Sounds good," he managed to say, pleased that his voice sounded relatively normal. "Anytime."

She laughed. "I like you, Eli Pitts," she said. "A lot. If you ever find yourself in New York, please look me up."

"I will." He knew she had no idea how sad that made him. He'd never go to New York and felt pretty sure she knew that. "Just curious. How long are you here for?" he asked.

"I took a two-week vacation," she replied. "Though I'll ask to extend that unpaid if I have to. I can't leave until we find Charla."

Playing devil's advocate, he had to ask, "What if your boss says no? What will you do if he tells you either come back or lose your job?"

"She," Jackie corrected. "My boss is a woman. And honestly, I can't see her doing that. She knows what's going on and how important it is for me to find my sister."

"But what if she has to?" he pressed. "If work is piling up and they really need your warm body there to help out."

She glanced sideways at him, a slight frown creasing her brow. "Are you asking me if I'll stay here if they fire me?"

Put that way… "Sorry," he said, feeling sheepish. "I guess I was. I have no idea how it works in your line of work. I know when I worked for a large corporation, if I asked for too much time off, they would have fired me."

"Well, I'm hoping that's not the case with my employer. I love my job and I'm damn good at what I do. I've been doing some editing remotely and I can always pick up more. If that's not enough, I'll deal with that bridge when we cross it."

Now he felt like a jerk for even bringing it up. "Look, I shouldn't have said anything. I guess I was just wondering if there was any scenario that would have you staying in Getaway indefinitely."

"Eli…"

He gave her a rueful smile. "I know, I know. Still, you can't blame a guy for trying." He'd already revealed far more than he knew he should about his growing feelings for her. The last thing he wanted to do was to scare her away. "The lovemaking was really awesome," he added, hoping she'd think sex was all he cared about.

"Ahhh, now I get it." Her brow cleared. "You know, since you feel that way, I'm sure we can get together again at some point."

Glancing at her, he grinned, relieved to see the matching sparkle in her eyes. "I'd like that," he said. "A lot, actually."

The sound of her laughter made everything right with the world. Or at least as right as it could be with his son and her sister still missing.

The thought sobered him. He'd always considered himself an optimistic person, but Charla and Theo's prolonged absence had made even him begin to imagine worst-case scenarios.

"They'll be all right, you know," he said, aware she'd know exactly what he meant. "They have to be, because nothing else is acceptable."

"I know." Her quiet reply matched her determined expression. "I won't have it any other way."

Spoken as two people who believed they had total control of not only their own destiny, but that of others. He could only hope they were right.

His cell phone rang.

"It's Rayna," he said, his heart skipping a beat. After a quick deep breath, he answered.

"Are you sitting down?" Rayna asked. "Is Jackie with you?"

Not sure how to take this, he answered in the affirmative.

"Put me on speaker," Rayna demanded. "I want Jackie to hear this, too."

Quickly, he did as she requested, filling Jackie in.

"Can you both hear me?" Rayna asked. She continued without waiting for an answer. "We have Theo." Her triumphant tone made her sound fierce. "Safe and unharmed."

Stunned, it took him a second to find his voice. He glanced at Jackie, who had her hand over her mouth and tears in her eyes. "How? Where?"

"One of Charla's friends brought him in. It seems Charla left him with her last Saturday before she went out and never returned to pick him up." Rayna paused, and then continued. "Apparently, this is not unusual and this friend has watched Theo for several days before. Charla pays her well, she said."

"What friend?" he asked. "Do I know her?"

"I don't think so. She lives in Abilene. Her name is Natalie. When Charla didn't pick up her phone or return her text messages, Natalie drove here with Theo to find her. When she couldn't do that, she contacted us."

"Where is Theo now?" Eli asked.

"Here at the police station," Rayna replied. "Though Delia is on the way to pick him up."

Heart pounding, he swallowed. "Tell Delia I'll be there as soon as I can."

"Will do, but I'm going to need you to stop by and talk to me first." Rayna's tone had gone grave. "Because Natalie had quite a bit to say about why Charla left. Apparently, she felt threatened by you. She told Natalie that she believed you wanted to kill her, so you could have sole custody of Theo."

He opened his mouth, but no words came out. "That's ridiculous," he finally managed, horribly aware that Jackie had gone stiff and still in the seat next to him. "You know that, Rayna. Don't you?"

"I know you're a good man," Rayna replied. "I know how much you love your son. But we still don't have any idea where Charla is. And now I can't discount the possibility of foul play. While we don't have any evidence, I'm thinking we might need to turn this search in a new direction."

"What's that mean?" Jackie asked, the sound of her broken voice shredding his insides. "Do you mean you're now considering this a homicide investigation?"

"Not yet," Rayna hastened to reassure her, her tone soothing. "We have nothing to base that on."

"Like a body?" Jackie finished flatly.

Rayna paused. "Yes. We have no reason yet to believe Charla met with serious harm."

"Yet. Except for the text she sent me, saying she was in danger. And now her friend says she felt threatened by her ex-husband, the man I'm currently alone with in the middle of nowhere."

"What do you mean?" Rayna asked. "Where are you two?"

"Driving back from Big Bend," Eli answered. "We followed up on a lead. Someone said they thought they saw Charla hiking a trail up there."

"Charla hiking?" Rayna made a dismissive sound. "I can't see that happening."

"Me neither." Eli glanced at Jackie. She stared straight ahead, refusing to look at him. Her entire posture radiated anger and something else.

"We're on our way back," Eli said. "I'll text you when we're getting close."

"Sounds good."

Eli pressed the button to end the call. He glanced at Jackie, but before he could speak, her phone rang.

"Hello?" she answered. "Hi, Mom." Then, raising a brow at Eli, she pressed the button to put the phone on speaker.

"That man killed your sister," Delia said, her voice full of venom. "I hope you understand now why I didn't like you hanging around him."

Eli started to speak, but Jackie held up her hand to silence him. "We don't know that Charla is dead," she said, her voice full of pain. "And until we know that for certain, I refuse to hear anyone say such a thing."

Delia went silent. "I agree," she finally said, much more subdued. "I have Theo with me."

"That's what Rayna said," Jackie began.

Eli couldn't take any more. "I want to talk to my son," he said. "Please put Theo on the phone."

"You're with *him*?" Delia screeched. "How could you?"

The rueful look Jackie shot him told him he should have kept his mouth shut. He acknowledged she might be right. With emotions running so high, no way in hell would Delia allow him to talk to his son right now.

Why would Charla say such a thing? He'd never threatened her, and the last time he'd seen her, things had been cordial. At least as cordial as it could be with her inebriated and upset about her two boyfriends coming to blows. He hadn't engaged with her, simply listened as he drove her back to her apartment. She'd made sure to tell him Theo was with a sitter she trusted and while he'd wanted to ask her why she hadn't asked him to keep their son, he knew drunk Charla might be apt to take the question the wrong way, so he hadn't.

He listened as Jackie attempted to calm her mother down. But Delia wasn't having it. She began to swear, calling both Eli and Jackie several colorful terms, until Eli decided he'd had enough.

"Delia," he said as loudly and firmly as he could. "Not. In. Front. Of. My. Son."

In response, she ended the call.

"Jackie," Eli said, reaching out to touch her with one hand, meaning only to console her.

"Don't touch me," she said, jerking away. The look in her eyes as she pressed herself into the passenger door shattered his heart. "Not right now."

Chapter Nine

When Eli reached for her, Jackie gasped out loud, instinctively shrinking away from the man she'd just made love with. All along, her gut had told her one thing and common sense another. Maybe because she trusted her instincts, she'd managed not to listen to common sense. Now she was trapped in a moving vehicle with the man who might have harmed her sister. *Might have* being the operative words. She took several deep breaths in an attempt to calm herself down. Just because her mother had gone off the deep end didn't mean she had to.

At her instinctive reaction, Eli's tortured expression made her feel a twinge of remorse, which she quickly squashed. She needed to keep her head clear and try to look at this objectively.

"Sorry," she muttered. "I just don't know what to think."

"What Charla's friend said, you know that's not true, right?" he asked, his husky voice breaking. "I would never hurt the mother of my child. I'm not sure why Charla would even say such a thing, or if she even did, but I've never done anything to threaten her. Not once, not even when I learned she'd cheated on me multiple times."

Keeping her own face neutral, Jackie nodded. Truthfully, right now with her head spinning and her stomach churning, she wasn't sure how to react or what to think. "I understand," she said, trying not to reveal her inner trepidation. Had this man, this man she'd begun to fall in love with, done something to harm her sister? Was that why he'd been so certain they wouldn't find Charla in Big Bend? She wanted to ask him, but then again, she didn't. Because of course he would say no and if she couldn't convince him she believed him, would he hurt her, too?

"Do you?" A hint of bitterness crept into his voice. "Because I'm getting a totally different vibe from you. Come on, Jackie. You've gotten to know me pretty well. Do you really think I'd hurt Charla?"

She sighed. His pointed question put everything in focus. "I'd like to think no, but if there's ever been anyone who had a better reason, I don't know of them. She was awful to you, you had to constantly worry about your son and from all accounts, you were the last person to see her when you picked her up at the Pub on Saturday night. Plus, according to all the true-crime dramas and books I've read, if the wife goes missing or has been harmed, the husband or the boyfriend or ex usually did it."

"For real? And do you actually believe that? About me?"

"I did at first," she admitted. "Now I'm not so sure." Possibly foolish, but as she'd gotten to know Eli—and who was she kidding? The spark between them had become an inferno—she'd found herself believing there was no way he could ever do such a thing. Maybe her attraction to him blinded her; perhaps she'd one day come to regret her naivete, but for now she'd go with that. Innocent until proven guilty. The Eli she'd gotten to know, the ruggedly tender man in whose arms she'd just spent the night, would never have hurt her sister or any woman. She couldn't be wrong. Dear heaven, don't let her be wrong. Because if she was, more than just her heart could be at stake.

"I believe you," she said softly. "Unless you give me a reason not to."

Keeping his gaze on the road, he nodded. "Thanks. I won't."

They both lapsed into silence, broken only by the monotonous sound of the tires on the pavement. She wondered what he might be thinking. She could only imagine the relief he felt knowing that his son was okay.

If only she could say the same about her sister.

Half turning in her seat, she studied Eli's rugged profile. While she couldn't help but wonder if she was letting her attraction to him blind her, she also trusted her gut. And right now, every instinct told her this man hadn't harmed her sister. Then why did she have to keep convincing herself of that?

She took a deep breath, aching to be back on comfortable ground. Her conciliatory nature had been one of the things her mother and sister considered a flaw, though Jackie disagreed.

"I'm sorry for doubting you. You must be overjoyed

knowing Theo is safe," she said, offering a verbal olive branch. "I'm really looking forward to finally meeting him."

"I am," he replied, shooting her a quick glance. "And relieved. More than anything, I want to gather him up and hug him. Only then will I know it's actually true."

Touched, she swallowed past the sudden lump in her throat. "I can imagine. I only wish Charla would be there, too."

"She'll turn up," he said. "She always does."

More silence. A quick glance his way revealed he stared straight ahead as he drove, noticeably lost in his own thoughts.

"Do you know this Natalie person?" she finally asked. "Did she often babysit Theo?"

"No." Expression remote, he barely took his gaze off the road. "I've never met her. Hell, Charla never once mentioned her name. I'm glad she took care of Theo, but I have no idea why Charla would make such a claim. Assuming she did."

"Assuming she did." She mulled that over for a moment. "What reason would Natalie have to lie?"

"I don't know." A hint of anguish had crept back into his voice, and the tight set of his jaw revealed his inner turmoil.

"I'm sure Rayna will figure it all out," Jackie said. "She seems good at what she does." Despite everything, or maybe because of what they'd shared, she had to push down a strong urge to comfort him. Finally, she decided the hell with it, and squeezed his shoulder. He reached up and covered her hand with his. They rode several miles that way, each lost in their own thoughts.

"I'm glad you're still on my side," he finally said, removing his hand, which made her feel oddly bereft, so she moved hers, too.

"Does my opinion matter that much to you?" she asked, genuinely curious.

He grimaced. "I like you, Jackie. More than like you. I get that you'll be returning to your job and the east coast once all this is over, but this thing between us—whatever you want to call it—is unreal."

"It is." Still, that skeptical part inside her wondered if he was deliberately highlighting their mutual sexual attraction to ensure she stayed on his side. After all, she'd all but admitted she felt the same way. But now she'd be a fool not to have some doubts. She couldn't help it—she'd only known this man a short period of time. He was her sister's ex, after all. Now someone had actually said Charla felt threatened by him. Was that what she'd meant when she'd texted Jackie that her life was in danger?

And how awful was it that even now, when Jackie looked at him, she still wanted to kiss him?

Concentrating on the road, Eli drove fast, his quiet competence and concentration reassuring. Theo had been found. But where was her sister? Would Charla really willingly leave her son for so long?

Jackie knew Charla had grown up spoiled. As the older sister, both she and their mother had doted on her. From the moment Charla could walk and talk, Delia had made it clear that Charla's wants and needs had precedence over anyone else's. Wanting to be a good big sister, Jackie had willingly gone along with this plan. With Charla merely two years behind her in school, Jackie had gladly done without so that Delia could afford to buy Charla the latest fashions, the expensive makeup and designer purses. In truth, Jackie hadn't cared about any of that stuff anyway.

Looking back now, she could see that she'd allowed herself to enable Charla's bad behavior. Jackie had done late homework for her and had even written more than a few of Charla's term papers. A doting—and blind—Delia had refused to give her darling younger daughter anything resembling a curfew, so Charla had taken to partying and even experimenting with drugs.

That was where Jackie had put her foot down. To her surprise, Charla had gone along with Jackie's demands to not partake of the drugs, though she'd balked at the request to make new friends.

Which was why, when Jackie had graduated at the top of her class and had made plans to go to Tech, she'd been dumbfounded at Charla's demand that she remain here in town instead.

When Jackie had attempted to explain, Charla had refused to hear a word she said. Instead, all Charla could think about was herself. "You *owe* it to me to stay until I finish high school," Charla insisted. "You can always go to college later."

After Jackie had left for school and her dorm room, both Charla and Delia refused to speak to her for months. Instead of being proud of her elder daughter, Delia believed Jackie was being selfish.

When Jackie came home for Thanksgiving break, the ice had barely thawed. While away, she experienced the normal freshman homesickness, but when she was back home she'd begun rather quickly to plan her escape.

Things had improved slightly when she returned for winter break. She'd taken Charla shopping, purchased her lots of small gifts that she could barely afford, and as long as she did whatever her younger sister wanted, things were fine.

Looking back, Jackie could see the pattern. Charla took; Jackie gave.

Which was why Charla hadn't bothered to attend Jackie's college graduation. Delia had shown up begrudgingly, explaining away Charla's absence with shrugs and a vague explanation. Because she knew her sister's nature and loved her anyway, Jackie had pushed away her own hurt feelings. When she'd returned home after graduating, Charla hadn't even congratulated her. Jackie had known she should have confronted her, but she'd once again let it slide. After all, she was busy, applying for jobs at various publishers, hoping to put her degree to good use.

It wasn't until Jackie had accepted her editorial assistant job in New York that she'd actually come to understand how self-centered her baby sister had become. Excited to share her good news, Jackie had informed her mother and Charla at the same time. Delia had simply stared, before mumbling a congratulatory phrase and turning away. Charla had turned almost purple with rage. She'd thrown a fit.

Jackie had stood in stunned disbelief as her sister

stomped around their small kitchen, yelling out curse words, calling Jackie names, accusing her of being too big for her britches. Charla sneered as she broke a few plates by hurling them at the wall. Instead of reprimanding her, Delia had simply left the room. Frozen, Jackie wasn't sure what to do. She hadn't expected this reaction at all. She foolishly believed her own sister would be happy for her.

Finally, Charla had given Jackie an ultimatum. Stay in Getaway or consider all ties severed between them. "Stay and do what?" Jackie had asked. Charla didn't have an answer so Jackie had simply shaken her head and continued making her plans to move to the east coast.

Though Jackie had assumed Charla would get over her pique with time, she hadn't. In fact, the first Christmas when Jackie had called her mother to see about making plans to come home, Delia had told her not to bother. It would be too upsetting to her sister, Delia had said.

This had hurt, naturally, but really shouldn't have come as a surprise. Jackie had gone on with making herself a new life in New York, trying not to feel like an orphan.

Looking back, Jackie realized both she and her mother had become Charla's enablers, always making excuses for Charla's bad behavior and questionable choices. Since she never had to face any consequences, Charla had never had the opportunity to learn from her mistakes.

She must have been shocked when Eli actually gave

her some pushback. Evidently, becoming a mother had done nothing to curb Charla's narcissistic tendencies.

And still, despite her sister's refusing to have anything to do with her for three years, Jackie had dropped everything and rushed home when she'd received Charla's text message. Only to learn that instead of finally growing up, Charla had clearly gotten worse.

What a mess. Jackie couldn't believe she'd actually thought she'd be able to fly out here and do what she'd used to do—fix her sister's problems. Instead, she'd managed to create a few of her own.

When she'd stormed out to Eli's ranch, she hadn't expected the flare of instant attraction. He was her sister's *ex-husband*, for Pete's sake. She also knew if she were a disinterested third party on the outside looking in, she might be tempted to think she was a fool, easily swayed by a handsome, sexy man.

Maybe she was. She wasn't sure of anything anymore. Her head began to ache as she continued to gaze out the window at the rugged landscape. Part of her wished she could hightail it back to New York and lose herself in her work and her social life. Once Charla was found, of course.

The other part of her, a part she hadn't even known existed, ached to remain here and explore her developing relationship with Eli. Even allowing herself to think this blew her mind. Talk about complications, not to mention high drama, especially once Charla returned. And Delia…

No. This line of thought had to stop right now. She'd returned to town for one reason and one reason only—

to help her sister. If she couldn't manage to enjoy the company of a handsome cowboy without getting her emotions all tangled up, then she'd need to establish a safe but friendly distance.

Decision made, she relaxed as they drove past the starkly beautiful landscape and wide-open sky. West Texas wasn't for everyone, but anyone who'd grown up here knew they'd always belong.

OVERWHELMED WITH JOY at the knowledge that he would soon see his son again, Eli tried to process the rest of what Rayna had said. It made absolutely no sense. This woman Natalie's claiming that Charla had been afraid of him, worried that he would hurt her, might as well have been another language, with something vital lost in translation.

He wasn't a violent man. Never had been. Even in the darkest part of his marriage. When it seemed he couldn't even look at Charla without provoking an argument, he'd hung on tight to his temper. He'd rarely raised his voice, never mind his hands, no matter how much she'd provoked him. And as addicted to drama as Charla was, she'd deliberately provoked him a lot.

He'd actually been relieved when she'd declared she wanted to move out. But only if she'd left their son. Seeing how much that meant to him, she'd refused. She'd actually laughed when he told her he'd intended to fight her for custody.

When he'd lost, she'd laughed again. His steadfast refusal to visibly show his frustration had made her lose interest in tormenting him further, and they'd settled down to work out the details of his visitation dates with their son.

Oddly enough, while his and Charla's marriage hadn't worked out, they'd actually gotten along better as coparents. She'd been free to live her life unfettered by a husband. He'd never once passed judgment on her lifestyle, other than the times he'd expressed concern about their son. She'd always insisted Theo was being well taken care of, knowing Eli had no choice but to believe her.

So why would Charla—or this Natalie person—make such a bogus claim? He supposed he would be finding out shortly. At least he had the small comfort of knowing how good Rayna was at her job.

The most important thing was that Theo was safe. Delia might try to give Eli a hard time when he went to pick him up, but in the end, she'd have no choice but to release the boy into his father's custody.

The closer Eli got to home, the more his impatience had him rattled. The drive felt as if it took far too long, and he caught himself pushing ninety miles per hour more than once, though he immediately adjusted his speed as soon as he realized. Though Jackie never commented, she seemed a bit fidgety, too.

Her first reaction to hearing this Natalie person's lies had cut him to the core. He understood, and actually couldn't blame her. At least once she'd thought things over, she was willing to give him the benefit of the doubt.

While Eli had his son back, Jackie's sister was still

missing. He could imagine how disappointed she must be that Charla hadn't turned up with Theo.

Again, he wondered where Charla had gone. If she'd really stolen from her employer, did she truly value money more than her son? Clearly, since she'd left him with a friend and never gone back to pick him up.

Unless...what if she truly considered her life in danger? After all, she had sent a text to Jackie stating that. Maybe Christopher Levine had gone after her, once he'd learned of her embezzlement. And then there were her warring boyfriends, one of whom might have decided to make her pay for cheating on him.

To be honest, while Charla had a lot of friends, she'd also made quite a few enemies. Christopher Levine's wife, for one. Eli couldn't imagine she'd been happy to learn about her husband's mistress. The fact of that same mistress stealing from them might have been the last straw. No doubt Rayna had already made a similar list, just in case.

They arrived in town just before dinnertime. He drove straight to the sheriff's department as Rayna had requested, though he really wanted to go directly to Delia's and hug his boy close.

"Let's do this," he told Jackie, swinging into a parking spot. "The quicker I can get this over with, the sooner I can see Theo."

Rayna waited for them in the reception area. The rest of the sheriff's office had emptied out, leaving only the much smaller night crew on duty.

Unsmiling, Rayna nodded at them as they walked through the door. She wore her fiery red hair in a neat bun, and her flinty gaze meant she was in professional law enforcement mode. "Come back with me to my office," she ordered. "I have a few questions to ask you."

Eli nodded, resisting the urge to check his watch because he knew Rayna wouldn't appreciate it. With Jackie right beside him, he followed Rayna back to her office.

Back behind her desk, Rayna waited until they were both seated before dropping into her own chair. Again, she outlined what she'd already told them on the phone. When she'd finished, she sat back in her chair and stared hard at him across her desk. "Eli, do you have any idea why Charla would say such a thing?"

"No." He inhaled. "In fact, I'm not entirely sure she did. What do you know about this Natalie person who Charla entrusted with our son?"

"We checked her out. She has a clean record, no prior arrests. Works a steady job and appears to be an upstanding citizen. She's older than Charla, and says she picks up extra money by taking babysitting jobs." Rayna tilted her head. "Are you sure you've never met her? Tall, leggy brunette with bright blue eyes?"

Why did he feel like that last question might be a trap?

"I don't recognize the name or the description," he said cautiously. "Why do you ask?"

"Because this woman had quite a bit to say about you," Rayna responded. "None of it positive. She talked as if she knew you well, not just on hearsay from Charla. And she seemed very adamant in her statement that you were a danger to her friend."

Not sure how to respond to that, Eli settled on a careful shrug. "I honestly have no idea who she is or why she would feel that way. Let me set the record straight. I never threatened Charla or gave her the slightest indication that I'd ever hurt her. She and I had a friendly divorce and despite the disagreement over who should have custody of Theo, once the decision was made, I accepted it."

"But you didn't like it," Rayna pressed.

Aware of Jackie quietly watching, Eli nodded. "No. I did not. Theo comes first with me. I didn't—don't—believe that Charla feels the same."

"Which might imply motive," Rayna drawled. "However, right now all we have is hearsay. I know you, Eli, and I'd like to think this woman is wrong. We will continue looking for Charla. As long as we find her alive and well, you have absolutely nothing to worry about."

Beside him, Jackie stiffened. Since he knew her absolute worst fear was that something awful had happened to her sister, he decided not to protest. He nodded instead. "Thank you. If we're finished here, I'd like to go see my son. I've been worried sick. I need to see for myself that he's all right."

"Go ahead." Rayna stood, smoothing down the front of her uniform. "Do you want me to go with you? Delia is aware of the accusations Natalie made. I'm thinking she might refuse to let you have your boy."

"I don't think that will be necessary," he began. Jackie placed her hand on his arm.

"Rayna needs to come," she said, her eyes full of concern. "You've seen a brief glimpse into how dramatic—and crazed—my mother can be. You heard her on the phone earlier. If she truly believes you've touched one hair on my sister's head, she'll be out for your blood. Seriously."

Realizing she might have a valid point, he agreed.

"I'll drive right behind you," Rayna said. "When we get there, I'll hang back, unless there's trouble."

Trouble. He thought of how Delia had screamed curse words over the phone. His gut clenched. Around his innocent little boy. Theo had to already be confused and afraid with all the changes and not seeing his mother for so long.

By the time they pulled up to Delia's small house, his insides were churning. All the lights were on and the front porch was well lit. Eli and Jackie got out and waited for Rayna to catch up. Then, all three of them walked up the sidewalk and climbed the three steps up to the front door, though Rayna hung back, waiting on the edge of the front porch, as she'd promised.

Taking a deep breath, Eli pressed the doorbell, listening as the chimes sounded inside. They waited a moment, and then two. No one came to the door. He glanced at Jackie, letting her see his frustration and the worry he tried to suppress. What if Delia refused to come out? Was it possible she wouldn't let him see his own son?

"Let me call her," Jackie said, her voice soothing, apparently noticing his rising panic. "Clearly, she's home."

She pressed the button to dial her mother, putting the call on speaker. Three rings in and Eli began to worry

Delia wasn't going to answer. But midway through the fourth ring, Delia picked up.

"What do you want?" She sounded tired. In the background, Eli could hear his son chattering in toddler-speak.

"We're outside, Mom," Jackie said. "Me and Eli and Rayna. Could you please answer the door?"

"I'm not giving my grandson to the man who might have harmed my daughter," Delia declared. "And you can't make me."

Rayna spoke up. "Actually, Delia, we can. Eli is Theo's father. Eli has not been charged with any crime and he has every right to have custody of his son. You need to turn the boy over or I will have to arrest you."

In response, Delia snarled several harsh curse words. But a moment later she yanked open the front door.

"Wait out here," she demanded, the tight line of her mouth and her furious gaze matching her angry voice. "I'll bring Theo and his bag out to you. I don't want any of you people setting foot in my house."

Jackie started a little at that. *You people* apparently included her own daughter.

"Mom," Jackie began, but then shook her head when Delia wheeled around and glared at her. "There's no reason for you to act like this."

Delia's lip curled as she faced Jackie. "How dare you," she snarled. "You'd better be careful, girly, or Eli will do to you whatever he did to Charla. Though you'll actually deserve it for being stupid enough to trust him."

Narrow eyed, she swung her gaze to Eli. "And when they arrest you and throw you in jail, I'll be raising your son anyway. I'll make sure and tell him all about what kind of person his father turned out to be."

With that, she stomped back inside her house, slamming the door behind her.

Eli briefly closed his eyes, trying and failing to let her vindictive fury wash over him and away. He needed his mind clear of turmoil for his son.

"Don't take her too seriously," Rayna said softly from behind him. "She's just worried and hurting right now. She'll come around eventually."

Jackie didn't say anything. Judging from her strained and hurt expression, her mother's words had cut her deeply. Though Eli knew she, too, worried about her sister, at least she didn't truly believe he'd done something to hurt Charla. He was thankful for that at least.

A moment later the door opened. Delia stood framed in the doorway, still scowling, holding Theo's small hand in hers. At the first sight of his son peering around at them in confusion, Eli thought his heart would explode. "Theo," he said, holding out his arms. "I'm here. Daddy's here."

The instant he caught sight of his father, Theo froze. "Daddy?" he asked, the uncertainty in his small, wavering voice tearing at Eli's heart.

Immediately, Eli crouched down, putting himself at the same level as his son. "It's me, bud," he said. "I don't know where you've been, but I've sure missed you." He continued to hold out his arms, willing to wait until his boy came to him.

Theo jerked his hand free from Delia's and launched himself at his father. Easily, Eli caught him, swinging his boy up and out and around, making Eli squeal with joy. Then, after making two full turns, Eli gathered the toddler close and hugged him tight. Tears pricked at his eyes. His son. Alive and safe.

At that, Delia shoved a small suitcase and a car seat out onto the front porch and closed the door just short of a slam. A moment later they all heard the sound of the dead bolt clicking into place.

Little Theo flinched. "Gamma?" he asked, his plaintive tone tearing at Eli's heart. Judging from his scrunched-up face, Theo was trying to decide whether or not to cry.

"She's okay," Eli soothed. "I promise. Your gamma is fine."

"Come on," Rayna said, putting a hand on his shoulder. "Take your son home. Get him settled. If you need anything, you know how to reach me." Turning, she headed back to her patrol car. "As for me, I've got to get back to work."

Jackie picked up the suitcase and the car seat and took them over to Eli's truck. "You'll have to put this in there," she said, holding up the car seat. "I'm afraid I don't have the slightest idea how."

Though Theo clung tightly to him, Eli managed to untangle himself and handed his son over to Jackie. "Hang on, Theo," he said. "Let me get your car seat ready, okay?"

Thumb in mouth, the toddler nodded. Shifting him to one hip, Jackie rocked him side to side while Eli made short work of installing the child safety seat. He gently took Theo back from Jackie and got him buckled in. "Ready to go to Daddy's house?" he asked, ruffling his son's hair.

Eyes wide, Theo nodded. "See Mama?" he asked.

Feeling as if he'd just been sucker punched, Eli swallowed hard. "Not just yet, little guy. Just me and you and your aunt Jackie here." He glanced at Jackie. "Do you mind coming back to the ranch with me?" he asked, keeping his tone casual. "Or if you'd rather, I can drop you off at the Landshark."

She glanced from him to Theo, who appeared to be on the verge of falling asleep. "I'd like to come with you," she answered softly. "It's about time I get to know my nephew."

Eli tore his gaze away from his son long enough to smile at her. "Great," he said, his heart full. "I'll introduce you. Let's go."

Chapter Ten

Jackie's stomach did a dip the instant his eyes connected with hers. Warmth bloomed inside her, the same aching sense of need she always felt around him. Damn. What was it about this man?

During the drive out to his ranch, she noticed the way Eli constantly watched his son in the rearview mirror. The absolute love and tenderness in his expression told her more about what kind of man Eli Pitts truly was than anything else.

When they finally made the turn onto the rough gravel road that led to his place, she couldn't suppress the feeling she was going home.

Home. That word again. Growing up, Getaway had been the home she couldn't wait to get away from. Often, she'd believed that was why the dusty little west Texas town had been given such a moniker; because people couldn't wait to leave it behind. Despite the town's official story that the name had been chosen by early settlers to keep people out, she'd always believed this.

The past three years she'd slowly made New York

City her home. When she'd first moved there into her small apartment with a roommate she hadn't known, she'd found the crowded chaos both terrifying and lonely. It had taken her a while to make friends, to develop a social life, but she'd finally found her groove. She loved her job, loved the hustle and bustle of the city, and even if she was still single, she'd learned being alone didn't always equal loneliness. She'd dated a few times, nothing serious, but she hadn't actually been looking for that anyway. She wanted to focus on her career.

Now back in the place she hadn't been able to wait to leave, she found herself finally able to see the charm of small-town life. Though honestly, she knew Eli Pitts had a lot to do with that. She shook her head, mentally chastising herself. She'd never been the type of woman who'd let a man derail her from her chosen path.

Jackie had been surprised when Eli asked if she wanted to come back to the ranch with him. She'd actually expected him to drop her off at the motel so he could spend some quality time with his son. The fact that he'd allow her in his special family moment made her feel all squishy inside.

Theo was absolutely adorable. He'd certainly received the best attributes of each parent—Charla's thick platinum-blond hair and long-lashed baby blue eyes along with Eli's features. This child would be a heartbreaker someday, making her wonder what Eli had looked like as a toddler.

Eli. Everything always came back to Eli. Clearly, she had it bad. When she wasn't worrying about her missing sister, she couldn't stop thinking about him. Or aching for the slightest contact of her skin to his, even if it was just a bump of their arms. She'd actually caught herself imagining a life on the ranch with him, even though staying in Getaway had never been something she'd ever even remotely considered.

Charla would be found, she knew. She had to be since the alternative simply wasn't acceptable. And when she returned, she'd be facing charges of theft and embezzlement. Would she have to go away to prison if convicted? Jackie might not know much about her sister anymore, but she did believe someone like Charla would wilt away if confined to a prison cell.

Glancing at the child now soundly asleep in the back seat, she turned to Eli. "Do you think Charla might have gone on the run because she knew Christopher Levine was about to find out what she'd done?"

Keeping his voice pitched as low as hers, Eli answered, "I'm pretty sure that's the situation. I'd guess Rayna's working with that scenario in the back of her mind."

Once he'd pulled up in front of his garage and parked, Eli turned and watched his sleeping son. His unguarded expression, so full of wonder and love, stirred an ache low inside her.

"I wonder if we can get him out of that car seat and into the house without waking him," Jackie said.

"I've done it before." His quiet confidence was even more endearing.

She got out, closing her door quietly, and stood back, watching while Eli carefully unbuckled his son and lifted him from the car seat. Holding him close to his chest, he handed Jackie the keys so she could unlock the front door.

Once inside, Eli carried Theo down the hall into his bedroom. Gently, he cradled his son in one arm while pulling back the covers. To Jackie's amazement, the little boy continued to remain deeply asleep, even when Eli removed his shoes and covered him with the sheet and blanket. Meeting her gaze, Eli motioned at her to follow him. On the way out, he turned off the light.

Instead of immediately leaving, Eli stood in the doorway of his room for a few minutes, just watching him sleep. Jackie stood next to him, memorizing the tender look on his face as he gazed at his son. Finally, Eli put his arm around her waist and tugged her with him. "Come on," he murmured.

Though she'd half expected they'd go to his bedroom, he led her down the hall toward the living room instead. But they'd only taken a few steps when he pressed her against the wall and covered her mouth with his.

As always, passion flared at the first touch of his lips to hers. She got a sense of celebration in his touch; joy, too. His boy was safe. Now, if she could just say the same about her sister.

The thought acted like ice water on flames. She wiggled out from under him, marching down the rest of the hallway and into the kitchen. He followed, equally out of breath, his arousal straining the front of his jeans.

Though her entire body ached for him, she managed to avert her eyes. "I'm starving," she declared, a little more breathless than she would have liked. "Could we make a couple of sandwiches, maybe open a can of soup?"

His bemused expression almost made her crack a smile.

"Sure," he replied. "Go sit and I'll make us something. Would you like a beer?"

Almost tempted to offer to do it herself, she nodded instead. "Sure. Thanks."

He handed her two and then began rummaging in the cupboards.

Carrying them with her, she took a seat at the kitchen table and popped the top on hers, taking a long drink. She was all too aware she'd end up staring at him too closely, so she pulled out her phone and checked social media. She needed something to distract her from her craving for him. Even so, she couldn't resist looking up frequently, watching him as he moved around the kitchen, preparing their meal. Despite her every intention, being here with him in his kitchen felt incredibly intimate. All she needed was for him to put on some soft music and they'd be dancing around the room.

The random thought made her smile and she glanced back at her phone, scrolling past the constant parade of pets and scenery and memes.

"Here you go," Eli said, sliding a plate with a sandwich in front of her and another opposite her seat. "Soup coming right up."

His warm gaze heated her blood. She put down her phone, debated jumping to her feet to see if she could help and decided to remain seated. Watching him, his quiet competence sexy as hell, desire thrummed through her blood. She drank another sip of beer to cover it.

After carrying two bowls of soup over, he sat. "I thought you were hungry."

"Oh, I am." She picked up her sandwich, ham and Swiss with mustard on wheat bread, and took a bite. Looking up, she found him watching her, his own meal uneaten in front of him. The heat in his gaze made a shiver snake up her spine.

Unbelievably, she blushed.

"Do you mind sleeping in the guest room tonight?" he asked. "Because the only way I can take you back to the motel is after Theo wakes up, which probably won't be until morning. Are you okay with that?"

Images of him sprawled in his bed, with her tucked in beside him, flashed through her mind. "The guest bedroom will be fine," she said, refocusing her attention on her food.

After they ate, she offered to do the dishes, but he insisted. Once again, pleasantly full this time, she sat and watched him, admiring the way his jeans rode on his narrow hips, and the shape of his butt.

He checked on Theo again before asking Jackie if she wanted to watch TV. She agreed, feeling both relaxed and oddly on edge. She kind of liked feeling so cozily domesticated here in his home with him, but knew she shouldn't.

When she took a seat on the couch, he joined her, though he sat at the opposite end. Though he'd picked up the remote, he made no move to turn the television on.

"Where do you think Charla is?" she asked. "I don't get why she'd leave her son."

Eli opened his mouth and then closed it. "I'm not sure," he finally answered. "From the way she's been acting lately, I think she might have decided she couldn't live her best life and take care of a toddler, too."

"Her best life?" she echoed. "What do you mean?"

Again, he considered her, appearing to weigh his words. "If Charla did steal from Levine's, and say the amount was…substantial, she might have decided to take the opportunity with the stolen money to reinvent herself somewhere else. She always seemed to be struggling with what kind of person she wanted to be."

"True. I get that. But what would make her decide to become a thief? I know my sister likes to party and could be superficial and shallow, but to steal from her employer?" And abandon her child, she added mentally. Not to mention dump a man who, from all appearances, had made a pretty fantastic husband and father.

Or, she reminded herself, it could all be an act.

"Earth to Jackie," Eli said softly. "I don't know where you went, but as far as your question about what Charla was thinking, we won't know until we can ask her." With that, he turned on the TV.

"Anything in particular you want to watch?" he asked, scrolling through the offerings on Netflix.

"I've just finished a couple of shows," she replied, deciding not to tell him she'd binge-watched them. "How about a movie?"

They settled on a light romantic comedy that had good reviews. As the movie began, she found herself wishing he'd slide over from his end of the couch and sit closer to her, but figured in the end it might be best if he didn't.

Evidently, he felt the same way, because he kept a good bit of distance between them the entire movie. As the ending credits rolled, she got to her feet and quietly asked him if he'd mind showing her where she'd be staying.

"Sure," he said. "There are already clean sheets on the bed. I keep it made up just in case."

The small room had been simply decorated. A double bed, a single nightstand with a plain lamp, and a dresser were the only furniture. A few generic framed prints hung on the walls, and three colorful throw pillows brought a touch of color to the room. Eyeing them, Jackie realized she could see her sister choosing them. At least at one point, Charla must have tried to decorate the house.

"I'll leave you fresh towels in the bathroom," Eli said, his tone formal. "Is there anything else you need?"

Without turning to look at him, she slowly shook her head. "I'm good, thank you."

He turned and left without another word. Aching, she closed her door and turned down the covers.

When she woke the next morning, she sat up in bed blinking, looking around the unfamiliar room, disoriented. Eli's guest room. And judging from the absolute silence in the rest of the house, everyone else must still be asleep.

Needing coffee, she tiptoed toward the kitchen, stopping short when she caught sight of Eli rocking Theo in a chair she hadn't noticed in one corner of the den. Eli crooned wordlessly to the dozing toddler.

Heart struck, she froze, unable to speak past the lump in her throat.

As he glanced up, a slow smile spread across his face. "Hey," he said softly. "Good morning. He woke up hungry at five, so I changed him and made him breakfast. He'll sleep for an hour or two and then I can take you back to the motel."

She nodded and cleared her throat. "Sounds perfect." Not trusting herself to speak again, she turned and made her way to the kitchen.

Though it felt like she was hiding, she sat at the table and drank her coffee. Her equilibrium couldn't take seeing Eli and his son right now. Emotion washed over her as she thought of her sister and the bad choices Charla had made.

Once she'd finished her coffee, she went back to ask Eli if he wanted her to make something for breakfast. She couldn't make herself just rummage in his fridge. But when she got to the den, he and Theo were gone. Listening, she thought she heard them down the hall in Theo's room. A rush of overwhelming longing hit her, so hard she momentarily couldn't catch her breath.

Suddenly, she wanted to get out of there. As soon as possible. She'd shower once she got to her motel room.

Heart pounding, she forced herself to walk down the hallway toward Theo's room. Eli had gotten the boy dressed and right now had knelt down to tie his shoes.

"Hey," she said, standing in the doorway. "Would you mind running me back to the motel?"

Looking up, Eli studied her. "You sure you don't want to shower and have breakfast first? Theo's already had his bath and I showered earlier."

"No, thank you." She kept her tone polite. "I've got a few things I need to do today, so I'd really like to get back."

"No problem," he replied. "Let me grab the keys and we'll head out."

When he dropped her off at the Landshark, Theo giggled and blew her a kiss from his car seat. Touched, she blew him one right back. Eli smiled. "I'll touch base with you later, okay?"

"Sure."

Back inside her room, she rushed through her shower, planning to go out and grab a meal somewhere. After blow-drying her hair, she got dressed. She felt oddly lethargic, as if she'd spent the entire night making mad, passionate love with Eli. As if.

Her cell rang. Rayna. Jackie answered on the second ring.

"Hi, Rayna. What's up?"

"Can you come downtown?" Rayna asked. "I have something here that you need to see."

"Of course," Jackie answered. "Should I tell Eli?"

"Not this time," Rayna replied, surprising her. "I'd like to talk to you alone."

Jackie promised to be there in fifteen minutes. She finished applying her makeup, slipped on a pair of flats and grabbed her keys. She made it to the sheriff's department in ten.

The receptionist smiled at her as she walked through

the door. "Go on back," she said. "Rayna is expecting you."

As usual, Jackie found the door to Rayna's office open. The sheriff sat behind her desk and looked up at Jackie, unsmiling.

"What is it?" Jackie asked, dread coiling low in her belly. "Is something wrong?"

"This came." Rayna held out an envelope. Jackie recognized Charla's distinctive, almost childish, handwriting on the outside.

"Go ahead," Rayna urged. "It's addressed to me, but I think she meant part of this for you."

As Jackie accepted it, her heart pounding, Rayna touched her arm. "A word of caution before you read it," Rayna said. "I'm not sure I believe what she wrote at all. Keep that in mind, okay? There's no reason to freak out. Especially if you notice the postmark date."

Slowly, Jackie opened the envelope and pulled out a single sheet of paper. Definitely her sister's handwriting, though clearly Charla had made an effort to tone down her usually exuberant scrawl.

If you're reading this, most likely I'm dead. Jackie gasped aloud, raising her gaze from the paper to meet Rayna's.

"Keep going," Rayna urged, the set of her mouth grim. "Like I said. Take it with a grain of salt."

Heart pounding, Jackie nodded. *I had an arrangement with a friend to mail this if they didn't hear from me by Wednesday. I think my ex-husband is working with Christopher Levine to have me killed.*

Now Jackie understood Rayna's comment. Her skepticism made sense. Only someone as self-involved as Charla would try to make anyone believe those particular two men would work together for anything, never mind murdering her.

She continued reading. *My son is with a friend of mine named Natalie Beaumont. My mother will need to raise him. I know she'll make sure he remembers me. And if my sister showed up after I sent that text—which I doubt—tell her too little, too late.*

But I want Eli and Mr. Levine punished for taking my life.

Promise me you'll do this, or I swear I'll haunt you.

AFTER DROPPING JACKIE OFF, Eli took his son to the Tumbleweed Café for breakfast. He knew just about everyone in town had been worried about Theo and it would do them all good to see him in person.

From the back seat, Theo chortled. He'd brought along one of his favorite toys, a stuffed alligator with whom he liked to converse in his own mostly unintelligible language.

After parking, Eli unstrapped Theo and carried him inside. As usual, the café was packed. Several people looked up when he entered, and then did a double take when they saw his son.

On his way to the table, he stopped and talked to several people. Once he and Theo were seated, he requested a booster seat and ordered breakfast. Theo wanted pancakes, so he got those, plus a fried egg platter for himself.

He'd just pushed his plate away when his cell rang. His heart skipped a beat when he saw the caller was Rayna.

"Any news?" he asked, hoping she'd gotten a lead as to Charla's whereabouts.

"Sort of," Rayna replied. "But not what I think you're hoping for. I've got Jackie here with me. Christopher Levine is on the way, and I need you here, as well."

"What's going on?" he asked, more intrigued than alarmed.

But Rayna had already hung up.

Quickly, he signaled for the check and paid, leaving a generous tip. After cleaning off Theo's face and hands with a baby wipe, Eli lifted him out of the booster seat and carried him inside.

The instant he stepped into the sheriff's office, the receptionist waved him past. He hurried through the open area, back to Rayna's office. When he arrived, he knocked on her closed door.

"Come in," she said.

Inside, Rayna sat behind her desk. Jackie sat in one of the visitor chairs, while Christopher Levine sat in the other.

"About time you got here," the jeweler muttered, eyeing Eli with a sour expression.

As for Jackie, she wouldn't meet his eyes. Judging by her tightly crossed arms and her defensive body language, she wasn't happy with whatever news Rayna had shared.

"This came today," Rayna said, handing him a photocopy of a letter. He recognized Charla's swirly handwriting immediately.

Only then did he realize that both Jackie and Christopher also held copies.

Reading it quickly, when he got to the end, he shook his head. "This is not true. At all."

Now Christopher smirked at him. "That's exactly what I said. Why would I kill her before I got back what she stole from me? I think she's setting us up."

"You may be right." Judging from Rayna's noncommittal tone, she'd set up this meeting just to see what bringing them all together might shake out.

Jackie spoke up for the first time. "Actually, you both have motive. Charla stole from you, Christopher. And Eli, she took your son away."

When Eli opened his mouth to reply, Jackie held up her hand. "I'm not finished. Personally, the more I've come to learn about my sister, the more I've come to realize she wasn't a very nice person. One thing I do know for sure is I don't think there's any way in hell the two of you would work together since I know Charla had an affair with you, Christopher, while she was still married to Eli."

Though Christopher flushed, he didn't deny her observation. How could he, when it was true?

"Then what could be Charla's motive?" Rayna asked, her gaze briefly settling on each of them in turn.

"Faking her death to disappear with my money," Christopher replied. "Come on. It's pretty damn obvious."

Though his comment earned a scowl from Jackie, she didn't dispute his statement.

"That's one possibility," Rayna chimed in, once

again the voice of reason. "The other, though doubtful, is that Charla really has met some sort of serious harm."

No one responded to this, though Jackie sighed.

"Does anyone have any other suggestions?" Rayna asked. "Because after looking over the records Mr. Levine has provided, due to the amount of money missing, this is a felony."

"Does that mean you'll be calling in the FBI or the Texas Rangers?" Jackie asked.

"No." Rayna smiled. "Those agencies are busy with other larger crimes. They don't like to deal with business crimes. Embezzlement is much more common than you realize."

Christopher opened his mouth as if to protest, and then closed it.

"However, since Mr. Levine has pressed charges, I've been able to put out an APB on Charla. This will help get other state police departments on alert. If they see her, she will be arrested."

Jackie turned to face Christopher. "If you don't mind me asking, exactly how much money did Charla steal?"

He swallowed hard. "Over the last three years, it's half a million dollars."

Shocked despite himself, Eli glanced at Jackie.

Jackie sat back in her chair. "I..." she began. "I don't know what to say."

"Yeah," Christopher said, glum-voiced. "I trusted her. I really trusted her. I still haven't told Kim."

His wife. Eli wondered if Kim knew about the affair. Since it wasn't his business, he decided not to ask.

"Does Kim know about you and Charla?" Jackie asked, evidently feeling no such constraint.

Christopher blanched. "No. And I'd like to keep it that way. Charla and I ended things and we were just employer/employee for a good while. When she returned to work after having her son, one thing led to another and..." He shook his head. "Looking back on it now, I think she used that to distract me so I didn't notice her stealing from the company."

"Any other suggestions?" Rayna asked, clearly trying to bring the discussion back on track. "I've already spoken with Delia and asked her to provide me a list of places Charla might have talked about visiting. I'd like the three of you to do the same. In the meantime, I have friends who work for the Houston Police Department. They have contacts in Galveston and Corpus, in case Charla might have fled to the coast."

"Do you really think she's still in the country?" Eli had to ask. "Because it seems to me more likely she might have taken off for somewhere like the Bahamas or Grand Cayman. It'd be much easier to disappear, especially with that much cash."

Though Rayna nodded, Jackie stubbornly shook her head. "Even though you're running with the theory that my sister cut and ran, promise me you're still looking into the chance she might have come to harm. Between the text message, her friend Natalie and this note, it seems to me that's still a very real possibility."

"Of course." Rayna nodded. "One thing I've learned since beginning work in law enforcement is never to close my mind to any scenario."

Eli felt compelled to speak. "One thing I can say for certain is that I didn't harm Charla in any way."

"Me neither," Christopher seconded. "I just want my money and my missing gemstones back."

Looking from one man to the other, Jackie didn't speak.

"All right," Rayna said, pushing to her feet. "I've got to get back to work. I'll keep you all posted if I learn anything."

Waiting while they all filed out, Rayna held out her arms to Theo. "Come see Auntie Rayna," she crooned.

Eyeing her with suspicion, Theo squinted at her. Then, either remembering her or just deciding he liked her, he giggled and leaned toward her. Eli passed him over, conscious of Jackie standing behind him and quietly watching.

"Let me walk you out to your truck," Rayna said, still bouncing Theo. "You, too, Jackie."

Jackie nodded. "Sounds good."

"Where's Christopher?" Looking around, Eli realized the other man must have already gone.

"He took off the second I ended our meeting," Rayna responded. "I'll definitely be keeping an eye on him."

Once they were outside, Rayna continued to hold Theo while Eli unlocked his truck. She then handed him over, watching while Eli buckled him into his car seat. "Jackie, wait," she called out. "Come here for just a second. I have something to say to Eli and I think you need to hear it."

Though her reluctance shone in her face, Jackie complied.

"I want you to know I'm not only going to be watching Mr. Levine," she said. "I'll be keeping an eye on this one, too. But honestly, I truly don't think Charla is in any danger. My best guess would be that she took the money and ran. I wouldn't be surprised if she hasn't left the country already." Looking from Eli to Jackie, she nodded. "Either way, we will find your sister. You can count on that."

"Thanks." Jackie nodded. "I appreciate that. Have you mentioned this latest letter to Delia yet?"

"Not yet."

"I'd appreciate if you'd hold off," Jackie asked. "I understand if you feel you can't do that, but Delia is already out for blood. Charla can do no wrong as far as she's concerned. I'm afraid something like this might send her over the edge."

Rayna nodded. "I figured. I'll keep this to myself for a while longer. Y'all have a good rest of your day, all right?" With that, she turned and went back inside.

Without looking at him, Jackie also took off, hightailing it to her rental car. Eli thought about calling to her and decided against it. They'd all had a bit of a shock this afternoon. Each of them had their own way of dealing with things. He'd leave Jackie alone and let her figure this out on her own. After all, she knew how to reach him.

Chapter Eleven

Driving through downtown Getaway, sleepy and quiet in the sunshine, Jackie didn't know what to think or how to feel. This was absolutely insane. Everything she'd thought she knew or believed about her sister had been turned upside down. On the one hand, she'd much rather believe Charla to be safe somewhere, maybe lounging on a beach, even if she'd stolen a huge amount of money and abandoned her son. On the other, she couldn't quite discount the possibility that her sister might have actually come to some harm.

The letter had been the tipping point, at least for her. It was complete and utter nonsense. No way would Eli and Christopher Levine have worked together against Charla. If Charla truly thought anyone would believe such a thing, she'd guessed wrong. The only person Jackie could think of who might would be Delia. Which was why Jackie had asked Rayna not to share it with her yet. All they needed was Delia going off on another frenzy.

The only thing Charla's letter had accomplished, as far as Jackie was concerned, was that she actually felt sorry for both Eli and Christopher Levine. While she couldn't deny that the jewelry store owner had done wrong by having an affair with his employee, he didn't deserve to lose half a million dollars.

And Eli, poor Eli. From the various clues she'd been picking up ever since she'd met him, he'd at first been blinded by Charla's beauty and her fake charm and had never seen the true Charla coming. She managed to completely upend his life, leaving a trail of destruction behind her like an EF4 tornado.

She made it back to the motel and let herself into her room. Housekeeping had already made the room up, which meant she wouldn't have to worry about being disturbed.

Head pounding, she decided to try and take a nap. She hadn't slept well in Eli's guest bed and there'd been too much emotional drama in the past twenty-four hours. She'd barely crawled between the sheets when her phone rang. Fumbling in the dark room, when she saw Eli's name come up on caller ID, she declined the call. She didn't really feel up to talking to him right now. She needed both time and space to clear her head.

An instant later her phone chimed, indicating a voice mail. She debated, but in the end decided to go ahead and listen. "I need your help. Your mother is here. She's demanding I hand over my son and is refusing to leave until I do, which isn't happening. I thought I'd try you before I called Rayna. I guess I have no choice."

Muttering a curse word, she hit Redial. Eli answered immediately. "I stupidly let her into my house because she apologized and seemed normal. She is Theo's grandmother after all, and I felt like she has a right to see him. But then she went into his bedroom and started packing him a bag. She got loud and hostile, which scared my son. He's crying, I'm trying to calm him down and she's refusing to leave without him. I can tell you right now, that isn't happening."

"I'm so sorry," Jackie said, her headache intensifying. In the background, she could hear Theo wailing and her mother ranting and raving. "I'm on my way. But since I doubt she'll listen to me, go ahead and call Rayna." After ending the call, she grabbed the car keys and ran to her car.

Though she drove as fast as she dared, by the time she pulled up to Eli's ranch house, a sheriff's department cruiser was already parked next to her mother's red Camaro.

With a dread settling in her chest, she got out and climbed the steps to the front porch. While she still grappled with her feelings for Eli, in the end he was Theo's father, and Delia had no right to try and take his son from him. Her mother appeared to have completely gone off the rails.

As she raised her hand to ring the doorbell, she heard Delia shouting inside. Jackie tried the knob and finding the door unlocked, simply walked into the house. Immediately, she saw the sheriff, back to her, facing off with Delia. Eli and Theo must have gone to another room.

Rayna turned, relief flashing across her face. "There you are," she said. "Maybe you can talk some sense into your mother before I have to arrest her."

"For what?" Delia bellowed. "I haven't done anything wrong. In fact, I seem to be the only one here who hasn't lost their damn mind. I want to save my grandson's life. How can anyone deny me a chance to do that?"

"Mom." Jackie moved forward. "You've got to stop this. We have no proof that Eli did anything to Charla. He's Theo's father, so he has every right in this situation. You don't."

"Traitor," Delia sneered, her lip curling. "You've always thought you were so smart, such an intellectual, looking down on me and your sister. Now that man has you wrapped around his finger, blind of anything but how badly you want to—"

"Stop." Eli entered the room, cutting off Delia. "I'm going to ask you nicely once again to leave. If you refuse, I will press charges for trespassing and ask the sheriff to arrest you."

"You can't do that," Delia protested. Her gaze swung to Rayna's. "Can he?"

"Yes. And since I sure hate the idea of you riding to the jail in the back of my patrol car and all the gossip that will come from that, I'd suggest you do as Mr. Pitts asks and leave."

"Right now," Eli added for emphasis. "I finally got Theo calmed down. I don't need you riling him up again."

Looking from one to the other, at first Delia didn't move. Glancing from Eli to Jackie to Rayna, she appeared to be weighing her options. For a second, Jackie feared her mother might make a mad dash toward Eli's room in an attempt to snatch him up and run.

Finally, Delia shook her head. Muttering under her breath, she marched toward the door. When she reached Jackie, she stopped and looked her older daughter in the face. "I think you should take a long, hard look at how you're acting here. You need to be thinking more about helping your sister and less about yourself."

Then, head held high, Delia sailed away.

A moment later they heard her car rumble to life. Spinning her tires in the gravel in a final show of defiance, she took off.

Jackie let her shoulders sag with relief.

"That was intense," Eli said, his expression troubled. "I know Delia tends to be dramatic, but that was bizarre even for her."

"She's worried sick about her daughter," Rayna pointed out gently. "I think she feels like she should be doing something, anything. In her mind she honestly feels there's a very real possibility you might have harmed Charla. She told me this. She even said she could hardly blame you, after the way Charla treated you."

"Delia spoke to you about her feelings?" Jackie asked, hardly able to believe it. "When?"

"She stopped by my office bright and early this morning." Rayna met Jackie's gaze before doing the same with Eli. "And for the record, I had to show her that letter from Charla. I couldn't lie to her. She broke down and wept."

"That's what set her off." Eli dragged his hand over his chin. "Considering I went through hell just getting

Theo from her last night, I couldn't figure out why she was already back at it this morning."

Rayna grimaced. "She told me she was going home. That she was going to go by Jackie's room at the Landshark so they could talk, maybe work out a plan of action. I take it she didn't come by there?"

Feeling like a deer caught in the headlights, Jackie shook her head. "Not while I was there, at least." She hoped Rayna didn't ask her to elaborate, because even though her overnight stay at Eli's place had been innocent, she doubted anyone would believe that.

Luckily for her, Rayna didn't press. Instead, she told them to let her know if they needed anything else and left.

Drained, Jackie turned to do the same.

"Wait," Eli said, touching her arm, his gaze pleading. "Can we talk? Please? I put Theo down for a nap and I'm thinking we might need to clear the air after all that."

Slowly, she nodded. "Look, Eli, I'll be up-front with you. I feel as if you are being put in an awful position here and you don't deserve that. Right now, I wish my sister would just show up and admit to what she's done wrong and get some help. But I think we both know that's not going to happen."

Cautiously, he agreed.

"That said, until she can see and talk to Charla, my mother is going to think the worst of you. I'm not sure why, as she's known you longer than I have, but that's clearly how it's going to be."

His expression darkened. "I can't have her upsetting

my son. Theo's been through enough in the last couple weeks. He needs stability and calmness. All that shouting and screaming had him shaking and sucking his thumb. That's not acceptable at all."

Her heart squeezed at the idea of that precious little boy quaking in terror of his own grandmother. "I agree," she said. "Once she's had time to calm down, I plan to have a word with my mother, though clearly she thinks I've gone over to side with the enemy."

Gaze locked on hers, Eli nodded. When he looked at her like that, with his heart in his eyes, she couldn't think, never mind speak a coherent sentence.

"You're probably right," he said, his voice dejected. "I'm sorry you got dragged into the middle of all this, Jackie."

Stunned, she eyed him. "The fact that you're apologizing to me seems like almost a bitter irony. Especially since it's my sister and my mother causing all this."

"I have Theo back," he told her. "The rest of this is a fresh hell, but none of it matters now that my son is safe."

Did that mean he was washing his hands of everything else?

"Are you still going to help me search for my sister?" she asked. "Since you have Theo back and all, I wouldn't blame you if you decided you were done."

"Of course I am." His chin came up, his gaze steady. "I have to clear my name. Now that she's thrown around all these false accusations, I want to find her more than anything."

"Fair enough." She actually managed to smile at him.

For one awkward moment they stood there, separated only by a few feet, breathing the same air. She had the sense that one move toward him on her part and she'd find herself wrapped up tight in his arms.

The sound of car tires on gravel jerked them back to reality. Eli went to the window and swore. "She's back. Your mother. I'm not going to answer the door." He pulled out his phone. "Should I call Rayna? This is ridiculous."

"Not yet." Rolling her shoulders to try to relieve some of the tension, Jackie took a deep breath. "Let me go outside and talk to her. Maybe I can convince her that this is a huge mistake."

"I'll go with you," he decided. "I won't hesitate to call Rayna if Delia tries to start more trouble."

"Let me try to handle this alone first," she insisted. "I'll call you if I need you." Not giving him a chance to argue, she slipped out the front door and waited for her mother on the porch, heart pounding.

As Delia slowly got out of her car, Jackie debated whether to go down and intercept her on neutral ground. In the end, she decided to stay where she was, ready for anything. For all she knew, her mother might have decided to resort to physical violence. She hoped not.

"Are you still here?" Delia asked, seemingly surprised, though so far her tone sounded reasonable.

Instead of answering, Jackie gave her mother a stern look. "What are you doing, Mom? There's no sense in stirring up more trouble. I know Rayna doesn't want to arrest you, but she will if she has to."

"I came to apologize to Eli," Delia responded. "And

since you're here, to you. I'm out of my mind with worry. I don't know how I'll go on living if Charla is dead." Her voice shook. Then, covering her face with her hands, she started sobbing. Loudly and noisily.

Now Jackie left the porch to put her arms around her mother's shaking shoulders. "She's fine, Mom. I truly believe she's fine. I still intend to find her."

The front door opened and Eli stepped outside, just in time to hear Delia's last statement.

"Me, too," Eli said, the sympathy in his deep voice bringing tears to Jackie's eyes.

Delia looked up, still crying. "I'm sorry for how I treated you, Eli. You didn't deserve that. Neither did Theo. When Rayna showed me that letter Charla had mailed, I lost my mind."

"I understand." Eli didn't move. "But you cannot ever do that to Theo again. He's very uncertain due to all the changes he's been through. You coming here and screaming and cursing made him shake and cry. I had a tough time getting him settled back down. I can't allow you to be around him at all if you can't act like a responsible adult and a loving grandmother. Do you understand?"

Wiping away her tears, Delia nodded. "I'm sorry. It won't happen again, I promise."

Though he didn't appear convinced, Eli finally nodded. "What about your other daughter?" he asked, nodding toward Jackie. "You owe her an apology, too."

Delia's jaw tightened, making Jackie realize for whatever reason, her mother found saying she was sorry to Jackie more difficult. "I shouldn't have said what I did," Delia admitted. "You've always been so smart, so accomplished. Charla and I always felt somehow less around you."

Stunned, Jackie wasn't sure how to respond. She'd never ever treated either her mother or her sister as if she considered herself better than them. In fact, she'd always secretly envied the close bond they'd shared, their vivaciousness and blond good looks.

When she said this out loud, Delia appeared shocked. "Honey, I had no idea." She reached out and pulled Jackie in for another hug. Not a social hug, or a for-appearances'-sake hug, but a genuine let-me-offer-comfort hug. For the first time since Jackie could remember, she allowed herself to lean in and hug back. It felt pretty darn good.

Delia then stepped back and looked at Eli. "Since we're admitting truths, I should tell you that I had high hopes when Charla married you and got pregnant. I figured if anyone could help that wild child settle down, it would be you. Don't think I didn't see how she treated you."

He opened his mouth to respond, but Delia held up a hand. "I'm not finished. Despite all that Charla put you through, I noticed how you responded. You never once raised your voice or your hand to my daughter. That's why I know you wouldn't have hurt her, no matter what her letter says."

Eli smiled wryly. "Thanks, but like any married couple, we argued. I'm sure I might have yelled once or twice. But the other, no. I was raised to understand that a man never hits a woman."

Nodding, Delia turned to face Jackie. "Your sister is up to something," she said. "I understand she might have stolen a lot of money from Levine's. It's been all over town. People are speculating that she might have escaped to the Caribbean, but I know for a fact that Charla never got around to getting her passport. That makes her leaving the country highly unlikely."

Fascinated, Jackie tried to understand her mother's mercurial change of heart. She wasn't entirely sure Delia was sincere. "How are you so certain that Charla is okay?" she asked. "Barely an hour ago you were convinced Eli had done something to her."

Delia lifted her chin, looking from Jackie to Eli and back again. "Because I know my daughter. Charla was always into those true crime television shows. I think she's trying to make people think she's dead so she can get away with stealing that money. And sadly, she's trying to make either Eli or Christopher Levine take the fall."

Struggling to process this, Jackie shook her head. "To do that, she'd need a body. They'd have to match the DNA to hers. How on earth would she pull something like that off?"

"There are a lot of ways." Suddenly the expert, Delia spoke with more confidence. "She and I used to discuss this all the time. Like I said, she was fascinated by the subject. Her personal favorite was an explosion with fire on board a yacht in the ocean. As long as there was enough proof she'd been on board, she wouldn't need a body."

Frowning, Eli shook his head. "That sounds complicated. That'd be a lot of work. I don't think Charla could manage that alone."

"That's just it," Delia replied. "She wouldn't be alone. I didn't mention this to anyone before because quite frankly, it didn't occur to me, but Charla had met a man online. I'm not sure where he lives, but I remember her saying it was on the coast."

"There's a lot of coast," Jackie said slowly. "Gulf coast, east coast, west. Is there any way you can narrow it down?"

"I can." Voice triumphant, Delia nodded. "It has to be the Texas coast. Charla always said she'd never date anyone but a Texan."

STEPPING OUT OF the room, Eli phoned Rayna and filled her in. "There's a lot of coast in Texas," he said. "I wish we could have more specifics, like which city."

"We need access to Charla's online dating profile," Rayna said. "There are a ton of different services, so it would help if Delia can narrow it down to one or two." She paused for a moment, clearly thinking. "It'd be even better if we had access to Charla's computer. Now that Mr. Levine has pressed charges, we'll get a warrant to search her apartment. Hopefully, she'll have left something behind."

"Sounds good. What, if anything, can I do to help you?"

"Just sit tight," Rayna responded. "I promise I'll keep you posted. One more thing. I probably don't have to say this, but watch out for that Delia. She's not stable. The wild mood swings have me worried."

He glanced back toward the house. “Right now all is quiet, but I get your point.”

The front door opened just as he ended the call. He shoved his phone into his pocket as Delia hurried out. She stopped short, obviously surprised to see him. “I’d wondered where you’d gotten to,” she said, smiling. “I hope you won’t hold my hysterics earlier against me. I’d like to see my grandson again. Jackie said he was sleeping and she didn’t want me to wake him, but will you bring him by my house sometime?”

“Sure.” He dipped his chin, thinking not any time soon. He had no idea what Delia might be up to, but he didn’t entirely trust her. As Rayna had mentioned, Delia wasn’t stable.

“That was weird,” Jackie said as soon as he walked inside. “At first, I so wanted to believe her. The little kid in me, I guess, still craving her mother’s love.” She took a deep breath. “But this feels off.”

“I agree.” Walking to the back, he checked on Theo, still sound asleep. When he returned, he motioned for Jackie to follow him into the kitchen, so he could fill her in on his conversation with Rayna.

“I think it’s important we continue to play along with your mother,” he continued. “Maybe you can call her and ask her if she knows what dating services Charla used.”

“I can do that,” Jackie replied. “One thing, though. I don’t think you should allow Delia anywhere near Theo until Charla is found. I know she might have seemed sincere in her regret and all, but I have no idea what might set her off again. She might suddenly decide you shouldn't be raising your son and cause another big scene."

"Agreed." Unable to resist, he crossed the room and pulled her into his arms. She wrapped her arms around him, and they stood that way, each silently drawing on each other's strength.

"This is one big cluster," she murmured, her face pressed into his chest. She felt good, nestled against him, her soft curves molded into his.

Inhaling the sweet scent of her hair, he agreed. At least he had her, at least for now. Jackie in his life might be only temporary, but she was the best thing that had ever happened to him, other than his son.

In fact, he knew he'd fallen hard for her. His ex-wife's sister, who happened to live all the way across the country. Talk about poor choices. He grimaced. As if he'd had a choice. The instant he'd seen Jackie, standing on his doorstep with fire in her eyes, he'd been lost.

When she finally moved out of his arms, her expression looked as bleak as he felt inside. "I'm sorry about all of this," she said softly. "It seems my entire family has gone off the deep end."

He tried to lighten the mood. "Unfortunately, we don't get to choose our relatives."

"Truth," she replied, though she didn't smile. "I'd better be going. I want to see if Rayna would let me help look at Charla's computer, if they find one. I'm a bit of a computer nerd and I think my skills might be helpful."

He had some horse training and barn cleaning to do. He usually just set up a playpen and put Theo in it where he could keep an eye on the toddler. But lately, at least according to Charla, Theo had been climbing out of the playpen on his own. This wouldn't be good around horses.

He eyed Jackie, wondering. "I need a favor first," he said. "If it's not imposing too much. It'll probably take Rayna a bit to get a judge to sign off on that search warrant. I'm wondering if you'd mind watching Theo while I work the two horses I have here to train. I also need to clean out a couple of stalls."

"I can do that," she said. "How long are you thinking?"

"Maybe three hours, four tops." Bracing himself for her to decline, he exhaled in relief when she nodded. He couldn't really afford to slack off with his work. Though he'd been paid a retainer, he wouldn't receive the balance until he had these two horses trained.

Thanking her again, he hurried out the door, intent on getting right to it. He saddled up the first horse, a beautiful palomino gelding the owner had nicknamed Johnny, and rode out to the outdoor arena.

The work went well, with Johnny responsive and seemingly eager to learn. Once Eli had removed the saddle and put the horse on the electric walker, he went to retrieve Ro, the other gelding. He rode Ro back into the arena and began to put the animal through his paces. Ro had a different personality than Johnny, more skittish and a bit antsy, though still responsive and willing to learn.

Movement over by the railing had Ro sidestepping, showing the whites of his eyes. Eli glanced over, surprised to see Jackie standing there with Theo in her arms, pointing out his daddy on top of the horse.

For an instant, just one flash of time, Eli could picture a future where this scenario was a regular part of the day. Doing what he loved to do, working a horse, with Jackie and his son looking on.

Even knowing damn well that such a thing wasn't realistic didn't stop the rush of yearning for it to be.

When Eli finished with Ro, he unsaddled him and put him on the automatic walker, while he took Johnny to brush down. By the time he'd taken care of both horses, Jackie and Eli had returned to the house.

He rushed through mucking out the stalls, something he usually had one of his part-time helpers do. When he'd finished, he walked back to the house, dirty and sweaty and in need of a quick shower.

Smiling, Jackie agreed. After a quick, restorative shower and some clean clothes, he returned to find her in the kitchen, feeding Theo macaroni and cheese in his high chair.

"There's more on the stove if you're hungry," she said, the warmth in her gaze letting him know she liked the way he'd cleaned up. Naturally, his body responded immediately.

Grabbing a bowl, he helped himself to some cheesy carbs and sat down next to his son. Theo grinned, clearly happy to see him, and began talking his particular brand of toddler gibberish, punctuated every now and then by an actual word.

Jackie stood for a moment, watching them, and then checked her watch. "I've really got to go."

"Of course." Looking down to give himself time to mask his disappointment, Eli stood. He debated kissing her goodbye, but ended up thanking her politely instead. For a second he thought he saw a flash of disappointment cross her face before she nodded and smiled.

"No problem," she replied. "I enjoyed hanging out with Theo and getting to know him."

As if he understood exactly what she'd said, Theo waved his arms and chortled, making Jackie laugh. Her laughter, joyful and unaffected, made him happy. Hell, just breathing the same air as she did brought him joy. Sometimes, the thought of how much she'd come to mean to him so quickly terrified him. Right now, he wished he could preserve this moment forever.

She caught her breath. "Eli? Are you all right?"

Blinking, he nodded. "Yes. Why do you ask?"

"I don't know." She shrugged. "Maybe because you seemed a thousand miles away."

"I…" Deciding to be honest, he took a step closer to her. "I was wishing this could be a regular thing. You, me and Theo. I know, I know." Grimacing, he held up a hand. "Can't blame a guy for wishing."

This time her smile seemed tinged with a bit of sadness. "I get that. Spending time here today with you and Theo made me—" She stopped, shaking her head. "I'd better get going."

Reaching out, he touched her arm. "Made you what?" he asked.

"Made me long for something that isn't possible," she whispered, her eyes huge.

He kissed her then, crushing her to him and taking her mouth as if this might be the last kiss they ever shared. She opened to him, her small tongue driving him wild. Only the sound of Theo chortling in the background kept him from deepening the kiss.

They both were breathing hard when they broke apart. Blindly, Eli turned away, desperate to hide his massive arousal. When he did, Jackie slipped from the room. A moment later the front door opened and closed. Bereft, he gripped the sides of the counter and tried to regain his composure.

"Dada?" Theo's hesitant voice came from behind him. "Dada?"

Instantly, Eli turned to his son, pushing away his own issues and focusing on Theo. "I'm right here, Theo," he said, making his voice both gentle and reassuring. "Do you want some more macaroni and cheese?"

After Theo finished his lunch, Eli watched him play for a little bit before he noticed Theo's eyes drooping. "Time for a nap, little man," he said, scooping the toddler up and carrying him to his room. Once there Eli changed his diaper, helped him get settled in his bed with his favorite stuffed animal and kissed his soft, chubby cheek. As Eli turned out the light, he caught himself wondering once again how Charla could bear to leave their son. As long as he lived, such a thing would be beyond his comprehension.

What would happen once Charla returned? He knew she'd be arrested and in the end, would most likely serve time for her crimes. His heart ached at the thought of possibly having to take Theo to visit his mother in prison, but then again, maybe Charla wouldn't want to see him.

No matter how this ended up shaking out, Eli would never understand how Charla could abandon her son. He might not have agreed with her lifestyle choices, but he'd never in a million years have guessed she'd be a thief and a fugitive.

At least his son was safe. That was what was important here. He knew he needed to focus on the positive. After all, no matter how much love he might offer Jackie, he couldn't make her stay. She had to choose Getaway—and him—for herself.

Chapter Twelve

After leaving Eli's, with her insides a jangled mess of raw emotion, Jackie drove around town for a bit. Now that downtown had been almost fully restored, Main Street had a homey, welcoming feel. For a moment she could see herself staying there, making a life in Getaway, with Eli and Theo at her side.

And then she thought of her mother and Charla's return, and that particular fantasy came crashing down. While New York and her life there seemed light-years away, she loved it there. If she kept herself busy to ward off the occasional loneliness, she didn't think that was unusual. She adored her job, her tiny apartment, the hustle and bustle and how she could always find a new place to eat just by taking a random walk. Where at first she'd found the crowds intimidating, she'd gotten used to moving effortlessly among them. She no longer heard the constant cacophony of horns and vehicles. In short, she'd adapted.

Then why did returning to Getaway feel so much like she'd come home? She had a feeling the real reason might be Eli. The more time she spent with him, the more she wondered how she'd survive without him.

Passing Serenity's, the metaphysical bookstore that had fascinated her when she'd been a teen, she made an impulsive U-turn and parked across the street. Ever since she'd talked to Charla's coworkers at the café, she'd meant to stop by and see if the store's proprietor, a self-proclaimed psychic named Serenity Rune, might be able to help with figuring out where Charla might be. Not only did everyone in town go to Serenity for help with various personal problems, but Serenity had also always been kind to a much younger Jackie, so she knew asking wouldn't be a problem.

Stepping through the front door with its jingling set of bells, Jackie inhaled the strong scent of incense and looked around. The place looked pretty much the same as it had back in the day.

"Welcome," a rich, feminine voice drawled, coming out from a back room. A moment later, Serenity came into view. Her eyes widened as she caught sight of her visitor. "Jackie? Jackie Burkholdt, is that you?"

"Serenity!" Smiling, Jackie walked into the other woman's hug. In her flowing, colorful caftan, bracelets jingling and dangly earrings swaying, Serenity didn't appear to have aged a single year.

"I heard you were back in town and I wondered when you'd stop by." Serenity grinned, her eyes sparkling. "Come into the back room with me. I just made a pot of tea and we can catch up."

"I can't stay long, but I'd love to." Following the older woman, she found herself in a crowded stock room of sorts, with a table and chairs, a small refrigerator and a microwave.

"My home away from home," Serenity chirped. "Have you heard anything from that sister of yours?"

"Not a thing." Settling into one of the chairs, Jackie watched as Serenity loaded up a silver-plated tray with a ceramic teapot and two matching mugs.

"Earl Grey all right with you?" Serenity asked as she poured.

"Yes, thanks." Never having asked for anything psychic related, Jackie wasn't sure how to begin, or even if she wanted to.

Once Serenity had filled two cups, she offered Jackie a small bowl with packets of both sugar and artificial sweetener.

"None for me, thank you." Picking up her steaming mug, Jackie blew on it, inhaling the distinctive scent of the tea. "I wanted to ask you if you've *seen* anything?" she asked, feeling slightly foolish. "Psychically, I mean."

Serenity eyed her over the rim of her own cup before taking a small sip. "I see you're on the verge of finding the joy you were always meant to have," she said. "Your sister has gone in pursuit of the opposite kind of joy. I'm not sure her choice will make her happy."

Though her face felt on fire, Jackie nodded. "Are you able to see where Charla might be?"

Closing her eyes, Serenity took one more drink before setting the cup on the table. She kept her eyes closed, swaying slightly from side to side, humming some sort of off-key, esoteric melody under her breath.

Jackie shifted uncomfortably in her chair, not sure what she should do, if anything. Apparently, this was what Serenity did when she wanted to have a vision or whatever she called it.

Sipping on her tea, Jackie began regretting her impulsive decision to stop by.

After a minute Serenity stopped humming and opened her eyes. "Your sister is near a beach," she said, frowning. "There are palm trees and those exotic drinks with umbrellas in them. I can't see who she's with, but I didn't get the sense it was a man."

Heart skipping a beat, Jackie leaned closer. "So Charla is alive and unharmed?"

"Yes, she is." Serenity appeared surprised at the question. "She seems pretty relaxed, without a care in the world."

"Seriously?" Jackie asked. "You've probably heard by now what she's been accused of doing."

"I have." Picking up her tea, Serenity took another sip. "I don't understand why she would steal from her job, but more importantly how she could leave her own child."

"I don't get it, either."

Serenity sighed. "The things people do constantly amaze me. How is her little son holding up?"

Again, Jackie blushed, for no reason that she could tell. "He seems good. I watched him for a little bit this morning while his father worked on the ranch. I don't know much about toddlers, but he appears to be a happy little thing."

"And how is Eli doing?"

Face on fire, Jackie pretended a sudden interest in her tea. "He seems good, too."

Serenity sighed. "Be careful what you throw away, my dear. A career won't keep you warm at night."

Jackie snapped her head up. How had she known? Maybe there really was something to this psychic stuff.

Suddenly, desperately, she wanted to ask the older woman for more advice, but she wasn't sure what to say. "I barely know Eli," she began. "But it feels as if we've been together forever."

"That's good, isn't it?" Serenity asked. "Rare, even."

"Maybe. I don't know." Miserable, she met Serenity's serene gaze. "He's my sister's ex-husband. When I came here, I'd convinced myself that he'd hurt or killed her. I couldn't have been more wrong."

"Then what's the issue?" Serenity's tone was gentle. "From what I can tell, your sister doesn't give a rat's ass about what happens to him."

The choice of words made Jackie smile. "Maybe not, though my mother has made it clear she highly disapproves."

Serenity snorted. "Delia has no room to talk. She hasn't entirely treated you well over the years."

Not sure how to respond, Jackie simply shrugged.

"Do you really care what your mother thinks? No judgment here, I promise. But if you're still trying to win her approval now, as an accomplished grown adult, I think that ship has sailed."

This comment made Jackie smile. Serenity's no-nonsense advice combined with her uncanny psychic abilities was one of the reasons so many people supported her business.

"It's not only that," Jackie admitted. "I live in New York. I have to return when all of this is over."

"Oh." For the first time, Serenity appeared troubled. "I'm sorry. I don't see that. I don't see that at all."

A bit nonplussed herself, Jackie frowned. "What do you mean? You don't see me going back to my life on the east coast?"

The lines in Serenity's face smoothed. "You know what, dear? We all have our own choices to make, our unique paths to follow. Sometimes, my visions are foggy and unclear and I must interpret them as best I can."

Though Jackie wasn't sure what to make of that explanation, she also believed in free will. No matter what anyone said, she made her own choices.

She just wished sometimes they weren't so damn hard to make.

Checking her watch, she was surprised to realize a half hour had passed. "I've got to go," she said, genuinely regretful. "I need to run by the sheriff's office and talk with Rayna."

"I understand." Serenity got up with her and walked her to the door. "Please don't be a stranger. Stop by again."

Promising she would, Jackie got into her rental car and drove the few short blocks to the sheriff's department.

This time no one manned the front desk. Jackie waited a few minutes and then took herself into the back and toward Rayna's office. Since the door stood open, Jackie tapped lightly.

"Jackie!" Rayna looked up from her computer. "What brings you here?"

"I thought I'd check to see if you'd had any success getting a search warrant for Charla's apartment," Jackie said.

"I did. I have people over there right now."

Disappointed, Jackie nodded. "You're not handling this yourself?"

Rayna's gaze sharpened. "I can assure you that my deputies are well trained and well qualified. They'll bring back any evidence they find for me to review."

"I'm sorry. I'm sure they are more than capable." Jackie dropped into one of the chairs. "It's just that I was hoping to go along with you when you searched her place. If my sister left a computer behind, I'd like to offer my assistance at going through it. I'm pretty skilled at that sort of thing. Even if Charla thinks she wiped it clean, I can find whatever she might be trying to hide."

"Really?" Rayna cocked her head, appearing interested. "That's not something anyone in my department can do. If we happened to locate one, I was going to have to send the CPU over to the FBI, which, as you might be aware, could take some time."

"Which we might not have."

"Very true." Considering, Rayna finally nodded. "Let me call and check with my guys. If they did locate a computer, once they've brought it here, I'll give you a call."

"Thanks." Jackie jumped to her feet, disappointed Rayna hadn't offered to let her meet her people at Charla's. Maybe doing so would compromise the investigation. "I'm hoping we can find Charla before I run out of vacation time. I only had two weeks. I had to buy a round-trip ticket, so I fly back home on Sunday."

Rayna's brows rose. "That's not all that far away. Any chance you can ask for an extension?"

"I might have to try." Jackie thought for a moment. "Even if it's unpaid. My boss is really understanding. But you can see why I seem in a bit of a rush to help. The sooner my sister is located, the better." Even though inside, she truly wanted more time with Eli.

"Completely understandable." Rayna picked up her phone. "Let me call. If Charla did leave a computer behind, I'll have Bill run it over here right now."

Still standing, Jackie thanked her. Listening to Rayna's side of the conversation, it sure sounded as if Charla had left behind a desktop computer. Which was slightly disappointing, since most people these days tended to use their laptop for just about everything. Jackie said as much to Rayna once the sheriff had finished with the call.

"I know. But it's all we have. The rest of the apartment seemed pretty clean. No receipts, no credit card statements, though we haven't had a chance to check her mailbox. She didn't leave behind any jewelry, though she left most of her clothes. I think she was trying to make it look as if she was grabbed, which would go along with the scenario she appears to be attempting to set up."

Jackie nodded. "What will happen once we find her?" she asked.

"She'll be arrested and charged. Depending on how good of an attorney she retains, she'll probably post bail, if a judge allows bail to be set. That might not happen, since certainly, she's a flight risk."

How odd to be speaking of her sister as if she were a criminal. Though technically, she sort of was.

"What kind of prison sentence will she get if she's convicted?"

Rayna shrugged. "That depends on the judge. She's a first-time offender, but the amount of money is astronomical, so there's no way to know. I'd guess at least five years, maybe longer."

Five years. "I can't even picture Charla making it in prison."

"She's a charmer," Rayna responded. "People with her type of personality tend to do well." She indicated the chair Jackie had just vacated. "You might as well sit. It's going to take a few minutes before Bill gets that computer back here. There's a pot of coffee on in the break room if you want some, though I can't guarantee how fresh it might be."

"Thanks, but I'll pass." Jackie grimaced. "I had enough caffeine over at Eli's earlier. I watched Theo for him so he could get some work done. I wonder what he's going to do for a sitter once I'm gone."

Rayna glanced up, her sharp gaze missing nothing. "You two seem to have become close in the short time you've been here."

Not trusting herself to speak, Jackie slowly nodded.

"Eli Pitts is a good man," Rayna continued. "Your sister did a number on him, but he behaved honorably, trying to do what was best for his boy. That's why I never believed, not for one minute, that he'd ever do something to hurt Charla. With all the things she put him through, if he was going to snap, he would have done it long ago."

Not sure how to respond, Jackie looked down at her hands instead.

"Are you okay?" Rayna asked, her voice soft. "I know this entire situation has been stressful. Your mother's behavior hasn't helped, either."

Jackie raised her head. "It has been stressful," she admitted. "Though not because of my mother. She's always been dramatic and distant." Not sure how much more to divulge, she sighed. She liked Rayna and in other circumstances, believed they could be friends. "Things have gotten complicated."

"Because of Eli?"

"You're very perceptive," Jackie said.

"It kind of goes along with the job," Rayna relayed. "Does he feel the same way?"

"I think so." Shaking her head, Jackie corrected. "Actually, I *know* so."

Sitting back in her chair, Rayna regarded her. "What are you going to do?"

"Now, that, I don't know. I'm hoping I'll figure it out soon."

"I'm sure you will." Rayna's phone rang. "Just a second. I need to take this." Answering, she listened for a moment. "Sounds good. I'm on my way."

Hanging up, she pushed to her feet. "I'm sorry, but I have to run out to Charla's apartment. Bill can't bring the computer right now. Something else came up."

Alarmed, Jackie stood, too. "What is it? Can I go with you?"

"Not this time," Rayna responded. "This is an official investigation. I can't let a civilian, never mind a relative, contaminate any possible evidence."

"*Evidence?* As in of another crime?"

"Exactly." Ushering Jackie toward the door, Rayna pursed her lips. "I'll fill you in when I can, but I can't discuss this yet. And when we do get that computer over here, I'll give you a call."

WITH THEO NAPPING, Eli did a few loads of laundry and some housecleaning. He didn't want to run the vacuum and take the chance of waking his son, but he dusted and swept and mopped the kitchen and bathroom. There were still a million other things he could be doing outside, but he couldn't leave his son unattended. Instead, he went online and ordered a toilet training potty and some toddler training underwear. Might as well make plans to start Theo on that and wean him away from diapers.

Even though Jackie hadn't been gone long, Eli already missed her like crazy. He fought the impulse to call her just to hear her voice, wondering how he'd managed to fall so crazily deep in such a short period of time.

He had it bad.

Filling in time, he passed the rest of the day with

other household chores and playing with his son. Theo always woke up grouchy and could only be mollified with fruit or cereal. After he had his snack, his mood always improved.

Eli loved taking care of his boy. He'd actually missed Theo far more than he'd missed Charla when they'd split up. He'd begged her not to take Theo with her when she left, having already gleaned an idea of how she felt about motherhood. But like Delia, Charla was all about appearances, and she knew leaving her son would generate a lot of gossip in town. Now, clearly, that no longer mattered to her.

That evening, as he made dinner, again he considered calling Jackie to see if she wanted to come share the meal. In the end, not wanting to impose any more than he already had, he didn't.

Once the dishes had been done, Theo played in his playpen while Eli watched TV. As soon as Theo started nodding off while still sitting, Eli got him into the bathroom and helped him brush his teeth before changing him into his pajamas. Though he usually bathed the toddler before bed, he decided this time he'd do that in the morning.

Kissing his sleepy son on the cheek, he turned out the lights and went back to the TV. A couple hours later he turned off all the lights and went to bed.

A weird sound, likely a creak in the floorboards or a tree branch scraping the side of the house in the wind, woke him sometime in the middle of the night. He sat up, listening, trying to decide if he could go back to sleep or if there truly might be a cause for alarm.

He really should get a dog, he thought, his thoughts still fuzzy from sleep. A dog would bark, warning him if there was anything actually wrong.

His bedside alarm clock showed 2:13 a.m. Yawning, he waited for the sound to come again. The fact that it didn't alarmed him more than it should. Better go check on Theo, just in case.

He threw back the covers and barefoot, padded down the hall toward his son's room. The past couple of nights, Theo had experienced a few nightmares and woken crying for his mother. Eli had comforted him and ended up letting him sleep in Eli's bed, which seemed to help.

But tonight his son was quiet. Maybe the out-of-place sound he'd heard had been his own imagination.

A rustle of clothing, a movement, made Eli freeze just outside his son's door.

"Gamma?" Theo's high-pitched voice, thick with sleep. And then someone else, whispering, telling his son to be quiet.

What the actual hell? Heart pounding, Eli rushed into the room and flicked on the light. Eyes wide and looking like a deer caught in headlights, Delia stood in front of him, holding Theo protectively in her arms. She glanced left, then right, at the window and back at Eli.

Luckily, he stood between her and the door. Not wanting to alarm his son, Eli kept his voice calm and reasonable.

"What are you doing, Delia? How did you get into my house?"

Instead of appearing sheepish or even ashamed, Delia

raised her chin, her expression belligerent. "Charla gave me her key. It's your own fault for not changing the locks."

Carefully moving toward her, Eli lifted his boy out of her arms. He half expected her to resist or try to move away, but she surprisingly released Theo without any fuss.

"I don't want any trouble," Delia said, backing away, her hands raised. Then she shoved past him and sprinted for the door and down the hall. A moment later he heard the sound of her Camaro starting up and realized she'd parked it a bit down the drive, so the noise wouldn't wake him. Stunned, he tried to process what had just happened.

Delia had actually tried to kidnap his son.

Theo made a sound, both bewildered and sleepy. "Gamma?" he asked, gazing up at Eli with his eyes at half-mast. "Dada?"

"I'm right here, Theo," Eli said softly. "Your gamma went home. Are you okay?"

Yawning, Theo appeared to be trying to go back to sleep. Eli gently placed him in his bed, drawing the blanket over him. With a sleepy and trusting smile, Theo closed his eyes all the way. In an instant he'd drifted off.

Eli stood for a moment just watching him, trying to slow his heart rate. Multiple emotions crashed through him—fear and disbelief, but most of all, anger. Undoubtedly, everything Delia had done earlier had been an act. So she could let herself into his house, steal his son and then what? No way would she have been able to keep Theo undetected.

Leaving the room, Eli locked the front door and then braced a kitchen chair up against it for good measure. He'd call a locksmith in the morning. Deliberating a moment, he heaved a sigh and phoned Jackie.

"Hello?" she rasped, obviously, barely awake.

He filled her in on what had just happened. "I wanted to let you know before I called Rayna. Delia's going to be arrested. She went too far this time."

Silence while Jackie digested this. "I agree," she finally said. "But a thought occurs to me. Hear me out and run it by Rayna and see what she thinks. What if Delia was trying to grab Theo and take him to Charla?"

At first, the possibility made no sense. After all, Charla had been the one to run off without her son. He said as much to Jackie.

"Maybe she regrets that," she responded. "It's entirely possible that Charla didn't realize how much she'd miss Theo."

"Possible, but unlikely. He'd put a serious crimp in her style."

"Not if she had a built-in babysitter," Jackie said.

"Delia." Everything clicked into place. "And all that sincerity and love she exhibited earlier was just a show."

"Are you surprised?" Jackie didn't even sound bitter, just certain. "It would have been extremely naive to think my mother could change her entire personality just like that. Yet, we both fell for it, hook, line and sinker."

He ached to be able to hold her. Though she put on

a brave front, her mother's continued rejection had to wear at her.

"Go call Rayna," Jackie said. "Though I'm sure she won't be overjoyed to be woken up with this news, she needs to arrest my mother before Delia skips town. Even though she wasn't successful at grabbing Theo, she most likely will still go to Charla."

"I have a better idea," he said slowly. "Delia could lead us to Charla. Maybe Rayna could follow her at a safe distance."

"Or we could." Jackie sounded wide-awake now. "Don't call Rayna. My mother doesn't know what kind of rental car I'm driving. Throw some clothes and stuff in a bag and get Theo ready. I'll swing by and pick you up."

"What if she's already gone?"

"Then we're out of luck. But I have a feeling she went back home to regroup and let Charla know she couldn't get Theo. She'll probably head out soon, though, just in case you send Rayna to arrest her, so we need to hurry."

Though he couldn't help but wonder if this would turn out to be another wild-goose chase like their Big Bend trek, he had to admit Jackie's theory had a certain kind of logic to it. He grabbed enough clothes for a couple days, packed the same amount for Theo, plus diapers. On an afterthought, he packed a few more of the latter. He really needed to start getting Theo potty trained. Carrying the bags to his front door, he went out to his truck and removed the car seat. If they were taking Jackie's vehicle, he'd need to install it in her back seat.

A few minutes later he checked the front window, relieved to see headlights making their way up his drive. She pulled up, got out and gave him a quick hug and then popped her trunk so he could load his bags.

He got the car seat installed and then returned for his boy.

Theo stirred groggily when Eli lifted him from his bed, but he barely woke, even when Eli strapped him in his car seat. "Do you want to drive first?" she asked. "I thought we could take shifts."

Surprised, he shrugged. "You sound as if you have an idea where we might be going."

"Don't you?" She pushed back her long dark hair with a graceful gesture. "Even if my mother was lying yesterday, I have a feeling she might have been truthful about Charla heading to the Gulf Coast. And while she might have gone to another state, I'm thinking she'd stay in Texas. Now, that could be anywhere, South Padre, Galveston, who knows. I'm sure that's what Charla would be counting on, being able to disappear seamlessly in one of the tourist locales."

"What about Mexico?" he asked. "You don't think she'd look for an opportunity to vanish in a foreign country?"

"Maybe, but not only does she not speak Spanish, but she'd stand out more there. That's why letting Delia lead us to her is our only real hope of finding her."

"That's a lot riding on a hunch," he said. "I still think we should tell Rayna and see what she thinks."

"Fine, call her on the way. We're running out of time. Here." She tossed him the car keys. "You drive first. Let's cruise over to her house. If we're lucky, she's still there."

Getting in her car, he started the engine. He wasn't sure why he believed her scenario. Common sense said Delia would have hit the road the second she'd grabbed Theo. Otherwise, she'd run the risk of having the sheriff's department descend on her to get the toddler back.

Either way, an Amber alert would have been issued, and there wouldn't be any place Delia could hide once that went out.

When he said as much to Jackie, she nodded. "I'm sure she and Charla had something planned to deal with such a contingency."

"Maybe, or it's entirely possible that Charla didn't know Delia planned to snatch Theo. That makes more sense. After all, Charla made it clear she was done being a mother." As soon as he voiced the thought, he knew he was right.

"Are you serious?" Jackie stared at him.

"Yes. In fact, I'm positive. Delia acted on her own when she tried to grab my son."

Though she shook her head, Jackie didn't argue the point. He supposed by now, nothing her mother did surprised her.

They pulled up on Delia's street.

"Now what?" he asked, slowing. "Do I kill the lights and park somewhere? Or do you just want to drive by?"

"Just cruise past," she said. "We need to at least get an idea if she's home or not."

To his surprise, though the house appeared dark, Delia's beloved Camaro sat parked in the driveway. He slowed and then parked, killing his headlights but not his engine.

"She is using another car," Jackie insisted, her voice flat. "That customized paint job she has is too darn recognizable. Plus, I know for a fact she always keeps that Camaro parked in her garage. If she left it out, it's because she wants people to think she's home. She's already gone."

"That's a lot of speculation," he pointed out. "Don't you think we should at least make sure?"

"Maybe." She fidgeted in her seat. "But how do we do that? Oh, wait. It's a long shot, but she always used to keep a spare key under that gnome statue in her flower bed, in case she accidentally got locked out. Since she felt free to break into your house, she shouldn't mind if I do the same with hers."

Uneasy, he considered. "I don't like it. I don't want you to put yourself in danger."

"Danger?" she scoffed. "She might be a pain, but she's still my mother. Plus, if she's in there, she won't have any idea that I know what she did. I can come up with some other BS reason for being there."

And then, without waiting for him to agree, Jackie slipped out of the car and strode up the front sidewalk toward Delia's house.

Chapter Thirteen

Though Jackie had pretended to be cool, calm and collected, in reality her heart was tripping in her chest like a mini jackhammer. Delia wouldn't take too kindly to her intrusion if Jackie happened to be wrong.

Luckily, the streetlight helped illuminate parts of the front yard. She located the little stone gnome she remembered from her childhood and lifted it. Sure enough, a spare key sat in the dirt underneath.

Turning, she flashed Eli the thumbs-up sign and then went to the front door. As a precaution, she went ahead and rang the doorbell, listening as the chimes echoed through the small house.

Then, before using the key, she took out her phone and called her mother. The call went straight to voice mail and she left a message. "Hey, Mom. Just wanting to touch base with you. I couldn't sleep, and I thought you might be up worrying, too. Call me when you can."

That done, she used the key, unlocked the front door and slipped inside.

Though she tried to move as quietly as possible, her footsteps seemed to echo in the too-silent house. She went from room to room, moving slowly but carefully, saving her mother's bedroom for last.

As she'd suspected, the house was empty. In her mother's room, the bed sat neatly made, though the closet door stood open. Checking that, Jackie saw evidence of missing clothing, items grabbed off hangers that now hung askew.

She'd been right. Delia had switched cars and run. Jackie's quick surge of triumph was followed by the crushing knowledge that she'd been too late.

After locking up, she replaced the key under the gnome and returned to Eli and Theo. A quick glance revealed the baby still slept. Keeping her voice low, she recounted everything she'd seen.

"Time to let Rayna know," Eli said, already pulling out his phone. "Though I hate to wake her, this is something she definitely needs to be aware of."

Jackie listened as he filled Rayna in. By the time he'd finished with the fact that they were sitting outside Delia's house, Jackie figured the sheriff had to be wide-awake.

"Sure. We can do that," Eli said, ending the call. He turned to Jackie, grimacing. "She wants us to meet her at the sheriff's department in twenty minutes."

This made Jackie perk up. "I wonder if she finally got Charla's computer. She promised to let me have a crack at it."

"In the middle of the night?" Eli asked.

"Sure, why not? I mean, she probably intended to call me in the morning, but with everything that's happened so far, it couldn't hurt. At least we might be able to get an idea where they might have gone."

Hearing herself, Jackie couldn't help but marvel at how quickly things had changed. She'd returned to Getaway thinking her sister's life was in danger. Now that same sister was on the run from the law.

"One thing still doesn't add up," she said out loud. "Why did Charla send me that text? She didn't want anything to do with me for the last three years. Why involve me now?"

Shifting into Drive, he kept his foot on the brake. "Because she was trying to engineer an elaborate setup to make it appear as if she'd been murdered. She figured your presence in town would help push that story along."

They pulled out onto the street, driving past the town's only all-night gas station and mini-mart. Jackie glanced over, spotting one customer in the blinding lights, walking from the building to her black pickup truck parked at the gas pumps.

Her heart skipped a beat. "Eli," she said, still low voiced, "I just saw Delia getting gas back there. She's driving a black pickup. You need to pull a slow U-turn so we can see which way she goes."

Eli immediately complied, without asking a single question. They were almost at the station when she spotted the pickup pulling out, luckily traveling in the same direction they were now heading.

"There." She pointed. "I wonder where she got that truck. I hope she doesn't notice us. It's not like there's a lot of other traffic out this time of the morning."

Intent on driving, he kept a fair amount of distance between them and Delia. "That'll change once we get to the interstate. I think she'll take I-20 east and then some of the smaller routes south, most likely US87 if I remember right. Either way she's got to go through San Antonio. Once she gets there, it'll depend where on the coast she's headed as to what route she chooses."

True to his prediction, Delia took the entrance ramp onto I-20. They followed. Jackie was glad to see the increase in traffic, even though it mostly seemed to be eighteen-wheelers.

They'd gone about five miles when Eli cursed under his breath. "We forgot about Rayna."

"I'll call her really quick and tell her what's going on," Jackie volunteered. "Once we get a better feel for where Delia's headed, maybe Rayna can call the police there and give them a heads-up."

"Maybe." Eli glanced at her, still keeping a fair amount of distance between them and the black pickup. "But I'm thinking Rayna's not going to be happy about this."

"You might be right, but I don't see what else we could have done," Jackie argued. "If we'd gone to meet Rayna, we would have missed the opportunity to follow Delia. At the very least, we know what kind of vehicle she's driving."

"I agree," Eli finally said. "Though Rayna might not see it the same way."

"Probably not." Jackie considered. "But the end result is what really matters, right?"

"Maybe. Except we don't work in law enforcement. That's going to be Rayna's big sticking point."

Turning her phone over in her hands, Jackie shrugged. "Right now all we're doing is following my mother. We're not committing a crime."

"True. You're stalling. Why?"

With a sigh, she admitted the truth. "I want to make sure we're far enough out that Rayna can't catch up to us. If Delia were to get one hint that anyone—especially the sheriff—was onto her, there's no way she's going anywhere near Charla."

This made him laugh. A startled bark of laughter, but not the reaction she'd expected. "What?" she asked. "What's so funny?"

"You think of everything." He changed lanes, passing a slow-moving semi before dropping back into the middle lane, keeping a couple of vehicles between them and Delia. "I never once considered that Rayna might want to follow us or take over the pursuit."

For whatever reason, this observation pleased her. "I edit a lot of romantic-suspense novels," she said. "I guess I kind of have a feel for how this sort of thing works."

Again, he laughed, the rich, masculine sound making her smile.

"Go ahead and call Rayna," he said. "By now she's probably wondering where the hell we are."

As if on cue, his phone rang. Keeping his eyes on the road, he passed it over to Jackie. "Looks like she saved you the trouble."

Making a face, she answered.

"Where are you?" Rayna demanded. "I'm not a fan of coming into work in the middle of the night unless absolutely necessary."

"Following Delia," Jackie replied. "We were on the way to meet you when we happened to spot her at the Quick Gas station. She's driving a black pickup. I have no idea where she got it or who it belongs to."

Rayna went silent, clearly processing this. "Why?" she finally asked. "What are you hoping to learn?"

"We think she's going to lead us to Charla."

"But she didn't get the baby," Rayna said. "Why would Delia go to Charla since she failed?"

Jackie explained Eli's theory that Delia had acted on her own, trying to grab Theo.

"That makes more sense," Rayna agreed. "Since Charla clearly doesn't want her son."

For whatever reason, Jackie felt compelled to defend her sister. "She could have changed her mind, you never know."

Eli shook his head at that, but didn't comment.

"Anyway," Jackie continued, "we think Delia is headed to the coast. Where exactly, we don't know. But we're hoping she's going to join Charla."

Eli chimed in here. "We'll know more depending on which direction she goes once we reach San Antonio. I agree with Jackie. Delia is going to join Charla."

"Either that, or she decided to take a quick vacation after what she did," Rayna said. "Though that's unlikely, it's entirely possible. Just don't let her see you and stay safe. Keep me posted."

Jackie agreed and ended the call. She looked out the

window, realizing sunrise was still several hours away. Glancing at Eli, concentrating on the road and maintaining a respectable distance between them and Delia, she felt a rush of emotion and immediately tamped it down.

"Whichever way Delia chooses, it's going to be a long drive," Jackie commented. "I hope you packed accordingly."

"I can always buy more if we need it," he responded. "There never seems to be enough diapers, so I figured I'd need to get more at some point."

"Like if we need a potty break?" Jackie asked.

He grimaced. "That's the thing. Since she left in the middle of the night, I figure Delia intends to complete the drive without stopping much to rest. But I'm thinking she'll have to stop sometime to use the restroom."

"True." Jackie nodded.

"She'll have to refuel at some point," he continued. "And so will we. That's going to be the tricky part. We can't use the same station to fill up since we'll run the risk of her seeing us. And if we use another place, there's always a chance we could lose her."

Jackie sighed. "We'll have to be careful," she agreed. "But if she uses one of those super stations, we could be at one end with her at the other and she'd never see us."

They made good time, reaching San Antonio shortly after seven, which meant they'd get through before rush hour got fully underway. Once they hit the loop, she took I-10 toward Houston.

"At least we'll miss the worst part of morning traffic," Eli said. "We should get to Houston around ten or ten thirty. Though traffic is going to be bad no matter what."

"She's going to Galveston," Jackie speculated. "It's a straight shot down from Houston."

"What are we going to do once we get there?" he asked quietly. "We aren't cops, so we can't just bust in wherever Delia is holed up and arrest her. And since Theo is with us, there's no way I'm letting her get anywhere near him."

"Good question," Jackie replied. "I'm thinking we call Rayna and have her alert Galveston PD. It's too convoluted a story for us to try and explain it to them."

Shortly after they reached Houston and heavy traffic, her boss called. Jackie answered with more than a little trepidation.

"Just checking in with you," Prudence said. "Your two-week vacation is almost over and I thought I'd see how things were going."

"We still haven't found my sister," Jackie admitted. "But we're getting really close." She took a deep breath and then decided she might as well bring it up now. "In fact, I might need to extend my time off. I'll need another week, though two would be optimal. I would be using up my vacation and personal days. After that, I could take a leave of absence if necessary. Or I can work remotely, if you'd allow that. But I really don't want to leave until Charla is located and everything is settled here."

Eli glanced at her when she said that. She made a face at him and waited to hear what her boss would say.

Prudence's extended silence sent a prickle of unease

up Jackie's spine. "I'm not sure that's going to be possible, though we'll definitely try to figure it out," Prudence finally said. "I'll check with Lennon and get his thoughts, but with those two big book series coming up, we need all hands on deck, so to speak. Our department is already shorthanded, as you know. And it's unfair to shift your workload off to another editor who is already overloaded." She sighed. "You know we'll do our best to help you out. I hope you sister is found soon."

Heart pounding, Jackie tried to think of something to say. As senior editor, Prudence Jones had been the one to hire her. She'd been a great mentor and boss and completely understood how badly Jackie had wanted this job.

Still wanted it, right? Of course she did. Except suddenly, she wasn't sure. Head spinning, she reminded herself she didn't need to make a major decision right this instant.

"Thank you," Jackie replied quietly. "I've still got a few more days left on my vacation. Hopefully, my sister will be found before then."

"Agreed. But if she's not? What will you do then?"

Jackie didn't want to lie. "I'm not sure. But I promise, I'll let you know. In the meantime, send me some work. I'll get as much done as possible."

"I appreciate that." Prudence paused. "I'll need your decision as soon as possible."

After ending the call, Jackie tried not to hyperventilate. She was about to lose her job. Her *dream* job. She still had time left on her leased shared apartment, a tiny bedroom full of her own furniture and a life she loved back in New York City.

While here… She closed her eyes. She could honestly see herself making a life with Eli and Theo on his ranch. Assuming he wanted that, too.

But what would she do for a job? She'd worked hard to get her degree, and she'd set her sights on eventually getting promoted from assistant editor to editor. She knew if she continued to excel, she'd eventually get it.

And what about Charla? Jackie's sole reason for even being here in Getaway. Her head spun. Her sister had turned out to be someone utterly different from the person Jackie remembered. From all appearances, she'd not only lied to her husband, mother and friends, but also abandoned her son, stolen from her employer and was now what? Planning to fake her own death so she could disappear with her stolen money? How crazy was that?

Her stomach churned. She was about to find her sister, end this crazy charade. Then she'd have some hard decisions to make. She didn't want to give up her job, but conversely, how could she say goodbye to Eli?

Conscious of him quietly sitting beside her as he drove, she felt lucky he didn't press her with questions. She appreciated him giving her space. Since he'd heard her side of the conversation, she figured he had a pretty good idea what the call had been about.

Turning her face to look out the window, she felt too stressed to even cry. This—the search for Charla, the reason she'd come back to Getaway in the first place—was almost over. Before nightfall she guessed her sister would be arrested, maybe her mother, too, depending on if Eli pressed charges.

And then what? Shake hands with Eli and return to her former life, trying to pretend nothing had happened, that this man hadn't upended her world as she knew it?

What were her options here? Go home and work and fly back on the weekends to try and spend time with him? She didn't really have the funds for that kind of thing. She suspected he didn't, either.

"Are you all right?" Eli asked quietly.

Without looking at him, she nodded. "I'm fine," she replied. It was the first and only time she'd ever outright lied to him.

ONE THING ELI knew for a fact was that Jackie was *not* fine, no matter what she said. Though she tried to hide it, the sudden stiffness to her posture, the way she kept her face averted and the odd hitch to her breathing told him she struggled to keep her emotions under control.

Judging by what he could hear of the phone call she'd taken, she'd been told to either return to her job or lose it. What he couldn't figure out was why that upset her. It wasn't as if such news could have come as a surprise. And as far as timing went, it would appear as if that had worked out, as well.

Undeniably, this thing with Charla was about to wrap up. Her sister would be located unharmed, and handed over into police custody. He hadn't decided yet whether or not he wanted to press charges against Delia for breaking into his house and attempting to kidnap his son, but he probably would. That woman, like her daughter Charla, needed to understand there were consequences to her actions. He only hoped Jackie could understand and accept his decision. Because even if he never saw her again, he cared about her and how she regarded him.

A quick glance in his rearview mirror showed Theo still slept. Riding in the car always lulled him to sleep, though Eli was surprised he remained that way for so long.

Jackie caught him watching his son and smiled. "He's a good little traveler," she said. "You're so lucky."

Right now, in this instant, this moment in time, he felt lucky. The two people he cared the most about were with him in this car, his ranch had begun to be successful and life truly appeared to be looking up. If only Jackie wasn't going to be leaving soon.

The instant he caught himself longing for something he couldn't have, he pushed the thought away. He had no choice but to take this time with her as it came and try to let her go without regrets. Charla's mysterious disappearance was about to be solved, and soon he could resume his life. With Theo, but without Jackie.

As they drove across the causeway that took them to Galveston Island, he eyed the bright blue water, wondering why he didn't feel more of a sense of closure.

Glancing at the beautiful, kind and sexy woman who continued to gaze out the window, lost in her thoughts, he knew he had to let himself acknowledge that the thing that had developed between them had likely come to an end, as well. She'd be gone by the time the weekend ended, and most likely would never look back.

The aching sense of loss such a thought brought felt staggering. The idea of never seeing Jackie again, hearing her voice, seemed unfathomable. Yet, she either had to return to New York or lose her job. He already knew which one she'd choose. She'd made no bones about that from the first moment they'd gotten together. He just hadn't expected it to hurt this much.

Briefly, he entertained the idea of following her to New York, though he had no idea what he'd do there. Plus, he didn't want to raise his son in the hustle and bustle of a northern city. Theo had been born a Texan and would be raised a Texan. Just like Eli had been, and his father before him.

Focus, he reminded himself. Focus on the present. There were still two cars between Delia's truck and theirs. So far she'd given no indication that she knew she was being followed.

As they entered Galveston proper, instead of going to one of the many motels, hotels or condos, Delia drove to a large restaurant and bar located on Seawall Boulevard called The Spot. The impressive building with lots of glass and wood had open-air seating and views of the gulf. The lunch crowd had just started arriving, and the parking lot was not yet crowded, though he suspected it would be soon.

Delia parked her truck, got out and disappeared inside the restaurant.

"Odd," Jackie mused. "I would have thought they'd meet up at Charla's hotel room."

"I'm guessing Delia is hungry," Eli replied. "She didn't eat much on the drive down."

Her stomach chose that moment to growl, reminding them both that they hadn't eaten, either.

The sound made Eli chuckle, breaking up the gravity of the moment. And now that they were no longer driving, Theo woke up and began crying.

"He probably needs a diaper change," Eli said. "For right now let me give him some juice and a snack." He rummaged in his pack, locating both and passed them back to his son. Then, while Theo contentedly ate and drank, Eli turned back to Jackie.

"You're so good with him," she couldn't help but comment.

This appeared to surprise him. "He's my son," he replied.

"As if that explains everything," she said.

"Doesn't it?"

A slow smile spread across her face. "You know what? In a way, I suppose it does."

He wanted to kiss her then, but he resisted. Neither of them needed any distractions right now, and he knew how quickly a simple press of their mouths together could fan the flames. Would he ever get used to this constant ache for her? He wondered how long it would take to abate once she left.

"What do we do now?" she asked, gesturing toward the restaurant, clearly unaware of his thoughts. "Obviously, we can't stroll on in there and grab a bite to eat."

"Sit tight and let me call Rayna. She'll let us know how she wants us to proceed."

She nodded. "Okay."

Eli put the phone on speaker and made the call.

When Rayna came on the line, she sounded both tired and relieved. He quickly filled her in.

"Do not go inside the restaurant," Rayna ordered, once he'd finished talking. "I'll notify Galveston PD, but you need to let them handle it. We don't even know for sure that Charla is inside. And if she is, they generally prefer not to make arrests in crowded public places."

"Then maybe we should wait to call them," Jackie interjected. "A large police presence will definitely scare Charla off."

"How about this?" Rayna suggested. "I alert them and we'll see how they want to handle things. I don't want you two getting any further involved. I'll call you back and keep you posted."

After Rayna had ended the call, he and Jackie exchanged looks.

"How about you sit here and watch for them and I'll go get us something to eat," she said.

"Where?" Looking up and down Seawall Boulevard, he didn't see any other restaurants within a quick walking distance.

"In there." She pointed to The Spot. "The place is packed now. Surely, they have a take-out counter or something. If not, I can always go into the bar and order something to go."

"No." He immediately discounted that plan. "It's too risky. Delia or Charla might see you."

"I'll be careful," she said. "Really. Aren't you starving?"

"I am, but not enough to risk everything. I packed

a bunch of snacks for Theo. How about we eat something from there? It should be enough to hold us over until we can grab a real meal."

She sighed, but finally gave a reluctant nod. He reached into the back seat and grabbed his backpack, extracting a box of assorted breakfast bars. "Chocolate chip or strawberry?"

"Chocolate chip please."

They munched on those, plus a handful of trail mix he'd brought. He'd even had the foresight to pack several plastic bottles of water, though they weren't ice-cold.

"Wow. You thought of everything," she said, smiling.

A police cruiser pulled into the parking lot. Swearing under his breath, Eli froze. "I was hoping they'd wait."

"Me, too." Jackie shook her head. "I'm thinking it might be okay. When they walk into the restaurant, neither Delia nor Charla will have an idea they've come for them. I mean, police officers eat lunch, too."

Watching as the police cruiser parked, Eli shook his head. "I wonder if they're going to make the arrest inside. If so, I really wish we could see it."

"Me, too," she said. "I'm half-tempted to slip inside and watch for myself. I know, I know." This as he started to speak. "I won't. For all we know, those officers might be here to eat lunch."

A few minutes after the first two officers went inside, a second police car pulled into the parking lot.

"Either this place is popular with law enforcement for lunch, or they called for backup."

In the back seat, Theo had grown restless. Squirming and asking to be out of the car seat. Eli found one of Theo's favorite games on his tablet and handed it to him. He didn't like to let his son spend too much time playing with electronics, but if ever a situation called for a distraction, this one did.

When the second pair of police officers got out of their car, they didn't go inside. Instead, they stood near the entrance, one on either side. They didn't have their weapons drawn or anything, but they appeared intent.

"Waiting there in case someone tries to make a run for it?" Jackie ventured.

He shrugged. "Maybe. Who knows?"

Watching and waiting for something to happen felt anticlimactic. While he knew the takedown probably wouldn't be dramatic, like something from a TV show, he'd definitely expected things to move a little faster.

Finally, after what seemed like a long time, the first two officers emerged and conferred with the second pair.

"Where's Delia?" Jackie asked. "And Charla? I figured they'd come out with those two in custody."

Confused and more than a little concerned, he shook his head. "No idea. Maybe the first two officers really did just go there to eat. Is it possible they have no idea Charla and Delia are inside?"

Chapter Fourteen

Jackie had never been a patient sort of person. It took every ounce of self-control she had to keep herself from getting out of the car and striding over to question the police officers. But she knew if they were waiting for Charla and Delia to emerge, the sight of her would definitely jeopardize the actual arrest. This entire situation felt surreal. Sitting in a rental car in a seaside parking lot, the cheerful sounds of a toddler's game playing in the back seat, waiting for her sister and her mother to be arrested.

"The suspense is killing me," she mused out loud. "Are the police really going to just stand around and wait for them to come out?"

Arm on the back of the seat, Eli faced her. "It looks that way. They probably don't want to cause a huge disruption inside the restaurant, so they're planning to nab them when they leave. And if you think about it, they haven't been in there long enough to have a meal."

He had a point. Especially since Charla and her mother had a lot of catching up to do. Not surprisingly, she felt a twinge of pain at the thought. On the flight west from La Guardia, she'd envisioned an eventual joyful reunion between her sister and her. To be fair, she'd also seen herself in the same role she'd always played, swooping in to save Charla. Now she'd gradually come to realize that her baby sister had become an adult and had to bear responsibility for her poor choices. It just wasn't easy to watch.

Theo made a sound from the back. She turned and realized he was still intent on his game. Such a cutie, his curly blond hair and bright blue eyes fixed on the tablet, his little tongue peeking out one corner of his mouth.

"How could she leave him?" she wondered softly. "I just don't understand it."

"I don't, either," Eli admitted. "She fought me for custody, claiming he belonged with his mother. When she won, I watched her as she continued to party every single weekend, even the ones where she had him. It just about killed me. My only consolation was that she seemed to love him. At least in front of me, she doted on him."

Heartbreaking.

"Look." Eli pointed, his voice hushed. "Something is happening."

The first two officers stepped in front of two people while the second pair slipped in behind them. Though Jackie sat up straight and tried to see, due to all the movement, she couldn't make out either her mother or sister.

"They're arresting them." Pain tinged Eli's deep voice.

Just then, the police moved enough for her to see he

was right. Charla and Delia stood, expressions shocked, unresisting while they were handcuffed. Jackie assumed they were also being read their rights.

"What do we do now?" she finally asked, not bothering to hide how shaken all of this made her.

"I'm calling Rayna." Eli already had his phone out. "She wanted to be updated."

Numb, she watched while her sister and mother were marched over to two separate police cars and loaded inside. Meanwhile, Eli told Rayna everything that had happened.

"Ask her if I'm allowed to go see Charla," Jackie interjected. "I'd like to talk to her now if possible." Damned if she wanted to go back to Getaway with no idea of how long it would be before Charla made it back. Especially since Jackie had a plane to catch this coming weekend.

"Thanks, Rayna." Eli ended the call. "She says to go by the Galveston police station and ask. They might make you wait until she's been booked in and transferred to the jail, but at least you'll know."

Tears inexplicably stinging her eyes, she nodded. "Thanks. I really don't want to leave Galveston without seeing her."

Gently, he squeezed her shoulder. "I understand. If it's going to be a few hours, I really want to show Theo the beach and the ocean."

When the two squad cars pulled out of the parking lot, Eli swung into place behind them, following them to the police station. Once there, they parked and watched as once again Charla and Delia, still cuffed, were led inside.

Jackie got out of the car slowly, her heart beating rapidly. She had no idea what to expect, seeing her sister for the first time in three years, under such circumstances. She suspected she knew how her mother would rcact, and then realized she really didn't care. She'd come back to Getaway for her sister, and now they'd finally get the chance to talk.

"Are you ready for this?" Eli asked, lifting Theo from the car seat. "Oh, wait. I need to change him." He laid his son on the back seat and made quick work of changing the diaper.

Once again, Jackie found herself awed by his quiet competence. Something of her thoughts must have shown on her face, because when he glanced at her, her shook his head and grinned. "Single dads have to learn how to do this stuff, you know," he said. "It's really not a big deal."

Now that Theo had been changed, Eli hoisted him up on one hip. "Though I really want to ask her why she was setting me up in her fake murder thing, I think I'm going to wait with Theo in the waiting area. I'm not sure how I feel about him seeing Charla and then having to be taken away from her."

Though she nodded, because she got it, she really did, another part of her ached for her little nephew and what he was going through. Theo had no idea what his mother had done. He loved her, the way all innocents did, and would no doubt cry for her if he caught sight of her. "No sense in putting him through that," she agreed quietly. "Especially since he wouldn't even begin to understand why he had to leave her again."

Surprise flickered across his expression, though he hid it quickly. She guessed he hadn't been expecting her to agree with him. Once, she wouldn't have. Now she was no longer on Charla's side.

Walking inside, Jackie resisted the urge to clutch Eli's hand. Little Theo looked around him with interest, his bright blue gaze inquisitive. "Mama?" he asked, his high voice hopeful. "Mama."

Eli cursed under his breath. The shattered look on his face matched the way hearing her nephew's plaintive voice made her feel. Once again, she found herself wondering how her sister could do this to her own child.

Shaking off her emotions, she marched over to the front desk and let the woman know why she'd come.

"This is highly unusual," the older woman said with a frown. "But I'll let them know. Why don't you have a seat and someone will be with you shortly."

After thanking her, Jackie returned to Eli and Theo. "Hopefully, they'll let me see her," she said.

"I think they will," he replied. "If not, you can always call Rayna and ask her to intervene."

She nodded. The idea of having come all this way, gone through all she had in her search for her sister and then having to fly back to New York without seeing or talking to her seemed unthinkable.

"Ms. Burkholdt?" A uniformed officer called her name. "You can come on back with me. Since your sister is going to be here until transport arrives to take her back to your local jurisdiction, I see no reason why you can't speak with her and your mother. Your sheriff explained your particular circumstances." With that, the officer glanced at Eli and Theo.

"We'll wait here," Eli said. "I really have nothing to say to either of them."

"I really just need to see my sister," Jackie said. "If that's all right with you."

"Certainly. You were going to have to see one at a time anyway as we're keeping them separated."

Following the officer, Jackie took deep breaths, trying to maintain some semblance of composure. Three years had passed since her sister had cut her out of her life, and surely, the person Charla had become bore no resemblance to the baby sister Jackie remembered. She still loved her fiercely, of course—love didn't die simply because of someone's bad choices. She just wasn't sure what to expect.

"You're going to have to speak with her with glass separating you," the officer said, stopping outside a heavy-duty door with a card key lock. "A guard will be present with her at all times and your visit will be limited to twenty minutes. There are phones you can use to communicate. Do you have any questions?"

Taking a deep breath, Jackie shook her head. She waited while the guard unlocked the door and stepped back, motioning her into the room.

A single plastic chair sat in front of a battered Formica counter, with a dirty glass partition that went all the way to the ceiling. Charla sat on the other side, unsmiling.

Still standing, Jackie took in her baby sister. She still

looked the same, though she'd evidently spent a lot of time in the sun, judging by the rich tan color of her skin. She stared at Jackie, her blue eyes cold.

Picking up the phone, not sure what to say, Jackie dropped into the chair. She waited until her sister did the same. "Charla. I'm glad you're all right."

"Are you?" Voice dripping with disdain, Charla scrunched her face exactly the way she used to do as a child. "From what Mom's been telling me, you've taken up with Eli. Is that true? Are you sleeping with my ex?"

"I got your text," Jackie said softly instead of answering. "I dropped everything, took my vacation and flew home. I was worried sick about you—and your son. I demanded the sheriff's department open an investigation, interviewed your friends and coworkers and accused Eli of hurting you."

"That's exactly what you were supposed to do," Charla said, sneering. "What went wrong? My saintly ex-husband couldn't keep it in his pants?"

Again, Jackie ignored her. "Then I learn you were not only having an affair with Mr. Levine, but you embezzled and stole from his store."

Expression unchanged, Charla shrugged. "Your point?"

"Why?"

Now Charla leaned forward, her voice fierce. "Christopher owed me that money. For years, starting when I was too young to know better, he took advantage of me. He kept promising he'd leave his wife, and I believed him. It wasn't until I wised up and told him it had to stop that I started taking money. A little here, a little there."

"Half a million dollars, Charla. That's a lot."

Charla's mouth twisted. "Listen to you, Miss Holier-Than-Thou. You got out. You got away. And you left me there to rot in that Podunk little town."

Shocked, Jackie gripped the phone. She wasn't even sure how to respond to that. She'd urged her sister to finish high school, go to college, in short, to follow a similar path as she had.

"I knew you'd show up when I sent you the text," Charla continued. "The guilt over abandoning me must have been eating you alive. So imagine my surprise when Mom told me you've been fooling around with Eli."

"Your ex-husband," Jackie pointed out, still reeling from Charla's earlier comment. "The one you tried to set up for your fake murder."

"He deserved that," Charla said, lifting her chin. "He broke his promise to me. When we married, he swore to stay by my side no matter what."

Not sure how to react to that, Jackie sighed. "I thought you were the one who asked for the divorce since you didn't want to be married anymore. Plus, you had all these guys on the side..."

"That was all a test of his loyalty."

It began to dawn on Jackie that her sister had become a complete narcissist. Heck, she'd probably been that way all along and Jackie had been too blind to see. "I understand. What about Theo? How could you just leave your son like that?"

Charla shrugged. "Motherhood isn't really for me. I don't have the time or the patience to deal with a kid."

"Then why did you fight for custody?"

"I had a couple of reasons," Charla replied, her lip curling. "One, I wanted to keep Eli under my thumb. I knew he really took being a father seriously. The other was Getaway itself. You know how people gossip in that town. It would have looked terrible if I'd given up custody of my own child. They would have turned up their noses at me."

In Charla's world, everything was about her.

"What about stealing from Levine's? You know Mr. Levine pressed charges for both the money and the diamonds. You know you'll probably go to prison for that, right?"

"Prison?" Charla laughed, amazingly carefree. "That's all a misunderstanding. Christopher and I were in on this together, so it wasn't stealing. He was going to leave his wife and meet me in the Bahamas. Setting it up to make it look as if I was a thief was all his idea."

"I hope you have proof," Jackie pointed out. "Because that sounds weak even to me."

Charla shrugged. "It'll all work out in the end for me. It always does."

"Mom's in trouble, too, you know. She tried to snatch Theo out of his bedroom at Eli's house. Eli walked in on her and stopped her."

For the first time Charla appeared surprised. "What? Why would she do that? I certainly didn't ask her to."

"I don't know. Maybe because she loves her grandson." Though in all probability, Delia had felt Theo needed to be with his mother.

"Mom is a fool." Charla shook her head. "She's more

like you than I realized." With that, she hung up the phone on her side of the partition, indicating to the guard that she wanted her visit to be over.

Still holding her own phone, Jackie sat frozen and watched as her sister was escorted out.

"Ms. Burkholdt?" One of the guards had opened the door. "Are you all right?"

Slowly, Jackie replaced the phone in its cradle and got to her feet. "I'm fine," she answered, though in reality she still tried to make sense of the entire conversation she'd just had.

Following the guard back to the waiting area, her chest tight, she tried to force a smile for Eli though she knew he'd see right through her.

As she approached, he stood, shifting Theo from his lap back to his hip. "Come on," he said, taking her arm. "Let's get out of here. I think it's time to grab something to eat and then take a walk on the beach. Let's show Theo the ocean and see what he thinks."

ELI KEPT UP a steady stream of chatter as he walked out to Jackie's rental car. She hadn't been able to hide her shock and devastation, though she'd clearly tried. He waited until they were in the car and driving to find a parking spot on the seawall near a restaurant before he brought up what had just happened.

"Are you okay?" he asked, checking on Theo in the rearview.

Jackie shrugged. "I never really understood that my sister was a textbook narcissist. Everything is about her.

She honestly thinks she can get out of the embezzlement and theft charges with more lies. I wish her luck."

Ahead, a small sports car pulled out. Feeling lucky, Eli got the space. "Here we are," he said. "This isn't as crowded as it would be if we went to one of the beaches. There's just enough sand and waves for us to walk."

"Do you mind if we eat first?" Jackie asked. "That restaurant is close."

"Food, then beach," he replied. "Sounds good."

Clearly still lost in thought, Jackie nodded and got out. He wanted to ask what Charla had said to her, but figured if she wanted him to know, she'd say so. He got Theo out of the car seat and carrying him, walked with Jackie over to the restaurant, a place called Miller's Seawall Grill. Since it was in between the lunch and dinner rush, they didn't have to wait and were shown to a table on the outdoor patio with a view of the sea.

The ocean looked peaceful, perfect waves rolling gently in, the bright sunlight making the blue water sparkle. Jackie appeared to notice none of it, still mulling over her conversation from back in the jail.

"Don't let her get in your head," he said instead. "You came all this way to help her. Nothing she says can take that away from you."

"I know." Blinking, she smiled at him. "I hope the food is good here. I'm seriously starving."

The waitress came over, bringing menus. "Do you have good burgers?" Jackie asked without even opening hers.

"We do," the young woman answered, smiling.

"I'll have a cheeseburger and fries." Eyeing Eli,

who'd grabbed the menu, looking for the kid section, she smiled. "Do you have hot dogs on the kids' menu?"

"We do. They come with fries or macaroni and cheese."

"Fries," Eli put in. "And I'll have the bacon cheeseburger."

They also ordered tea. Once the waitress moved away, Eli shook his head and laughed. "You're a little impatient there, aren't you?"

Appearing not the least bit contrite, she made a face, wrinkling her cute nose. "I'm sorry. It's been forever since I've eaten and I'm a little bit cranky. I get like that if I let it go too long between meals."

"I'll have to remember to keep that in mind," he said before he thought better of it. He found himself wondering if this would be the last meal he shared with her before she left. Surely not. Though now that she'd seen her sister, she really had no more reason to stay.

"Did Charla ask about her son?" he asked, pretty sure he already knew the answer.

Glancing from him to Theo, Jackie slowly shook her head. "Everything was a means to an end as far as she's concerned. A baby becomes a bargaining tool in her world. And from what I could tell, she expected you to be her doting sidekick no matter what she did. She even went so far as to blame me for her own poor choices. She regards me leaving town as the ultimate betrayal, which is why she hadn't spoken to me ever since I left."

He hated seeing the raw pain in her eyes. "Unfortunately, none of that comes as the slightest surprise to me," he said.

Jackie leaned forward, her gaze intense. "If you knew what she was like, why'd you marry her? Did you think you could change her?"

The waitress brought their drinks, promising their food would be out soon, and then left.

Eli gave Jackie's question the careful consideration it deserved. "I've wondered that myself recently," he admitted. "You know that old saying *love is blind*? I thought I loved her and I really believed she loved me back. Clearly, I ignored the warning signs that were there in the beginning. When she got pregnant with Theo, honestly, I was really happy. I figured a baby might just be what she needed to finally settle down. I was wrong."

Jackie's troubled gaze met his. "How do you know when love is real?" she asked quietly. "It might all be smoke and mirrors. You could be risking your heart. So how do you know, Eli? How can you be sure you won't make that same mistake again?"

This might be the most important question she'd ever asked him. He needed to think carefully on how to frame his response.

Except he didn't want to. Instead, he answered from the heart. "Sometimes you just have to take that chance. We all have our own ideas about what love is, but for me it's more than physical. It's when you're attracted to more than just that person's brain, or their beauty, and when all you want to do is make them happy."

Her eyes got huge as she stared at him.

Aware he might have just revealed far too much

about his feelings, he looked down. Luckily, the waitress chose that moment to arrive with their food.

Theo seemed thrilled to see his hot dog, refusing to allow Eli to help him eat. He did a good job of dipping his fries in ketchup, though more of it seemed to end up on his face and hands than in his mouth.

Smiling, Jackie leaned over and wiped Theo's little face with her napkin, making him grin as he happily continued to eat.

Only then did Jackie dig in to her own meal.

It struck him then that this was the sort of thing parents did—put their child's needs ahead of their own. Jackie was only Theo's aunt, but she cared enough to take care of Theo first. Eli recognized that he did that instinctively on a regular basis but Charla never had. Everything in dealing with her son appeared to irritate or inconvenience her. How could one sister be so different from the other?

As he slowly ate his burger and watched Jackie alternate between devouring hers and helping Theo, he realized he truly loved her. Not the superficial infatuation he'd felt for Charla, but a deep and certain love.

That love was the reason he wouldn't tell her how he felt. He knew how badly she wanted to return to New York, how happy her job and her life there made her. Loving someone meant not being selfish, but wanting the best for them even if it meant letting her go and breaking his own heart.

They finished the meal, Theo eating most of his hot dog and half his fries. The waitress cleared the table and left the check. Heart aching, Eli watched as Jackie cleaned his little boy's face and dropped a quick kiss on the top of Theo's head.

Somehow, he forced himself to smile. After leaving cash on the table to cover the bill and the tip, he reached for his son. But Theo leaned away, holding up his arms to Jackie.

Jackie laughed, unbuckling him from the child seat and lifting him in her arms. "Do you mind?" she asked, meeting Eli's gaze and making him wonder if something had shown on his face.

"Of course not," he said. "But let me know if he gets too heavy."

It turned out to be a moot point. In the fickle way of toddlers, they'd walked halfway to the door before Theo squirmed in Jackie's arms, crying out for his daddy.

As Jackie handed over his son, Eli shook his head. Together, the three of them walked out into the bright sunshine, a little family that could never be. He vowed Jackie would never know she'd broken his heart.

As they took the concrete steps down to the sand, Jackie looked at him and smiled. She took out her phone and snapped a few photos. "With the wind in your hair and the sea in the background, I want to always remember this day," she said.

Spoken like someone who would soon be leaving. Which she would. He knew better than to hope she'd stay.

"Let Theo walk in the sand and see what he thinks," Jackie suggested. "Maybe we can even take him in at the edge of the waves."

Since he figured the sand might be hot, he left Theo's

sneakers on as he lowered him to the ground. He took one hand and Jackie took another since Theo was apt to take off running. This new situation appeared to confound him. Small brow furrowed, Theo looked from the sand to the water and back to Eli. As they approached the water, Theo pointed, his attention riveted on the waves. "Go there," he said, clear as day.

"I wish we had flip-flops," Jackie mused. "We either have to take off our shoes or get them wet."

"Or not walk in the water," he added, wondering how they'd clean all the sand off before getting in the car.

She shot him a look of patent disbelief. "We drove hours to reach the ocean. You have to let Theo feel the water on his bare feet. How about we all take our shoes off and leave them up on the sand."

Not entirely convinced, he decided to let his son decide. Once he'd stepped out of his shoes and removed his socks, he helped get Theo out of his. Jackie grinned at him and did the same.

"Ah," she exclaimed. "Nothing like the feeling of toes in warm sand."

Though Eli disagreed, her excitement was contagious and he found himself smiling back. "Let's do this," he said, motioning for her to grab Eli's other hand again. Together, they lifted him up, to his giggling delight, and walked over to the edge of the surf.

When they lowered him down, still holding tight to his hands, his little feet were in the frothy water. Not much—just enough to cover his toes, but he let out such a loud squeal full of joy that Eli found himself laughing. "Come on," Eli said, encouraging his boy to take a step on his own. "It's the ocean."

Theo tried to tug his hand away, clearly wanting the freedom to play in the water, but Eli held on tight. Jackie didn't. She let him go, bending down to show him how to splash in the waves, laughing as he crouched down and mimicked her. In one quick movement, he spun and splashed his daddy's leg.

Though Eli continued his grip on Theo's hand, by the time they were ready to leave, Theo's entire outfit had gotten soaked, as well as Eli's jeans. Somehow, Jackie had managed to remain mostly dry.

Watching her frolic in the water with his son, Eli couldn't help but notice the way the tension seemed to melt off her. With sunlight making copper fire in her dark hair, the shocked look vanished from her eyes. She laughed and splashed and Theo ate it all up. In that moment Eli had never loved her more.

Another family came over, setting down beach towels and an umbrella, turning their radio on and playing loud country music. Eli and Jackie exchanged looks, silently agreeing their own respite should end.

They collected their socks and shoes and walked barefoot back to the seawall. Depositing Theo on a bench, Eli asked Jackie to look after him while he went to fetch some baby wipes, a fresh diaper and a change of clothes.

It didn't take long for Eli to get his son cleaned up. He and Jackie used the wipes to get as much sand off their own feet as possible before slipping their socks and shoes back on.

"What about your wet jeans?" Jackie asked, her eyes still shining, her hair wild from the wind.

"They'll dry," he told her, still aching with the love he felt for her. His reply made her laugh again; her entire face lit up.

"The ocean was good for you," he said as they got back into the car.

"It was. I might be a west Texas girl at heart, but I sure do love the sand and the sea."

A west Texas girl. Not a New York girl. Not sure what to make of that comment, he pulled out into the road and headed back toward home.

"What about you?" she asked, marveling at all the fully restored mansions as they drove up Broadway. "I see all that playing in the sun and sea spray wore little Theo out, but did getting out there near the gulf help you at all?"

"*You* helped me," he told her, deciding to be honest. "Through all of this, you've been your sister's fiercest champion, but your support of me and now my son, never wavered. I don't know how I ever can repay you, but it meant the world to me. Thank you for that."

Glancing at her as he spoke, he couldn't decipher the emotion that flickered across her expressive face.

"You're welcome," she replied quietly, averting her face, but not before he saw the sheen of what looked like tears in her eyes. Since he had no idea if something he'd said had hurt her feelings, he decided it'd be better to be quiet, so he turned up the radio and concentrated on his driving.

Chapter Fifteen

Though Jackie knew he'd meant it as a compliment, Eli's words had gutted her. Nothing romantic about them, he'd more or less complimented her for being a good friend.

Was that how he regarded her? A female friend with whom he'd shared occasional benefits? This knowledge made her feel even more foolish for even considering staying.

Except for one unalterable and certain fact. She loved him. With every fiber of her being, with all that she was. She loved him. This didn't feel like a passing infatuation, but a deep and certain love, the kind upon which futures could be built. Watching him with his son today had cemented it, erasing any lingering doubts she might have had. She loved Eli Pitts. And his adorable little son, Theo, her nephew.

She might only have known Eli two weeks, but she felt as if she'd been hit by a lightning bolt. Cupid's arrow. The thought made her smile. Cheesy, maybe. But a feeling this strong and sure was definitely worth exploring and seeing where it could go.

Maybe even forever.

Such a thought stunned her. She'd been in love before, or thought so at the time. But she'd never met someone with whom she could imagine spending the rest of her life. Even here in Getaway, in the town where she'd grown up.

Except she wasn't sure Eli felt the same way. Which should make her decision all that much easier.

Her head began to hurt as much as her heart. Too much sun, most likely. Eli had gone silent, so she decided she would, too.

For the next several hours she alternated between dozing and trying to figure out her future. When they stopped for gas in San Antonio, she offered to drive since Eli had driven the entire way down, but he'd insisted he did better when he had something to do. So with her head throbbing and exhaustion coloring the edges of her vision, she let him, turning her face to the window.

Amazing how in such a short time, her outlook on life had changed. Her once beloved New York no longer held as much appeal as it had before. Glancing at him through her lashes, she eyed the ruggedly handsome man behind the wheel, turned to view the adorable toddler sound asleep in the back seat. She couldn't imagine leaving them. The idea made her feel as if she'd be ripping her heart clean out of her chest.

She honestly didn't know how the hell she would be able to do it.

However, Eli hadn't asked her to stay. He hadn't even hinted. When he'd given her his thoughts on what love meant to him, she'd nearly swooned right there at the table. Luckily, their food had arrived and she'd been able to focus on devouring her hamburger.

Then, at the beach, she'd felt part of a sweet little family of three. Something she'd never even realized she'd wanted, never mind the brief flash of longing to have her own baby. Until then, after practically raising Charla, she hadn't been certain she even wanted children.

New York, with its constant activity, rushing from one thing to another, now seemed as if it belonged to another person. She could imagine how wonderful it would be if she had someone like Eli to share that life with, but she knew he wouldn't flourish in the city. He belonged in Getaway, in dusty west Texas, with his horses and his ranch. She wasn't even sure where she'd fit in his world. Or if he even wanted her to. After being burned by her sister, she couldn't blame him for being gun-shy. Especially since they'd only known each other a couple of weeks.

Again, she peeked at him. Strong jaw clenched, he appeared to be concentrating on driving.

Summoning up her courage, she almost asked him if he could ever imagine her having a place in his life. But saying that not only felt presumptuous, but made her feel raw and exposed, too, so she didn't. Something like that couldn't be prompted or forced. If he truly wanted her to hang around, he'd have to say so of his own free will.

Sometime between San Antonio and Abilene, she actually managed to fall asleep. And naturally, she dreamed of Eli, holding her close and professing his love. In her dream she asked him if it wasn't too soon and he responded by telling her he'd known the first moment he'd seen her. When you know, you know.

She woke with that phrase echoing in her head. Dream Eli had been right. Too bad real Eli didn't feel the same.

"Hey there." Eli smiled at her. "Did you enjoy your nap?"

Covering her mouth to stifle a yawn, she sat up straight. "I think so. Wow. I've never been able to sleep in cars or planes. It's so weird that I did."

"You must be really tired. I know he is." He used his head to let her know to check the back seat. When she turned, she saw little Theo, still fast asleep in his car seat.

"I am. Finding my sister sure didn't end like I hoped it would. Instead of becoming close, she made sure to burn all remaining bridges."

He nodded. "What about your mother? I know you didn't actually speak with Delia while we were in Galveston, but are you going to be upset with me if I press charges over what she did?"

"No." She didn't even have to think about her answer. "She and Charla are much more alike than I realized. They both need to understand there are consequences for their actions."

"I can't even imagine going through that hell again if she'd succeeded in snatching my son," he told her. "When he was missing before..."

Reaching out, she placed her hand on his shoulder

and squeezed. "I can't imagine. I'm so sorry my sister put you through that."

When he turned to look at her, the raw need in his face made her catch her breath. "Will you stay with me at my ranch for the rest of the time you're here, Jackie? I know you're planning on leaving this weekend."

Her heart, which had leaped at the first sentence, stuttered at the rest. "Of course," she replied, wondering how she'd endure the heartbreak. "I wouldn't have it any other way."

By the time they pulled off the highway, taking the exit that would lead them to Main Street, the entire town had shut down. Though the streetlights were lit, all the store windows were dark and the parking lots empty, except for the Rattlesnake Pub. "Does that place they called The Bar get a pretty good crowd on weeknights?" she asked, curious.

He shrugged. "I don't know. It's not like I do a lot of bar hopping these days. And I'm more of a Pub type of guy."

As they pulled up in front of the Landshark Motel, parking under a streetlight, her weariness threatened to overwhelm her. "I'll wait here while you grab your stuff," he said. "Theo is still asleep."

On the verge of asking if she could wait until morning to stay at his place, she realized they were in her car and if he went home without her, she'd be left here without a vehicle.

With her back stiff, she got out and went inside to collect her belongings. The melancholy affecting her had to be due to the long day. She didn't want it to ruin what little remaining time she had with Eli and Theo.

It only took her a few minutes to throw everything into her suitcase. She cleaned out her toiletries, too, deciding she'd check out in the morning. Once she'd done a complete sweep of the room to ensure she hadn't left anything behind, she took a deep breath, straightened her shoulders and went back out to the car.

Catching sight of her, Eli grinned, the streetlight illuminating his face. She felt the power of that smile all the way to her toes. He popped the trunk and she stowed her luggage there, closing it quietly and carefully. Climbing into the car, she glanced into the back seat where Theo still slept; she gave Eli a quick thumbs-up before securing her seat belt.

Once they reached the ranch, she grabbed her bags while Eli carried his boy inside. Waiting in the living room, she wondered if she'd be sleeping in the guest bedroom or with Eli. She stretched out on the couch to wait and closed her eyes, intending to merely rest them for a moment.

She must have fallen asleep again, because she woke with Eli nuzzling her neck as he murmured her name. Smiling, she pulled him down to her, kissing him with as much sleepy passion as she could summon.

"Your choice," he said, mouth against hers. "You can sleep here, or in the guest bedroom, or with me."

"As if there's even a choice," she scoffed, holding his gaze. "I want to be with you."

Still kissing, stumbling toward the bedroom like a pair of punch-drunk lovers, they fell onto his bed, passion flaring hot, heavy and all-consuming. He had enough self-restraint to grab a condom, but once he'd done that, he was insatiable.

Finally, that particular hunger slaked, he cleaned up and then returning to bed, wrapped himself around her to sleep.

The next morning, waking up in his arms, Jackie gazed at the sleeping man beside her and sighed, her heart full. She didn't want to move, didn't want to do anything to disturb this blissful moment.

"Mornin'," he said softly, opening his impossibly blue eyes. He twisted slightly, nudging her with his fully aroused body, which made her melt.

After he grabbed a condom from his nightstand, they made love again, slowly instead of the rushed, passionate frenzy of the night before. They explored each other's bodies as if they had all the time in the world. The thought made Jackie's heart ache, even as she arched her back, her pleasure coming in waves as she found release. Eli followed an instant after, and then they simply held each other. No words were necessary or wanted.

Jackie wished they could stay that way forever.

In his bedroom, little Theo started calling for his daddy. Eli hollered that he'd be right there, kissed Jackie and got out of bed. "Let's have breakfast at the café this morning," he said. "I'm going to clean up really quick and get Eli ready. While I'm doing that, why don't you go shower and we'll meet in the kitchen."

Stretching lazily, she gave him a sleepy smile. "Sounds perfect." She couldn't resist eyeing his sexy butt as he headed toward the bathroom.

Later, craving a cup of strong coffee, she hurried into the kitchen. The sight of Eli, sitting on the floor, playing trucks with his son, stole her breath away. This man, this handsome, ridiculously sexy cowboy, had so much tender patience and love inside him and he wasn't afraid to show it.

He looked up when she entered, his blue gaze warm. "There she is," he told Theo. "Your aunt Jackie. You ready to go get some breakfast?"

Theo nodded vigorously. He pushed to his feet, a little wobbly, but strong. Gaining momentum, he barreled toward Jackie in what looked like a drunken run. Just as he reached her, she scooped him up and swung him around, which made him squeal with glee.

As usual, the Tumbleweed Café parking lot had very few empty spaces. Eli found a spot and they all got out. For some inexplicable reason, Jackie felt nervous, as if people could look at her and know exactly what she and Eli had been doing.

They lucked out and were shown to a booth near the front window, with a view of the parking lot and Main Street. All around them, conversation hummed. Several people greeted Eli by name and a couple of older ladies stopped by and cooed over Theo, eyeing Jackie with open curiosity. Eli introduced her as Charla's sister, which inevitably led to Charla's disappearance. Eli informed everyone that Charla had been found and that Rayna or one of her deputies would be bringing her back to Getaway. The two women rushed away, as if they could hardly wait to start spreading the gossip.

"That's why you wanted to come here, wasn't it?" Jackie asked.

"Partly," Eli admitted. "I wanted to clear my name, and the fastest way to spread news around Getaway is tell people here at the café. A few well-placed words and everyone in town will know before nightfall."

During their breakfast a few other people stopped by the table and each time, Eli managed to work something into the conversation about Charla. By the time the waitress dropped off the check, Jackie figured he'd accomplished what he'd set out to do.

Rayna walked in just as Eli was paying the check. She headed straight for their table. "I've already had three phone calls asking me if it's true that Charla and Delia are in jail down in Galveston," she said. "I'm guessing that's why you're here?"

Eli grinned. "You caught me. I wanted to clear my name and fast. Plus, we needed a great breakfast after the day we had yesterday."

"Brilliant strategy," Rayna agreed, laughing. Her gaze slid to meet Jackie's. "Hey, just in case I don't see you before you leave, I wanted to tell you goodbye. I hate to see you go. I really wish you were here permanently."

Again, Jackie felt that twist in her heart, though she took care to hide it. "Me, too," she replied, jumping to her feet to hug the sheriff as she threw out a hint to Eli. "Take care."

Rayna moved on, heading toward the takeout counter, evidently to pick up her own breakfast.

"Are you ready?" Eli asked, wiping off Theo's face before lifting him out of the booster seat.

Jackie nodded, taking one last look around the packed restaurant. She found it strange how three years ago she couldn't wait to see the last of this town. Now she found herself dreading leaving.

As they walked outside to Eli's truck, she wondered if she should go back to her motel room for her last two nights. Maybe making a clean break would hurt less than dragging it out.

But as she buckled herself in, she looked at the man she now knew she loved and shook her head. No point in trying to fool herself. She wanted to spend every minute she had left with Eli and Theo. No matter how much harder it would be to go.

"We need to swing by the motel," she said. "Since I'm staying at your place, I need to check out. There's no point in paying for the room when I won't be using it."

At the Landshark, Eli and Theo waited in the car while she took care of checking out. When she returned, feeling somehow lighter now that she'd finished that final chore, she impulsively leaned over and gave Eli a kiss.

"What do you want to do today?" he asked. "We can do anything you want, just name it."

"Are you not working?" she countered. "I can watch Theo if you need to work around the ranch."

Expression incredulous, he eyed her. "That wouldn't be fair. I'd feel like I'd be taking advantage of you."

"Not at all," she replied, meaning it. "I enjoy spending time with Theo and I love helping you. Go ahead and get your work done." She couldn't bear to ask him what he'd do for childcare once she'd gone.

Pulling into the ranch drive, he shook his head. "Work can wait. I want to spend the rest of the time you're here with you."

Once again, like a fool, she caught herself waiting for him to say more. Almost as if she held herself still enough, he might actually ask her to stay.

But he didn't and she knew she'd need some time to regroup and get her emotions under control. "I appreciate that," she finally managed to say. "But a couple of hours of work won't hurt anyone. Go get it done. I promise I'll be here waiting when you get back."

WALKING TOWARD THE barn and leaving Theo with Jackie, Eli tried to settle his mind so he could think. Jackie filled his thoughts. Jackie smiling, her eyes shining as she gazed at him. Kind, tenderhearted Jackie, so strong and brave and beautiful. She'd befriended him, her sister's ex, supported and helped him and even shared her body with him. Despite the intensity of the heat that flared between them, she'd made no bones about her leaving, honest and up-front about everything. Unlike her sister, Jackie was real.

It might only be wishful thinking, but part of him couldn't shake the feeling that she might actually be willing to stay. The other, more rational side of him figured he thought that because he wanted it so badly. She'd lose her job if she did, and he couldn't bear the thought of her giving up everything she'd worked so hard for.

Either way, he planned to sound her out about it at dinner that night. There had to be a solution, some sort of compromise, if they both wanted it enough. This thought gave him hope. He might only have known Jackie a short time, but he couldn't imagine life without her.

He worked the two horses and then did a rushed clean-out of their stalls. His part-time worker would be there tomorrow, so he'd have help with some of the grunt work, but he'd need to find someone who could look after Theo at least part-time.

Rayna called just as he was finishing up. "I've sent Sam down to Galveston to bring Charla and Delia back," she said. "I thought you might want to be the one to tell Jackie."

"Thanks."

"How's she doing?" Rayna asked. "It's got to be rough, learning both your sister and your mother are under arrest and possibly going to serve time."

"She seems okay," he replied. "That meeting she had with Charla really opened her eyes. As for Delia, that woman has apparently always treated Jackie like dirt."

"Still," Rayna persisted, "she is her mother."

"Is this your way of hinting I need to think about dropping the charges?" he asked. "Because even Jackie feels her mother needs to learn there are consequences for her actions."

"I agree. And no, I'm not hinting about anything. I'm just throwing that out there in case Jackie might be having trouble dealing with all this. It's a lot."

"I agree. I'll take care of her. She's staying with me

at the ranch until she leaves." Just saying the words made his heart ache.

"Good. Oh, and I do have other, nonrelated news." Rayna's deliberate tone warned him she'd carefully considered her next words. "Normally, I try to mind my own business. But even I can see the connection you and Jackie have. So I thought I'd pass along that Myrna Maples is looking for a ghost writer and editor. Not only does she want to hire someone to take over writing her advice column, but she wants to write a memoir. Since Jackie is an editor at a book publisher, I immediately thought of her."

Myrna Maples, the syndicated advice columnist, was the most famous person in Getaway. She'd almost died at the hands of her serial killer son, though Rayna had saved her. The two women had become friends after that.

"I can put in a word with Myrna for her, if she'd like," Rayna continued.

Hope flared, though he quickly extinguished it. "Thanks for letting me know," he said quietly. "I plan to talk to her tonight to explore what options we have of continuing this relationship."

"At least you can let her know she might have a job here."

"True. And thank you," he said. "I'll have Jackie contact you if she's interested."

After ending the call, he mulled over what Rayna had said. While he knew Jackie was a book editor, he had no way of knowing whether or not she'd be interested in working for Myrna Maples. He'd have to figure out a way to ask her without putting pressure on her to stay.

Back inside the house he headed directly to the shower to wash off the smells of horse and barn. When he emerged, hair still damp, he followed the infectious sound of Theo's laughter to the kitchen, where he found Jackie sitting at the table playing with Play-Doh. They'd made all kinds of interesting things, from snowmen to what appeared to be horses.

The moment Theo caught sight of his dad, he lifted up whatever he'd been making and squeezed it in his little hand, crushing it. "Come see," he said, startling Eli. His son hadn't spoken much yet and despite his urging Charla to have him tested, she'd never done so. Eli figured he'd get that done, too.

"What do you have there?" Eli asked, crouching down next to Theo. "It looks like a big dog."

Theo shook his head. "Horse," he said clearly, beaming.

Amazed again, Eli glanced at Jackie. She grinned, noticeably proud.

"Have you been coaching him?" Eli asked, his heart full.

"A little," she admitted. "Right, Theo?"

At that, Theo laughed, a boisterous, joyous sound that made Eli smile. Jackie leaned close, her mouth to Eli's ear. "I think he's been starved for attention. He'll flourish now that he has you."

And you, he wanted to say. But he didn't. She'd be leaving soon, so it wouldn't be true. She got up and moved away, back to her chair.

"What would you two like me to make for dinner?" he asked, jumping to his feet. "Let me look and see what I've got to work with."

"No need," Jackie interjected. "I took out some chicken legs and used the microwave to defrost them. I was going to make oven-fried chicken."

"You don't have to cook for me," he said.

"I know that. Maybe I want to." She got up, moving gracefully. "Why don't you sit and play with your son and let me get the meal prepared."

Slowly, he nodded. Smiling at Theo, he reached out and grabbed a piece of the soft clay. "I'm going to make a horse," he announced.

Meanwhile, Jackie bustled around the kitchen. Once she'd put the chicken in the oven, she came back to sit at the table. "Chicken and roasted veggies," she announced.

"Sounds great," Eli responded. "But next time I want to cook for you."

She grinned. "That sounds like a plan."

When the meal was ready, they all sat at the table and ate like a family. More than anything, Eli found himself wishing they were.

For the rest of the afternoon and evening, Eli allowed himself to wallow in the comfortable feeling of family, even though he doubted Jackie even knew she brought it. Things had never felt so cozy and domestic, not even during his brief marriage to Charla. Jackie hummed to herself as she worked, slightly off-key, and a soft sort of happiness radiated from her. All smiles, Theo clearly picked up on it, too.

Damn, he could get used to having her around. Especially with the sexual tension running just underneath the surface, heating his blood and making him envision what he wanted to do to her once they went to bed.

Assuming she wanted to share his bed.

Later, after he'd bathed Theo, read him a bedtime story and tucked him in, he rejoined Jackie in the living room. She'd poured herself a glass of wine from the bottle they'd opened to have with dinner, and he grabbed a beer before taking a seat on the couch next to her.

"Hey there," she said softly. "It's been a really nice day. Thank you for inviting me into your life."

"Are you still planning on going back to New York?" he asked, inwardly wincing at his bluntness. He'd meant to try and ease into the subject, be casual. Instead, he'd blurted it out without warning.

Her head snapped up, her gaze flying to his. "I'm not sure," she said, choosing her words carefully. "Do you not want me to?"

"I want you to do whatever makes you happy," he said. The flash of disappointment that crossed her face made him wonder if he was going about this all wrong. He decided to say what was in his heart. "I want to be with you, Jackie. To see where *this*, whatever this is, takes us. I'm in love with you. But I can't ask you to give up your job, your life, just for me."

Slowly, gaze locked on his, she nodded. "I get that. I want to be with you, too, Eli. I'm in love with you, too."

He froze. Opened his mouth, tried to speak and failed. This gift he hadn't even dared to hope for filled him with wonder and joy, and a rush of desire so strong he could scarcely think.

He wanted to pull her into his arms, crush her to him and kiss her senseless. But that would all have to wait until later. This moment was too damn important to both of them to be rushed or turned into something else.

Looking down at her hands, she took a deep breath. When she raised her head again, he saw determination in her face, that strong and steady will that he'd come to love. "I never in a million years expected something like this to happen. Knowing you has changed my life. It's a difficult choice."

"It doesn't have to be." He took a deep breath, suddenly certain. "I'll do whatever it takes to work this out. If you can't stay, I want to go with you. I'll sell the ranch, move to New York and find work there."

Clearly shocked, she slowly shook her head. "No, Eli. I can't ask you to do that. This ranch is your life," she said, her voice as fierce as her expression. "You belong here, Eli. In Getaway. Not in New York."

Though he knew she was right, he meant what he'd said. Life with her, wherever that might be, was infinitely preferable to the bleakness of imagining a life without her.

"Then help me figure out a compromise," he replied, reaching for her hand. "Help me figure out a way to stay together."

"I want to be with you," she told him, lacing her fingers through his. "And part of your life here, on this ranch, in this town. Theo deserves the chance to grow up in Getaway. He belongs here as much as you do. And honestly, I can actually see myself living here with the two of you. Maybe even someday we can have one or two babies of our own." She blushed, though she kept her steady gaze locked on his.

He grinned. "I'd like that very much." And then he kissed her, a deep, sensuous kiss that left no doubt how he felt about her.

When they finally broke apart, he eyed her swollen, soft mouth and dazed expression, aching. "I love you so damn much."

Her smile bloomed, lighting up her face. "Right back atcha, Eli Pitts. I'm going to call my boss tomorrow and give my two-week notice. I'll have to go back and work those weeks, box up my things and see if I can get out of my lease."

"That's understandable." And who knew, but maybe her boss would cut her loose before the two weeks was up.

"Once all those details are taken care of," she continued, "I'm going to need to figure out what kind of job I could find here. Except for retail or food service work, it's always been kind of slim pickings in Getaway."

"I think Rayna might know something you'd like to do," he said, and then passed along all the info Rayna had given him earlier.

"Wow." After sipping her wine, Jackie shook her head. "Like everyone else who grew up here, I've always been in awe of Ms. Maples. I even wrote to her once, when my mother made me wear these awful patent leather shoes to the first day of middle school.

While she didn't use my problem in her column, she did write back."

"What did she say?" he asked.

"She was very nice. Sympathetic. She said something about how my mother just wanted me to look pretty. I let that one slide, because she didn't know my mother." Jackie shook her head. "She bought Charla the expensive, name-brand sneakers that everyone else was wearing. I got stuck with the cheap patent leather because Charla lied and told her I wanted them."

Shaking his head, he took her wineglass from her and placed it on the coffee table. Then he pulled her into his arms and proceeded to try and make her forget about the past. They had an entire future to look forward to together. Everything else would simply fall into place.

* * * * *

JOIN THE
MILLS & BOON
BOOKCLUB

* **FREE** delivery direct to your door
* **EXCLUSIVE** offers every month
* **EXCITING** rewards programme

Join today at

Millsandboon.co.uk/Bookclub

OIN US ON SOCIAL MEDIA!

Stay up to date with our latest releases, author news and gossip, special offers and discounts, and all the behind-the-scenes action from Mills & Boon...

millsandboon

millsandboonuk

millsandboon

might just be true love...